*Two Girls, Fat and Thin*

*By the same author*

**BAD BEHAVIOR** (short stories)

# TWO GIRLS, FAT AND THIN
## *Mary Gaitskill*

**BANTAM BOOKS**   *New York  Toronto  London  Sydney  Auckland*

*TWO GIRLS, FAT AND THIN*
A Bantam Book / published by arrangement with Poseidon Press

Printing History
Poseidon Press edition published 1991
Bantam edition / June 1992

Grateful acknowledgment is made for permission to reprint the following:

Excerpt from *Speak, Memory* by Vladimir Nabokov, copyright 1947, 1948, 1949, 1950, 1951, © 1967 by Vladimir Nabokov. Reprinted by permission of Alfred A. Knopf, Inc.
"Reach Out In The Darkness" words and music by Jim Post. Copyright © 1967 Lowery Music Co., Inc. International Copyright Secured. All Rights Reserved. Used by Permission.
"Love Is All Around" written by Reg Presley. Copyright © 1967 Dick James Music Limited. All rights for the United States and Canada controlled by Songs of Poly-Gram International, Inc. (3500 West Olive Avenue, Suite 200, Burbank, CA 91505). International Copyright Secured. All Rights Reserved. Used by Permission.
"Happiness Runs" by Donovan Leitch. Copyright © 1968 Donovan (Music) Ltd. Sole Selling Agent: Peer International Corporation. International Copyright Secured. All Rights Reserved. Used by Permission.
"Straight Up" by Elliot Wolff. Copyright © 1988 Virgin Music, Inc., and Elliot Wolff Music. International Copyright Secured. All Rights Reserved. Used by Permission.

*Library of Congress Cataloging-in-publication Data*
Gaitskill, Mary, 1954–

    Two girls, fat and thin : a novel / Mary Gaitskill.
       p.   cm.
    ISBN 0-553-55004-7
    I. Title.
PS3557.A36T96 1992
813'.54—dc20

                           91–41876
                           CIP

Published simultaneously in the United States and Canada

Bantam Books are published by Bantam Books, a division of Bantam Doubleday Dell Publishing Group, Inc. Its trademark, consisting of the words "Bantam Books" and the portrayal of a rooster, is Registered in U.S. Patent and Trademark Office and in other countries. Marca Registrada. Bantam Books, 666 Fifth Avenue, New York, New York 10103.

Printed in the United States of America
OPM  0  9  8  7  6  5  4  3  2  1

*For my parents, with gratitude for*
*their love and support.*

*I would like to thank Henry Dunow, Ann Patty,
Dave Barbor, Marc Glick, Robin Desser,
Irini Spanidou, Monique Miller, Amy Scholder, Tom Beller,
and especially Kathleen Anderson
for their kind and intelligent commentary.*

*I would also like to thank
the Dorset Theater Colony,
Cummington Community of the Arts,
the Ragdale Foundation, Yaddo, and Centrum.*

All one could do was to glimpse, amid the haze and chimeras, something real ahead, just as persons endowed with an unusual persistence of diurnal cerebration are able to perceive in their deepest sleep, somewhere beyond the throes of an entangled and inept nightmare, the ordered reality of the waking hour.

—VLADIMIR NABOKOV, *Speak, Memory*

# PART ONE

*I entered the strange* world of Justine Shade via a message on the bulletin board in a laundromat filled with bitterness and the hot breath of dryers. "Writer interested in talking to followers of Anna Granite. Please call—." It was written in rigorous, precise, feminine print on a modest card displayed amidst dozens of cards, garish Xeroxed sheets, newsprint, and ragged tongues of paper. The owners of this laundry establishment seem to have an especially lax policy when it comes to the bulletin board, and upon it any nut can advertise himself, express an inane opinion, or announce a slogan amid a blathering crowd of ads for Gorill-O-Grams, lost cats, plaintive George (wearing a tiny amethyst earring, gray leather boots) searching for "provocative boy in tight silver pants who asked tall black man for fabric softener," Micro-Cosmic Orbit Meditation Lessons, Yes Sir!: The All-Boy Maid Service, and Spiritual Karate for Women. That day there was even an especially sinister card bearing an invitation to submit to tests that would determine whether or not your suicidal depression could be alleviated by "the latest medication" or hypnotic technique—an invitation evoking images of bulimic girls held prisoner in somebody's basement, drug-addicted prostitutes confessing to severe men in white coats, electrodes wired to the naked bodies of frightened volunteers, rec rooms erupting with violence, all made doubly queasy by their proximity to wretched George with his laundry. Nestled in this shoddy configuration of suggestion, promise, and nightmare, the writer's card implied a lone kook gripping a grimy sheaf of papers, philosophical tracts, and paperback books, her jaw clenched, her face unnaturally pale. This is the kind of image that is, no doubt, associated with Anna Granite in the dull minds of those who peruse such bulletin boards carelessly, half-registering the muted snarl of urgency and need—but I knew differently.

I shifted my recalcitrant laundry in my arms and snatched the card from the board, not caring if anyone else wanted to read it or not. I went home, put away my laundry, and sat brooding with coffee and card. It had been years since anyone had expressed professional (or was it professional?) interest in Anna Granite, philosopher and literary genius. I read the card repeatedly, trying to deduce something from its hieroglyphical simplicity. Granite had enemies, even in death. I had made the mistake of talking to them in the past, seduced, as all of us were, by the glamour of flashing lightbulbs, microphones, hysterical questions, and so on. But that had been at least fifteen years ago, and this "writer" seemed too insubstantial to bear the weight of such mania.

Why talk to an insubstantial person? I finished my coffee, ate a Gruyère brioche, and left the apartment to go to work. I am thirty-four years old and I live in Queens. I am a proofreader on the midnight shift at a Wall Street law firm, and the hour of my departure for work is bleak and dark. That night the street featured only a few abstracted pedestrians: a guarded young woman in a raincoat carrying a brown-bagged carton of milk, a pair of subdued boys coming around the corner with their hands thrust into their pockets, a dog-walker clutching a wad of paper towels, and a moody doorman pacing in a vigilant circle. I entered a delicatessen which displayed boxes of detergent, stomach medicines, and bottled spring water in its windows. I purchased a handful of rum-flavored marzipan candies, each wrapped in bright red tinfoil bearing a picture of a mysterious brown-haired Victorian lady in décollétage, then I stepped into the street and hailed a cab. The driver and I exchanged mumbles, his ticking metal box lit up, and I sped to the office where my booth awaited me, nestled amid the flanks of word-processing machines, all faithfully burning their little green lights.

But I couldn't forget "writer." As I re-entered my apartment at 9:00 the following morning, I felt the harsh splendor of Granite's presence arrayed through all my rooms. I had never forgotten her, of course. Her books were all upright on my shelves, and the mighty power of her ideas continued to form the undercurrent that bore along the details of my uneventful and increasingly rancorous life. But Anna Granite had died two years earlier, and I had been disassociated from the remnants of her dwindling movement for longer than that. This was the first time in years that I had felt the almost visceral sensation of the woman's presence, which was nothing short of a shimmering, diamond-studded aurora borealis. It was as if this star system had become hidden, bound in a thick skein of ordinariness, and that "writer," with his/her innocuous request, had peeled off a corner of the binding, causing all that I had never really abandoned to come tumbling into my living room.

As I lay in my bed in my plaid flannel nightgown, Granite's characters crowded round me. Solitaire D'Anconti, oil magnate and lonely woman, paced the room in her black plunge-necked jumpsuit, one arm wrapped around her own slim waist, the other holding the cigarette which issued the snake of smoke that was coiling around her. Bus Taggart, the hood who worshipped her, sat on the windowsill, struck a match against his shoe, and sighed. Skip Jackson, newspaper baron and Solitaire's lover, leaned against the wall, watching Solitaire with a savage smirk on his face. What were they going to do? Eustace Kwetschmer, editor of a rival newspaper, had started a series of stories exposing Solitaire's connections with Bus; she had been subpoenaed to testify before a grand jury. Skip was willing to fight back on her behalf, even if it meant destroying his own newspaper empire. Solitaire, who scorned public opinion, was pleading with him to stay out of it. Meanwhile, the world was on the brink of destruction.

I got out of bed and went into the kitchen to look at the card. It seemed foreign, forlorn yet compelling for an index card. I returned to bed with it and snuggled under the blanket; I had been working the graveyard shift for six years, but my body still contracted at various crucial points in my neck, pelvis, and shoulders after staying up all night. I tried to relax my spastic muscles and lay on my stomach to reach for the sleek pink phone beside my bed. I dialed the number offered by "writer." There was no answer, not even a recorded voice informing me that its author could not "come to the phone right now." I hung up, relieved; my mental state, induced by such sudden contact with

Granite's fictional universe, was not one that could be shared with the prosaic writer.

I dug back into bed, cozily rubbing the inevitable granules away with my feet. In my mental parade, Granite's characters were followed by the four-square humans who had surrounded her, and the sensational drama of her life began to merge with the drama of her books. I saw Granite at the podium, her eyes storming as she lashed out at an idiot heckler from the audience who had stood during the question-and-answer period to say, "Doesn't your insistence on strictly objective truth lead to a kind of authoritarianism that—" "You are an authoritarian of the worst kind!" snarled Granite. "The authority of ignorance, of nothingness, of hallucination!" The article that appeared in *Demograph* that month read: "With a voice that would tuck a dog's tail between its legs, Miss Granite scourged the few non-believers who managed to get a word in edgewise," and the photo that accompanied it showed a homely little woman who could barely make herself seen behind a podium, pointing her thick finger at the world. I saw the journalists, who were allowed to attend the early meetings, clustered in their cheap suits, frowning with the greedy outrage of the self-righteous as they hunched and scribbled Granite's words on their pads of lined paper. Large, old-fashioned cameras emitted sour blooms of light as stern, unblinking Granite marched by, her purple-lined cape streaming behind her. I felt her outrage as columnists and third-rate thinkers denounced her everywhere. And I felt her glory as I beheld her, bedecked in a necklace of heavy turquoise, on the arm of Beau Bradley, her devastating raven-haired lover. Her short frame lengthened and liquified, her ruddy skin paled, her tight mouth swelled into a vicious pout as I watched her transforming into her creation Asia

Maconda, the international beauty and art critic who was swept off her feet by the brilliant sculptor, Frank Golanka, even as she fought to discredit him socially. I heard her rough, sorrowful voice, the Romanian accent that made her sound as if she'd swallowed a mouthful of ground glass and been surprised by how good it was. I saw myself, a near-psychotic child cuddled in the melancholy armchair in my father's room, dappled by splotches of sunlight through the cheesy curtains veiling the windows.

When I woke late in the afternoon, I called "writer" again. Again, no response. Instead of relief, I felt irritation. Why had this person put his/her number on a bulletin board if he/she didn't have a machine to take calls? I called twice in the following three days and was rewarded only with ringing. My irritation increased; still I was grateful to the nincompoop who didn't answer the phone. My life, divided into habitual motions of eating, reading, shopping, carrying loads of laundry back and forth on the same street, taking cabs to work, clutching my bags of snacks, had become laconic and disconnected; my strongest feeling in this scheme of things was the settled sense in my stomach when I sat before my desk at work. "Writer" had sent a current quivering through my quotidian existence, and now everything was significant. As I rode to work at night, I saw New York from Granite's perspective for the first time in eight years. The buildings of Wall Street became symbols of conquest, power, and money, the luscious fruit of life lived in the solid truth. The men who drove cabs and manned the rickety wooden candy/newspaper stalls were soldiers in the battle to uphold these standards. Mary, the white-haired word processor who works with me, was transformed from a cranky old woman into a fighter for the cause of concrete ideals; she was an excellent and compulsive worker who skipped lunch breaks, eating instead from a green box of Mystic Mint cookies in her drawer. Opposite her was the enemy, Joan, the complaining young woman who let her stomach hang out, who wrote articles on leftist painters who "challenge even our most basic assumptions about what is moral," and who would sneak away from her machine whenever she could to call her boyfriend and yell at him.

My almost daily calls to "writer" took on the ritual quality of my calls to Dial-A-Horoscope. It was a useless gesture and I knew it, yet somehow it was satisfying, a duty performed, a pretension of contact. I was taken off guard when she finally answered.

"Hello?" Her voice was flat, nearly metallic, except for the high pitch that made it the voice of a prematurely serious child. She said she was a free-lance journalist and that she wanted to write an article on Granite's philosophy, Definitism.

"I've just recently realized what an impact it has had on this country's psychology," she said solemnly. "It's quite remarkable. I don't think any other novelist has done anything comparable."

We talked enough for me to feel reassured that she wasn't one of Granite's enemies. I was lulled by the expressionless, melancholy quality of her voice.

"There's one thing I'd like to know," I said. I paused. "Let me preface this. During the beginning stages of the movement, there were a lot of people attracted to it who were a bit crazy. They would come to the meetings and say things about banding together and going off to an island to build a Definitist society—crazy. Granite was very kind to them of course, but she wasn't interested in those people. And I don't think their nutty ideas were any reflection of

Definitism. I just think that any major movement will attract its share of fanatics."

"Oh, I agree."

"And I wondered if those were the kind of people you've been seeing, so far."

The voice retained its flat thoughtfulness. "Well, I haven't done an interview yet. On the phone a few have sounded a little unhinged, but most of them seemed pretty ordinary, as far as I could tell. But I'm the last person to make judgments of other people's sanity."

"Yes, there is always that," I agreed. "There have been times, in the past, when I was a little bit . . . crazy myself. But those days are over. In any case, it wasn't the craziness in me that was responding to Anna Granite. It was the sanity."

"Well, seriously, I expect most Definitists to be quite sane," she said.

I was pleased after we hung up, and ready to start the project of the interview. I wrote "Justine Shade—10:00 A.M.—interview" inside one of the red-numbered squares on my calendar.

That was how it began, although to an objective party, it might look as though I were the strange world into which Justine unwittingly pitched herself. In any case, her effect on my mind and heart was immediate: the sad, voluptuous memories of Anna Granite would become, in the three or four days that would pass before the interview, memories of my childhood, as well as other things I don't like to think about. I spent hours before my legal documents, in my bed, and in the dream state of my cab rides, speculating on what kind of person Ms. Shade might be. I hadn't had a conversation about Anna Granite in at least eight years; in fact I couldn't remember the last time I'd had a genuine conversation at all. I invented possible scenarios daily, growing more and more excited by the impending intellectual adventure.

My wildest invention, however, didn't prepare me for what actually happened, which was mind-boggling even in the context of my circuitous and exhausting life. I had thought of Anna Granite as the summit of my life, the definitive, devastating climax—and yet perhaps she had only been the foreshadowing catalyst for the connection that occurred between me and Justine, the bridge without which our lives would have continued to run their spiritually parallel courses. But that is probably just the way it looks now.

*J*ustine Shade *was a neurotic,* antisocial twenty-eight-year-old. She had few friends, and as she saw them infrequently, her main source of entertainment was an erratic series of boyfriends who wandered through her small apartment, often making snide comments about her decor. She was serious about her career as a journalist, but she sold very few articles. This was because she got ideas at the rate of about one a year, and once she had one, she went through a lengthy process of mentally sniffing, poking, and pinching it before she decided what to do with it.

To support herself, she worked part time as an assistant secretary for a doctor of internal medicine. The job was lulling and comfortingly dull. Dr. Winkgard was an energetic, square, bad-tempered, good-hearted man, and his wife Glenda was a beautiful forty-year-old whose bright, erotic spirit, in combination with the stubborn way she held her mouth, made Justine think of a pungent, freshly cut lemon. The living room-like office was furnished with proud armchairs, a fiercely thin-cushioned sofa, a drawing of a geometric cat, and a radio that perpetually leaked a thin stream of classical music. The black-and-white striped walls and the purple carpet haughtily complemented each other. This office was the last place Justine would have expected to get an idea. But the fateful article on Anna Granite, which would, in an entirely unforeseen fashion, alter the course of her life, was born as she sat behind her desk, peacefully sorting papers.

She spent much of the day behind this desk with Glenda, welcoming the patients as they teetered in on their canes, hats listing on their heads. She wrote down their names, addresses, and birth dates on large index cards and guided them down the treacherously rumple-rugged hall to the electrocardiogram room, where she got them to take off their clothes and lie on the table so she could wire them to the machine. The EKG was a uniquely intimate process. The old, often odorous and clammy body lay spread out before her, affable and trusting, willing to let her squeeze blobs of white conducting glue on its ankles and wrists. Women lay docile as she lifted their limp breasts for the little red suction cups, even if there were lumpy brown sores beneath them. She saw eczema and swollen ankles and fragile chests bearing terrible scars. A lady with one eye blinded by milky fluid showed her the dainty bag of protective talismans she kept safety-pinned to her dirty bra.

One day she asked a fat, sweating woman how she was, and the lady burst into tears. "My husband, he is beating me," she said. "I am bruised, see?"

Justine was alarmed to see brown and purple splotches on her chest and stomach. Her alarm flustered her, and she didn't know what to say. "Why don't you hit him back?" she asked idiotically. "You're pretty big."

"Oh, he would kill me, he would crush me! He was in the army, he is strong, he knows how to kill!"

"Can't you leave?"

"Where would I go? I have no children. I have no one. He is going to kill me!" The weeping little eyes were finely shot with yellow veins.

Justine handed her a box of Kleenex. She took the EKG printout into Dr. Winkgard's office. "I think something terrible is happening," she said. "Mrs. Rabinowitz says her husband is beating her."

"Mrs. Rabinowitz is crazy," he said. "It's a very tragic case. She has a brain disease."

"But I saw bruises."

"Well, he does beat her sometimes, but she exaggerates. Sometimes she thinks the pills I give her are poison and she won't take them. It is a tragedy."

He went into the cardiogram room, and Justine heard him ask in his vibrant red ball of a voice, "How are we today, Mrs. Rabinowitz?" She took the manila folders of patients already seen and went back to the reception area. Mrs. Winkgard was picking the wilting blossoms from orchids in a vase, her head tilted slightly in appraisal.

"Glenda, Mrs. Rabinowitz just told me something terrible. She says her husband beats her. I told the doctor and he—"

"Yes, yes," said Glenda. "I know the situation. It is very sad. Both Jonathan and I have spoken to Mr. Rabinowitz. It seems to help for a while, but then he reverts. We've spoken to her as well. The problem is, she is as disturbed as he is."

"But it seems that something—"

The buzzer rang, and Glenda put a finger to her lips. It was Mrs. Wolfen, Mrs. Rabinowitz's sister. Her entrance, a dour presentation of ragged gray overcoat, folded hands, and disapproving jowls, effectively ended the conversation.

Sometimes a young person with a delicate heart would come to the office. If that person was a young woman, Dr. Winkgard would poke his smiling head out of his office to watch her advance towards him, his grin-wrinkled face set in the gloating, indulgent expression of a client just introduced to a teenaged prostitute. If it was a young man, the doctor would grin a more robust, less liquid grin and swing his hand through the air until it violently connected with the patient in a handshake of health and camaraderie that would have floored an oldster.

"It is good for him to look at a young body for a change," said Glenda.

It was from one of these diversionary young bodies that Justine got her idea.

He was a small nervous boy with a large round forehead, a saucy jawline, palpitations, and shortness of breath. Justine took him into the EKG room and closed the door. He took off his shirt and lay down; the little room became their private planet, with Dr. and Mrs. Winkgard hovering in the distance like friendly stars.

"What do you do?" asked Justine.

"I'm a writer," he said, "although I've never been published." He lifted his pretty head and looked at the painless clamps on his wrists and ankles.

"It'll only take a minute," she said.

He dropped his head back on the institutional pillow. "The thing is, I find it so hard to concentrate. I haven't written anything for a while."

"I write too," she said.

"Oh, then you understand."

The machine began to whirr; the thin needles jerkily sketched their abstract of the boy's heart.

"What do you think of Anna Granite?" he asked.

"I've never read her."

"Really? Oh, you've got to read her. She's the most unique writer. Of course, I don't believe in what she says politically, but still she's so powerful. Especially now, when people are so into whining and abdicating responsibility, it's good to read somebody advocating strength and power, and doing things. She had a lot of influence on me. I even thought of joining a Definitist organization."

"A what?"

"You know, the groups they used to have in the sixties where they got together and studied Granite's work. They're still around."

"You're kidding." She cut the printout on the tiny teeth of the machine and stuck it on the mounting paper. "I mean I knew she was popular, but—"

Dr. Winkgard entered with a broad flap of the door, shoulders squared in his white coat. "Come, Justine, what is taking so long?"

She returned to the stack of papers at her desk and brooded excitedly. It is hard to say why the Anna Granite story had impressed her, but almost immediately on hearing it she formed the tiny damp mushroom of an idea. Justine was morbidly attracted to obsessions, particularly the useless, embarrassing obsessions of the thwarted. She could not help but be drawn to the spectacle of flesh-and-blood humans forming their lives in conjunction with the shadows invented by a mediocre novelist.

"Glenda, have you ever read anything by Anna Granite?"

"Ah yes." Mrs. Winkgard nodded, her stubborn mouth set in admiration. "Very good writing, very dramatic. The clarity, the way she states her case. I read *The Bulwark* at a time when I was undergoing a crisis, and it gave me such moral support to read about those strong characters doing great things."

When Justine left work she bought a bag of cookies and rode home on the subway eating them with queenly elation, impervious to the crumpled bags and bad smells, the empty soda cans rattling about her feet. When she entered her apartment, she stripped off her pantyhose and called an editor she knew at *Urban Vision*.

The next day, she placed brief ads in *Manhattan Thing*, a monthly, and the weekly *Urban Vision*. To be sure she reached the serious nut population, she made up several index cards bearing a neutral statement which she placed on bulletin boards in rightwing bookstores, cafés, and an NYU building. She serendipitously stuck one on the wall of a laundromat in Queens where she had gone to argue with an exboyfriend before loaning him some money. Then she bought all of Granite's books, and started reading *The Last Woman Alive*, the story of a young woman caught in the grip of a socialist revolution in an imaginary society.

On Thursdays she went to the library with her notebook under her arm and did research. Granite had cut a colorful path through the media, starting with a few mild reviews of her early short-story collection, building in the seventies into lengthy, incredulous, outraged reviews as well as full-blown features about the "Stern Young Cult of Anna Granite," eventually culminating in sarcastic editorial denunciations by Austin Heller, Shepard Shale, and Michael Brindle, the foremost magazine intellectuals of the left and right wings. The last little noise was a long obituary in

*Opinion* by Heller, in which he told the story of their tentative friendship and eventual violent feud, after which Granite refused to be in the same room with him. He gloatingly referred to a time Granite "bawled" at a party after being insulted by a professor.

Justine left the library feeling as though she had been reading one of Granite's novels—the proud declarations, the dedicated followers, the triumphant public appearances, the controversy, the feuds, the denunciations, the main character storming from the room with her cape streaming from her shoulders after a violent confrontation with archenemy Austin Heller.

She began getting answers to her ads. The voices sounded like young, cramp-shouldered people taking their lunch breaks in cafeterias lit by humming fluorescent lights. She pictured women with sad hair in flower-print dresses and men with fleshy chests and hands. They all described what Granite had done for them, how she had made them value their lives, how she had inspired them to strive for the best they were capable of, whether as secretaries or as engineers. She made appointments to interview some of them, including one fellow who claimed to be a "Definitist intellectual."

Meanwhile, Katya, the heroine of *The Last Woman Alive*, had refused to join the Collectivist party, and had subsequently been thrown out of the academy, where she had been studying higher mathematics. She had been forced into an affair with the philosophically wrong Captain Dagmarov in order to save the life of her lover, Rex.

A week after the dissemination of the cards, she received a call from someone with a high-pitched voice that reminded her of a thin stalk with a rash of fleshy bumps. His name was Bernard, and, in addition to giving her the address of a study group that he attended in Brooklyn, he supplied her with the phone number of Dr. Wilson Bean, Granite's "intellectual protégé."

Bean's voice sounded as if it were being dragged along the bottom of an old tin tub. He didn't want to be interviewed; he spent minutes castigating the press, which he said had "crucified" him in the past, yet he continued talking. She pursued him down the center of his defense with the laser of her cold, clear voice, and she could feel herself contacting him. Grudgingly, with a lot of rasping around the bottom of the old tub, he agreed to talk to her again after she'd read *The Bulwark* and *The Gods Disdained*. He also advised her to attend the annual Definitist conference in Philadelphia, which would take place in a few weeks.

She hung up elated; the phone rang immediately. It was another Granite fan, a woman with a voice that, although riddled with peculiarity and tension, stroked Justine along the inside of her skull in a way that both repelled and attracted her. She said her name was Dorothy Never and she sounded like a nut. She'd been calling for days, she said, and she was so glad to have finally gotten through. Justine, trying to infuse her voice with seriousness and authority, was genuinely excited to hear that she had been a member of the original Definitist movement and had personally known Anna Granite, Beau Bradley, and Wilson Bean. She seemed not only willing but pathetically eager to be interviewed. They arranged a time, and Justine hung up full of amazement at the desire some people have for attention and publicity.

In the meantime, Katya had perished on an ice floe

in an effort to escape to America, Captain Dagmarov had killed himself on realizing that he was philosophically in error, and Rex, having been broken by the collectivist society around him, was writing pornography for a living.

*J*ustine Shade's voice sounded different in person than it had on the phone. Floating from the receiver, it had been eerie but purposeful, moving in a line towards a specific destination. In my living room, her words formed troublesome shapes of all kinds that, instead of projecting into the room, she swallowed with some difficulty. She sat in the least comfortable chair, blinking frequently under the squalid intensity of city sunlight pressing through my curtainless windows. She glanced surreptitiously at the horrified woman on the gold cover of *Night Duty*, the paperback on my coffee table. She picked at the dainty fried snacks I had placed between her seat and mine as I traveled from kitchen to living room arranging our tea things.

"I've been looking forward to this," I said. "I was dying to meet someone interested in Granite now, when it's no longer fashionable. Someone who isn't a zealot of some kind."

"Well you realize I'm not a Definitist," she said. She placed her narrow hands on the top knee of her crossed legs and tilted her small head away from her body, giving herself a neurotically asymmetrical but graceful appearance. She was a pretty woman, once you got used to her. Her skin was very white and clear, her small, finely shaped skull was set off by pale blond short-cropped hair. Her prominent cheekbones, strong chin, and high forehead complemented a face marred only by thin, tight lips and huge black glasses that sat crookedly on her small nose. I was a little disappointed by her. I had imagined a mature and handsome woman wearing a tailored gray suit and black stiletto heels carrying a small tape recorder. Justine dressed like a college kid: tight jeans, pointy red shoes, and a T-shirt with an indecipherable picture and the words "Girl World" on it. She held an already scrawled-in notebook on her knotted-up lap. She'd said that she'd written mainly for *Urban Vision,* and it was entirely believable to me that a *Vision* writer would look like this.

"But you seem to take Definitism seriously," I said.

"Oh, I do. Very seriously." Her wide gray eyes focused on me intently.

"Well, that means you respect it, and that's enough recommendation for me." I sat on the generous expanse of white-cushioned couch and spread my floor-length, bright-flowered dress around me. "Shall we start?"

"Okay." She smiled as this quasi word came from her mouth like a bubble that floated into the room and disappeared. "When did you first encounter Definitism?"

"As a teenager, when I read *The Bulwark.* I would say from about the tenth page on, it became the most important influence in my life—certainly the only positive influence." I paused. "Would you like tea?"

"Not now." She glanced with suppressed interest at my tea set. "Later I will."

"Let me explain what I meant by what I just said. I was a sexually abused child. I was forced to have an incestuous affair with my father, starting at age fourteen."

Her blank face registered nothing, but I could sense the telescope of her attention frantically adjust its gauge to examine my statement. "Have I upset you by telling you that?"

"No. No. I mean, yes. I mean it upsets me that it happened to you, but it doesn't shock me. I know it's very common. In fact, I was molested as a child." Slight pause, slight body recession. "When I was five years old, by a friend of my father's."

"Oh God."

"It didn't happen that often though. Maybe three or four times." Her face retained its serene surface. "I know that's not as awful as with your father because—"

"Stop. Don't deny your own experience. It's just not the kind of thing you can quantify. Any therapist will tell you that." I felt my face relaxing towards her in what I hoped was a pleasant way.

"I know, it's just that I can't imagine it happening over a prolonged period of time with your father." Her eyes flickered from me to the notebook; she paused, cheap ballpoint in mid-flight. Her attention zoomed at me like a bat. She tilted forward, her face shaded with melancholy puzzlement. What an odd little creature she was. "What I'm wondering about though, is . . . you know I'm writing an article for publication. Are you sure you want to be talking about this?"

"Oh, don't worry, I've done it before. I've been interviewed often in connection with Granite. A long time ago, but I'm quite used to dealing with it. I bring it up because it's important in connection with how Granite affected my life. And it's important to me to speak openly about it. But thank you. No one else in your position has ever thought to ask."

"Well, with something like this—I didn't know how experienced you were in an interview situation."

I thought I saw a shade of kindness in the dutiful shield of her expression. I felt a tendril of empathy appear between us. "It's all right. I know what I'm doing. I trust you."

"All right." Her pen was ready.

"So, anyway, by the time I was seventeen, I had a very negative view of life, and a horrific view of sex. Then I read Anna Granite and suddenly a whole different way of looking at life was presented to me. She showed me that human beings can live in strength and honor. And that sex is actually part of that strength and honor, not oppositional to it. And she was the first writer to do that, ever. To show that sex is not only loving but empowering and enlarging. Not only for men but for women. As you can imagine, this was a big revelation to me. And then the rest was just . . . the sheer beauty of her ideas. That morality is based on the right to choose for yourself, that your life is yours—she held up a vision for me, and her vision helped me through terrible times. I mean, by the time I discovered Granite, I had just about given up."

She glanced up at me with an expression that was impossible to read.

"I think I'm going to have some tea now." She scribbled wildly as I poured myself a cup of tea and stirred in the lumps of sugar and cream. I reached for a little boiled dumpling and reclined to eat it before going on.

"I finally escaped my father by going to a rather

strange little two-year college that I think has ceased to exist. But that didn't work out so well because I overloaded myself with a job and full-time classes, and I dropped out just before I would've graduated. It was around this time that I began attending Granite's lectures."

"What were they like?"

"They were wonderful, they were exciting. Beau Bradley was like one of her heroes. There were only about fifteen to twenty people in the original group, but that didn't diminish the sophistication, the intellectual thunder. I felt I was connecting with the life force of humanity. At the first lecture I sat there and wept. I just wept."

"What was Granite like?"

"My first reaction—I hate to say it but it's true—my first reaction was disappointment with her physical appearance. Everybody reacted that way. I was expecting—wanting—her to look like one of her heroines and here she was looking like a middle-aged housewife in a Chanel dress. No, no, she didn't look like that. I don't want that recorded."

Justine grudgingly gave her pen a token second of rest.

"She had beautiful lips and eyes, the most intense eyes. They were huge and soulful, and I have never seen a photograph that does them justice. She was a short woman, but she stood tall. She used to come to the meetings wearing this beautiful black cape with purple lining, and the moment she walked in, it was like magic." Images of Granite, Bradley, and his rosy-skinned wife Magdalen zipped through my mind in vivid succession, as if imprinted on bright, quickly flipped cards. "There was one time I especially remember that she came in wearing a pale blue dress and the most astonishing turquoise necklace you ever saw. This necklace was just so shimmering and so full of light, it was like the sun and stars combined. It was unreal. And another thing about that night"—I paused to adjust my dress, to tuck one leg safely under me—"she had just come back from a vacation in Jamaica, and she had this dark, beautiful tan. And it was impossible not to notice that Beau Bradley had a dark, beautiful tan, too, and that Magdalen did not."

Justine looked up with what was beginning to be an annoyingly impartial expression. "In some of the things I've read, it was implied that they'd had an affair, but I—"

"Oh, they did. It was obvious that Granite and Bradley had gone away that weekend. Poor Magdalen knew about it. That day after the weekend, Granite was just radiant, so triumphant, that it was even more obvious." I stopped to assess the effect of my words. "I know this sounds like trashy gossip. But I don't say it disrespectfully. The only reason I bring it up is because of how it fits in to what ultimately happened in the movement."

Justine looked at me with puzzlement; she unknotted her legs and shifted them demurely to one side. "My next question relates to that," she said. "How has the character of the movement changed in the last ten years?"

I did not see the relationship this question bore to my information, but I answered it anyway. "It's disintegrating without a strong center. The last Definitist meeting I went to was eight years ago. It was at the Centurion Hotel, as it had originally been, and Wilson Bean was speaking. It was nothing like the original lectures. It was so depressing. Poor Wilson stood up there, hanging on the lectern and blabbing, with his little twit girlfriend sitting behind him. What was especially significant to me—at the original meetings, there were these beautiful crystal chandeliers hanging from the ceiling and a lush thick carpet on the floor, and elegant, velvet high-backed chairs for the audience. And on every single chair was placed a pad of heavy vellum note paper and a thick silver pen. Can you imagine? Who else would go to such lengths? It was pure enchantment. And at that last meeting, they were using folding chairs and fluorescent lights. It was still the Centurion Hotel, but they'd rented a cheap room. That was it in a nutshell." I took an egg roll from my platter. "Don't you want anything?"

She looked quickly away from her notes. "I think I am ready to have a little bite." She zeroed in on a piece of sweet and sour pork that I suspect she'd been eyeing all along. She daintily dabbed her lips with the tip of her tongue. I finished my egg roll and poured another cup of tea.

"Have you met Wilson or any of the others who were around then?"

"Wilson Bean I've only talked to on the phone. One or two, I've met."

"What were they like?"

"Pleasant, polite."

"I'm glad to hear it." I tried to see an oddly pretty, coldly vulnerable little woman like Justine through the eyes of a male intellectual; yes, they'd like her all right. "Some of them weren't pleasant at all. I used to see some of Granite's followers do things like attack people who were basically silly and harmless and unable to defend themselves in front of Granite, to impress her. There was one fellow who publicly demeaned his girlfriend. There was a lot of sheer flirtation too. Lots of girls fell in love with Definitism because of the erotic power of the books. No one wanted to admit how important the sex was, but let's face it— the books were very erotic. There were all these intrigues going on, all these little girls wanting to satisfy their sexual cravings, and some of the men took full advantage."

I took a deep drink of tea. It was too sweet, and I enjoyed it as I enjoyed reconstructing the movement that had transported me from the evil universe of my childhood to the bland and benevolent planet of my Queens apartment, my cabs, my legal documents. "It's disturbing to me that there were cruel and exploitative people in the movement. And some of them were Granite's right-hand people, her intellectuals, for God's sake."

We regarded each other for a few seconds. She unfolded her legs, sat up straight, and asked, "How do you explain those kinds of people in Anna Granite's following?"

"I was going to get to that." I paused, and in that pause tried to gauge the hopefulness of conveying my meaning to this unresponsive creature. I saw Bradley and Granite before me on the lectern, saw Granite's meaningful look as she caressed Bradley's hand while handing him the notes for his speech, saw Magdalen's averted eyes and Bradley's manly coolness. "You see, Granite and Bradley were two rare creatures. They were of the same species. And that they should be sexually mated as well as professionally, philosophically mated—well, it was like the Definitist formula for matching components. According to Definitism, it was logically impossible for them not to have an affair. And it was equally impossible for Magdalen, as a Definitist, to refuse to accept it, as it was to her partner's highest good, and so on. But you see, it happened only because Bradley believed that sexual desire must spring from objective admiration. He believed he should desire Granite when he didn't. And she tried to demand from him that which can't be demanded. It became really awful to watch. She was a good twenty years older than he, and I think that, with a young man . . . well, it was just undignified somehow. It finally came to a head during a party at the Centurion. Bradley had foisted Magdalen off on a body builder who'd just joined the meetings"—a painful and acute flash of that melancholy muscle man, his hammy hands absently patting Magdalen's waist as her trembling body huddled against his bulk—"but instead of dancing with Granite he spent the whole evening courting a beautiful blond actress named Cheryl Bland. And Granite was furious. She finally ordered the music stopped and stalked out, her cape streaming behind her. The next day Bradley's Definitist Symposium was closed down, and Bradley was a broken man. I remember him that last day, leaving his office with a cardboard box of papers and books. He just kept saying, 'I'm sorry, I'm so sorry.' It was a permanent rift, and none of their ideas, however great, could help them." I paused, dizzy with the memory, the awful wrenching apart of these magnificent human beings who should've been together forever, yet never could. Justine's face had taken on a matte dreamy quality.

"Bradley nearly killed himself, but in the end he faced it, admitted his error, and rebuilt his life. He went to Canada and married Cheryl Bland—she was maimed two years later in a hunting accident, a tragic story. But Granite failed to examine what had happened. She hardened in her position that Bradley was a traitor to Definitism, and everybody around her had to harden theirs to suit her. By that time she had backed herself into a corner and surrounded herself with wimps and that's why she wound up playing Twenty Questions with sycophants instead of leading a movement."

I regarded Justine happily. She was scribbling dutifully. I had underestimated her. She seemed unresponsive only because she had been listening so intently, her attention too focused to allow outward expression. There was something wonderfully consistent about her. She was like Katya, the serious, doomed young heroine of Granite's early *Last Woman Alive*, Katya who never reveals her emotions, letting the nature of her thoughts and actions stand alone. I remembered that Justine was a molested child, and her methodical reserve became all the more poignant. I reclined and allowed a sensation of personal contact and intimacy to assail me. We could be friends. We could be more than friends; she could be the one to at last tell the truth about Anna Granite to an ignorant world. When she looked up at me, I was convinced of it; her demeanor was that of one who has just come to an understanding.

"So you still consider yourself a Definitist, even though you reject the idea of matching components?"

It was a disappointment, but I answered it.

"I don't reject it, I—" There was a twinge of hostility in my chest. "Look, you're really not getting it. The most important thing about Definitism isn't matching components, it's that it takes life seriously, which is rare. She said reality was definable—no one was saying that in the sixties. She said you were important in reality, that you could control it. She was the first person to tell me I was important and that I could come out and say so."

"Do you feel that fatalism was pushed on you in school or elsewhere?"

"Yes. One of my first memories is having to deny the concrete truths of my life, of denying the clear pattern of them. In school, everything was disconnected, you were never supposed to discover the way things interlocked."

I regarded Justine with dislike and awaited her next prepackaged question.

"Do you think all of the evil in the world can be attributed to denying an interconnected reality?"

"Evil comes from denying reality. Period. If my father hadn't deluded himself, he never would have been able to do what he did. You have to distort reality to rationalize evil acts."

I was suddenly very tired. A world had been created between this girl and me, a subtle, turbulent, exhausting world. I had not had such a long conversation with anyone for over two years.

"I think I will have some tea now," she said.

"Go right ahead. Although it's probably cold."

I watched her lean forward to fuss with the tea things. Her movements were careful and graceful. Perhaps I had reacted to her too harshly. She had, after all, just barely been exposed to the complexities of Definitism. There was ink on the tips of her blunt-nailed fingers.

She sat back in the uncomfortable chair and sipped her tea from the turquoise cup. The sun had moved, or been blotted by a cloud, and she was no longer so oppressed by its light. She looked at me frankly, perhaps a little sadly, as she placed her cup on the table and reclaimed her pen and pad. "I hope I'm not taking too much of your time," she said.

"Oh no. I don't work until midnight tonight so I have plenty of time." I omitted telling her that in my eagerness to speak with her I had stayed up past my bedtime, and that I was thus punchy and skittish.

"There's just a few more questions."

"All right."

"Why do you think Definitism frightens people so?"

"Because it's powerful. It glorifies the freedom of the individual, and nowadays that sort of philosophy is labeled fascistic. People think if you make moral judgments, or work hard for a goal and don't let yourself be deterred, if you accomplish something, that you're right wing and somehow unfeeling to other people's plights." I glanced out my windows into the health club across the street. The exercise class was starting. I could make out the dim shapes of thickset young men in shorts stretching themselves, posing on steely machines, prowling. "People made a lot of assumptions about Granite that simply weren't true. It's possible to have great humanity and be a Definitist. I once protected a prostitute from an abusive client—let her stay with me, helped her get back on her feet. And when people who knew I was a Definitist heard that I'd done that, they were shocked that I would protect such a woman, as if being a Definitist and a compassionate person were a contradiction in terms."

They were lining up, jostling into position like ponies, pointing their toes against the floor to flex their calves. The instructor stood by, slim hip tilted, indolently lifting and dropping a small barbell in one hand. I wasn't usually awake to see this class. They were restful and pleasing to watch when they did their exercises in formation: dozens of boys bending, stretching, and jumping in harmony, standing splaylegged to lift weights, or on their backs, rapidly curling and uncurling like wounded ants.

"People only accept the validity of movements that champion the underdog and scorn those that champion people of great accomplishment. You always have to take the dumbest as your lowest common denominator." The phrase caught in my throat; it had a hard, treacherous shape. I imagined my words tumbling atop each other, snarling together, forming a hostile tangle around my feet that I vainly struggled to escape as a chorus of Granite's enemies stood and pointed and said, "So! You despise the weak, the helpless . . ." "So people start to think that someone like me, a Definitist, would not feel sympathy for the weak and helpless. Well, they don't know what the fuck they're talking about. Pardon my French." I wrenched myself free of the trap and stood defiant, fists clenched at my sides. Justine stared at my sudden anger. "I had a friend once named Kim who happened to be retarded. We used to belong to a women's support group, and those women there, those Marxist, feminist bitches, they ignored Kim, they hurt Kim, they would kill Kim if they thought it would further a cause. They would victimize the weak and the helpless. Not me. And not Granite." Kim's loose-eyeballed face and pathetic form stood peeping from behind my defiant, fish-clenching figure.

The exercisers began their jumping jacks.

"How did Granite react to the press?"

"She was hurt by them. She could never really defend herself against them, especially after Bradley left. She was a tough lady supreme. But somehow her very toughness made her vulnerable to jerks. If she was wrong but thought she was right she would go to the death to defend it—and she did in the case of Beau Bradley. She was brilliant, she was powerfully sexual, and she spoke with a glamorous accent. When the average person sees a woman with all these qualities plus, he is going to be overwhelmed with how small he is in comparison. She scared the shit out of them. She believed in herself and they didn't believe in themselves, and they hated her for that. The critics gang-raped her. She tried to fight back but she just wasn't capable of dealing on their niggling, ugly level."

The boys across the street blurred before the vision of an elderly Granite on the dull gray box of my TV set. She was the guest on a talk show, sitting in a plush swivel chair. "Do you know what I have to say to those who don't agree with me? Fine, don't agree. But don't come on my show and ruin it for everybody else." The audience laughed.

I viewed the exercisers sadly. Justine followed my gaze. They were bending in unison in solemn, balletic toe-touches. We could faintly hear the sonorous thump of the disco music that bore them along.

"Do you see a contradiction in the sexual behavior of her characters—the pattern of dominance and submission that she says is, in other spheres, irrational? Do you find that the behavior of her female characters is a denial of themselves in reality—for example, when Skip beats up Solitaire and she likes it?"

The stupid and self-righteous nature of this question cast a grim shadow on my hopes for the quality of Justine's article. The sight of the joyful exercisers soured, as did the awful green of the instructor's sweatsuit. "Solitaire likes it, not because she's hit, but because it's Skip. It's totally different from the kind of neurotic masochism you're implying."

"Well, then, there's the rape thing with Asia Maconda and Frank Golanka."

"Look, I'm a sex abuse victim and so are you, and you ought to be able to understand. Asia is presented as having a problem, for one thing. She's neurotic and she needs this kind of crushing force to act upon her because she needs to be broken in a way, but it's got nothing to do with masochism. Asia is exalted when Frank Golanka takes possession of her. She is not demeaned. A masochist is somebody like my mother who was demeaned by her subservience to a cruel, dishonest, contemptible man. When the women in Granite's books submit, they do it out of strength, out of choice, as a gift. That's the difference between masochism and love, and if you don't see that, then you're crazy."

Justine's jaw muscles flinched spasmodically as she scribbled; her fingers were tight on her pen. She was skewed by a renewed blast of sunlight. Minute cinders of light darted and vanished in the air between us, the hallucinated discharge of my wrath. My head felt separated from my body; I floated, stretched out, calm and naked in a soothing space above our ugly disconnected conversation. Below, my intestines contracted into a malign snake. A large gas bubble solemnly floated up from my abdomen. The exercisers jogged gaily in place, hands flopping at their sides.

"I have to go to the bathroom," I said.

In the placid enclosure of aqua tiling, my intestines warred, suffered, and subsided. The fierce cylindrical lights on either side of the mirror above the basin revealed a surprising face; instead of the angry, adamant woman I had expected to meet, there was the porous, puffy, pink-splotched face of an exhausted person on the verge of tears. Only my bright eyes, shining bravely and a little too enthusiastically above dark and heavy skin revealed my fighting spirit. But who was I fighting? The collegiate mouse in my living room? I finished my ablutions in the aqua basin, opened the window a crack, and sat on the edge of the tub for a moment.

I returned to the living room to find Justine contemplatively eating an egg roll.

"I think you're misunderstanding me," she said. "I'm not asking these questions because I think those things about Granite's work. It's just that these accusations have been made against her, and if I'm going to write an article, I have to address them."

"But do you understand what I'm saying? I

wouldn't consider it demeaning to worship at the feet of a hero."

"I know what you mean. I even know what you mean when you say that Asia needed to have something taken from her by force for it to mean anything. I've had an experience like that myself."

All my eagerness to like Justine frolicked in the air between us. "Really?"

"It wasn't that I was raped or anything. Just that about three years ago I had a relationship with someone who sort of . . . in bed, opened me up in a way that I had no control over."

"Oh! Really?"

"And it was the most moving thing because I was never able to open up to anyone else before that. And no one else had been able to really penetrate me. I didn't have any choice either, the way he did it. He just made it happen."

"Oh!" I was intoxicated with the ravishment of Justine. I envisioned her, her nervous jaw relaxed, her neck arched, throat exposed, the brittle crust of her public persona broken and stripped off. What would you find under that crust? "Did he say anything about what happened?"

"No. We didn't talk about it."

"How wonderful of him not to say it!"

"I'm not sure he noticed, actually."

"Oh, surely he noticed! Are you still together?"

"No." She inclined her head downward, closed her notebook. "He was sort of awful, generally."

She put her red-shoed feet together and began to organize her papers. From the kitchen, the refrigerator whirred and droned. A gauzy float of dust twinkled in the fading sun. What did she mean, sort of awful?

"I just brought it up so you'd know that I understand you." She closed her notebook and put her pen in her small fat burgundy handbag. "I'm done interviewing you. Unless you have anything more you'd like to say."

"No, I think we've covered it." My body posed in a sore slump on the edge of the couch. Justine stood, glancing around as though she'd dropped something. "But if you'd like to stay and visit a while and help me finish these snacks, we could talk some more about some of the things we've started. Just in a personal way."

Her eyes widened and lightly filmed over, as though she had withdrawn behind a veil of polite embarrassment. "Thank you but I really can't. I've got a lot to do today and I've already spent more time than I'd planned. But thank you. It's been very interesting."

"Perhaps you'd like to come back tomorrow? Or the next day? We could have lunch."

"I don't know, I . . . maybe. I'm busy but I could . . . I could call you."

Her hand was on the doorknob. She was fleeing.

Every loneliness is a pinnacle. I opened the door for her. From the safety of the hall she promised to send me a copy of the published article, and then she was gone. I returned to the couch and sat on it. The rims of my eyeballs had dried out. My tail bone had become a focal point of exhaustion. But I knew I couldn't sleep. I sat for several seconds feeling the apartment recover from the presence of a stranger. While she had sat before me, a foreign vibration had quivered through the air, handling and examining everything it brushed against, subtly changing the attitude and appearance of my knickknacks and furniture, giving everything the stiff, careful quality of the scrutinized. Slowly, the room settled into ease as the last tremors of that inquisitive quiver subsided. The cool beige carpet crawled happily along the floor.

The refrigerator whirred. I turned on the television. It was *Firing Squad* with Austin Heller. His guests were Donovan Milundira, the exiled Czech author and somebody else, a dense old fellow with massive eyebrows and a hand lifted to dangle before his mouth. I sat on the floor to watch it, my back against the soft white plush of the couch, my legs stretched before me.

"So I am not exaggerating to say you despise Chernovsky?" asked Heller. He popped his eyes and rapidly flicked the tip of his tongue against both corners of his open mouth—a weird and unattractive habit he had developed recently.

I raised my baggy flowered dress and crept along the floor to the window. I stood upright on my knees and rested my arms on the ledge. The exercise class had ended. A few lone boys still lolled about, stretching and chatting. One leaned pensively on the window ledge, a fluff of blond hair across his sulky brow, his squared chin resting on his fist. Beyond him, in the fluorescent shadows of the gym, I dimly saw two boys standing to talk, their inclined hips almost touching. The taller one rested his thick forearm on the shoulders of the lighter boy, who looked shyly down. I dropped my eyes to the street below. Everywhere there were people with their arms around each other.

I picked up the bottle of Magic Bubble that I kept on the window sill, and removed the slim wand from the mysteriously blue, ether-smelling liquid. I dipped the wand again and leaned out the window with it; the iridescent chemicals that stretched invisibly across the wand's small hoop caught the sun and glimmered before I blew. A dozen bubbles floated free. They dallied wondrously in midair, as though unsure what to do with their new life, and then meandered on the wind, all the way to the corner below, into crowds of people waiting for the light with their briefcases and bags. The pedestrians looked up, confused, looked all around for the source of the bubbles, watching in fascination as the shiny circles drifted into the street to be murdered by traffic. I raised my wand and blew another doomed, shimmering flock.

I envisioned pale Justine in the arms of her powerful lover, her small head thrown back in surrender. I felt a pinch of pain. The pouting boy across the street had left the window. Only vague shadows were visible in the fluorescent depths of the gym. Every loneliness is a pinnacle.

I turned away from the windows and faced the room. I had wanted to tell Justine about my childhood.

# PART TWO

$W$*henever I think of the house* I grew up in, in Painesville, Pennsylvania, I think of the entire structure enveloped by, oppressed by, and exuding a dark, dank purple. Even when I don't think of it, it lurks in miniature form, a malignant doll house, tumbling weightless through the horror movie of my subconscious, waiting to tumble into conscious thought and sit there exuding darkness.

Objectively, it was a nice little house. It was a good size for three people; it had a slanting roof, cunning shutters, lovable old doorknobs that came off in your hands, a breakfast nook, an ache of dingy carpets and faded wallpaper. It was our fifth house, the one we collapsed in after a series of frantic moves which were the result of my father's belief that wherever he lived was hell. Eventually he became too exhausted to move again and made our sedentary status a virtue, gloating as he gazed out through the cracked shutters at the arrivals and departures of several sets of neighbors on both sides—the Whites, the Calefs, and the Hazens on the left, and the Wapshots, the Rizzos, and the morose, relatively stationary old Angrods on the right. "We live in a society of cockroaches," he said. "Scurrying all over the face of the map with no thought of community or family, nothing."

The Painesville house was the most significant point of my upbringing, and it unfolds from its predecessors with the minor inevitability of an origami puzzle in several pieces. With each house the puzzle becomes more sinister, then more sad, then simply strange, the final piece made from a grainy photograph of Anna Granite's face. I imagine Justine Shade picking up the various paper constructions to examine them, furrowing her brow, tapping her lip with her pen.

I was born in Blossom, Tennessee. I think of grape arbors, trellises clotted with magnolias, the store downtown that sold white bags of candy. (There actually was a grape arbor in our backyard in Blossom, but our second, more lived-in Tennessee house near Nashville had a square backyard full of short grass and festering sunlight.)

One of my succession of therapists used to say that "the body remembers everything," meaning that on some level so deep you don't even know about it, you've stored compressed yet vivid details of everything that's ever happened to you, including, she was later to assert, everything in your past lives. This could be true, I guess, but these bodily memories are so unevenly submerged and revealed, so distorted—as the deficient yard is garnished with imaginary arbors and trellises—that they may as well be completely invented; it's only the hideous physical shock that attends the mere shadow of one remembered gesture, that fraction of some past agony that reminds you they were real.

. . .

*M*y *mother, whose name* was Blanche, came from a poor but respectable matriarchal farm family. She was the oldest of three girls, but she was the shortest, the shyest, the one most likely to be teased. As the oldest she was responsible for taking care of her sisters, Camilla and Martha, when there was no school and their mother went into town to clean rich people's houses. This was a hopeless arrangement, as Camilla and Martha were strong, boisterous girls who banded against their sister, barred her from their games, and ridiculed her. They refused to get up to eat her carefully prepared breakfasts, they wouldn't help her with the dishes, they ran around the house like cats, knocking things down while she tried to clean. The sole factor that enabled the harried girl to maintain any order at all was her intense and agitated seriousness. Her idea of the world was a pretty picture of shiny pink faces and friendly animals in nature scenes, of dulcet conversations and gestures, a lively but always gentle and harmonious world that could not accommodate (and could be totally undone by) sarcasm or cruelty. Out of the need to impress a lacelike pattern on brutish reality came her unshakeable determination to clean and sew and mop the floor. She got up before sunrise to get cream and eggs. She wreathed her table settings with clover and daisies. She made jam and arranged the jars so that their colors complemented one another: mint, plum, cherry, apple. Her sisters' jeering hurt her, but it also roused and locked into position a surprising element of strength that dignified her melancholy zeal, which caused her unkind sisters to remember her, in their broken-down middle years, with pathos and respect.

The same frantic need to prettify informed her mothering. We spent a lot of time together when I was five, more than I spent with other children. On Saturdays, we sat at the kitchen table, intently drawing crayon animals in their jungles or under cloud-blotched skies. We made stories illustrated by pink-earred families of mice. We built homes for my animals that ranged across rooms, and my mother always consented to "hold" the wicked frog who lived in a penthouse atop my dresser. Or my mother would read *The Wizard of Oz* aloud. Other times we would sit on the couch and my mother would show me art books and prints, inviting me to invent stories about the little boy in red and ruffles standing alone with a bird on a leash. And at night, she would sit on my bed and tell stories of her girlhood. I would hold her hand as she constructed airy balloons that floated by in the dark, bearing glowing pictures of her and my father holding hands on the porch swing, or of her lying in a meadow of clover, dreaming and looking for fairies while horrible Camilla called her home.

My father entered this magic world in the evening, when he returned home from work in grandness, and our phantasms and elves stood at attention to receive his directions. He would put on one of his records—opera, marching music, or jazz—and turn up the volume so that it trumpeted aggressively through the house, ramming his personality into every corner. My mother worked in the kitchen, stirring a big pot of chili, or peeling potatoes, and my father would pace excitedly between kitchen and living room, drinking beer after beer and eating the dry roasted peanuts, sliced Polish sausage, and hot green peppers that my mother had arranged in little dishes as, against a thundering soundtrack, he expounded upon his day. He was an office manager in the clerical department of a sales firm in Nashville. He would talk about the office intrigue as though it were symbolic of all human activity, as though he were enacting daily the drama of good versus evil, of weakness versus strength, of the fatal flaws that cause otherwise able men to fail, of the mysterious ways of the universe that make the rise of "bastards" possible. He would start on some tiny incident—how "that socialist shit-ass Greenburger" had tried to undermine the unfortunate clubfoot Miss Onderdonk in order to cast favor on a pretty new typist, and how he was publicly exposed and deplored— and then link this to some greater abstract principle, cross-referencing it to events in his childhood, or his stint in the army, as though one had led, inexorably and triumphantly, to the other. The room filled with overlapping scenarios from the past—his past, as created by me—that appeared in a sweet-smelling, melancholy wave of events, picnics, days at school and old ladies that had clasped him in their perfumed arms before slipping away forever, carrying on its crest, and depositing safely in our living room, the scene now transpiring.

He paced as he talked, now and then walking close to the windows to peer out, rubbing his fingers together as though grinding something to powder, nibbling zestfully at the snacks that occasionally dropped down his shirt front, and drinking beer. My mother moved about the kitchen in a frilly apron, her hair bound into a ponytail with a rubber band garnished with large plastic flowers. She listened enthralled to the stories of betrayal and redemption, nodding vigorously, shaking her head in disapproval or agreeing, "Absolutely! That's right!" as the music underscored her husband's stirring rendition of his eventual triumph. "You can't throw your weight around like that in my office, buddy. It's okay to be a tough guy, but you'd better be sure I'm not tougher. And nine times out of ten I am." I would listen gravely as they talked.

It seemed as though they were arranging the world, making everything safe and understood. By the time we sat down to dinner, life was friendly and orderly, and we could regally feast on chili over spaghetti noodles, with chocolate ice cream in little ceramic cups for dessert. Then there would be TV—soldiers winning, dogs rescuing children, criminals going to jail, women finding love—and then my mother would carry me to bed singing, "Up the magic mountain, one, two, three. Up the magic mountain, yessiree."

*When I was five years old,* my mother had a friend named Edwina Barney who came almost every afternoon to teach her how to drive and later, how to swim. She was tall, slender, and gracefully slow-moving; she had a large benign face with slightly pouchy cheeks, a relaxed mouth, and heavy-lidded eyes that, in glasses, had a slightly crocodilian look. She wore loose clothes with big, bright patterns on them and sandals with red cherries on the toes. She towered over my nervous-moving little mother. When I went with them to the "Y" for the swimming lessons and sat in the tiled "pool area," rolling ungnawable jawbreakers from cheek to cheek, I admired her gliding through the pool like an imperious seal, my mother dog-paddling behind, her sincere obedient head lifted tensely out of the water. After class, Edwina drove us home with one long arm hanging halfway out the open window, talking about small subjects with a manner that made them big, all her words planted firmly in the low, relaxed sound of her voice. When we got home, she and my mother would sit in the kitchen drinking coffee, their swimsuits hanging on chairs placed before the stove, Edwina stretching her legs out over an extra chair, talking in her strong, melodious voice that my mother's voice responded to or complemented rather than met. It was clear to me where the authority lay between them. Our family was self-contained and hoarding, with a clear sense of separation from other people, and Edwina was like an emissary from another kingdom, an ally who traveled through the chaos of cars and strangers and traffic systems to share this authority with us, this quality that enabled her to say whatever she wanted to say and have it be so. That, along with her physical grace (and in my eyes, beauty), made me love her. I rushed to meet her when she came to the door, I introduced her to my stuffed animals and showed her my drawings which she would study and say, of my portrayal of a lion, "That's a real lion all right. It may not look exactly like a real lion, but that doesn't matter because it's got lionness," and it would be so.

I loved her even when, one day after class when we were all in the kitchen, there was a sudden change in the tone of conversation, and Edwina jerked her head in irritation and said the word "stupid." I was busy working on a drawing and I didn't hear the entire sentence, but I knew from the way my mother suddenly turned her head and reflexively picked an already chewed nail that she had been called stupid. There was only a moment of silence, and then they went on talking, my mother moving with stiff animation when she got up to get a plate of cookies for them to eat. Edwina sat with her head and face presented regally to the room, her oddly self-righteous expression that of a person who has successfully imposed her personality on someone else.

Like Edwina, my father could say it and it would be so. Sometimes he would come home when Edwina was still visiting and he would say, "Hey, it's old Ed Barney!" and invite her to stay "for a few brews." When that happened, we would all move into the living room, and my father would put on a record, and they would talk, each telling truths and agreeing with one another, organizing the world with their words and deciding what was right or wrong as the music ranted. "That's right," one would say to the other, as they all vigorously nodded their heads. "You're absolutely right."

Once though, Edwina did not agree with my father. He sat in his chair with his neck craning angrily forward, rubbing his fingertips together as though crushing something into powder. He used words I didn't understand in a tone of voice that filled the room and pressed down on my neck, making me want to compress my bones and breath. My mother said, "Oh Al." He ignored her, crushing her voice with his yells. Edwina sat stiff and bristling in her chair, her long hands deliberately loose on her wrists. She talked, and he interrupted her. He stamped over her words, but her face and body held the weight of his voice off her, and she occupied the little space around her with the same imperious face she'd made when she called my mother stupid. My father strained forward as though he would spring.

"I'm not going to stay and listen to this," she said, and she stood, knocking over her glass of beer. As she walked to the closet to get her coat, my father did spring, and I was shocked to see Edwina break into a run, which she controlled almost immediately. My father followed her out the door yelling at her, his fists balled. I understood that he was telling her she was bad, evil, she had aligned herself with the terrible things in the world. I don't remember if I felt anger or sadness or fear. I can only picture myself frozen and compressed, staring at my crayon drawing. I can't remember what my mother did.

It was a long time before Edwina came to see us again. When she did, she and my father were friends again, but their faces held little reservations that prevented total agreement. He would look at her as though she were a naughty but lovable child, and she would look at him as though he were not as smart as she was but that she liked him anyway. There was no change between Edwina and my mother.

*This and every other* image from that time is faded, small and surrounded by a thick border of fuzzy, quavering blackness. The images aren't connected; there are large spaces between them filled with the incoherent blackness. The emotions belonging to the images are even more unclear; they seem a slur of abnormal happiness, as if my childhood were characterized by the cartoons I watched on TV. This is probably because the adults around me, believing childhood to be a pretty thing, encouraged me to feel that way, talking to me in baby talk, singing about itsy-bitsy spiders and farmers in the dell, laying an oil slick of jollity over the feelings that have stayed lodged in my memory, becoming more and more grotesque as time goes on. But the feelings continue to lurk, dim but persistent, like a crippled servant, faithfully, almost imbecilicly trying to tell me something in the language of my childhood, my own most intimate language which has become an indecipherable code.

*I remember the time* a kid fell off our porch and cracked his skull. It was Halloween, and I wasn't allowed to go out because my mother thought that, at five, I was too young. My mother dressed for the occasion in her red terry-cloth robe that reached the floor and made her look thick and imposing. The ordinary packaged candy looked special in a large crystal punch bowl. She handed it out with a gently officious air, enjoying herself as my father sat quietly in the shadows of the dim, radio-mumbling house. Most of the kids in our neighborhood were close to my age, and they stood bashful and ungainly in their monstrous wings and clown feet, incredulous and feeling slightly guilty that a stranger had put on a ceremonial dress to give them handfuls of candy. Sometimes a crowd of big kids would come and bellow "trick or treat" like a threat, or even thrust their masked faces into our living room to scream right at my mother, who screamed in return and hurriedly thrust the candy at them. It was during one of these screaming moments that we heard the real screams of a small child who had just fallen off the porch. There was a scramble of movement amid masked children in the dark, and then the boy was in our bright kitchen, sitting on a stool, bundled in a blanket, sucking his thumb. Probably his parents were there somewhere, but I don't remember them. My mother was on the phone to the hospital, picking her nails while my father paced in and out of the room, coughing and wiping his mouth. He said something that made me think we could get into trouble because the boy fell off our porch.

I was frightened and fascinated by the boy. It terrified me to think that you could be standing on a porch, my porch, receiving official candy in a spirit of goodwill and then, with one wrong movement, be pitched into darkness, cracking your head in way that could kill you. I stared at his eyes. They were a garish painted mask of red and blue, his sole costume. His lashes were long and beautiful, his eyes serene and wide, completely undisturbed by the large red gash in his head. I stared at the gash and at the brown hairs mashed around in the blood. I thought I was looking right into his brain. It seemed glowing and wonderfully mysterious. I felt very close to him. I wanted to put my hand in his head. We could get into trouble for this.

He started to whimper and tremble and to suck violently on his thumb. My mother got off the phone and came to him. "Poor little one," she said. "Soon everything will be all right." She put her arm around him, and suddenly I wanted to do the same, to protect and heal the boy.

I ran out of the kitchen and got my stuffed animal, a little limp dog named "Greenie." I thrust it at the boy and said, "Take Greenie." He did. He held Greenie tightly with one arm, sucking his thumb, quiet again, his beautiful eyes looking at me with what seemed like curiosity. I stared into his deep red brain until my mother bundled him in her sweater and took him to the hospital.

I let him take my toy. I felt that Greenie had helped him in some way, and it made me feel good to think that I could help a person, especially a person whose brain I'd seen. When I got Greenie back the following week, I valued him all the more as a healer and personal emissary of my goodwill.

When it was over, my father held me on his lap. He held me as though he was frightened of what had happened to the boy and thought I must be frightened too. The house was dark, the radio was singing to us in the background. His hands encircled the ankle of one of my legs and the knee of the other, and I rested in his body as though it were infinite. He said, "The Daddy will never let anyone hurt his little girl." He said it as though the sentence itself was grand, as though saying it turned him into a stone lion, immobile but internally watchful and fierce.

. . .

*O*nce *my father took me with him* to watch a basketball game. These were the games he talked about when he walked around the house, rubbing his fingers together and saying "the Mighty Reds" or "Hey hey! What do you say? Get that ball the other way!" as though the words were inflatable cushions of safety and familiarity with which he could pad himself. The Reds were clearly one of the good forces in life, playing basketball against bastards and viciousness. Even my mother said their name in the way people talk about doing right; it wasn't fun, but you had to admit it was important.

The game wasn't fun either. The auditorium was hot and muggy, full of muffled senseless noise and strangers with invulnerable gum-chewing faces. Sweating men ran with meaningless urgency, straining to prevent each other from doing something that changed from moment to moment. Strangers sat on benches roaring at intervals. My father sat with his neck stretched forward, his face set in the expectant, placated look he had when the world was forming a pattern he approved of.

When it was over we walked home in the dark. "The old Reds won," said my father. "Don't you want to cheer?" I cheered into the damp night as I ran up the sidewalk. The houses and trees were remote and strange in the dark, the mailboxes lonely and disoriented on their corners. Cars swished by in mournful sweeps of light, and we walked in triumph.

At home there was cinnamon toast and hot chocolate and my mother in her special white Chinese robe with black dragons on it. We marched into the rec room, Daddy carrying me on his shoulders, my legs dangling down his chest. Fat old Walnut the cat thumped behind us, his tail low and steady. My father put *Carmen* on the record player, and I darted around the room, swirling in an invisible lavender skirt. Daddy and Mother kissed on the blue-flowered sofa. Mother's legs were folded and tucked against her body like the wings of a plump bird, and I saw the jagged shred of toenail and the hard little callus on her pink incurved baby toe. Her husband's hands covered her face as he kissed her. "Olé, olé!" shouted prancing me. Scornful Carmen, with an aquiline nose and a rose in her teeth, silently leered from the velvety dark of her album cover where she sat propped sideways against a tall blue lamp. She had been stabbed to death by the time Daddy swung me into his arms. "Up the magic mountain, one, two, three. Up the magic mountain, yessiree." We left Walnut curled beside the heat vent. Mother followed behind, smiling at my head as it rested on Daddy's shoulder, hitting light switches as we passed from room to hall to room to staircase. "She's going to sleep with Mama and Daddy tonight because the Reds won and because she is such a good girl."

My memory of that night is a swollen, rose-colored blur that shades every thought venturing near it. The pink bed was massive. The quilts and blankets were rumpled into low mountain ranges with frowning indentation eyes and brows that stretched and melted when Daddy pulled the blankets over me. Tiny curls of hair and granules were the worms and earth of the pink bed world. The smell of Daddy's hair oil and Mama's perfume penetrated me like a drug too strong for my system to metabolize.

I lay cuddled in the arms of my softly pajamaed father, waiting for Mama, who was lazily brushing her hair at the vanity table. The rest of the room with its furniture, curtains, glimmering bottles, and snakes of Mama's jewelry was a dream of objects that claimed to

*J*ustine Shade *had unusually* attractive parents, something she came to hold against them for reasons unknown to her. Even when she was five, she says, she
knew that they were socially beautiful, although that
concept is foreign to five-year-olds. They weren't exquisite or perfect, but they had a reassuring, big-
boned blondness (her mother), an elegant, slouching,
Cary Grantesque authority (dad) that people responded to as though a cerebral complacency-center
was stimulated by the mere sight of them.

When Justine thought of her childhood with them,
she thought of the shoeboxes of color photos stored
in a living room closet in their Deere Parke, Michigan,
home. As an adult, Justine used these photographs as
a set of icons, talismans against her fear that there had
been something unusually nasty about her childhood.
She would take the photographs out of their
shoeboxes and vinyl albums and arrange them in bou-
quets that spanned the floor before her as she
hunched near the radiator, holding her white-socked

feet for warmth as she brooded over these proofs of family happiness and genetic beauty. There they were, eager, rosy, smiling young parents, kneeling to hold their tiny daughter upright between them as she stood on her unsteady legs like a worried poodle, her face quizzical, solemn, and concentrated. At age four, she was caught in a wild charge across the living room in her white gown, her cheeks pink, her eyes glittering with a flashbulb-induced diamond pupil. She smiled on a swing set. She squatted shyly in a sandbox, squeezing the ruffles of her red swimsuit; she stood with her slender legs in bathing beauty position, one hand on her hip, her face demurely composed as an uncouth neighborhood child holding a garden hose gaped. At nine she dolorously examined the contents of an Easter basket; beyond a piece of cockeyed floor, tilted by her mother's weird camera angle, her pajamaed father sat on the edge of a couch, holding a green coffee cup with both hands and looking bitterly into space, his glasses on the end of his nose. She stood in the doorway, a princess in gauze and yellow spangles, a delicate rhinestone tiara, and cheap sandals spray-painted gold, holding her Halloween bag and smiling as her mother captured her creation on film.

She could find nothing to link the charming world represented by her little photographs with the squalid, sweaty-pantyhose situation that became her adolescence—even though the pictures taken of her adolescence recorded a smiling, vulgarly pretty, confident young girl surrounded by friends wearing white lipstick and flowered miniskirts, her handsome, bemused parents in the background. Justine hated to look at these pictures, which, in her eyes, had the queasy, urgent, side-tilted quality of a dream that is rapidly becoming a nightmare. Her earliest memories though, weren't as clear, and she was thus completely seduced by the bright old photos.

*When she was five,* they lived in Lancelot, Illinois, in a large apartment with two floors. Her father, having just graduated from medical school, was in residence at the hospital there. She pictures him returning home in his white coat, exuding safety, duty, and cheer. He is sitting slouched before the coffee table with little Justine tugging at his pant leg, a tuna sandwich on the plate before him. He is talking about important things. He sounds angry, but the anger is sleek and shaped to look like something else; it makes Justine feel afraid and reassured at once. Her mother replies as though she knows exactly what he means and has known all along. Her voice isn't angry. It's strong and almost proud, yet it has a curiously unstable quality as though the strength can't sustain itself but needs to plant itself in some other form of energy to thrive. It makes Justine feel uneasy and confident at once. Their voices weave in and out of each other; they construct their conversation like a bridge of concrete high above Justine's head. She watches solemnly.

They got up at five for breakfast because Dr. Shade had to be at the hospital at six. There was less talk then; Daddy was grumpy, not triumphant. He would say, "Lorraine, these eggs are mucusy," or "How do you expect me to drink this?" The anger pulled against its sleek shape, and Justine held her breath. Her mother was subdued and obedient, but the strength in her voice was vibrant, as though rooted in her husband's peevish demands. As to a corporal in the army, obedience to a respected superior was not degrading, rather it ennobled, it scornfully subsumed feelings that didn't serve it, it gave a hard, elegant shape to every movement and object that embodied it. Mother's grace and efficiency as she moved to pour the juice, the beautiful, fragile flowers in the vase, the stirring classical music coming from the radio were all performing a duty, augmenting and uplifting the campaign to get Dr. Shade out the door in the morning. Yet all this beauty and order could be disturbed by mucusy eggs. Her daddy could still get out the door, but it would be that much harder to do the important things. It was a puzzle.

When Daddy marched out in his white coat, Justine and Mama went into the living room to do their exercises. It built discipline, said Mama in a voice of conviction that had its roots in something Justine didn't know about. Mama would change from her robe into her leotard, and Justine would stay in her pajamas. Mama would put on the exercise record of surging yet sedate music supporting a man's voice which said, "Up ladies! Down ladies! Very good ladies!" Justine loved the record. The man's voice had a mysterious foreign accent, and on the cover were pictures of a beautiful serious woman wearing a gray leotard, who was swinging her legs or touching her toes or kneeling and putting her head to her knee, just like the foreigner said. Justine and her mama would face each other as the music began, they would move up and down and back and forth together. Mama's chest would get red and blotchy where Justine could see it exposed by the plunge-necked leotard, but her chin and face remained upright and intent as she rose and sank or knelt and swung. "We must learn to push ourselves, Justine," she said.

After twenty minutes, the record was dispensed with, there was five minutes of stretching and then the mysterious pleasure of a "spit bath." They would strip off their sweaty clothes and hang them on a towel rack to be hand-washed later that night and stand naked to the waist (except for Mother's richly embossed brassiere) before the mirror, daubing their armpits and necks with washcloths and deodorants. Sometimes Mama would let Justine daub her back while she applied her modest lipstick and mascara, her face absorbed by the mirror as she licked her fingertips to remove the stray smudges of makeup from her eyes. During the winter, the rattling electric heater would be on, and the windows would fog, and the smell of their sweat would rise off their bodies like the sighing sounds you make in sleep. Justine hated leaving this warm, safe room to go out into the world. She wanted to stay with her mother always.

But they would get dressed and into the car, and Mama would drop Justine off at kindergarten and then go to work herself.

She remembers this morning ritual with great vividness, probably because they repeated it so unwaveringly for so long. Most of her other memories are snatched in arbitrary fragments from the deep past and fraught equally with emotion and meaninglessness as they float by for her half-conscious perusal as she lies daydreaming on her back.

She remembers the way her mother would push white wax suppositories into her ass with a slow gentleness that made her feel her body was being turned inside out. There was no place in her body where she could hide from the feeling. Her mother's face wore the pursed look of duty it had when she made breakfast or put on her makeup, and the memory of the expression combined with the inexorable, horrible gentleness filled the adult Justine with loathing.

She remembers the way her mother came to her at night, with her nightgown undone so her moist breastbone gleamed in the light from the hall. Her blond hair would be rumpled, her unmadeup eyes tired, with damp little bags under them, her body warm and vulnerable, totally unlike the brisk pink Mama who did squats and knee-swings and made breakfast with the same purpose and strength. There was a different strength here, a kind that didn't have to be planted in anything else to survive but rather infused her mother's body and voice like blood. She put her arms around Justine, and stroked her face and told her stories. She was like a mama tiger licking her cub, and Justine never wanted her to go away.

Then there were the walks in the park on Sunday when they would lead the ducks on a bread-crumb parade, Daddy showing the way. They were admired; Justine especially was admired standing next to Mama in their almost-matching yellow dresses. There were spaghetti dinners while they listened to classical music on the radio and pretended they were in Italy, and Daddy stood at the table to conduct the orchestra while Mama cried, "Bravo, Dirk!"

Sometimes Daddy's colleagues would come to the house for drinks. They stood in the living room, dark pant legs and deep, utterly sure voices, holding the drinks. Mama would stand in her flowered dress with her hands folded, her voice ringing with approval, and Justine would climb on the men's laps. There was one she liked to climb on in particular, a man named Dr. Norris. Dr. Norris didn't speak or move in quite the same confident way of the other doctors. He was somehow tentative, with numb, helpless-looking hands and eyes that seemed to defer to whomever he was with. Justine climbed on his lap and said, "If I were in trouble would you come like Popeye?" and he said, "Yes." Mama told Justine in passing many years later that he liked her "especially," and that he spent a lot of time with her. Justine remembers this; she remembers one time in particular.

They were walking in the park with him and his son, the contemplative, nose-picking Sam. They were by the swing sets when she told Dr. Norris she had to go to the bathroom. He asked which kind, and she said to pee. He took her hand, and they walked for a while until they were away from people. He began to take off her pants. She didn't stop him because he was an adult, a gentle adult she trusted. But she didn't want to take off her pants in public, even though there were no people around. She felt horrible standing naked except for her shoes and her shirt. He told her to spread her legs and pee on the ground. She spread her legs, but her whole body was suddenly stiff and she couldn't pee. It felt so stiff it felt like wood. Even her face felt like wood. There was something wrong, but Dr. Norris didn't seem to know it. "This will help you to pee," he said. He said it in his kindest, most deferential voice. He knelt before her and licked his fingers and rubbed her between her legs where she would pee from. Her abdomen contracted like a crouching insect. Her bladder was full and it hurt. She looked at Dr. Norris's face. He was looking between her legs with his numb eyes, and she saw that he knew there was something wrong but that he was going to do it anyway. He rubbed her briskly and numbly, and he talked to her, his voice coated more and more thickly with an expression she had never heard before. A strange and horribly powerful sensation flexed its claws in her body.

Many years later, when she told a man about this incident, he said he believed that child molestation was bad only because of the negative social rules that made the child feel sullied. Otherwise, he said, it would be good because it could only give the child pleasure, and children didn't have reservations about pleasure until they were taught to. Another man told her it was good that she'd had the experience because "that man taught you something." She didn't argue with either of them because she didn't know how to explain that this uncomprehended attack of invasive sensation had not felt like pleasure at all but rather like the long claws of some unknown aggression that had gripped her organs and her bones and never quite let go.

Dr. Norris and his son and she went to the park after that, she doesn't remember how many times. Once she told her mother that "Dr. Norris touches me here," and pointed to show her. Her mother was standing in the kitchen making dinner. She didn't stop what she was doing. She said, "He just doesn't know that little girls don't like to be touched there."

$M$*y family moved to Ohio* when I was seven. We lived in a large, cool, damp house outside Cincinnati. I couldn't walk to school anymore and instead rode a bus with other children who sang, "The worms go in, the worms go out, the worms play pinochle on your snout." There were lots of tornado warnings. Sometimes they would be followed by local news footage of some neighboring town that had been devastated. These broadcasts thrilled me; I loved to look at the destroyed houses and ripped up trees, the dazed, unkempt victims standing around in overcoats, mumbling for the spruce newscaster who asked them how they felt.

Once there was a tornado warning when I was at school, and the teachers led us all down the hall into the bomb shelter and kept us there an hour after school, talking about what to do in case of nuclear attack and singing about bottles of beer on the wall until the warning was over. We rode home in the twilight, exhilarated by our brush with death, loudly bawling the worm song. When I got home, my mother said, "I didn't know they'd held you at school. I waited at the bus stop for half an hour. The wind whipped my legs until they were red and sore. I was terrified when you didn't come." She said this in the same girlish voice that she used to tell stories of Motherdear and Joedaddy, punctuating certain words with a tight, up-lifted voice, as if she were describing a tasty dessert. Her voice wasn't angry at all, which made me feel un-easy; it seemed as though she should be angry. I asked her why she hadn't gone home. "Because I had to be sure you were safe. I stood there and stood there and my legs just burned."

I hastily constructed a fantasy in which I came sail-ing through a full-blown tornado on the bus. (They'd tried to hold me at school, but I'd faced the principal with tears in my eyes and pleaded to be allowed to go home and be with my mother. He understood; gruffly he allowed me to go, and the bus driver, the old salt, was so overcome by the spirit of this brave, lone child that he volunteered to take me. "You're mad!" cried my teacher, Miss Clutch. "Well maybe I am, and maybe I ain't," he said. "All's I know is, I gotta kid, too, an' if there was a tornado, I'd want 'er to be with 'er ma.") In one version of this fantasy, he and I leapt from the bus together, he scooping my swooning mother into his arms and carrying her home, me clinging to his pant leg as we struggled through the fe-rocious wind. In my preferred version, I leapt out alone, and the driver tootled off into the tornado, waving a leathern hand and wiping a tear from his eye. Supporting my fainting mother on my shoulders, I struggled mightily through the storm, despite her gasps of "Leave me! Save yourself!" When we got home I bundled my mother in a blanket and bathed her short, plump legs in bubble bath.

I liked this fantasy so much I kept it nearby all day, and by nighttime, I no longer believed that my mother had suffered at the bus stop.

My mother always came to say good night to me when I was in bed. She would lean forward to kiss me as a prelude to leaving, and I would grab her robe and say, "Wait, I have to tell you about the squirrels versus the cats in school today," or, "Tell me about when you and Daddy skipped school." She stayed and stayed, and it never did any good. No matter how many stories she told or listened to, no matter how many times she stroked my back with her fingertips, I felt the same emptiness and panic when she left. I didn't even enjoy her stroking; I devoured it with feverish passivity, my mind lunging forward ahead of her fingers to consume her touch before it came. She'd leave and I'd be left with my hideous, rearing thoughts. I would fixate on the strip of light coming from my partly open door, listening to the TV and radio voices, trying to figure out where my parents were and what they were doing from the sound of their footsteps, chair-creakings, and voices. Then they went to bed and the light was gone. Some nights I lay in such anxiety that I could sleep only when morning came. Throughout the day, the residue of the night's tension stayed in my body.

*My father didn't like* Ohio. It was only two states away, but to him it was the last decisive step away from civilization into gum-popping, transistor-blasting subhumanity. He saw evidence of this everywhere. He'd go to the drugstore, and sullen teenagers, smirking and scratching themselves behind the counter, would rather tell each other jokes than wait on him. When he said "Thank you," they didn't an-

swer him. The clerks at the grocery store didn't answer him either, and once one of them rang up his
bill wrong and then was rude about it. None of this,
he said, ever happened in Tennessee. "And that's the
last of Alfred A. Footie's business those sons of bitches
will ever get."

At night he'd put on a marching record and walk
up and down talking the same way he had at the
house in Tennessee, only now it was more desperate
in tone, as though everywhere the bastards were gain-
ing ground. The music battered the walls, and my
mother moved in the kitchen as if his voice were the
force behind her movements. During dinner my father would talk about moving back to Tennessee and
tell stories about ordinary people foiling criminals:
Gas station attendants had sprayed a thief with gas
and threatened him with books of matches until the
police arrived. A husband beat his wife's escaping rapist half to death. An entire family ran out of their
house and pounded a youth who was wrestling an old
lady for her purse. "A society," he warned, "has to protect itself. Just like old Jim McCann and that big bastard in the south of France. The big sonofabitch stood
outside his tent for half an hour calling him filthy
names because Jim was a nice little guy and he didn't
think he could do anything about it. But he did. He
came out of that tent in the goddamned rain and beat
that bastard's ass. And that's just what I'm going to do
to anybody who thinks I'm not big enough to fight
back. Knock their teeth down their goddamn throat."

In awe, I locked the gray, twilight scene in my memory. The morose sheet of rain, the small decent man
roused from his sleep by the ominous shadow outside.
The outpouring of vileness, the weary flap of the tent,
the squaring off in the dark, the fight to the finish in
the mud. My father had been there. He hadn't taken

part but he'd observed righteousness taking place, he'd recorded it, he'd approved of it. It was like *Combat!* on TV.

We watched *Combat!* every Tuesday. I loved the theme from *Combat!* and can remember the final bars even today. The theme was about fighting and winning but it was also about something more subtle and intimate, something voluptuous. I didn't know exactly what this something was, but it had a lot to do with Lt. Hanley. Lt. Hanley was a slim, boyish person with large, flowerlike eyes. He was always getting captured or wounded. Even when he wasn't getting captured, there was something about him that made his capture seem imminent. Episode after episode featured Lt. Hanley bound on the floor or to a chair while a large German stood over him, arrogantly resting his jack-booted foot on a table or something. ("Why does he put his foot there?" I asked. "Because Germans love their boots," said my mother. "They love to show them off.") Of course, Sgt. Saunders, a grizzled, stocky man, would come rescue him, and they would go on with the plot, but there was always a small moment when it was so nice to have Lt. Hanley tied up and looking at his captor with those brave, flowerlike eyes, and somehow the music referred to that moment. It was a very human theme song, I guess.

*It was in Ohio that* I developed what my mother came to call my "unattractive habits." First, I stopped brushing my teeth, except on rare occasions. All at once, I hated putting the paste-laden brush into my nice warm mouth and scraping the intriguing texture of food from my teeth, annihilating the rich stew of flavors, the culinary history of my day, and replacing it with the vacuous mint-flavored aftertaste, the empty cavern of impersonal ivory. So I did it as infrequently as possible, even though the girl down the street called me "green teeth." In addition, I began giving in to gross and unhealthy cravings: candy bars, ice cream, cookies, sugar in wet spoonfuls from the bowl, Hershey's syrup drunk in gulps from the can, Reddi Wip shot down my throat, icing in huge fingerfuls from other people's pieces of cake. Like my mother's presence at night, it was never enough, and no threats or shaming lectures could stop me. The most offensive habit, at least according to my mother, was my way of deftly peeling back the edge of one nostril and delicately stroking the soft hairs inside. "If you do that in public," said my mother, "no one will want to be your friend. They'll think you're a nose-picker." I tried to wait until I was alone to feel the tiny hairs, but sometimes I would emerge from a daydream in, say, the middle of the A&P, to find a hand blissfully at a nostril.

It wasn't until years later that I realized I'd gotten this hair-stroking habit from my father, who did it as he absently wandered the house.

*When Justine was seven*, she ordered the Catholic boy who lived down the street to tie her to his swing set and pretend to brand her, as she had seen Brutus do to Olive Oyl on TV. Sometimes she made him chase her around the yard with a slender branch, whipping her legs.

His name was Richie, and she remembers he was Catholic because his mother, faceless in memory, told her that if she lied there'd be a sin on her soul and she'd have to go to hell.

"Mrs. Slutsky is a good woman, but she is ignorant," said Justine's mother. "You must be kind and respectful to her, but don't listen to anything she says."

But Justine liked listening to Mrs. Slutsky talk about hell and encouraged her to do so every Saturday morning when she went to play with Richie. The Slutskys' apartment was close and ramshackle. Once Justine put her finger on the wall and dirt came off on it; she felt like she was in a story about poor people. She loved the picture of the beautiful doe-eyed Jesus with a dimly flaming purple heart wrapped in thorns adorning the middle of his chest which hung in Mrs. Slutsky's bedroom. She loved the ornately written prayer to the saints in the den. She loved to stand in the kitchen, which smelled of old tea bags and carrot peels, and question Mrs. Slutsky about hell.

"What if you do something bad but you believe in God? What if you believe in God but you're always doing really bad things? What if you do something bad but you're sorry?"

Mrs. Slutsky would explain everything as she did the dishes or ironed or smoked, expansively delineating the various levels of hell and purgatory. Sometimes Justine and Richie would sit at the kitchen table and draw pictures of a smoking red hell with the victim's snarled-up arms writhing skyward. Justine liked to draw angels floating at the top of the page, looking down in sorrow and raining pink tears of pity into hell.

She and Richie spent hours watching Saturday morning cartoons on the Slutskys' sagging, loamy-smelling green couch. She wanted to be tied up and whipped after watching cartoon characters being beaten and tortured by other characters for the viewer's amusement. She watched the animated violence with queasy fascination, feeling frightened and exposed. It was the same feeling she had had when Dr. Norris touched her, and she felt a bond with docile, daydreaming Richie, simply because he was near her while she was having this feeling.

When she began making him tie her up, she couldn't tell if he wanted to do it or if he were passively following her lead. She recalls his face as furtive and vaguely ashamed, as though he were picking his nose in public.

One day she saw a cartoon about hell. In it, a wily

dog with paw pads like flower petals plotted against a kitten he was jealous of. He locked the kitty out of the house in a snowstorm, then settled down to rest before the fireplace. He fell asleep before the fire and suddenly, through a series of hallucinatory sequences, he went to hell. Hell was very hot and populated by demon ice cream vendors who sold blazing Popsicles on which the desperate dog burned himself while seeking relief; it was overseen by pitchfork-wielding devils who chased the hound, breathing fire and stabbing his bottom. He was tormented, howling and weeping, from one end of hell to the other until a coal leapt out from the fireplace and awakened him from the nightmare. He raced to rescue the kitten, but the happy ending did not mitigate Justine's dismay at seeing an eternity of torture and punishment presented as an amusing possibility. She sat with the now familiar sensation of violation coursing through her body as if it could split her apart.

She was at home when she saw this, and she ran to her mother, crying.

"And they stuck him with pitchforks," she wept. "He tried to buy a Popsicle and it burned him and they laughed!"

"That is very bad. They shouldn't put things like that on television."

Her mother consoled her with statements that cruelty and violence are wrong, and then helped her to write a letter to the TV station on the widely lined manila paper she used in school, in which she told them how much the cartoon upset her.

It had upset her, but she thought of it again and again. At night she would lie in bed and imagine being tormented forever because you had envious thoughts or were angry at someone. She didn't have the vocabulary to express, even to herself, the feeling these images evoked in her; it was too overpowering for her even to see clearly what it was. It seemed to occupy the place that all her daily activities and expressions came from, the same place Dr. Norris had touched. It felt like the foundation that all the other events of her life played upon.

Of course, she didn't think of it like this until much later, when she could only look at the ancient, entrenched feeling as an animal looks at a trap on its leg. At the time she soothed the demanding feeling by tying herself to her bedpost, gagging herself, and forcing morose but compliant Richie to beat her, or to pretend to.

Some time after she wrote the letter to the station, she received a reply from them apologizing for the cartoon and thanking her for writing. Her mother read it aloud to her when it came and then again at the dinner table.

"This is very good," said her father. "It is a civics lesson. She can see how she can affect her environment, make her views known. Isn't that right, Sugar?"

Justine nodded even though to her the letter was a surprising but irrelevant development that had nothing to do with affecting her environment.

*When Justine's father went to work* in his own private office, Justine's mother went to work with him as a receptionist. This was ostensibly to save money but was in truth because Mrs. Shade could not bear to be away from Dr. Shade during the day. On the rare occasions when he went somewhere without her, she would clutch his shirt and look at him with an expression that seemed to come all the way from the back of her head. She would ask when he would be back in a way that made Justine wonder if he might not come back at all. He would answer with a hearty certainty that did not acknowledge the expression in his wife's eyes, as if it were normal for her to look at him that way. Then he would turn to leave. Justine's mother would let go of him and turn back to Justine, the boundless need in her eyes replaced by her usual brisk confidence, as if she had stepped out of one world and into another.

But this didn't happen often as her mother usually accompanied her father to work. Sometimes her mother left the office early so that she could be home when Justine arrived from school. Other times her mother stayed late, and Justine came home to Gemma, the housekeeper. Justine would then call her mother at work and ask when she was coming home. "Soon darling. Can't you go play with Richie?"

"I don't want to play with Richie."

"Well then do your multiplication tables with Gemma."

"I already did," she'd lie.

"Sweetheart, I cannot stay on the phone. I am a receptionist. Keep busy and I'll be home in an hour or so."

"But Mama, I want to tell you what Miss Grub said today."

"Were you good in school today?"

"Yes, but—"

"The phones are lighting up, darling, I have to go."

Sometimes she would only be on the phone for bare seconds before her mother's voice would swell with threat and rejection. Other times she could stay on the phone for a long necklace of lovely minutes, shifting her weight from hip to hip, relishing her mother's words. It was hard to say what made her mother respond differently.

When she hung up, she'd go to her room and change her clothes, feeling like a survivor in a spaceship after a meteor storm. Then she'd drag through the house looking for something to poke into or violate. Without her mother there, her vigorous energy connecting every object with a bright ribbon of purpose and sense, the stark utilitarian furniture seemed alien, ugly, almost frightening. This was especially true in contrast with her hours in school, sitting in rows of desks, each desk and its inhabitant a world with its own system of tasks and exercises. Justine regarded other children as spacecraft one could signal to, either peacefully or in war, and school, with its organized hours and lunch period, facilitated this impression. She wandered the apartment, wanting to smash a vase or carve something on a table. She was so lonely.

She would try to think of other things, or tell herself a story to keep from calling her mother again, and sometimes it worked. Other times she held off making the call, as she'd sometimes hold off going to pee—the mounting pressure, so uncomfortable it made her squirm, doubled the voluptuous pleasure of letting go, or of rushing to the phone to obtain the loved voice, no matter how scolding.

"Justine, really, you cannot do this to me. I told you, I will be home. The more you call, the more you delay me."

She sounded angry, but Justine had once heard her talking on the phone to Mrs. MacCauley about how Justine called her at work, and she'd said, "Yes, but it does make one feel good to know one is wanted." Thus, although her mother would speak angrily, and Justine would apologize and whine, she knew they were simply having two conversations: the one on top in words and the one underneath, which was conducted in tones of voice, silences, and breaths. Still, it was humiliating to have to make these calls.

Sometimes she would go sit in the kitchen with

Gemma, who would be moving around the stove making dinner or sitting at the table, reading a paperback and smoking a cigarette while a pot of food simmered. Gemma was a young black woman with luminous purple-hued skin, a straight slim back, and serious, silent eyes. She would talk to Justine and occasionally play cards with her, but she always held Justine away from her, somehow using the very words of their conversations as a fence to emphasize the stretch of territory between them. Justine often felt that Gemma did not like her, and further, that her dislike had nothing to do with who Justine actually was. Sometimes this made her want to charm Gemma, to make her like her. Sometimes it made her want to hurt Gemma. She couldn't get near enough to do either.

One night when her mother had come to say goodnight to her, she said, "I don't think Gemma likes me."

"Why do you think this?" Justine could hear an unfamiliar element in her mother's voice. "Has she been unkind to you?"

"No. I just don't think she likes me."

"Nonsense dear, I'm sure she likes you." Her mother patted her vigorously for a second, and then the movement of her hand slowed and strayed over her leg, as though uncertain and considering. Then she took it off Justine altogether and put it in her lap. "I am going to tell you something very adult." She paused again and Justine nodded. "Negroes are not in a good position in our society because at one time they were slaves. A lot of white people believe that they are inferior because they are dark-skinned and do things to hurt Negroes. They keep them out of restaurants and jobs and sometimes hurt them and kill them. We do not think this way. We believe all people are equal. But because of these prejudiced white people, many Negroes do not like any white people. You cannot do anything about this. You must respect Gemma and be extra kind to her, but you cannot have a normal relationship with her because of this. The lives of white and Negro people are very separate. But there must be politeness and decency between them. Do you understand?"

Justine nodded, unhappily regarding this bloodless world of decency and politeness that had just opened before her.

"But if Gemma is ever rude to you, you must speak to me immediately."

Justine nodded again; she could no more imagine silent, gliding Gemma being rude than she could picture Miss Grub, her teacher, taking her clothes off in class.

"And you must never, ever repeat any of this conversation to Gemma. Do you understand?"

Justine thought of Gemma's dark, veiled glance, which was piercing and indirect at once. It made her puzzled and sad that they could only have politeness and decency between them.

After this conversation, she watched Gemma and her mother together with interest. Her mother would usually come home as Gemma was getting ready to leave. She'd sweep into the kitchen with Justine at her heels and say, "Hello, Gemma, how are you?" and then look all around the kitchen, seeing what Gemma had done and what she had cooked for dinner. She might say, "Gemma, do you think you could bag the garbage a little more securely?" or "Would you have time to mop the floor tomorrow?" or "Gemma, you've done a wonderful job, I don't know what I'd do without you." And sometimes they would stand at the back door talking about an advance in pay that Gemma needed or a possible day off. Justine would look admiringly at the two tall women, especially her mother, who could tell another person what to do and have her do it.

But sometimes it worried her to see the two of them together, Gemma speaking from behind the shield of her cold dignity, her mother from the height of her impenetrable politeness. She wasn't sure that Gemma knew that her mother wasn't one of those white people who hated Negroes. How could she know for sure when her mother told her to bag garbage and mop floors? Justine wanted to tell Gemma that her mother liked her and that she did too.

Then other times it would seem to her, from the way Gemma nodded and answered her mother, that Gemma understood this perfectly, that the talk the two women had in the kitchen was a code for some other kind of conversation, like when Justine called her mother and her mother pretended she didn't like it.

Into adulthood, she remembered Gemma's still face, her measured voice, and the words that disappeared in the air between them. Their empty companionship was like a small void in the larger emptiness of the house without her mother.

*Her father said that* she was lonely after school because she didn't have enough to do, and it was decided that she should take piano lessons three times a week.

"We will see if she has inherited my gift for music," he said, referring to his brief fling at composing before medical school.

After school Gemma would take her to Miss Elderblau's apartment, a few blocks away. Miss Elderblau was a thin, short, nervous woman who wore a black leotard and heavy blue eyeshadow around her large brown eyes. The way she looked fascinated Justine: she was nearly as old as Justine's mother, but she had no breasts and almost no hips, and her brown hair was practically as short as a boy's. Her living room fascinated Justine too. It was square and bare-walled except for two posters, one a set of bright stripes and the other a close-up of a crying woman holding a pistol against her cheek. There was almost no furniture, just a couch, a table, a stereo, some records against a wall, the piano, and a big stone horse. Miss Elderblau (who turned into Judith later on) smoked cigarettes and sat at the piano with her slight body in a graceful, seemingly spineless droop, speaking with toneless gentleness as she guided Justine's hands over the keys.

After a half hour she'd say, "Ready for a break?" and they'd have tea, sometimes with frozen cake, sitting on big pillows on the bare wooden floor. Miss Elderblau would talk to Justine about her childhood, in which she had been a misfit. Justine had never heard the word "misfit" before, and Miss Elderblau used it constantly. "If you're smart, you're almost always a misfit," she'd say. "And when you're young that can be tough. But when you get older, you can make the world into what you want it to be, not the other way around. Remember that." She asked Justine questions about her life, asked so seriously that it made Justine anxious. Miss Elderblau seemed to think that they were both misfits linked in a secret understanding, which was nice because Justine liked her piano teacher, but mystifying as no one had ever considered Justine a misfit. Miss Elderblau listened to what Justine said carefully but strangely saying "That's right," and, "Of course," and, "Isn't that just the way?" or chuckling knowingly at junctures that could be interpreted as examples of Justine at odds with the world. Instead of asking why or making it harder for Miss Elderblau to do this, Justine exaggerated the things that she knew would elicit the most response just because it was so nice to have a sense of understanding with this breastless woman, even if it was groundless.

She had been taking lessons for a month when her father said it was time for "a performance." After dinner one night, the three of them rolled the top up on the old piano in the dining room, and Justine played while her parents had their coffee. She played a whole song, with only one mistake and one fumble. When she was finished they applauded loudly and her father yelled, "Bravo!" and called her to him to give her a kiss. As he cuddled her against his leg, he said to her mother, "She is like me. Competent and quick, but she doesn't really have anything."

*One night Justine dreamed* about hell. She dreamed hell was right under her backyard, and in the dream she saw the devil come out of a trap door in the lawn while she was hiding behind a bush. He was small and red, and if you hadn't known he was the devil, he wouldn't have looked so bad. She decided she wanted to break into hell. She opened the trap door and snuck down a long flight of stairs, prying large jewels from the walls as she went. When she reached the bottom, she found a comfortable room. There were bookcases, a roaring fireplace, ornate furniture. And, in an armchair that fortunately faced away from her, sat the devil, reading a book. Behind the chair was a bag of treasure. She tiptoed up and grabbed the bag and ran

*When I was nine I read* "The Little Match Girl," the fairy tale about a starving child who freezes to death outside the home of a middle-class family as they eat Christmas dinner. I read with growing horror as it became clear that no elf or genie was going to appear to take her to a magic land or grant her wishes. She used the last of her pathetic matches to warm her fingers and finally lay down in the snow to die. For days I was obsessed with fantasies in which I appeared in the story, a wealthy child philanthropist, to sweep the match girl away to my opulent home. Then I switched to a fantasy in which the match girl appeared huddled in our backyard one snowy night, and I took her in and fed her bowls of Cream of Wheat. We gave her clothes and money, and in the end adopted her. She slept in my bed with me, her bony back pressed against my front, my arm wrapped around her waist.

"Mama, if we found a girl in the yard who was starving and cold, we'd take her in, wouldn't we?"

"Of course we would."

"We'd feed her and let her spend the night?"

"Yes, but there aren't any starving people in our yard. Why do you ask?"

"Well, in case there was."

"People don't starve nowadays, honey. Everyone has enough to eat."

"Even poor people?"

"Yes, even poor people."

Still, I clutched the fantasies to me for days and kept them within reach when, months later, the idea of the dying girl would pierce me.

*It was during the summer* of that year when we moved to Chiffon, Michigan, a suburb of Detroit. We moved because my father had spent the happiest summer of his boyhood there with an aunt before his parents sent for him in Tennessee. We drove to Chiffon during a noisy downpour of rain. I sat between my parents in the front seat, comforted by the moist car-warmth of fresh sweat and damp vinyl. A friendly little snake of scent (apple cores, old potato chip bags) crawled out of the plastic Disposan bag that dangled from the knob of the glove compartment. The windshield wipers rubbed the water back and forth on the glass, and Michigan appeared to us through rivulets and teardrops as we slowly toiled towards Chiffon.

My father hunched over the wheel, squinting and talking about how wonderful life in Michigan would be. My mother sat cross-legged in her see-through raincoat and yellow paisley head scarf. For months I had been imagining this place of big beautiful snow and houses with front porches, where trees dappled the streets with their shadows in the summer and grocery clerks were your friends.

When we arrived at Chiffon, I was surprised to see

rows of houses more squat and symmetrical than those in our neighborhood near Cincinnati. They each had a small square of concrete for a porch and short starved trees in their yards. My disappointment rose up like a silent creature staring at me from beneath the filmy green surface of a pool. But I put a sheet of optimism and determination to like the neighborhood over my feelings, and the creature sank. The square sod yards were very green, the tree bark was slick and black in the rain, and, before our house, there was a crabapple tree flowering in a dazzling pink burst, scattering its bright petals in the grass.

Exultant, my daddy took me in one arm and his umbrella in the other and carried me over the Lysol-smelling threshold. I ran across the thin maize carpet yelling "We're here, we're here!" my voice echoing from one square beige room to the next.

The next few weeks were a paradise of trips to the grocery and take-out dinners eaten in the basement rec room before the TV. We couldn't get into a normal routine; there was so much to do. My father scanned the local newspapers for coupons and announcements of bargains, cut them out and saved them until he was ready to hit three or four stores at once.

"Well," he'd say, walking into the kitchen, "are you ready to loot Farmer Jack's and A&P and Kroger's for all the ice cream and Kleenex and chicken pot pie we can carry?"

Or my mother and I would take a walk after dinner, through blocks of identical houses, with identical shrubs planted in each yard, to a stretch of dirt road that led to a little cluster of stores, one of them a drugstore with an enormous fluorescent-lit candy counter. We'd buy Almond Joys, Mallomars, Mellomints, and licorice ropes and walk back in the dark as the street lamps winked on. Kids standing on the sidewalk in groups would stop talking and turn to watch us, their expressions dimmed by the evening.

When we got back to the house, my father would be sitting in the dark in the living room with a flashlight at his feet. We'd come in and he'd flick it on, shining it in our faces, momentarily blinding us. "Were they friendly at Baker Drugs?" he'd ask.

During these first weeks I saw very little of the other kids in the neighborhood because I almost never went out alone. They would sail by on bicycles, watching but keeping their distance whenever they saw us. Or I would hear them calling each other in a ritual singsong voice that scorned door bells and intermediary parents. The neighbors on either side of us (the old, grinning, big-nosed Sissels and the faded Catholic Kopeikins) had introduced themselves, but the Sissels had no children and the Kopeikins had only two squeamish myopic girls who wore matching flounce dresses, watched soap operas, and were given Saltines to eat when they were especially good.

One day when we'd been there almost a month, I was sitting in the front yard in a lawn chair reading *Tarzan and the City of Gold* when two boys pulled up on bikes and looked at me.

"Hey kid," they said. "Where're you from?"

"Cincinnati, Ohio."

"Ohio's a queer state."

"What does 'queer' mean?"

"God!" They looked at each other in disbelief. "You don't know what 'queer' means?"

I shook my head. Their voices were sarcastic, with a hard quality that didn't allow for softness at all.

"It means retarded. Ohio's a retard state."

I felt my parents' house behind me, and it felt vulnerable and weak. "Then what's Michigan if Ohio's a retard state?"

"Michigan's a cool state. What's your name, kid?"

"Dotty Footie."

"God!" They looked at each other and rolled their eyes. "See you around, kid." They got on their bikes and pedaled away.

I folded the lawn chair and went into the house. My mother was sitting on the hard new orange couch, reading a magazine, so I asked her what "queer" meant.

"It means odd, or unusual. Why?"

"Some boys came up while I was reading and said Ohio was a queer state."

"They just means they don't know much about Ohio."

I didn't go out and read again. But when I went with my parents for bargains or sight-seeing, I looked at the kids in the street more closely. I noticed that the boys and girls played separately, the boys standing in groups or walking with baseball equipment, the girls sitting on the concrete stoops with Barbie dolls, their blue plastic Barbie homes and accessories laid out in a format. I told myself that I was just the kind of person who liked to stay inside a lot.

"Territory is very important," said my father. Somebody had thrown a paper cup on the edge of our yard, and he'd brought it in and put it on the kitchen table. "That's why people have yards and fences and decorations and flowers in their yards. To establish a territory and mark it. Whatever bastard threw this on our yard has violated our territory, and if I see him do it again, I'll kill him."

Before the summer ended there was a serialized TV special on Anne Frank. We all sat in the basement and watched it in the dark, eating plates of cookies my mother made when *The Wizard of Oz* or something special was on. The Anne Frank show was a live play on a bare set of rooms with actors and actresses who had lines on their faces and pieces of hair hanging on their foreheads. It was preceded and followed by a man sitting in a chair talking about Nazis. They showed concentration camp footage at the end, as they were rolling the credits.

I loved the Anne Frank show. It made me feel something for other people, an awful connection with dead strangers more intimate than any relationship I had with my living peers. It made me feel vindicated and angry and self-righteous. The television presentation padded it enough so that it induced a mild feeling of sorrow and sensitivity instead of actual pain. After all, the actress who played Anne Frank had said in the end, "I believe people are basically good," and the announcer had talked about the triumph of the human spirit, even though there were all those corpses.

*In September I had to go* to school. The trip to school was a gray sleepwalk through bathroom and breakfast, then through a neighborhood that was by now as familiar as a bad taste, surrounded by groups of other children who swung their lunch boxes and ferociously snapped their gum. In memory I see it from an aerial view; the square green lawns, the rooftops with the same chunk of space between them, the maze of sidewalks, the little human clusters progressing through the maze like disease moving through the body in a science diagram. The sight of myself—the lone toiling dot among the lunch box-swinging clusters—instantly recalls the fear and isolation that I took to be a normal state when among people other than my mother and father.

The school was a low concrete building surrounded by asphalt that had seesaws, swing sets and other iron instruments of play welded on to it. The halls were wide and monstrously echoed the shouts of children. We were assembled in the "Multi-Purpose Room," given speeches, and told where to go. There were roughly thirty children assigned to big, full-skirted Miss Durrell, who had brown eyes and a burst of pimples arrayed across her forehead.

The days were defined by the tasks we had to accomplish such as making numbers jump over and under lines on the blackboard, reading about people on the Prairie, memorizing the imports and exports of Nicaragua, or why people in Turkey no longer had to wear fezzes. A map hung over the blackboard at all times to remind us that other countries were delineated by particular shapes and distinguished by different colors. At intervals we were made to go out on the asphalt where, for the most part, boys would run up and down screaming and fighting and girls would huddle by the door talking in low voices. The most formidable group was made up of big girls in short skirts that cut tight across their thighs and clung to their buttocks, who had hair that was teased and knotted until it stood straight up on their heads. I was afraid of them and I walked out to the edges of the playground and daydreamed until it was time to go in and memorize something else.

At the end of the day I would go home, strip off my dress and leave it on the floor of my room, put on pants, and go sit in the basement rec room watching *Wagon Train*, *The Twilight Zone*, and *Hullabaloo* until dinner was called.

During the first week I made friends with Eileen

Iris, who sat next to me. She was a small, sedate child with long wavy brown hair who wore a pale pink sweater with white sequin leaves on it, which seemed the essence of femininity to me. Soon we were exchanging "friendship bracelets" made of fake shells, walking together on the outer reaches of the playground, collecting pretty pebbles, and eating the tiny strawberries to be found in the fitful undergrowth. She introduced me to tiny Darla Rice, a brown-skinned girl one grade younger than us whose short dark hair was set in a fashionable adult style. Her mother took the three of us to the wonderful Ice Capades in Detroit, to watch skaters in ballerina attire or grinning papier-mâché heads glide and leap to solemn recorded music as they were raked by mystic blue and white spotlights.

My friendship with Darla and Eileen did not, however, ease my feeling of isolation as I sat in class or walked home alone from school. It was like an aberrant pocket of comfort that could not emit enough warmth to extend into the coldness surrounding it.

I was still afraid to venture out of the house into my neighborhood, although I didn't think of it as fear. It felt more like a natural aversion; the very air outside our door seemed unbreathable, the voices of the neighborhood children, hard and bounding as rubber balls, cut into my sphere and left no space for me. Where were the friendly Michiganders my father had spoken about so confidently? I watched him and waited for an answer, which came in the form of a speech. "They've ruined everything that Michigan ever was," he said. "They ripped down the old buildings and paved over the old roads and put crap up all over everything. It's terrifying."

He spoke in the dark of evening after dinner, from

his vinyl reclining chair. My mother sat on the edge of the couch, examining her nails.

"It's all part of the general trend," he continued. "I thought Michigan would've escaped it, but I was wrong. We're being destroyed, like the Romans." He was answered by the tiny click of my mother's thin nails being peeled into her cupped palm.

He said these things again on many other nights as he paced through the house like a soldier, rubbing invisible granules and making bitter comparisons between our neighborhood and the Michigan of his happy summer, sometimes punctuating his words by rushing out into the yard to seize a piece of litter or a crumpled beer can which he would bring in and hurl onto the kitchen table. His words seemed to hover over the house in a useless attempt to shield it.

Then it was October, and we found out about Devil's Night. There had been a Devil's Night in Ohio, too; the night before Halloween, teenagers could go around ringing people's doorbells and throwing toilet paper over trees, and nobody would mind. In Chiffon, it wasn't just one night. It started a whole week before Halloween, and it wasn't just ringing doorbells and throwing paper. Gangs of kids would wander around, rubbing layers of soap onto people's windows and walls, setting fires on front stoops and splattering the houses of unpopular people with eggs.

Our house was "egged" the first night, and my father screamed with rage. "These are the people who pick on old people, who terrorize the small and the defenseless!" The next night he turned off all the lights and, with me at his side, waited in the living room for the next pranksters. We hid behind an armchair together with a flashlight, some crackers and peanut butter—our "rations," just like in the army. I was proud to be part of my father's battle against juvenile delinquents. The first pranksters were a gang of doorbell ringers whose faces registered shock as my father burst out upon them with his machete, who scattered and fled in all directions as he chased them down the block shouting, "Come back and fight, bastards!"

By this time my parents had made friends with the neighbors on both sides of us, the Sissels and the Kopeikins. They had put on their bathing suits and gone to swim in the Sissels' pool; my mother had many afternoon snacks with bespectacled, limply grinning Mrs. Kopeikin. But for me the friendly presence of these kind people was only a thin layer of civility that could be peeled away to reveal the gangs walking the streets on Devil's Night, or, on the next layer, my father and me crouched behind the armchair, waiting.

*My mother and I* began having story times again, mostly on the weekends. Our favorite thing to do was sit at the kitchen table with paper and crayons, drawing stories for each other. If we couldn't think of a story, we'd draw heaven. My mother's heaven was blue and almost empty except for one or two angels with yellow hair, large silver stars, and a rainbow of many colors that she would work on for several minutes, slanting her crayons on their sides for more subtle hues. My heaven was full of grinning winged children, candy bars, cake, ice cream, and toys. When we were finished drawing, we would put our best pictures on the wall with Scotch tape and sit admiring them over dishes of cake and ice cream.

At night on Sunday, she would read me books like *My Father's Dragon*, *Little Witch*, and *Peter Pan*. When she read *Peter Pan*, I stopped drawing pictures of heaven and began drawing Never-Never Land. Never-

Never Land was pink and blue and green, it had trees with homes inside them, cubby holes and hiding places, tiny women in gauze robes, and flying children with rapiers in their elegant hands. Its very name made me feel a sadness like a big beautiful blanket I could wrap around myself. I tried to believe that Peter Pan might really come one night and fly me away; I was too old to believe this and I knew it, but I forced the bright polka-dotted canopy of this belief over my unhappy knowledge. And I tried to conform the sub-urban world around me to the world of Victorian London described in the book—which resulted in a jarring sensation each time I was forced to look at my true surroundings.

My mother's presence protected me from these moments. Sometimes when we would go out on our drug-store errands—sailing forth in the car with our elbows thrust out the window, the radio playing cheerful music—we would encounter kids my age slouching in a group outside the store, teasing their hair, gnawing their gum, and they would turn to look at me, and I would see myself in their eyes, a fat girl wearing white ankle socks and heart-shaped sunglasses. If my mother hadn't been there, they would've made jokes about me. But she was there and she bustled by them wagging her hips, saying, once we'd reached the store, "Do you know those girls? They look like gun molls!"

My closeness with my mother was physical as well as emotional. She washed my hair and rubbed my feet, and at night she would rub my back as I lay in bed. Occasionally, she would have me bend over her lap and, lifting my cotton nightie, she would spread my hips and check to see if I had worms up my ass. I could've questioned why she thought this was possible, but I didn't. The certainty of her movements made it seem perfectly natural that I'd have worms in my ass and that she'd better check. It was to me as normal as the massages she gave my father almost every night.

I would often say good-night to them as my father lay in his reclining chair with my mother kneeling at his bare feet with a bottle of baby oil. Or he would be lying on his stomach on the floor in his pajama bottom with a sheet spread beneath him while she knelt over him in her nightgown with her bottom facing toward his head, rubbing his back, bending forward so that her long, loose hair brushed his hips.

Sometimes I would be allowed to take part, and we would both sit on Daddy in our gowns, massaging him with oil while he said, "Oh, that feels so good to the old father." We would change positions often—I'd start at his feet and she at his shoulders, and then we'd switch. His skin would glisten with cheap oil, and he'd give off a hot, glandular smell that mixed with the smell of my mother's light sweat and perfume. The little gold locket she wore around her neck swung back and forth as she moved, and her nightgown came away from her body so that I could almost see her breasts. I loved massaging my father with her.

*When I started the sixth grade,* our neighborhood was rezoned. Eileen and Darla now had to take a bus to a school half an hour away, and I was transferred to yet another school. The new school was filled with crowds of strangers with ratted nests of bleached hair, makeup, and breasts. The girls wore pointy boots and stood with their legs apart and their hips thrust out; the boys wore cleats and had faces like knives. I once saw two boys standing in the hall by their lockers, one boy passive and expectant, the other gently holding the passive one's face with his palm, and then, with a sudden movement the touch turned to a slap, leaving the slapped face hot red. This caress/slap was repeated again and again, with varying gradations separating the caress from the slap, on one cheek and then the next. The slapped boy's expression remained impassive, even insolent.

Both boys and girls covered their notebooks with drawings in hot Magic Marker and decals. Their drawings were of monsters with dripping fangs, long, roiling tongues, bugged-out veiny eyes, and short hairs all over them. The monsters were surrounded by Magic Marker words in huge ornate Gothic letters— "Cool," "Eat Me," and "Suck." Almost everyone drew, with the same ornamental flourish and precision, a huge swastika or Maltese cross in some central place on his or her notebook.

It was pretty much the same situation as the last school except this one had more audiovisual aids, and instead of the teacher giving the usual talk during science period, she'd have one of the boys wheel in a television, and we'd watch a program called *Adventures in Science*. It was awful, and during the first week, a girl behind me said "I'd rather fart than watch *Adventures in Science*."

I asked my mother what "fart" meant, and she said it was "a vulgar word sailors use when they mean to say 'poot.' "

Sometimes on my way home, I'd see the fart girl walking a block or so ahead of me. She was big, with adult hips brutishly packed into a tight skirt, large knees with raw bumps on them, and eyes that wandered blankly as she gnawed her gum. Her name was Barbara Van Bent, and I was surprised when one day she waited for me to catch up to her on the sidewalk and said "Hi." She was the kind of girl I was naturally afraid of, the kind of girl who pushed me out of the lunch line. But she said "Hi," her eyes avoiding mine in the guarded, deferential way some children have of making friends.

She lived in my neighborhood, and the next day she waited for me to walk with her. I went to her house, and she showed me her autographed pictures of pouting boy rock stars and television personalities. She showed me her collection of naked bug-eyed rubber dolls with stand-up hair, and she shared a bag of orange and pink candy with me. Her mother, a big woman with stiff hips in stretch pants, gave us sloppy Joes on paper plates. She came to my house, and my mother made us hot chocolate and gave us paper and crayons. Barbara seemed surprised by this, but she took her paper and made drawings of girls with breasts wearing white go-go boots and boys with big eyes in Nehru jackets. I drew a picture of Never-Never Land and explained it to Barbara, as she had never heard of Peter Pan. I think she said "Cool," but I don't remember.

I can barely remember her face, just her mouth, full, dark-colored, and often slightly open, her fingers pulling and pinching it together. Her mouth could slide sideways in an expression of such sudden disdain that it would frighten me—then I'd silence my discomfort, and she'd be my friend again. I told her I never wanted to grow up. She said she did. I asked her why, and she said because then you could wear lipstick and sexy pants. Once I heard a boy say, "I'd like to make Van Bent strip," and I imagined her naked. Later I saw him trying to pull up her dress on the playground. She tilted her hips and defiantly posed.

The last time she came to my house, we went into the backyard. Wretched pocked hunks of leftover snow sat near the house. Barb wore tight stretch pants and a blue ski cap with a big pom-pom. She wanted to throw snowballs at a target on the fence. I didn't want to because I wasn't any good at aiming or throwing, but I did it to please her. Her snowballs almost always hit; mine fell apart in the air. She got bored and didn't want to play, and I felt it was because I wasn't good enough. We stood talking in the damp yard, shifting our weight from leg to leg. She told me about the Nasty Club. She said it was she and three other girls who got together and showed each other pictures of naked people, or whatever else they could find that was dirty. Becky Pickren had once brought a rubber cock she'd found in her mother's drawer, and Marsha Donnelly brought a used condom. To get into the Nasty Club you had to strip from the waist down in front of everybody, and according to Barb, Denise Biddle had hair between her legs.

Hearing about the Nasty Club shocked me and made me uncomfortable. My mother would hate it if she knew I was listening to such things. Why did they want to see these things? It seemed violent and humiliating to me. I tried to ignore these feelings. I tried to make Barb think I liked the Nasty Club.

For a while I didn't see Barb after school; I'd wait for her in our usual place, but she didn't come. Then I saw her walking a few blocks ahead with Sharon Ringle, a girl with a pushed-in face who I didn't like. I quietly settled into my disappointment. I didn't look at her in class, she didn't look at me. "I didn't think she was a nice girl anyway," said my mother. "She just didn't seem like a very high type."

Then one day in the hall, someone said to me, "Hey, Footie. Van Bent says you're a sweathog. She says you believe in Peter Pan."

"Hey," said a girl on the playground, "do you believe in Peter Pan?" I knew what had happened and I could see how the Peter Pan stuff sounded. I wanted to explain that I didn't believe in it exactly, it was

more that I wanted to believe it. But I didn't know
how so I just said "No." That didn't make any difference. The next week I was followed home from school
by three big girls who walked right at my heels saying
things like "Sweathog," "Retard," and "Hey, where's
Peter?" Barb was one of them. I didn't turn to look at
her or speak. I couldn't even separate her voice from
the others.

The next day there were five or six girls walking a
foot behind me yelling "Footie is a sweathog!" over
and over again. I tried to leave school ahead of them;
I walked so fast my forehead sweated in the dry winter
cold. Most of the time I escaped them, sometimes not.
Sometimes I would see them blocks behind me, fes-
tively waving their Monkees or Barbie lunch boxes,
confident as buffalo, and I would feel, for all my bulk,
empty.

I told my mother what was happening. "Hood-
lums!" she said. "Ignore them, honey, just pretend like
you don't even see them." What she said was stupid,
but I could hear that she was angry and hurt for me,
and this caused me pain. She called Barb Van Bent's
mother and talked to her about her daughter "picking on" me. She called the school and tried to get
them to protect me. My father said, "You've got to
fight dirty with thugs," and told me to smash their in-
steps and kick their shins.

The crowd continued to follow me down the
street. My mother began walking to meet me after
school. She would come marching up the block with
a tight, upcurving smile that wrinkled her face and
made naked the expression in her small gray eyes,
twinkling with succor and cheer. There was nothing in
her expression that acknowledged what the other children were saying to me—and continued saying, in her
presence. She would bring me home for cookies and

tea and put on a recording of a Broadway musical about a tropical romance, where soldiers and grass-skirted girls sang and danced in formation under coconut trees.

Part of me accepted my mother's comfort, shutting out, with a huge effort, the rest of the world. But another part of me saw that the world created by my parents and me was useless. It was not translatable into the language of the tough, gum-popping kids around me, and it failed to protect me from them. I dimly recognized this world as pathetic, functional only in my parents' house, but as there was no bridge between it and the outside, I had nowhere else to go.

One day when I was being followed by a group of five or so, one of them pushed me. This was too much and I turned, terrified but unable to stop myself. I faced startled Nona Delgado, a strong athletic Cuban girl with a soft mole on her cheek who, because of her beauty, style, and quick mouth had a place among the coolest in spite of the dark skin that relegated the few other Latinos to social obscurity. I had never looked at her up close; I had a second to register her sleek brows, the tiny white fleck caught on an eyelash, the parting of her dark colored lips, the glimpse of wonder and vulnerability that flared in her large eyes, momentarily stripped of their tough kid sheen. She was beautiful, and I felt a second of bitterness that this beautiful face was my enemy, then I punched her nose. She opened her mouth and stared. Convinced that I was about to be beaten by them all, I hit her again and again—about five times before she dropped her books and fought me. Surprise one: she did not know how to fight at all. Surprise two: her friends did not jump on me. They stood around us and yelled "Get her Nona!" while I, a fat girl, pounded her. After I recovered from my fear and anger, the fight became a squalid embarrassment I couldn't find a way out of. We rolled and sweated on the ground, my Sears coat torn, her nose and tender mouth ribboned with blood. Finally a housewife came out and told us to stop fighting in her yard. As I walked away, my enemies stood around the angrily weeping Nona. One of them shouted after me "You fight like an animal, Footie!" My mother and father praised me for fighting, and I was glad I had. But I was only glad in the abstract; I was sorry I'd hit Nona, who I'd always secretly admired. I felt she couldn't really be my enemy; she had simply been drawn into a bad crowd. I remembered the feeling of my fists on her face with a strange mix of disbelief, repulsion, and pride. Her tears and blood I remembered with tenderness. When I thought of her, I didn't feel contempt or anger or triumph; I felt warmth and unhappiness. One or two times after our fight, I saw her face in the hall in school and saw in its sudden stiffness that I had affected her. It made me feel excited and troubled.

One night almost a month after the fight, I called her house. Mrs. Delgado, who had her daughter's large liquid brown eyes, answered and told me Nona was skiing. I said, "Tell her that Dotty Footie called. Tell her I'm sorry I fought her."

The next time I met Nona in the hall, I was shocked to see her look directly at me, her eyes holding an almost unbearable expression of receptivity and humanity. "Hi," she said, and disappeared into the yelling mass of kids. I felt as if I had been stripped of clothing; her second of kindness pierced me and touched a naked private place so unused to contact that I cringed with shame and discomfort, as if a stranger had put a hand down my pants.

And it didn't stop there. To my dismay, Nona began calling me at home and inviting me out to play. My mother was delighted; even I could see that here was a chance to make a friend. But I didn't want to. I didn't want to go out into the barren squares of neighborhood snow and play with this television-beautiful person in a pink ski cap. I didn't know how.

But I couldn't refuse, so out I went. A nature walk, a game of catch, a cup of cocoa in Nona's pink room checkered with photos of rock and TV stars. Our activities were burdensome, tense affairs devoid of the girlish giggling and trash talk I had never learned how to do. I wanted to go back in the house and draw pictures of Never-Never Land elves or listen to a musical with my mother. Strangely, unbelievably, I had the feeling that Nona liked me. In her cautious conversation I sensed discomfort, curiosity, a sense of duty that had somehow been irrevocably triggered by my phone call. But I also sensed actual interest and liking waiting for me to show myself.

I wanted to show myself but I could not. I vainly groped for words that would let her see what I was like, things to say that she would understand. Desperately, I called other children "retards," "niggers," and "queers," something she seemed always ready to do. But when I talked this way, her face would become confused and remote, as if she knew these words from me were lies, and she didn't understand why I was lying.

The awful climax of our attempted friendship came in early spring, as we were crouched stiffly in my backyard near our shelterless wire fence, moving our naked rubber troll dolls around my mother's tomato plants. Suddenly, across the Sissels' exposed yard, I saw Barbara Van Bent and her gang. And they saw us. They paused for a second, registering the shock of seeing Nona in my yard with me. Then they began to yell, "Delgado is a spic! Delgado loves the sweathog!"

For a second I saw Nona's body fractionally withdraw from me; I saw she had been wounded by what they said. I saw her stop and pause. I saw her slowly return to me. I felt her stay by me, defying the other girls. On her face was a look of mild puzzlement, as if she couldn't imagine what she was doing in this situation.

I began turning down Nona's invitations, and soon they stopped. She kept looking at me and saying "Hi" in the halls, and this made me so uncomfortable that I avoided her the same way I avoided Barb and her friends.

One day just before school was over, something unusual happened. As I was struggling down the pavement on my way home from school, my fingers sweating around my lunch-box handle, I almost bumped into Barb Van Bent, who was hustling along almost faster than I was. It had been so long since I'd seen her alone, I didn't recognize her. She was completely different without her group. She seemed relieved when she turned and saw it was only me coming up behind her; her eyes had been uncharacteristically wide with terror. "Hi," she said.

I was so nonplussed I fell into step with her, and we walked at breakneck speed in sweating silence.

"Did you see Donnelly back there?" she asked. She meant her friend Marsha.

I hadn't.

"She says she's gonna beat my butt," explained Barb. "That Jew bag."

This was a very interesting idea and an altogether plausible one. Barb was a big girl, but Marsha was bigger, with huge, frozen-hamhock hands and tiny, brainlessly sparkling eyes flanking a giant nose that looked like it could live independent of her face. What was strange was that Barb should tell me about this. Was it a weird form of companionship? Or did she simply have no sense of irony? Did she not care that I saw she was even more cowardly than I?

Bewildered into silence, I listened to her describe Marsha's hideous body and warped personality. ". . . and she's got pimples on her butt and holes in her underwear," she said. "And she's a bitch. Do you know what she'd do?" Barb paused while a tiny kindergartner came within range and addressed herself to him. "She'd say, 'Get out of here you nigger lips or I'll beat your butt.'" The child fled. "That's what she's like," finished Barb.

By the next day she must've decided these qualities weren't so bad, because I saw them in the cafeteria together, giggling over their lunch boxes.

Summer came, and I didn't have to be afraid anymore. I never went out of the house. I stayed down in the basement rec room all day watching *Dialing for Dollars* and eating Sara Lee cheesecake, bags of potato chips, and diet pop. When that was over I'd watch the gladiator movie and then go upstairs to play with my troll dolls or draw pictures of Tarzan and the Lion Queen. Then I'd sit and talk to my mother while she made dinner, and then we'd eat in the anesthetic wind of three fans trained on the table as we watched Walter Cronkite. My father would walk around, talk. I'd see the kids of the neighborhood wheeling dreamily on their bikes in the lamplight and feel that all was as it should be. They were outside and I was inside. I gained fifteen pounds that summer.

*When Justine was ten* she read a poem about French resisters during the Second World War in her children's classics book. In it, a French hero was crucified to a barn door with bayonets and tormented by SS men before a crowd of weeping French patriots. The poet dwelt voluptuously on the hero's torment, and the poem climaxed with the death of the smirking SS captain. It excited her even more than the cartoons that had induced her to make Richie tie her to the swing set. She kept the children's classics under her bed so she could read it at night with a flashlight and masturbate.

They had moved from Lancelot to Action, Illinois. Richie was no longer at her disposal, and she hadn't yet found anyone to take his place.

Action was a thriving industrial suburb outside of Chicago. Justine's father was a successful cardiologist at the Action Medical Center, an interesting building that appeared to be made of plywood and concrete. Her father had told her mother that she couldn't be his receptionist because they already had a receptionist, so her mother did volunteer work at a center for emotionally disturbed children instead. Their house was a large, wandering, one-story with a flamingo worked into the aluminum grille on the front door.

They had moved there during the summer, when the sidewalks of the new neighborhood were alive with lounging, bicycling, roaming kids. When Justine ventured out onto the pavement, she was accosted by three gum-chewing girls who looked like they were trying to find something wrong with her. But suburban Michigan kids have almost the same laconic, nasal speaking style as the kids of suburban Illinois, and she was immediately accepted into the group.

Justine was drawn to the most sexual of the girls in the neighborhood, Pam Donovan and Edie Bernard, who wore the tightest pants and tightest shirts over their tough little chests. Edie, the blonde, was even sophisticated enough to wear pink powder and black mascara. Although their friends described them as "cute," they were not pretty. They were skinny and sharp-boned, with sullen, suspicious eyes, thin, violently teased hair, and faces generic to thousands of suburban little girls. But they were made beautiful by the erotic ferocity that suffused their limbs and eyes and lips.

Yet these girls, who harbored such power, were the most passive of the neighborhood gang. The three of them didn't like to play tag or baseball or even to ride bikes. They liked to sit on the small squares of concrete that were called "porches," sometimes getting up to walk around the block, getting whistled at and sprayed with light stones by boys. They talked about boys with a nervous mix of fear, disgust, and attraction, about girls with malice or displays of alliance, about their mothers with contempt, and about their bodies with a range of emotions from protective, reverent secrecy to loathing.

*There were race riots* in Detroit that summer and there was a lot of talk about that. Darcy Guido stood up to imitate Martin Luther King, tap dancing, rolling her eyes and pulling her lower lip down and sticking her tongue up to make weird wet lips that looked like the genitals of an orangutan. The day the national guard flew over their rooftops in helicopters, they stood in the streets and cheered. Even Pat Braiser's mother came out on her concrete slab and said, "That'll teach those animals to be decent!"

Justine sat quietly during the first days of the riot, hearing the distant people called animals and watching the genital-lipped, eye-rolling clowning. Her memory of Gemma rose up and stood mute, like a sign forbidding her to laugh at Darcy's joke, even when Pam, her best friend, nudged her and said, "Why don't you laugh?"

For days there were pictures of the riot on television. At dinner, Justine and her parents would sit at the table, eating and watching the dark figures run around on the screen while flames flickered in the blackened buildings. Her father would speak on the reprehensibility of rioting and violence, smartly wielding his utensils, the very posture of his haunches expressing the rightness of his disapproval. Her mother would agree, adding praise for Martin Luther King. The people on the TV apparently felt the same way; after showing clips of rioting or angry black spokespeople, they would console their viewers with old footage of Dr. King giving his famous dream speech. Justine became tired of seeing him, and of hearing him, and of hearing him praised. She didn't see what was so great about him.

Then the riots were over and it was time to go to the Wonderland Mall for clothes. Justine loved Wonderland. It was dotted with shrubs and waste containers, there was a fountain with a rusting cube placed in the center of it. Muzak rolled over everything, decorously muffling sound and movement. Huge square portals led into great tiled expanses lined with row upon dizzying row of racks hung with clothes. Signs that said "Junior Miss," "Cool Teen," or "Little Miss Go-Go" in fat round letters protruded from the tops of the racks, some of them illustrated by teenaged cartoon girls with incredibly frail bodies, enormous staring eyes, tiny O-shaped mouths and large round heads with long straight swatches of brown or yellow hair.

The dresses on the Cool Teen racks seemed to have been manufactured in a country where no one sat at home waiting for their mother; it seemed that in wearing the hot orange and yellow polka-dotted "hip-hugger" skirt with matching vinyl belt, the paisley jumper with purple pockets, or the high-collared chartreuse dress, Justine would suddenly occupy a place in which her mother didn't even exist.

She did real shopping, ironically, with her mother, but what she loved best was to go with Mrs. Bernard and Edie and Pam. All the way to Wonderland, she and her friends would lounge all over the back seat giggling about pubic hair or how stupid somebody was while Mrs. Bernard, a strangely thin woman with a face that looked like it was held in place with tacks, talked to herself in a low, not unattractive mutter. (Edie said her mother had a mustache that she tore off with hot wax, but Justine didn't believe it.)

Once at the mall, the four of them would comb the grounds like a gang of cats, rifling the racks, plunging into dressing rooms, snacking savagely between shops. Mrs. Bernard would wander ahead, continually bush-whacked by salespeople who thought her mutter was addressed to them, leaving the girls to stare and giggle, and to furtively admire the groups of tough older kids lounging on the public benches, smoking cigarettes and sneering. Sometimes glamorous older boys would follow them saying "I'd like to pet your pussy" and other dirty things; this was exciting, like the poem about the crucified man, only it made her feel queasier as it was real and in public. It was horrible to be in front of people having the same feeling that she had while masturbating and thinking about torture. She was sure that Edie and Pam didn't have feelings like that; probably they didn't even masturbate. They blushed and giggled and said "You guys better stop it," but they swung their purses and arched their backs, their eyes half-closed and their lips set in lewd, malicious smiles. Justine would imitate them, and when she did, sometimes a door would open and she'd step into a world where it was really very chic to walk around in public with wet underpants, giggling while strange boys in leather jackets and pointed shoes called you a slut. The world of Justine alone under the covers with her own smells, her fingers at her wet crotch, was now the world of the mall filled with fat, ugly people walking around eating and staring. It was a huge world without boundaries; the clothes and record and ice cream stores seemed like cardboard houses she could knock down, the waddling mothers and pimple-faced loners like dazed pedestrians she was passing on a motorcycle.

Once, at Sears, she was sullenly picking through the dressing rooms, trying to find a vacant stall, when she flipped back a scratchy yellow curtain and saw a strange person. She was about Justine's age and weird-looking, Justine thought, ugly, with pale cold skin, a huge exposed forehead, and blue plastic glasses on her face. She was fully dressed and slumped on the floor in a position of utter passivity and defeat, right against the mirror, staring at herself with the lack of expression that comes from extreme mental pain. Their eyes met for seconds—the stranger's face faintly reflecting embarrassed humanity—and then Justine backed out. The sight of such mute, frozen pain was stunning and fascinating, like an animal with its legs hacked off. Justine had never seen such a naked expression on her parents' faces, let alone on the face of a stranger. It made her feel queasiness and fear; it also made her want to poke at the queasiness and fear so she could feel it all the more. To see and feel something so raw in the mall was obscene, much more obscene than the whispering boys. She went to get Edie and Pam.

"Come and see," she said, "there's a drooling retard in the dressing room."

Naturally they hurried back. Justine had imitated her deranged slump with embellishments of jaw and eyeballs, and they approached the dressing room with a sense of cruel, illicit excitement. But when they got to the dressing stall and flung the curtain back, there was no one there. They sighed with disappointment and turned to go, and there was the girl again, standing up and peeping at them from behind the curtain of another dressing stall. Her face was accusing and almost snotty. Edie and Pam knew it was her, but somehow they couldn't make fun of her, even though they would've liked to; her staring face made them feel caught.

"God, what a queer," said Pam as they left the dressing room.

They found Edie's mother eating candy necklaces at the coffee counter of Woolworth's and left.

*When the first day of school* arrived, Justine had accumulated ten interchangeable outfits. And, in spite of all the fussing, picking, and mutual encouragement from her friends in the purchase of them, she was afraid that when she walked into the classroom she would be ostracized for fashion reasons that would become horribly clear to her as she made her way to her desk through a blinding sheet of jeers. What if none of her neighborhood friends were in the class, or even if they were, what if they turned out to be hopeless retards so low down on the social scale that association with them condemned her forever?

She was so numbed with fear that she accepted, without retort, her mother's breakfast table assurances that she looked "adorable" in her yellow and turquoise checked skirt and yellow knee socks.

The drive to school would've taken place in silence, if it hadn't been for infuriating *Adventures in Good Music*, which she hadn't the strength to object to, on the radio. She felt the whole magical summer of huddling safely with her friends, talking trash, and rejecting black people in a blur of hot bright days amid the changeless squares and rectangles of the trusted landscape had taken place in another world that would have no bearing on this terrible new place she was headed.

This was not true. The assigned classroom was filled with murderously aggressive boys and rigid girls with animal eyes who threw spitballs, punched each other, snarled, whispered, and stared one another down. And shadowing all these gestures and movements were declarations of dominance, of territory, the swift, blind play of power and weakness.

Justine saw right away that she'd be at home here.

When they were let out on the asphalt playground that morning, she found Edie and Pam, and they huddled together, chewing their gum and sending sharp stares of appraisal over their shoulders. They told each other who was cool and who was queer. By the afternoon recess, they had gathered three other girls about them, Debby, Dody, and Deidre. The D girls were all big and tough, charmed perhaps by Justine's sullen beauty and the sophisticated style of Edie and Pam.

Justine had made friends with Dody, the pretty one of the three. Her prettiness was of an unusual type in this time of anorexic cuties with ironed hair and white lipstick, she being a big raw-boned girl with large fleshy shoulders and hips, and big active hands and feet attached to long, confused arms and legs, multidirectional like rubber. Her eyes were extraordinary, huge and brown, shot with mad glowing strands of yellow and gold which, in conjunction with the tawny mass of hair sprawling frantic and uncontrollable on her head, gave her the look of a restless, fitful lioness. Her size and weight gave her no center; Justine's first retrospective image of her is of Dody splayed, arms and legs, as though in the middle of a tornado, only laughing, open-mouthed and loud. The next image is an actual memory of the time Dody, humorously displaying her size and strength, picked up a scrawny fourth-grader by a fistful of hair and swung her in a complete circle three times before letting the screaming creature fly. Justine remembers her strange vulnerability, her terror of thunderstorms and spiders, her moment of wide-eyed panic that time she and Justine were making out in the Mall restroom with two boys they'd met, when Justine had to hold her trembling paw. Ten years later, it had not surprised her to read by chance in the paper that Dody LaRec, college junior, had become an unusual statistic, one of the few females to commit suicide with a bullet to the brain.

The others, Debby and Deidre, were not pretty, but they exuded an awful cynicism that impressed people and they knew dirty things—Deidre claiming, at the age of eleven, to have "done it." Besides, they were brutal. The six of them terrified the other kids as they patrolled the playground, looking for trouble. In gym class they were always on the top team, hand-picking the ablest girls to be on their side, pitting themselves against the feeblest people, whom they happily pounded. Parents were always calling to complain about them pulling down their son's pants or dropping someone's lunch in the toilet. Teachers cajoled, pleaded, and occasionally ranted, but they couldn't do anything and they knew it. Justine believed teachers to be secretly on their side as they trampled the weak and the uncool, people adults have to accept, and, as a result, become like.

There was only a small group of boys who weren't afraid of them, on account of their being so tough themselves. They were small, sinewy boys whose main strengths were their monstrous voices and inhuman indifference to pain. They were always getting bashed with baseballs, splitting their skulls in rock fights, chipping their teeth, ripping open their elbows and knees, beating each other up as often as they beat retards and queers. They hung around with Justine and her group on the playground, pushing and pinching and pulling up their skirts. Sometimes they'd stand quietly and talk together, and Justine would feel her private torture feeling glowing through her lower trunk. She particularly liked little Ricky Holland, whose beautiful, almost dainty hands were such a contrast to his morbidly cruel personality. He was a loner within his gang, almost protected by the other boys in some unconscious way, as if they knew that just a slight shift in their perception would render him a victim rather than a cohort. He seemed happiest when torturing small animals by himself, yet he had an inexplicable kind aspect that appeared randomly and could lead him to risk rejection, like the time he protected a crippled girl who had been circled by the others. He was the first among them to smoke cigarettes, which, since drugs had not yet come to suburban playgrounds, was as chic as one could be. Justine loved his expressionless face, his blank, lusterless eyes. There was nothing in that face anyone could hurt or even approach. Love would find no opening there except perhaps in that quirky kindness which appeared for no reason and vanished again, too transient to support a reckless prepubescent ardor ready to crucify itself on a heartless boy. He paid no attention to her.

Meanwhile her mother worked at the home for emotionally disturbed children. This was very embarrassing to Justine, and she took pains to make sure her friends never found out about it, forbidding her mother to mention it in front of them. "I'd die if they know my own mom works with the 'tards," she said, hoping her mother would be ashamed. But her mother just answered, "There isn't any need for them to know. I understand darling, peer approval is very important at this age."

Justine alternately despised and admired her mother. It was hard not to admire this tall still-beautiful woman who dressed so well, who kept active, who led the dinner conversation with a ringing voice. Compared to other mothers she was an athlete, still rising in the morning to exercise in her leotard. She impressed all of Justine's friends, who thought she looked like somebody on TV. Her mother never told her she couldn't buy a dress because it was too short, like some mothers did. She did talk to her about being "nice" in reference to boys and to bullying other kids, but Justine understood from her tone of voice that "nice" had nothing to do with what anybody really felt or thought or observed but was something everybody had to pretend. Justine could also tell from her mother's voice that her mother believed this pretense was very important.

This was where she began to despise her mother; once she started she couldn't stop. She despised her earnest expression when she talked about a "breakthrough" made by some mental case at the center; she despised her straight posture, her diets, her exercises, her humming along to *Adventures in Good Music*. When they were in the same room together and her mother farted (silently, of course, but Justine could smell it), she felt such revulsion and hatred she wanted to hit her mother in the face. She wanted to see the attractive propriety of her mother's face collapse into tears, loud, ugly tears.

She never saw this, but once she heard it. She was awakened late one night by the sound of it, although at first she didn't know what it was; at first she thought the ungainly sounds were a dream. Then she heard her father's voice. He was angry. Her mother was crying, a deep moaning cry, saying something over and over again to him. Justine was stunned with horror and disbelief. Her father raised his voice and said a bunch of words, out of which Justine could only distinguish "stupid cow" and "off the floor." And then her mother was quiet. Justine's heart pounded deep and hard in her chest.

The next morning she watched her parents at breakfast. Her mother was pink and perfectly madeup, briskly leading the breakfast conversation as usual. What Justine now noticed was the reason she was leading it; her father, dourly pushing his eggs around on his plate, was making polite noises, not really responding to her. At first she thought it was because they'd had a fight, but as the week went on she realized he was acting as he always did. Justine thought: He doesn't like her either.

The thought was disconcerting, and she pushed it away, but it kept coming back, especially when her father began staying away for overnight conferences. Sometimes it would make her gloat, sometimes she'd try to hurt her mother with falsely innocent questions about where dad was. Other times she'd imagine her mother looking old and weak, crying on the floor while her father scorned her, and it would fill her with fear and pity. She would hate her father then and have fantasies of yelling at him, warning him to leave her mother alone. But she never heard him say those things to her mother again, although some nights she lay awake listening for it. Sometimes too, her father would stop ignoring her mother and would act the way he used to, smiling at her, hugging her shoulders, standing beside her, handsome and proud, calling her "my lady." When this happened, the things Justine had heard that night seemed like something that had happened between people who were only pretending to be her parents.

At the beginning of October a new kid entered Justine's class. Her name was Cheryl Thomson. She was big, she had acne, and she wore old plaid skirts what were obviously not from Sears or Wards. This would've been all right; some very cool kids—Dody among them—dressed this way. But they had a sloppy panache, a loose-limbed grace that made their flapping shirt-tails and shifting skirts seem sassy; halting, thick-bodied Cheryl did not. She sat in her seat with her stubby hands in her lap, talking to people politely before class, a dull dreamy look coating her gray eyes. Then the teacher came in and, in an innocent effort to help everyone get to know the new student, opened class by asking Cheryl questions meant to gently reveal her, for example, "What is your favorite food?" Cheryl did all right with that, but when asked about music, instead of saying "the Monkees" or "the Beatles" she answered "country music," causing a ripple of disbelief to alert the room. From that point on, every answer she gave confirmed her to be a hopeless alien in the world of primary-colored surfaces. She wanted to be a fire fighter when she grew up! Her favorite TV show was *Andy of Mayberry*! She liked to go fishing! Every answer seemed to come out of some horrible complex individuality reeking with humanity, the clarity and trust in her soft voice made them squirm with discomfort.

In the lunchroom, everybody was talking about how queer she was. Her second day at school, somebody tripped her in the hall; the following week somebody put a tack on her seat. When she sat on it, she cried, and little Marla Jacob sneered, "God, what an emotional!" From that day on she was known as "Emotional," the worst insult imaginable.

Her presence changed the whole composition of the class, uniting everyone, even other unpopular kids, against her. Everything she said became further proof of her stupidity, her social failure. Every ugly and ridiculous thing introduced into any discussion, in the classroom, on the playground, at the mall, was "like Emotional." She was most often taunted verbally, but there was also physical abuse—a shower of orchestrated spit balls, an ambush by a dozen or so boys and girls who struck her legs and arms with their belts.

Emotional's reaction was by turns angry, hurt, bewildered, but her most constant expression was one of helpless good nature. She was too even tempered to remain angry or brooding; she always tried to reverse the tide against her, to make jokes, to be positive, to join in. Once Justine saw a smiling face drawn in Magic Marker on her notebook with the words "Happy-Go-Lucky" written underneath and knew, sickeningly, that it was true, in spite of everything.

Of course, Justine took part in the Emotional pogrom. As with all the other little social massacres she'd taken part in, she was more a goader and abettor than an attacker; she was too small to be a real bully and not aggressive enough to be a ringleader. Besides, she was secretly too ambivalent. When she looked at the chalky, rigid face of some kid who was being shoved to and fro between Deidre and Debby, she felt deep, excruciating enjoyment as well as equally deep discomfort that she deliberately provoked, like she'd chew a cold sore. These two feelings met and skewered her between them while she giggled and cajoled and incited her friends to riot, making her feel monstrously alive and enlarged beyond the boundaries of herself, exploding into the world like her memory of tornado-splayed Dody—yet unable to bear being in the world, turning in on herself like an insect run through with a needle.

These feelings were magnified by Emotional, who, within a few months, became something other than human. Justine always joined in the teasing, yet the sight of Emotional's unhappy face brought darkness up from some thoughtless pit within her, made her turn away and frown when she should've been laughing. When she looked at Emotional she looked into the face of her most private fantasy, the victim crucified before a jeering crowd.

To Justine's discomfort, Emotional began appearing in her dreams. The most outstanding of these dreams featured her and Emotional in the front-line trenches of a war. There were other people in the trench, but there existed between her and the class queer a deep unspoken friendship that was expressed in meaningful glances and, at one point, a fraught hand clasping. The height of the dream was reached when Justine lay injured and paralyzed from an enemy blast, and Emotional ran to her side, ripping off a piece of her blouse to bind Justine's wounds.

It was perplexing: in many of the dreams Emotional helped or even rescued Justine in various ways, which in real life she couldn't possibly do. If anything, brooded Justine, she could help Emotional if she wanted to. *If* she wanted to. Of course, she didn't want to, but what if she did? She began to nurse strange fantasies of advising Emotional on how to improve her wardrobe, even accompanying her to the mall for a shopping trip, sitting with her at lunch, walking home with her, hearing the weird things that doubtless went on in her mind.

Emotional reappeared in her dreams, smiling and waving.

One morning after a particularly mysterious and moving dream, Justine found herself in a gym class that had been divided into groups, each group performing various athletic acts. Emotional was in her group. As usual, whenever it was Emotional's turn, the others would try to make her fail. When everyone had to jump over a pole held by two kneeling girls, all would finish their jump with a pause by a pole-bearer and a whispered "make Emotional trip!" Which they did; when Emotional made her jump, the pole came up mid-leap. There was an amusing facial wobble, a mid-air flounder, and Emotional thudded down on her hands and knees. She cried; everybody laughed and said, "God, Emotional!" But Justine, although she laughed too, felt unwanted remorse. This remorse became a secret weight of gentleness and sorrow within her which stayed, no matter how hard she tried to kill it. That afternoon she decided she was going to stop hurting Emotional.

She didn't want to voice her new tolerance to anyone at school, but what good was it if nobody knew about it? If Emotional didn't know about it? She would see Emotional and itch with curiosity about her. What did it feel like to be despised and victimized by everyone? How would Emotional react if she knew that in this nest of enemies she had an ally?

One day when Justine's pack of friends was not with her at the end of the day, she found herself a bare three feet from Emotional, both of them in the act of closing their lockers. Justine couldn't help it; she turned her head and held the other girl's flitting glance. "Hi, Cheryl," she said.

They left school together and continued walking for a few blocks before they had to part. Justine did this because it was late and she didn't see anyone she knew and because the novelty of talking with this outcast was too fascinating to let go of quickly. But mainly she walked with Emotional because when she allowed contact to occur between them, she was touched by her in a way she had no experience with and therefore no resistance against. Every aspect of Emotional's body—the shy ducking motion of her head, her injured eyes, her small steps, her arms held protectively close to her body, her soft dislocated voice—was the manifestation of a deep woundedness which Justine, without the harsh interference of her friends, felt acutely. She wanted to salve this wound, to shield it. It was a feeling she hadn't had for a long time, not even

for herself, and it was such a tender feeling that she
wanted to prolong it.

That night as she lay in bed, she fantasized about
standing between Emotional and the whole brutish
world, protecting her, creating a little place between
them where she'd be free to like her hillbilly music
and wear her uncool clothes and nobody would mind.

She unexpectedly got the chance to act out this fantasy when the next day, before school, she was confronted during the usual pre-class homeroom melee
by Debby, Deidre and another girl with terrifying big
black hair. They wanted to know: "Are you friends
with Emotional?"

She was only telling the truth when she said "No,"
but then they wanted to know if it was true she'd
walked with her.

"I just wanted to see the queer kinds of things
she'd talk about. I just wanted to know what weirdos
say. I was pretending to be nice, but she could tell I
hated her."

Later that day she and Dody were alone, ratting
their hair in the rest room after school. "Do you really
hate Emotional?" Justine asked.

Dody stopped in midrat and stared. "Of course I
hate her, what are you, some kind of retard?"

"No really, why do you hate her?"

"Because she's retarded."

"Yeah but if she's retarded, shouldn't we help her?
Shouldn't we be nice to her if she can't help being
weird?"

"God, Justine, sometimes I wonder about you."
Dody produced a compact and vigorously ground
some pink grit into her skin.

The next day Justine had to put up with a lot of sarcastic comments. But she found that once she'd begun expressing what she felt, it was hard to stop; she

became reckless, irritated by the choke collar of public opinion. Although she was frightened, she couldn't help yanking against the restraint, and the more disapproval she got, the harder she tugged against it. A tough little person within her rose and asserted itself. She stuck by what she'd said, more and more vehemently, until finally she exploded. "I don't care what you douche-bags do. I'm not gonna hate Emotional anymore so just shut up, okay?" The other girls stared at her, shocked.

They began savaging poor Emotional even more viciously than before, especially in Justine's presence. But there was a lack of confidence in their voices as they picked and abused. After a few days it became half-hearted and then stopped. The subject of Emotional was all but dropped in the lunchroom, where Justine sat in her usual place among the others, defiantly eating her dried-up burger and fries.

It was during gym class that the miracle occurred; the girls were dividing into teams, the most popular ones ritually selecting their team mates, when Debby suddenly bawled out, "I want Cheryl! Cheryl Thomson!" There was a moment of silence, and then someone on the other team said, "Aw! I wanted her!" in a voice usually used to coo over the cuteness of babies and bunnies.

Emotional took her place on the team looking like she'd been hit in the head with a brick and was stoically preparing for another blow. She played her usual clumsy but serviceable game, and every successful move she made was wildly cheered with greeting-card enthusiasm while her fumbles were loudly excused in the same awful tone. Her expression throughout was the same as when she was abused: hurt, bewildered, remote. Did she have any suspicion that she was a new fad?

It lasted for a few weeks. In the lunchroom, in the halls, on teams of all kinds, Emotional was the hip thing. Her presence was demanded everywhere although she didn't say or do much but stare, sad and frozen. This was further proof of her exotic idiocy, and they cooed and twinkled over her as if she were a wounded animal in a box.

Justine didn't know what to think. She felt ashamed and angry. The sound of the others "being nice to Emotional" was even worse than their cruelty—her cruelty—which at least had been a clear, consistent message, potentially refutable by its recipient. This insulting mockery of friendship hadn't been what she had imagined when she'd resolved to be kind, but she was afraid to interfere again.

Mercifully, they soon got bored with it, and the gym teacher had once more to force a reluctant, groaning team to accept Emotional. There was some change, however; after such an elaborate show of friendship and kindness, it was hard for them to revert completely to all-out sadism, and all but the meanest kids pretty much ignored her. She finished out the school year as a lumbering ghostly presence, her humanity unknown and unacknowledged.

*When Justine started seventh grade* in the new junior high, Deidre, who had breasts and hair between her legs, began seeing a boy from the eighth grade. He went to a different junior high school across town; she had met him while sitting beside the copper cube fountain in the mall, smoking a cigarette alone. His name was Greg Mills. He had a concave torso, thin legs, narrow eyes, long lank hair, and red pimples which only added to his lurid charm. He wore a black vinyl windbreaker and spoke in monosyllables. Justine was secretly uncomfortable around him and wondered why, if he was so cool, he didn't have a girlfriend his own age.

Deidre described going with him and his friends to an empty housing development, breaking into one of the finished houses, and throwing a party with their transistor radios, smoking, drinking, making out, and doing it, leaving ashes and stains on the bedspread of the display bedroom. It shocked and thrilled Justine to picture them sitting in the cold deserted rooms with their jackets on, smoke and alcohol in their throats. She imagined Deidre pulling her ski pants off, her bottom on the bedspread, the mattress naked underneath. She would be all goose flesh and tiny leg hairs sticking up, her feet clammy, her genitals hairy and weird between her big thighs. Did Greg pull her legs apart and look at her or did he just stick his thing (reportedly hairy itself) inside her in the dark? Did he take off his pants and show *his* butt or did he just unzip? Justine would look at Greg and decide that either way was nasty and exciting. She admired Deidre tremendously.

Diedre began asking if they wanted to come with her some time. "Not to some scuzzy development," said Justine. "I don't wanna freeze my butt." Neither did anybody else until one Saturday Deidre called Justine and Dody and told them Greg's parents had left for the day, that he was inviting over some really cute eighth grade guys, did they want to come?

Greg's house was just like Justine's and Dody's and everyone else's. Greg and Deidre were on the couch, and there were two other boys, one of them with the empty pretty eyes of a TV star. Justine saw, with a rush of excitement and fear, that they were drinking alcohol mixed with Coca-Cola. She didn't want to drink it, but she didn't want to say no in a prudish way, so when one of them offered it to her, she turned it into an occasion for sexual tension, saying, "Uh uh, I know what you guys are trying to do!" "Yeah," said Dody, taking her cue, "you wanna get us drunk and make us do things." She smiled in fake innocence, fake sophistication, and real sexuality. Her gold eyes were half-lidded and glinting.

The boys liked this. "You'd better be good," said Greg. "We're baby-sitting you seventh graders, and if you don't do what we say, you're gonna get it."

The game was on. They sat on the couch, moving closer and closer, the boys getting drunk, the girls getting giggly and excited. They teased and flirted and made fun of each other, the boys commanding the girls to do things, like pick a piece of paper up off the floor. The girls would fiercely resist and then do it, pouting and flouncing. There was a thick current of feeling coursing through the room, a wide band of glittering yellow-gold that swept them off the floor and into another sphere. At first Justine stood aloof and looked at this process with wonder; then she let it move her.

Greg and Deidre left the room, disappearing behind a closed door. The two other boys became rougher and more demanding; one of them told Dody to make him a drink, and when she didn't move fast enough, he grabbed her hair and pulled her toward the kitchen. "You leave my friend alone!" Justine yelled in the phony little-girl voice employed by sluts and whores the world over (and she an actual little girl!) as she leapt up to grab the boy's shirt, pummeling his back with deliberate futility. She and Dody overpowered him and pinned him to the wall, greedily savaging him with tickling fingers until his friend leapt off the couch and the girls ran screaming until they were cornered in a parental closet.

"You guys are really gonna get it now," advised the blank-eyed boy. "You have to stay in here and wait while we decide what we're gonna do. You have to stand back to back with your hands behind you."

The boys left the room, and they did as they were told, standing and telling each other how afraid they were in thrilled voices. "Do you think we should try and run for it?" asked Dody. "No, we'd better not," Justine said. "They'd really kill us then." Justine thought of her parents sitting at the table eating dinner, her mother daintily picking an errant morsel from her teeth, and for a minute she actually did feel afraid. What if she really was in another sphere and couldn't get back to the old one? Then she relaxed; but of course, it would be as simple as the times she lay in bed and, putting her hand between her legs, became a victim nailed to a wall, and then, as her body regained its tempo, became Justine once more.

The boys came back into the room. One of them said, "Okay LaRec, follow me." And Dody sneering, "Oh, I'm really scared," followed him into the bathroom, visible at the end of a short hall, leaving Justine to stare at this pretty-eyed creature with chiseled features, peachy skin, and no human expression. Her heart pounded. She wanted to sit down. He forbade her. He told her his friend was "going to strip Dody and finger her." Her underwear became wet. She told him Dody was probably beating his friend's butt, but no sound of butt-beating emanated from the bathroom. They stood silently, Justine's breath getting quicker and shallower, every detail of the boy's bored, sideways-looking face becoming larger by the moment. She felt as if he were right next to her, his breath filling her pores, his smell up her nose. The longer they stood the more genuinely afraid she became. The more afraid she became, the more bolted to the floor she was, her armpits damp, her throat closed, her pelvis inflamed and disconnected from her body, her head disconnected from her neck. She heard Deidre laughing in the bedroom.

The bathroom door opened, and Dody paraded out with her boy lurking and smirking behind. Her face was red but her body exuded pride.

"Come on," said Justine's boy, "your turn."

The bathroom was pink-tiled and green-rugged, the sink decorated with large, stylish shells and glass jars filled with bubble bath balls. The boy sat on the green toilet and looked at her. "You hafta get over my lap," he said.

Justine thrust her hip out and tried to look like she was making fun of him, but she didn't know how to do that without her friends. The music from a ball-point pen commercial was playing in her head, and she imagined huge-eyed Cool Teens dancing to it. "I'm not gonna do that," she said.

"You hafta."

Back and forth they went. Heat and tension sat between her legs; the rest of her felt cold. He grabbed her hand and pulled her face down across his lap. She tried to appear graceful, feeling heavy and fat on his slim haunches. She looked at the toilet cleaning brush in the corner as he pulled down her pants. Her breath held itself as his numb fingers pushed into her numb contracting body. He fingered her with strange mechanical movements. His hand felt far away even when his fingers were inside her, as if he were doing something someone had told him to do and was pleased because he'd succeeded in doing it, not because he liked it. His remoteness made him authoritarian and huge, like a robot in a comic book. It inflamed her. She thought of Richie whipping her at the swing set amid the red flames of her little cartoon hell. His fingers hurt her. She gripped his thighs—and, in contrast to his hand, felt him there, a quick boyish spirit in the warm, feeling body of a young human. "It hurts," she said.

Perfunctorily, he stopped, took his fingers out of her, wiped them on her bare ass and moved his hands so that she could stand.

She walked out of the bathroom feeling like a busty blonde on *The Man from U.N.C.L.E.*; womanly, proud, almost inert in the majesty of her dumb, fleshy body.

Then she and the D girls went to Dody's house and had ice cream and vanilla wafers.

She never saw those particular boys again but, although she had occasion to "make out" a few times after that, the boys who kissed her and felt her tiny breasts never made her feel the way she had felt while standing in Greg Mills's house. The only person who provoked that feeling again was girl—a girl she didn't even like much! She was Rose Loris, a mousey pretty thing with thin lips and eyebrows who wanted with fierce anemic intensity to be "in the group" and who was tolerated on the fringes because she was Debby's friend, although it was a friendship based mainly on Rose's devotion to Debby, who was always standing Rose up at the mall.

This intent yet drooping girl with the shoulders of a rag doll and the alert, quizzical head of a bird, whose sleepy limbs seemed at odds with her straight spine, followed Justine around wanting to be her friend. This annoyed or flattered Justine, depending on her mood. Rose was always saying weird things that she thought would sound cool, and it embarrassed Justine. Still, she sometimes went to Rose's house to watch television and to look at Mr. Loris's pornography collection.

Among the many magazines, postcards, and books,

Mr. Loris had a comic entitled *Dripping Delta Dykes* about two huge fleshy rivals who, through a strange plot with many perplexing changes of locale, battled each other in their changing lingerie ensembles. On the kitchen table, in the boxing ring, on tropical isles, in hospital rooms (where they worked as nurses), they met and settled one another's hash, the brunette, after a lot of hair-pulling, arm-twisting, and tit-squeezing, generally trussing the blonde up in a variety of spread-eagled poses so she could stick different objects into her vagina.

Although Rose laughed and squealed "Gross!" while perusing this book, Justine noticed she kept coming back to it over and over. Rose's reaction irritated Justine; it made her want to shove or slap Rose. Instead she said, "God, this is no big deal, I've done this stuff with Debby. It's fun."

Rose's stunned face seemed to fractionally withdraw, and for a moment Justine was embarrassed at her lie. But Rose drew near again. Then, as had happened in Greg Mills's house, they crossed a border together.

Justine went on talking, saying that not only had she and Debby done the things depicted in the comic but that everybody did this, didn't Rose know? She never knew if Rose believed her, but at the moment she also knew it didn't matter, that Rose was going to pretend she believed her. The torture feeling was roused and roaring as she wheedled and teased, moving closer to the agitated, awkward kid until she was all but cornered against the wall, pulling her hair across her lips, Justine whispering that Rose was a baby, a goody-goody, that she didn't know anything.

It took surprisingly little to get her in the basement bathroom, where they were least apt to be discovered.

It is with a mixture of incredulity, guilt, and conceit

that she remembers that dreamy session in the Lysol-smelling toilet with the concrete walls of a jail cell. She was incredulous at Rose's docility; every cajolement or command elicited another trembling surrender, and every surrender filled Justine with a boiling greed that pushed her further into the violation she'd started as a game. The occasional feeble resistance—Rose's pleading hand on the arm that rampaged down her pants—only increased Justine's swelling arrogance and made her crave to rip away another flimsy layer of the hapless girl's humanity. Justine felt her eyes and face become shielded and impenetrable as Rose's became more exposed; she felt her personality filling the room like a gorging swine. Rose was unquestionably terrified and doubtless would've liked to stop, but she had been stripped of the territory on which one must stand to announce such decisions, as well as most of her clothes. For although Justine had only meant to cop a feel, within a few delirious moments Rose was placed on the closed lid of the toilet, her pants and panties in a wad on the floor. Her shirt was pulled up to reveal her tiny breast mounds, her legs splayed and tied with her own knee socks to conveniently parallel towel racks, her hands ritualistically bound behind her back with a measuring tape, her mouth stuffed with a small roll of toilet paper.

Justine stood and surveyed her victim. She was shocked at the sight of the hairless genitals; they reminded her of a fallen baby bird, blind and naked, shivering on the sidewalk. It disgusted her to think she had something like that too, and she focused the fullness of her disgust on Rose. There were no more cajoling words, the mouse had been hypnotized, she was free to strike at leisure.

Fascinated by the meek unprotected slit but too appalled to touch it, she plucked a yellowing toothbrush from its perch above the sink—pausing to glance at herself in the mirror as she did so—and stuck the narrow handle into her playmate's vagina. From the forgotten region of Rose's head came a truly pathetic sound; her face turned sideways and crumpled like an insect under a murdering wad of tissue, and tears ran from her closed eyelids.

But it was not the tears that brought Justine to her senses, it was the stiff, horrified contraction of the violated genitals which she felt even through the ridiculous agent of the toothbrush, a resistance more adamant than any expressed so far. Suddenly she realized what she was doing.

She left the sobbing child crouched on the cold concrete floor, pulling on her clothes with trembling fingers, while she bounded up the basement stairs and out the back door yelling, "I'm gonna tell everybody what I made you do!"

But she didn't. Out of a muddled combination of shame and barely acknowledged pity, she kept it to herself, for her own frenzied, crotch-rubbing nocturnal contemplation.

Rose was absent from school for a week and then appeared like an injured animal dragging its crushed hind legs. No one remarked how her head, previously so busy and alert, had joined the collapse of her shoulders, or how her cheerful little spine had somehow crumpled. She avoided Justine and the gang, then tentatively approached and realized no one knew. She once accompanied Justine home from school in an abject silence that Justine was too embarrassed to break, except when they both mumbled "Bye."

Although Justine told no one, the other girls sensed some new vulnerability in Rose, unconsciously recognized the loss of that nervous puppy spirit that had been her particular charm. They became aggressive and cruel to her; Debby was especially unkind. Rose walked home with Justine one more time and, at the corner where they would've said goodbye, blurted out an invitation to Justine to come play the game they played before, in the bathroom. Justine snarled and turned away. Rose never came near the gang again. Since she was not in Justine's class, Justine only caught occasional glimpses of her in the halls or on the periphery of the playground, wandering by herself or standing with a crowd of other mousey unpopular girls.

This incident did not interfere with Justine's other make-out activities, except in one way: after a squatting self-examination over a mirror, she vowed that while they could touch it all they wanted, she'd never allow anyone to look at that ugly thing between her legs. But she was only eleven and knew nothing at all about her future, so one can't be too hard on her for breaking vows made at this time.

*My family moved to Painesville,* Pennsylvania, when I was thirteen. Physically, the neighborhood was as I had been expecting the neighborhood in Michigan to be. There were big trees, lawns, gardens, and a small main street downtown. Our house was a pointy-roofed charmer with shutters on the windows and rose bushes cuddling against the walls. There was a patio and a breakfast nook, and for months before we moved, my father walked around our house in Chiffon holding snapshots of the Painesville house and smiling. But, within months after moving in, he discovered we had been betrayed by the real estate people. The house was dark, drafty, weirdly put together. Doorknobs fell off, the basement tended to flood, and the roof was so moldy that a wind-blown seedling rooted in it and grew into a sapling. My father was bitterly disappointed, first with the house, then with the neighborhood, then with the town.

After Michigan, I was suspicious of Painesville's alleged splendor, and so I was not disappointed. I employed the same methods I had learned in Chiffon to chop up and organize my life to lessen the impact of the outside world.

In the morning I would roll from my bed without turning on the light to put on my turquoise polka-dot girdle, my pantyhose, and my dress. In the bathroom my father ran water, coughed, blew his nose, rubbed the radio dial back and forth, spat into the sink, and flushed the unhappy old toilet. I finished my reluctant dressing ritual as he burst from the bathroom in a cloud of steam, and went to wash my face, brush my hair, and pee. The toilet seat was moist with steam, the mirror fogged, the bath mat damply rumpled on the floor, and the sink blobbed with his thick discharges of toothpaste. I performed my toilet cocooned in my father's smell of hair oil, Old Spice deodorant, sweat, and faded urine, and then went to sit at the breakfast table with him. He hunched at his place eating his eggs while I chewed my cold cereal and my mother flitted from kitchen to table in her robe. On the radio was a morning show called *Put On a Happy Face*, hosted by a man who sounded as if he viewed happiness as the most hopeless, yet most necessary, form of human gallantry.

I rode to school with five other girls, whom I remember mainly as knees tinted beige by pantyhose and arms clasped around books. Four of us were ugly and unpopular. When the car pulled up at the school, the one pretty, popular girl would leap out and walk ahead with frantic briskness so that no one would suspect that she had any connection with us.

The rest of the day was divided into hours and rooms labeled "math," "social studies," etc. There were minutes of travel through teeming hallways and there was lunch. Of these divisions, I found the classroom hours the most painless because they were most controlled. I divided this time even further, first by the spaces between the clock's numbers, then by the gestures and whispered conversations that took place without any words suddenly leaping out to injure me, then by the written exercises to be performed. Between these markers I toiled, slowly connecting one to the other. The moments in the halls were horrible because they were not divisible and because I was exposed to a striding, grinning, shouting chaos of people, many of whom possessed an unbearable youthful beauty, all of whom were connected to each other by feelings and conversations I could not understand, people with whom I could never connect, except when someone screamed, "Look! It's Twiggy!" Lunch was less jarring, but, after I got through the various points in the line, there was no way to mark off my existence, and for a full half hour I was skewered by the sight and sound of others celebrating their youth and vitality. I began to eat my Choco Chunk bars and french fries in the bathroom in the company of two or three girls with nests of hair, threadbare skirts, and leather jackets. They drooped on the wall, put on lipstick, teased their hair, and smoked cigarettes, languorously blowing the smoke ceilingward as they talked about their boyfriends or how much they hated someone. I still remember, with useless clarity, the large pink bump that one of these girls had at the corner of her nose, a pimple that was always inflamed and set off by a delicate circle of orange makeup at its base.

The most rigid pattern was not the one imposed by the school system or the adolescent social system. It was the pattern I made of the people around me, a mythology for their incomprehensible activity, a mythology that brought me a cramped delight, which I protected by putting all possible space between myself and other people. The boundaries of my inner world did not extend out, but in, so that there was a large area of blank whiteness starting at my most external self and expanding inward until it reached the tiny inner province of dazzling color and activity that it safeguarded, like the force field of clouds and limitless night sky that surrounded the island of Never-Never Land. My mythology was based on images rather than words because I could not generally understand the conversation around me. A cluster of girls would sit behind me on the floor in the echoing hollow of the gym and say things about clothing—what they wanted to buy that spring, how much they liked pink or paisley or lacy cuffs, how cute Leslie's dress was, as opposed to how ugly Kitty's dress was (sometimes engaging in subtle battles over whether or not someone was acceptable through an exchange concerning her clothes)—what someone's boyfriend did to her the night before, or a television program. Then suddenly, one of them would bite out, "Oh God, we don't want that ugly scuz on our team," or some other comment that I could not associate with dresses or television programs. It seemed to me that the rest of the conversation had been a mere basket for the snake of cruelty coiling under the banal weave of words.

Yet I knew that these were nice girls. I sensed that if their mundane words covered cruelty and aggression, the cruelty and aggression covered other qualities. Vulnerability, tenderness, curiosity, kindness—I sensed these qualities in the child harridans around me, yet I could not experience them. Even more bewildering, it seemed that they did not experience them either. Perhaps this was because these softer feelings were so immature, so frail, and, if allowed their full measure of expression, so potentially unbearable that the girls instinctively protected their gentleness with impenetrable harshness, unconsciously fearing it would otherwise not survive. If this were true then the rigid and complex social structure they adhered to, with its confusing rules of dress and conduct, must be a code for the deeper reserves that lay beneath, and thus, if this code were cracked, it would allow access to that friendliness and compassion I saw them sporadically express. So I listened desperately and tried to understand the code. But I could not do it, and on the rare occasion that someone spoke to me, I was struck dumb by trying too hard to discover the correct response. Either that or, having stood within earshot of a conversation on the cuteness of a particular TV show or the sluttiness of a heavily madeup twelve-year-old, I would blurt out a comment that seemed to me very like everyone else's comments and be met with stares of incomprehension.

Thus the mythology.

There was a delicate underweight girl named Emma Contrell with round gray eyes painted stormily black and blue, and a curly bunch of short peroxide hair that made her small head heavy on her slight neck. She sighed and walked with her shoulders hunched and her arms held inward. She belonged to an elite band of girls who wore too much makeup and short skirts. They drank and smoked cigarettes and went to parties with seventeen-year-olds. They were gossiped about, envied, and feared. Emma was the frailest and dreamiest of these girls; even her vicious taunting of the wretched lone "special education" student was giddy and whimsical. She had a bad reputation with the other girls for being a "nympho" and she would've been outcast if she hadn't been protected by her formidable friends. I saw her lingering in the halls or in the parking lot with one large lumbering lad after the next; their big bodies and limbs seemed to menace Emma merely by close proximity to her. Emma always appeared to be under some terrible stress; she carried a large bottle of aspirin with her, her hands trembled, she had urgent whispered conversations with her friends in the toilet stalls. I sat behind her in math, and I once heard her whisper to the lewd, snide child next to her, "Don't you think Mr. Johnson has a fab bod?" Her voice was tiny and sharp, like an especially foolish bird. I decided from that moment on that Emma was in love with the cheaply suave math teacher and that she was involved with her apish series of boyfriends simply to kill her miserable passion under their stampeding bodies. But no matter how ardently they felt her up in the parking lot, her arched neck and open lips were not for them. Their fumbling paws only provoked her bitter longing for the math teacher until one day after school she put her hand on his thigh and gazed at him sorrowfully with her huge smudged eyes. He gloatingly took her hand and led her out to his car. He took advantage of the romantic child, enflaming her love and driving her to acquiesce even more frantically to her parking lot swains in an effort to divert public attention from her real love, in order not to destroy his family life and position, which he had warned her could happen. She was promiscuous also because he loved to hear her talk about her adventures in his overheated car.

I felt a throb of admiration every time I saw little Emma in the bathroom, her hands trembling as she applied pink lipstick to her plump lips. I pictured her clinging to the rutting math teacher in the back seat of his car, her face abandoned to love and despair, and I forgave her everything, even her cruelty, even the time she tripped my polio-crippled friend, poor dull defenseless Donna Doe.

I was astonished to hear one day, while sitting quietly on a toilet, a whispered conversation about the scandal at Bev Pawler's pajama party, when Emma was found kissing Mona Prescott. I was taken aback only for a moment; then my loyalty and devotion swelled like an infected gland. I imagined Emma and Mona Prescott (a coarse girl with pockmarked skin and blank, intent brown eyes, who once remarked, as Miss Vanderlust, the bowlegged gym teacher, relegated me to an unwilling volleyball team, "Oh no, not that fat weirdo") gazing passionately into each other's eyes. I imagined Emma, scorned by the boys who had used her, rejected by the math teacher, tormented by rude phone calls in the night. I imagined Emma crouched in her underwear, sobbing on the floor of the deserted gym class locker room. Mona's concerned face would appear from behind a row of lockers. "Hi. Wanna go for a swim?" They swam in the deserted pool, moving under the water in slow rippling bands of light. Mona, the stronger one, led the way. In my mythology, she had a large red flower tattooed on her inner thigh, exposed like a betrayed secret. Emma watched the flower through the rippling water and wondered how she could've overlooked it before.

I did in reality see them in the locker room together, padding around in their underwear, whispering and giggling. I did see them swimming together once, and perhaps, in some dim way, recognized two familiar prototypes as Emma, like my mother, paddled nervously behind while Mona, like Edwina Barney, cut through the water with brisk strokes. The rest of the class gamboled about them, their playful screams rising in the echoing air while I sat in my chair and watched with the silent group of girls who always had their period when a swimming class was scheduled.

There were many others about whom I formed such beautiful and elaborate fantasies. There were the

D'Arcy twins, tall and bony-legged girls with curly black hair and prominent ribs. Their strident athleticism, their barking voices, in which they talked of "really creaming" somebody made me envision them in white leather, armed with bows and arrows, smiling as they entered a field of battle and carnage, perhaps looking for souvenirs of teeth or buttons.

There was Jana Morgan, close friend of Emma Contrell and even more of a slut, a dumb-eyed girl with a big oval face, big lips, and a graceful, acquiescent neck. She was loud, foul, and kind, she wanted more than anything to attract the attention of everyone around her. She sat straddling her chair in her short skirt and badly run pantyhose, twisting her torso coquettishly as she whispered to a boy or passed a note to a girl; she popped big bubbles of gum and flirted with teachers. She often had to report to the principal's office, and she went with defiance in the swing of her hips, turning when she reached the door to whisper dramatically, "I'll never tell!" in imitation of those handsome and noble TV prisoners of the Gestapo who always escape over the barbed wire on their motorcycles. In the frequent wars of my dreams, she appeared as the most valuable prisoner in the enemy's detention system; she and I were among the unbreakable cadre that our captors had so far failed to brainwash. Although they led her away daily to be savagely interrogated, Jana still gallantly cried out, "I'll never tell!" and she looked at me with eyes of such understanding and connection that I awoke feeling deeply and tragically moved, as though someone I loved had died in my arms.

I attached these bright phantasms and others like them to the people around me, like exuberant billowing shadows more real than the flesh they shadowed, phantoms living full lives that I was excluded from, even though I had created them.

When I arrived home from school, my mother would be in the kitchen, preparing dinner. She employed the same energy with which she had once cleaned the house of her girlhood, stirring the pot, prodding the meat, peeling the potatoes with concentration and zeal. I hated the careful, exacting way she watched the food. I hated it when she patted my lower back or squeezed my shoulder and said, "Hi, honey" as I lumbered through the kitchen. My mother didn't care if I was fat and ugly. She seemed to like it in fact. In my diary I wrote, "I fear my father's anger, but I fear my mother's love." This phrase was destined to sink slowly and heavily to the bottom of my memory and to sit there, undulating like a baleful underwater plant.

For, in creating the imaginary world inside me, I had abandoned the world that had existed between my parents and me, leaving them alone with their chipmunks and their triumphant heroes. It was a silent defection but they felt it, my father especially felt it. He would watch me as I moved through the rooms of his house as if trying to decide if I were his friend or enemy. Step by step I moved further away, and he registered each internal retreat with growing outrage and fear.

Sometimes when I came downstairs for dinner, my father would be resting in his black leather armchair; he would raise his eyebrows in greeting as I stumped down the stairs. I would set the table and talk with my mother. Dinner would be accompanied by television voices and the sound of my father gnawing his steakbone. During warm weather, we would sit at the table long after we'd finished eating, with our chairs pushed out and our legs comfortably extended, drinking iced tea and watching television. I stirred so much sugar into my tea that it went to the bottom of my glass in a grainy swirl and sat there; I fished it out with a spoon and ate it when I had finished drinking. Newscasters would talk to us, and my father would translate, commenting on the bastards who were trying to undermine the United States in its fight to protect Vietnam from communism. Sometimes he would ask my opinion on what the newscaster said; I would give it and he would say, "Good comprehension. You're following it pretty well," and lean back in his chair, his mouth a satisfied line. Eventually, my mother and I would clear the table, scrape the food from the plates and load the dishwasher. My parents would move into the living room to concentrate on the TV, and I would go back upstairs to read. The evening would grade easily into night.

There were other evenings, though, when I lay upstairs trying to read while my parents' voices floated up through the floor. I would visualize a part of my mind separating from my body like a cartoon character, tiptoeing away from the rest of me to listen at the door with cupped ear and then hurrying back to tap the complacent corporeal reader on the shoulder, gesticulating wildly. They were talking about me. My mother was telling my father how rudely I had greeted her that afternoon, or how I had told her to shut up that morning. The cartoon character reported sentences in scraps; ". . . it's got to stop . . ." "What are we going to do?" "I just don't know." Soon my father would be pacing the living room to the martial bagpipes of the Coldstream Guards, ranting about "little shits" who deliberately rejected everything good and decent in favor of ugliness, who selfishly disregarded the feelings of those who'd sacrificed for them. In between declarations, he stamped up the stairs and into the bathroom, slamming the door so hard that my door trembled. His close presence came through my wall in a heavy wave, and I unconsciously padded the air for yards around me with numbness. When my mother called me for dinner, the table would already be set, and my father would be sitting at its head, watching me as I entered the room. His face was bitterly red, his eyes glassy, his hair stood away from his head in an oily halo gone askew. "There she is," he might say. "The one who doesn't want to be a part of her family. The one who ignores her mother and tells her to shut up." We would eat silently, my mother consuming tiny forkfuls, my father noiselessly but violently chewing, squeezing his napkin into a shredded ball with his free hand. Slowly, starting first with veiled attacks on "selfish turds" and "fat slobs," he began to tell me how awful I was. Soon he would be leaning towards me on his elbows, his mouth forming his words so vehemently that he showed his teeth. "You sit there on your fat butt night after night wearing the clothes I bought you, stuffing yourself with my food, stupid and ugly, contributing nothing." He paused to study me as I chewed. Tears ran down my face and over my lips as I ate, mixing in my mouth with my hamburger. My mother ate her salad and traced a little design on the table with her finger. "Not only do you contribute nothing, but you attack. You attack a woman who's never done anything but give you attention and affection." He retreated back to his plate to seize another mouthful of hamburger. I stared at my plate and wept.

Those dinner tribunals occurred with such frequency that I developed the ability to divide myself while they occurred; the external person who sat and cried while her father reviled her and the internal person who helped herself to more salad as he ranted, and noticed that the scalloped potatoes were particularly succulent tonight. With bitter pride I hugged the inner me to myself at night and thought how I had enjoyed dinner, no matter what. But my pride was marred by the dim awareness that it sometimes felt as though it was the external person who ate her dinner in dignified silence while the internal person hurt. "If you ever tell your mother to shut up again within my hearing, I'm going to knock you flat on your back. And if you get up, I'll knock you down again. Every time you get up, I'll just keep knocking you down." I rose to clear the table. "I'll help you, honey," said my mother, gently patting my elbow.

After the table was cleared, I went upstairs to lie in bed. I would lie in the dark, sensing my body sprawled out before my head like a country I had seen only on maps. My thoughts formed a grid of checkered squares clicking off and on in an industrial pattern of light and dark. Once this grid was in place, what had happened at the dinner table became a tiny scene observed from far away, and I would turn on the light and get my book and read, eating from a bag of orange corn curls I kept under my bed.

It seemed that part of my father wanted to destroy me for leaving him, and that another part of him, which I could sense only at certain moments, wanted to follow me into my retreat, to wrap his arms around me and never let me go.

Sometimes after I had put on my nightgown and gotten under the blankets to sleep, my father would come into my room. I would wake to find him standing beside my bed in the dark in his pajamas, looking at me with an invisible face, rubbing his fingers together. I would pretend to be asleep, feeling his presence and wondering if he was thinking about how innocent I looked in sleep. He would stay in the room for several minutes and then leave, nervously wiping his mouth with his hands before turning to go. I would lie there feeling a vague sense of vindication and satisfaction from this silent nocturnal contact. I thought he was trying to apologize.

He did apologize once. I had been sitting on the floor beside the heat vent in the living room reading a paperback called *Kennedy Days* while my parents talked, my father pacing the floor with a glass of beer, my mother sitting on the couch. They were talking about a journalist who'd hoaxed the country with a book on the life of a millionaire who, as it turned out, had never existed. The journalist had gone to jail and was now writing another book from jail called *Hoax*. He had been offered a million-dollar contract in advance, which made my father furious. He was talking about how the writer, Irving Wiseback, had cheated not only the public but the memory of people like Obie and Aunt Cat, people who would never have cheated anybody, who died poor but honest. "Anyone who would enjoy reading that garbage is as worthless a bastard as Wiseback—and there's one now. Look at her over there, reading that crap." This was so unexpected that I had no time to create a padding of numbness. I dropped the book and walked quickly from the room. "Al." My mother's voice was full of gentleness and remonstrance.

An hour after I had slammed the door to my room, my father came up the stairs with slow, soft thuds. He knocked on my door and opened it to find me sitting on my bed with a blanket wrapped around me. He came and sat on the edge of my bed. He said that sometimes he got so "goddamned upset at all the vicious immorality in the world" that he couldn't think straight, and that in his urge to punish it, he sometimes "lashed out" at people who weren't to blame at all, and that he actually found it commendable for a person my age to read about the Kennedys. I said it was all right. We sat on the bed, my father smiling tightly. I didn't want to swallow because I was afraid he would hear it, so I let the saliva build up in my mouth as we sat. I became warm, and the blanket dropped from my shoulders. My father wiped his mouth and coughed. "Would you like to go for a walk around the block?" he asked.

My mother looked away from the television and smiled as we filed down the stairs. "Just let me get a jacket," said my father.

Our walk was dreamy even though we both walked with habitual quickness, my father rubbing his fingers together and staring down at the sidewalk with distant intensity. The tall street lamps cast pools of light that graded gently into the dimness of street and sidewalk, then into the strange darkness of other people's yards. Our neighbors' front doors stood open, letting patches of weak light out onto their porches. I listened to the faint sounds of their televisions and their voices, occasionally a piece of laughter, with the covetous loneliness of an eavesdropper. We passed a group of adolescent boys lounging under a lighted basketball hoop nailed to their garage, and they stopped their conversation to watch the middle-aged man and the fat girl walk by. I had a moment of shame as I felt myself and my father perceived as the representatives of a world foreign to those agile basketball players with their easy limbs and voices, a stunted world of graceless movements, pathetic wants and weaknesses. I buried this feeling, and we passed the boys.

We talked about ideas and events; a new TV show, what I was doing in social studies, what had ever become of that awful little dog of the Rizzos. Brown toads hopped out of the grass and onto the pavement before us, oblivious to the threat of our oncoming feet. My father talked to me about the pressure of his job, how he had to fight with people all day in subtle battles of the will which were never named, in which enemies tried "to cut your throat." I saw my father in his office behind a desk, watchfully holding a sheaf of papers like a shield as another supervisor approached him. I admired him as he sat there, the cagey champion of the office, ringed by formidable opponents. I saw myself and my mother standing vigilantly in the living room at home, ready for him to arrive. I saw a group of girls in the high school lunchroom, sitting around a table, talking out of their smiling, chewing faces. They seemed trivial compared to the vision of my embattled father with my mother and me standing behind him. They were pretty and happy, but my father and I aimed for higher things; we had relinquished beauty and pleasure and turned our faces towards the harsh reality of the fight against cruelty and falsehood. I saw his face and mine in profile together, like John Kennedy and Martin Luther King on a postage stamp, pressed against the stark gray sky, our expressions sad, yet resolute. Then my father did something he hadn't done since I was a child: he took my lightly swinging hand and held it. I looked down smiling in embarrassment. He kept holding my hand, stroking it along its side with his thumb. I felt tension vibrating the length of his arm and hand, the tension of his complicated love for me, and I felt something like pity for him, as well as sorrow that I could no longer fully be a part of his life, nor invite him into mine.

Just before we reached the house, he stopped walking and I stopped with him. He released my hand and I looked at him. His face held an expression I had never seen before and which looked like the suppression of pain. He reached out, cupped my head in one of his hands, and pulled it towards him. He stung my cheek with a fierce kiss and roughly tousled my hair. As we approached the front door lights of home, I felt peaceful and happy.

The next day was a Saturday. My father and I spent the afternoon together watching *Eerie Hours*, four hours of old horror movies followed by *The Arena*, which featured gladiator movies hosted by a middle-aged man sitting at a desk in a gladiator outfit. My father sat in his black leather chair eating potato chips and drinking beer. I sat on the floor with Noxzema on my face eating popcorn, potato chips, corn curls, and diet grape pop.

I wished that I never had to go to school again. I wanted to spend all of my days in the comfort and safety of this living room with the dirty wool carpet, flowered couches with used Kleenex tucked into their cushions, crumpled bags of potato chips, and the little black-and-white TV. I went into the kitchen to see if there were any more bite-sized Heath Bars in the refrigerator and saw my mother standing by the sink, gazing out the window with her arms folded around her thick waist. In the light of the window, I saw the dust on her glasses. She stood in a bundle, her bell-bottomed legs and tennis-shoed feet together, her stomach sticking out. Her mouth was slightly open and her face abstract with bewilderment. I stopped on my way to the freezer. My mother turned and recovered her expression. "Can I get you anything, honey?"

One night my mother, calling up the stairs, asked me to set the table while I was on the phone talking with Donna Doe. I turned furiously from the phone, covered its receiver with my hand and bellowed, "Just a minute!" My mother called up again and I kicked the door shut. I snuggled against the wall and relished the phone. My father stomped up the stairs and opened the door so hard that the feeble old knob fell off. He tore the receiver from my hand, and Donna Doe became a planet hurled into oblivion by a tantruming god. He grabbed a fistful of my hair and dragged me from the room and out into the stairwell. I tried to steady myself by placing my hand on the wall; he took this as resistance and pushed me down the stairs. I tumbled briefly and broke my fall by grabbing a banister. He picked my hand off it and pushed me again. My mother sat watching quietly as he dragged me through the living room by my hair. "When your mother tells you to set the table, you move!" He shoved me against the dining room wall and yelled, "Do you understand?" again and again until I said yes. He let go of me, and I set the table.

I ate my dinner of pork chops and green beans in silence. My father and mother chatted amiably about our neighbors and the last letter they had received from Edwina Barney. There was boxed lemon chiffon pie for dessert.

I turned off my light earlier than usual that night, but I didn't sleep. I lay having a fantasy about Jana Morgan and Emma Contrell as French waifs during the Second World War who had been driven to prostitution by poverty, but who doubled as resistance informants. My fantasy decomposed as I wobbled towards sleep. I dreamed I was sitting in social studies, but instead of feeling the dread that I felt in class, I felt a sense of triumph. A popular song overlaid the class scene, not its sound but its evocation of friendship and the eventual moment when everyone drops their public pose and exposes the goodwill they've harbored all along. I sat erect in my seat, smiling at everyone. The song said, "It's so groovy now, that people are finally getting together."

I wobbled back into wakefulness. The room was

covered with sleep fuzz. My father stood before my bed. I closed my eyes, imagining my innocent face as it appeared to him. He sat on the bed next to me. I peeked at him. I was surprised to see that he wasn't doing the nervous things he usually did when he came to my room night; he didn't wipe his mouth or rub his fingers together, he just sat there exuding determined presence. I closed my eyes, feeling the tension and suspended contact. I remembered his nighttime kiss. There was a movement that seemed gracefully swooping and swanlike to me, even though I knew my father was pulling up his feet and awkwardly laying his body on my bed. My sense of anticipation, my feeling of intimacy, impending resolution, and fear almost nauseated me. When he put his hand under the blankets, I was surprised and opened my eyes. He was waiting for me. He put his fingers on my lips and said, "Shh." His eyes were bright and his forehead was lifted into friendly wrinkles. "I don't want to wake your mother," he whispered. "I just thought we could have a little talk." I nodded, feeling a sensation like warm tears trembling in my chest. It was as I thought: my father came into my room because he wanted to apologize. I felt so moved, I wanted to cuddle against his chest as I had done as a child, burying my nose in his warm, detergent-scented pajamas.

"I just wanted to let you know," he began, "that when you were born I thought you were the most beautiful little thing I ever saw. It wasn't just me either. Everybody in the hospital thought you were special. You had the intelligence, the sparkle, the beauty—you had it all."

I smiled spastically. My father twitched a grin and touched the tip of my nose with his finger. "And I still think so. Say, can I get under the covers? It's cold out here."

He kissed my face and neck as he had taken my hand during our walk: tenderly, the tenderness vibrant with inheld tension. He said how hurt he was when we "argued," when it seemed like I just didn't care about everything he'd fought for. I moved nearer him to protest that I did care, and I smelled him, the deep smell produced by his particular combination of organs and glands and the food he ate. He pulled me against him, crushing my face into the chest hairs exposed by his open pajama top. I felt the power and insistence in his embrace, felt how tight were the muscles of his embracing arm, and for a second I was afraid. Then with his other hand he caressed my breasts and nipples through my light gown. My breath stopped. Arousal rose through my body and seized it. My excitement terrified me and made me feel ashamed because I knew it was wrong to be excited. But underneath the fear and shame, underneath the excitement, it seemed that what was happening now between my father and me was only the physical expression of what always happened between us, even when he verbally reviled me, especially when he verbally reviled me. Tears came to my eyes; it seemed that his cruel words had clothed these loving caresses all along. I put out my hands and clutched his pajamas in my fists. "Yes," he said, his voice crushed and strange. "Yes." He moved his hand away from my chest, not loosening his grip on my shoulders. Through the gown, he touched between my legs. Shock impaled my body. As if he felt it, he snatched his hand away. He let go of my shoulder and lay silently staring at the ceiling with me paralyzed in a curl, my forehead touching his shoulder. At length he sat up and said, "Good night, Sweet Pea." He left, stopping in the bathroom to pee before returning to his bedroom. I heard him cough nervously before he closed his bedroom door behind him.

For a long time I lay curled in the position he had left me in, held by shock and smothered feeling. My heartbeat threatened to break open my chest. It was not the same as sex, I thought. And truly, what had just happened seemed to bear no relation to "sex": smiling big-breasted women in scanty bathing suits, modern couples winking and making jokes on television, boys whistling at pretty girls, the things I heard about Emma Contrell and Jana Morgan. This had been something secret, special, and symbolic; it had happened in a tiny place where only my father and I lived. I straightened my body and lay on my back, my breath returning. The room gradually slowed its disturbed pulsing. The shadows of branches moved back and forth on the ceiling.

During the day there was no external change in our behavior towards each other. But there had been a change. I felt it both awake and asleep.

*It was many weeks* before my father came to my room again. Then he began to come more frequently. Each time he touched me, the physical sensation I had felt the first night became more hardened with fear and shame until I couldn't feel it at all. I would think of my mother asleep in her bed, and she seemed as far away as when she sat and watched my father yell at me. Sometimes I would pretend I was asleep or ask him to stop, but he continued. I could not resist him anymore than that because with each visit my body seemed less mine and more his.

When I say to people that my father molested me, I visualize myself sprawled on the living room floor with my pants pulled down or my dress over my head.

My father storms around the room, gesticulating violently and shouting about something. My mother sits on the couch, looking into space. An almost visible bolt of horror and panic splits the room. This scene, even though it never occurred, is more real to me than what happened those nights in my room, mainly because my mind has flattened those real events, which now become three-dimensional only in involuntary screeches of memory. My father pressed tightly against my back, his hand pinching my jaw and mashing my lips together, his legs pushing mine apart. My flannel gown scrunched up around my shoulders and my buttocks rubbed by what felt like the blunt, hairless limb of a medium-sized animal. His fingers hard implements inside my body, gouging me.

The scene becomes static, frozen in flat subreality, a torn grainy photograph of my own stunned face. He is on top of me for several moments, breathing. He swings himself into a sitting position on the edge of my bed and sits there, both hands flat on the mattress. He seems to have forgotten about the glop he's left on my body. My held breath is an obstruction in my throat. My feet feel cold and far away. I watch him from my side-turned head. He clears his throat and sits in a hunched, unassuming position, as though puzzled by something. He turns, bends forward and kisses the back of my head. "Good night," he says. "Sleep tight." Then he leaves the room, closing the door carefully behind him.

I became conscious again as I sat in study hall the next day before a pile of books. My French book, a faded green thing with a broken spine, lay open before me, ignored. I was listening to the group of small, slender girls in bright dresses and paisley tights. Sally Rose was talking about how she let Chris Hannewald "finger" her, and Emma Contrell was saying she'd go all the way with Todd Welsh any time. I felt stupefied to think that I'd done the things they coyly talked about. Yet it was nothing like what they were talking about. An invisible square of definition formed around the circle of girls; another square formed around me. I imagined myself sealed in an enclosure of darkness that could be seen into but not out of, only in my imagination I was a tall, beautiful woman with waist-length raven hair. I was a space traveler sent on a dangerous mission and captured on a hostile planet. I was condemned to eternity in the impenetrable enclosure that would drift through space until I floated out of my solar system and into a black dimension. Space travelers would tell stories about the legend of the beautiful lady trapped in the impenetrable column. Those who had actually seen me could barely refrain from weeping at the sight of my beautiful face, frozen and transfigured by pain.

"No really," said little Emma. "I'd suck his thing, prob'ly."

*I* read 1984, *by George Orwell.* I read it voluptuously, loving the pitiless description of a panicked fat man weeping as he vainly tried to escape machine-gun fire, of a terrified woman trying to protect a doomed child with her body, of the toothless old whore that Winston had mistaken for a pretty child-harlot. It wasn't the brutality I loved, it was the bravado in Orwell's monotonous treatment of horror, and the pathetic human efforts to stand against it, or even to believe in the existence of something else. The outburst of humanity between Winston and Julia was a feeble blow against the malign forces of Big Brother, beautiful only in the moment it dared to come into being before crumpling and dying like a leaf. The unbeautiful monotony of Orwell's prose was like Winston's affair with Julia: a slight, spare poem pitching itself against the horror it evoked, and dying in the attempt.

I read planted on the couch in the living room, oblivious to the televised news, or crouched at the dining room table after dinner, eating a teacupful of sherbet, or in my bed under the blankets, a bag of corn curls at my side.

"Do you understand what it is you're reading?" asked my father. "Can you give me a plot summary?"

"It's about a totalitarian government—a communist government—that's taken over the world, and that controls everyone's minds. And there's two people—who represent individual freedom—who are fighting it."

"That's pretty good. You have better comprehension than a lot of adults." He looked out the window, frowning, pressing the tips of his fingers together. "It's a very important book, *1984*. It's a warning about what could happen if we don't keep the destructive bastards out."

As soon as I finished it, I began reading it again, from the beginning.

*A song began playing* on my transistor radio called "Love Is All Around," by the Troggs. "It's written on the wind," sang the Troggs, "It's everywhere we go. So if you really love me, come on and let it show." A slur of violins and guitars undulated around the words. It spoke to me of hopeless passion fluttering on a wind that would bear it to its death. I bought the 45 with its pale blue label and played it over and over again on my little plastic record player. "Why do you play that record so much, honey?" asked my mother. We stood by the kitchen sink, me peeling carrots while my mother scrubbed potatoes. "Don't you get tired of it?"

"It reminds me of Winston and Julia," I said. "In *1984*."

"But why? Love wasn't all around them."

I couldn't explain it.

I could hear my father in the dining room, shifting in his chair.

*I sat behind an invisible shield* while a classmate, possibly classmates, threw spitballs at me during intervals of lapsed teacher attention. Dozens of tiny white balls lay about my chair, like the seedlings for a field of white poppies. I thought of Hate Week. "You gave your promise to me and I gave mine to you," sang the Troggs. Of course, Winston had broken his promise to Julia, and she had broken hers to him. But I believed that under the destroyed integrity, the broken bones and humiliated character, the ghost of love flitted amid the ruins, moving from broken pillar to broken pillar, hiding behind a pile of rubble. On some deep, unfathomable level, where the pressure would burst human lungs and flatten three-dimensional bodies, where life took the form of eyeless, headless creatures with wobbling tentacles and undulating hammerlike tails, their love survived, faithful, luminous and totally useless.

My ear stung. Someone had shot a rubber band at me.

*My mother wanted me to make* lists of the things that made me happy and the things that made me un-happy. On the happy list I put "reading in bed," "talk-ing to Donna," "lime sherbet," "watching horror movies," and "George Orwell." On the unhappy list I put "walking to school from the car," "gym class," "study hall," "dinnertime," "going to bed," "getting up in the morning." My mother took the list and tacked it up on the inside of a cabinet door, along with newspaper recipes, a grocery list, and a reminder to call Dr. Adams.

*You are an argument* for abortion," said my father. "If I had known you were going to happen, I never would've had a child."

I sat on the couch with my face in a knot. My mother sat in the red armchair, her mouth determined and straight, her eyes as distant as though she had, by intense concentration, sent her mind to bathe in an ocean of neural bliss which was reflected, crystal ball-like, in the tranquil, unseeing gray of her eyes. "Don't sit there looking at me with that face. You attacked me, and when you attack me, I react. And when I react, I go right for the jugular."

He appeared in my bedroom again and again. The air filled with angry shapes that rolled around the room, tipping the furniture, tilting the floor, suffocating me as he held me against his chest. My nose filled with sweat and baby powder, his hands possessed my breasts. Our bodies became white, ectoplasmic forms that stretched and contracted; my arms and legs flew from my pinned body to the corners of the ceiling, then back into their sockets, then back to the ceiling. My head was a white round thing with black holes for eyes and a mouth that stretched until my whole face was a scream. The image snapped back into my head, which was still a hard little skull and a face with open, staring eyes and a closed, silent mouth irredeemably connected to an inert fleshy body with hands that gripped the sheets of my bed in the dark room, quiet and still except for the squeaking of the bed and my father's breathing.

*I sat in study hall.* The room was full of voices moving through the air like colored balloons. Urine trickled down the legs of my chair and made a puddle on the floor. No one seemed to notice. I delicately lifted one red and black shoe, shook it, and removed it from the puddle. It was a strange sensation to be doing such a private thing in public, even if I hadn't done it on purpose. I tried to tighten my collapsing bladder, but warm pee continued to trickle between my legs, into my pantyhose, and down my chair as the giggly words from the next table floated by.

My mother began taking me to see a psychiatrist named Dr. Eldridge Mars. I liked him. He was a tall, thin man with dandruff and madly optimistic eyes burning behind a pair of dust-covered glasses that sat, with affable kookiness, in the middle of his nose. When I went to visit him, my mother waited for me in the lobby along with other mothers and two plastic toys with grinning faces on wheels. The front wheels turned at radical angles from the yellow and chartreuse bodies, as though grinning horse and grinning dog had violently swerved to avoid a collision. Dr. Mars took me down a hall to a candy machine and bought me a chocolate bar. Then we went to his office and he asked me questions. Did I have any friends? Did I like school? What did I want to be when I grew up? Then he produced a dog-eared manila folder of pictures and asked me to imagine what was happening in each picture as he showed it to me. He showed me a cheap reproduction of an early Flemish family portrait: the exhausted mother and father in the dull gray background, the young daughter in a high-necked dress in the foreground. "The daughter has just been raped," I explained. "And she's wondering how to tell her parents."

*I began* reading *The Bulwark* during the winter of my seventeenth year. It was not exactly true that it became "the most important influence in my life" from the tenth page on as I would later tell Justine Shade, but I was deeply moved by the description of Asia Maconda and Frank Golanka, the proud outcasts moving through a crowd of resentful mediocrities, surrounded by the cold glow of their genius and grace. I was profoundly satisfied by the terse, brutal prose, blunt as a bludgeon. Granite drew ugliness and beauty with the same unveiling hand; there was no attempt at bravado, yet the elegant gesture with which she plucked off the obscuring extranea was exquisite. When I read the words of Anna Granite, I visualized a man with a splendid chest standing stripped to the waist in a moonlit snow-covered field. He stood erect, arms loose at his sides, fists lightly balled, waiting in the dark for something he alone understood.

"When I look at this stone, Miss Maconda, I see not only an object made up of mineral and material parts, but properties of color, curves and density that exist in their own point in space. This rock exists, Miss Maconda, because it exists. Not because I want it to exist, or because I imagine it exists, or because anyone else imagines it exists but because it does. And just as this rock and its properties exist, so do it and its properties exist on an abstract level. They are projected into being, Miss Maconda, by this mundane physical shape. It is those abstract properties that I represent in my work. As accurately and truthfully as I can."

Asia listened, her perfect head tilted coolly to one side, her long jade eyes half-closed in their usual mocking expression. Her fragile form stood at such an angle that she appeared to be supported by air. Only her dilated pupils betrayed the surge of emotion she felt at his words. She looked at the canvas before her—at the arrogant strength of the line, the elegant hauteur of the spare details, the distinct bold use of color. There was not one element in it that shrunk from the fullest statement of what it was. It was a gauntlet flung in the face of everything cheap, trivial and false. The thought of it in a gallery full of conceptual, cubist and surreal trash made her want to die.

It was the same brave evocation of beauty that I had loved in Orwell—except that this was strong, contemptuous beauty, a beauty indifferent to anything but itself and its own growth. In Orwell's world, beauty was unreachable, and the attempt to grasp it was fatal; the frail shadow you could hold in your hand was quite possibly not worth the attempt, however admirable that attempt might be. In Granite's world, it thrived, proud and undeniable. It could be had by the strong and at least admired by the weak. As I read, the actions and words of Granite's characters settled like a mantle over the people around me. Jana Morgan, Emma Contrell and the D'Arcy twins became spritelike partial elements of Asia Maconda: Jana the languid beauty Asia, sitting with her waist twisted so that her breasts were accented, not because she cared about making people desire her, but because she knew that Beauty is part of what makes life livable. Emma, the abandoned, passionate Asia, so deeply sensitive to the viciousness and dishonesty in the world that she would disfigure her own integrity and insult her body with subhuman lovers rather than let her natural purity exist side by side with corruption. The D'Arcy twins, one jumping into the air in a jackknife to slam a volleyball with two fists while the other bounded across the floor to help it over the net, were the vicious snakelike Asia who teases men and humiliates women.

And I myself was another aspect of Asia, as I sat silently at the dinner table while my father crouched above his plate, reviling me. I felt, in addition to the inevitable dislocated shame, a strange kind of pride; I was almost grateful to my father for hating me. I was accepting the discharge of an aggression that was an essential part of the life force.

The greater pain she was subjected to—every mediocre piece of trash she was asked to review, every fatuous ass she saw praised as a great artist, every empty conversation at every party, every night alone—only created a thicker wall between her and the rest of the world, a wall that protected her from being poisoned by its mediocrity. It was behind this wall that she really lived, in a small world of dazzling white. In this world, she was never cruel or cold, but gentle and wondering as a child in a garden. She was alone and lonely, and it was this cherished loneliness that gave her inner world its inviolate whiteness.

If I could see aspects of Asia all about me, even in myself, I could see Frank Golanka nowhere in my world. This did not make him less real than Asia Maconda—on the contrary. The absence of his reflection in my daily life rendered him exalted, immune to my vulgar fantasies, more inviolate than Asia behind her wall. His absence cast a silent spell over my world, he was all life's potential suspended in a state of constant possibility, the prince who could awaken me with a kiss. At any moment he could appear, but if he didn't I could spend the rest of my life caressing the possibility. Like Katya in *The Last Woman Alive*, I nurtured myself with dreams of what could be. On those nights when my father came to me, these dreams were the mainstay on which my listing comprehension attached itself, the immobile constant that stood watch while I struggled to maintain silence and stillness.

I didn't speak to Donna of my feelings about Anna Granite. I lent her *The Bulwark*, but she was unable to finish it; she returned it with an indifferent mumble about big words.

I spoke to Dr. Mars about it only once. "I want life to be like it is in Anna Granite's books," I said. "I want life to matter."

"Well, that's very normal," said Dr. Mars. "We all want life to matter. And sometimes it seems like it just doesn't."

"I want people to be like Anna Granite's people. Perfect and strong."

Dr. Mars nodded vigorously. "That's very normal adolescent idealism."

She crouched in the darkened room, her face almost contorted with fear. He stood still in the doorway, arms loose at his sides, an amused sneer on his mouth. She felt her lip curl. She darted forward and then she felt her body, helpless and frail, crushed against his chest. She felt her fists and elbows beating against his form. She thought she felt a deep, silent laugh well up in his chest. Effortlessly, he lifted her body and carried her to the stone

*The Shades moved again* right after the eighth grade year ended. Dr. Shade had been offered a prestigious position at a cardiology clinic in the lush suburb of Deere Parke, Michigan, and the Shades were ready to claim the rewards of his profession.

Kids in Deere Parke didn't hang out on the street, at least not thirteen-year-olds, so Justine didn't meet anyone the entire summer. This didn't bother her. She drifted into a pleasant world of television and magazines which led, to her surprise, to reading books. Each book was an invisible tunnel leading to a phantom world that existed silently parallel to real life, into which one could vanish then emerge without anyone knowing. Hardy, Dickens, Poe, Chekhov—she could barely understand the way the characters spoke, but it only made the experience more exotic, more secret, something to which no adolescent social rules applied. How had the hard-edged furniture, neon signs, and minimal hot-colored clothes evolved from the baroque book world, the complex, multilayered universe populated by people who spoke so elaborately and died of tuberculosis? It frightened her to think the world changed so quickly.

Her parents deeply approved of her reading, especially her father.

Her father had grown full and hale during the Action years. He presented himself with his chest pushed out, his eyes vibrant with outgoing energy that allowed nothing in. He came into rooms and clapped his hard little hands together and said, "Well!" His silences were imperious excretions that nobly enshrouded him as he read *The New York Times*. When they went to eat at restaurants, he gave loud speeches at the table. When they rented a cottage in the Upper Peninsula, he stood calf-deep in the waters of Lake Michigan in his bathing trunks and pretended he was conducting an orchestra while his wife and daughter lolled on the beach. Justine watched him jerking his arms above the waves and wondered why he didn't look ridiculous.

He took the entire summer as a vacation before beginning his new position, and Justine spent a lot of time with him and her mother. In Action an entire summer of this would've been unbearable, but in a new environment where no one was there to see, it was different. In the afternoon she went with her father on long car trips, during which they viewed the new neighborhood and discussed politics and art. He always wanted to know what she was reading and what she thought of it, what were "the main themes." He would listen intently, vigorously nodding his head. "All art should be about the world," he would say. "It isn't just some pretty story about what's going on in the artist's mind. It's about the universal truths, the social truths, the struggle toward decency and equality." The words awed her so, she didn't even notice that they were in distinct contradiction to what she read for. The stately lawns, delicate trees, and winding concrete walks of Deere Parke sailed past as though unfolding from her father's words, a splendid physical manifestation of his orderly sentiments.

At night she sat in the living room with her parents and watched newscasters tell stories illustrated by dramatic film clips of men being led away in handcuffs, men talking behind desks, men giving speeches, men angrily shaking their fingers, and, at the end, smiling women serving muffins to old people or playing with children. Her father praised her for taking an interest in the world. She liked to hear him praise her, but she vaguely knew that she didn't watch the news for the reasons her father thought she watched it. It simply relaxed her to watch the parade of events organized by newscasters who appeared in orderly sequence desk after desk. The nodding, smiling faces of posing politicians especially relaxed her. It was great to see these smooth-voiced gray images confirm that there existed an apparatus run by men in suits that on the surface had nothing to do with her life and yet supported everything around her—grocery stores, malls, schools—acting as a deep terra firma for her to run around on.

In mid-August the Shades joined the Glade of Dreams country club, and Justine briefly encountered her peers. They were older than she and tall, with round, buttery muscles, modulated voices, and oval nails with neat cuticles. They had none of the raw toughness of her friends from Action, and Justine, while not afraid of them, did not quite know how to approach them. She stalked around the pool in her tiny black two-piece, gloating when older men looked at her. The men were fat creatures mostly, baked pink and bearded, their self-satisfaction and arrogance expressed in their saggy-bottomed hips and their wide-legged stance as they stood staring, their thick pink lips smiling at thirteen-year-old Justine, as if they could know every single thing about her merely by looking at her in her swimsuit while they, on the contrary, remained sweating, lotion-oily sphinxes, about whom she could comprehend nothing, revelling in their complex ugly humanity. She looked at them with dumb, shielded eyes, an imitation of wide-eyed young girlhood she had seen in magazines. They were from the world of the evening news, like her father, part of the apparatus controlling even the little lapping lakes. They were hideous, she wanted nothing to do with them, yet she was happy to intersect with them in that way, playing a magazine girl, a creature they viewed with pleasure and relief. "You flirt well, Justine," remarked her mother.

*On the first day of school* Justine was scared. She stared at the mirror again and again trying to decide whether she was ugly or cute, applying another layer of white lipstick, then taking it off. She was confident as a result of her social success in Action, but deeper than that confidence was the fear that had also accompanied her on the first day of school in Illinois.

At first it looked as though her fear would be confirmed: after ten minutes of home room, she could tell that the kids here were different from the old Action crowd. She was too young to think in terms of economic class, but she saw that skirts were longer and modestly looser, makeup lighter, shoes cleatless. Only a few girls with dandruff and submissive eyes ratted their hair. Everyone seemed to be wearing huge sweaters with soft fuzzy hairs protruding from them. She sat sweating, waiting to be made fun of.

But she wasn't. All those hours spent running with mobs, tormenting other children, and having sex in bathrooms had created an aura of sensuality and mystique that she radiated without effort. Besides, she was pretty, even in her blobby eyeliner and subtly ratted hair.

In history class she sat next to an intriguing girl in the back of the room, separated from the distant teacher by rows of heads and a lazy cloud of whispers and note-passing. The girl's dress was a low-cut wisp of baleful black with a cinched waist, short flared skirt, and elaborate sleeves of lace and chiffon rolling off her shoulders in histrionic puffs. Her face was pale and intelligent, she had honey brown hair, an elegantly crooked nose, and wide, full lips. All of her features were larger and more adult than the pettishly powdered faces around her. She wore no makeup other than a set of obviously false eyelashes. She sat with her body twisted dramatically sideways, her long black-stockinged legs crossed once at the knee and again at the ankle, a Chinese puzzle of tension and beauty, while her torso leaned over the desk with exaggerated indifference. She was sketching in a sketch pad. Was she an artist? Justine noticed a huge book open in her lap, for the moment ignored. She was an intellectual! Her strange, temperate gray eyes met Justine's. "Hi," she said.

Within a week Justine was walking home from school with Watley Goode. Watley's house was decorated in lime green, yellow, and cream—except for Watley's room which was primary blue, red, and white. Watley's mother was a fashionable woman who wore checked pant suits and high heels, who made complicated three-tier cookies, watercolor paintings, and shellacked découpage lunch boxes plastered with images cut from magazines. She was a clinically diagnosed schizophrenic who had to take special brain medicine and who would sometimes go nuts anyway and suddenly start yelling things like "Penis!" or "Vagina!" in public. Justine was very impressed; it was the first time she'd met a mother as glamorous as her own.

Watley herself was more glamorous than anyone Justine had ever known. Instead of pictures of TV stars taped to her walls, she had glass-covered museum-size posters of an art deco peacock, a vase of flowers, a woman with large breasts. The antique four-poster bed frame, the satin sheets, the down comforters, the vase of lilies, the full-length gilt-edge mirror, an imitation twenties-style phone—all these things bespoke a level of elegance Justine had never encountered in a girl her own age. Part of her wanted to hold herself aloof and sneer at Watley—as she had heard some girls doing while she was sitting on a toilet—but she was simply too seduced to do so.

Watley didn't seem to care if she was being talked about; she simply did things and got away with it. She never made fun of the people everyone else scorned but instead reserved her considerable sarcasm for the set of girls she called the "vanilla wafers" who were as popular and formidable as Justine's little Action gang but without the swagger and sensual style.

She talked about sex as often as the girls in Action but differently. Among the D girls, sex was dirty and mean, like throwing a rock at an old lady; you did it for fun and to prove how tough you were. With Watley it was an act of high style, sophistication, and emotion. While Justine bragged about her experiences to her new friend, she cannily changed the settings from rec rooms and toilets to moon-drenched beaches, rugs before roaring fires, canopied beds. Watley nodded, obviously impressed. Her own experiences had all taken place in her rattling four-poster where she had, with much drama, finally allowed her boyfriend of the moment to take off her bra and then, with many expressions of adoration, put his hand down her underpants. Justine was spellbound; she'd never thought of it that way before. She had grown accustomed to dividing girls into two categories: thin-lipped bores who read books and had conversations, and cruel, lolling beauties with heat seeping from their pores. But Watley was neither, or both. She liked to talk about important subjects like racism, hippies, and presidential elections. She got A's on papers; she wanted to be a lawyer. She wanted to go out with a boy with whom she could discuss politics, not the greaseballs who tried to look down her low necklines and leered about her "advanced development."

This was perhaps the reason she had no boyfriend for her entire freshman year. Justine didn't have one either, and they spent most of their spare time together in Watley's room, measuring their breasts and talking about imaginary boyfriends.

Their boyfriends had shoulder-length hair, high foreheads, mustaches, muscles and mouths, tortured pasts, complicated feelings, swords of flesh, and souls of silk. They were as feverishly perfect as Mrs. Goode's découpage lunch boxes, festooned with gold unicorns, pink-faced harp-wielding girls, ladies with wigs and monocles, flying cherubs, rainbows, and wads of flowers, image after frozen image, cut with the tiniest of scissors so that no white edges showed.

They viewed their group-huddling peers with increasing scorn as the year went on. Justine occasionally received a flowered, coyly folded letter from one of her fading Action friends, tattooed with slogans like "Hippies are cool, greasers are fools." She answered one or two and then thew the rest away after reading them with quick disbelief, no longer able to connect herself with the world she had belonged to so completely less than a year ago. She did talk to Watley about Emotional and, to a much lesser extent, Rose Loris, but without telling her of the conflicted pain these people had caused her. They became unpleasant, minor incidents, having little to do with her. It would be years before she would realize these incidents were lodged in her heart like gristle, ready to pop up into her throat at any sudden slap on the back—and there were lots of those later on.

Her father was away from the house often; he was home most on the weekends when he slept his numb ten-hour sleep and then rose to pace the house with his chest puffed out, telling stories about what had happened at the hospital, how he'd been called in for an emergency consultation during an operation and had knocked down a nurse while running through the hall. The patient was saved; Dr. Shade swam a vigorous six laps in the hospital pool and bought a milkshake on the way back to the office. Sometimes a patient would die, and he would pace around flailing his arms. "You know when this happens, what do you do, Lorraine? You are so close to it, that space where death and life come together for an instant and then, suddenly, there is nothing." His hard eyes would shine with fierce opacity.

"He is so upset when a patient dies," said Justine's mother. "He cares so deeply."

And Justine would feel the way she did when there was a dying dog scene on TV; on one hand she could barely control her tears, on the other she felt like being really snotty.

She felt like being snotty almost all the time to her mother, who didn't have a retard center to work at and was thus at home a lot. Her mother suddenly wanted to be snotty to her, too. After ignoring the tight clothing and white lipstick worn by her daughter in Action, Mrs. Shade began to be obsessed with Justine's clothing, about which they fought on the stairway and in the driveway almost every morning before school. "Really, Justine, you look like a cow," her mother would snap as she regarded her daughter's slight, optimally revealed bustline. "What kind of attention are you trying to attract?" One morning, the dog-walking Mrs. Kybosh next door was treated to the sight of Justine's mother trying to pull Justine back into the house by her hair and skirt while obscenity-shrieking Justine beat her about the head and shoulders with her purse.

Her mother also censored the clothes she bought, leaning spitefully in the direction of sweaters and long plaid skirts—this when Justine was walking around with a girl like Watley! Justine was forced to shoplift chic ensembles, smuggle them to school in her big leather handbag, and change in the bathroom, stuffing her ugly plaids in her locker.

Once she adopted this strategy, there were no more morning battles, and the criticism shifted to Justine's laziness and poor posture. The connection between mother and daughter stiffened and frayed down to a wire sharp enough to cut your hand on; it was through a long dark tunnel that Justine viewed her parents as they moved about the house.

The connection between her parents had further frayed as well. Although unaware of it at the time, in retrospect she could see it clearly. As a young child she had watched her parents create constructions of concrete and steel with words that swung triumphantly upward; now they dug circuitous tunnels around each other, one every now and then setting up a cul-de-sac for the other to stumble around in while he or she ran off in the opposite direction. Her father would tell a story about something that had happened at the hospital, emphasizing a particular part with his voice. Her mother would respond to some other part, and he would continue as if he hadn't heard her. She would respond again to that part of his story he neglected, and relate it to some story of her own about say, a neighbor. He would discount her story by stating, "Mrs. Kybosh is a stupid woman," and then disappear behind his wall of important concerns. They seemed to want to create these mazes of cross-purpose and misunderstanding, and to need each other to do it, possibly because they needed the dry rasp of contact that occurred when they collided on their way to their separate destinations.

Justine's own mazes led away from them both, and she minced around their house like an heiress on an ocean liner. She stayed up late at night, crouched near her radio listening to rock music on "underground" stations and fantasizing about the soft-voiced disc jockeys who played it.

She remembers a strange thing she said one night at the dinner table, without knowing why she said it. Her mother asked her how school had been that day, and, recalling a study hall conversation, she answered, "Sally Hinkel is going to fuck Jim Thorn tonight." Her father's eyes widened in alarm, her mother's mouth opened in midbite, and a mallet of incomprehension flattened their previous conversation.

Perhaps it was this remark that prompted her father to ask her about Dr. Norris. She was in the car alone with him on a weekend errand. They were silently progressing on a scenic back road, when without any preamble he said, "Justine I want you to tell me what happened between you and Ed Norris."

She didn't say anything.

"There was an incident, wasn't there?"

"I remember something," she said.

"What? He touched you somewhere? Where did he touch you?"

Justine felt the full force of his surgical concentration, probing between her legs. His invulnerable eyes remained fixed on the sunny road. She held her breath.

"I want to know what happened, Justine, because I care for you. What exactly did he do?"

She remembered lying over the lap of some forgotten boy who stuck his fingers inside her. She thought of herself crouched over a mirror thinking how ugly her vagina was. Her pelvis became rigid. "He touched me between the legs. He masturbated me."

There was a moment of silence. "That is all?"

She said nothing.

"How many times did it happen?"

"I don't remember."

"I should kill him," said her father. "I should find him and I should kill him."

He sounded like he did when he complained about an incompetent orderly at the hospital. She listened, interested, but he said nothing more. She refrained from pointing out that it would be ridiculous to kill Ed Norris now, roughly ten years after the fact, if her father actually did mean to kill him, or even yell at him, which she knew he didn't.

They continued to drive along, her exposed pelvis constricted like an animal in a trap. They went home, and the discussion dropped silently into the deep pool of their three-way life.

Everything was fine until she was caught shoplifting a miniskirt. The store detective took her elbow with such insinuating intimacy that she jerked her arm away from him and gave him an eyeful of the special scorn adolescents reserve for middle-aged mashers before she realized she was staring at a badge.

All at once she was the delinquent kid in the manager's office, sitting with her legs crossed, staring at a corner and pulling her hair across her mouth. The manager, a thin stylishly suited woman, talked about juvenile correction facilities as she paced the office, adjusting papers and emptying the ashtray. "I could see it if you were some poor inner city kid who didn't have anything nice to wear," said the manager. "But for somebody like you to steal, it's sick."

Justine had to admit it was true. She felt ashamed, but the idea of being sick had a certain drama—or at least she could pretend that it did. Her mother swept in, Saks Fifth Avenue skirt swishing grandly. "Really, Justine, this is impossible," she said. Justine shrugged her shoulders and scowled while her mother and the manager agreed on how awful she was. Her mother seemed gratified to hear official confirmation that her daughter was bad.

From there, it was a short step to her mother's surprise visit to the high school, where Justine was discovered in an illicit outfit. She was summoned to the principal's office for a confrontation, then walked to her locker by both principal and parent, where the hideous cast-off plaid was disgorged. Before the whole milling between-class student body, she was forced to leave school with her mother, clutching the wadded up woolly jumper to her chest. To her irritation, she encountered Judy Hollis and Becky Tootle, two popular girls she and Watley made fun of and who made fun of them in return. She felt acutely the ridiculousness of her position as they stared at her with greedily mocking eyes that lingered with particular satisfaction on the jumper. She'd already heard herself sneered at for "sneaking in clothes and changing so she can parade around in skirts up to *here* and necklines down to *there*," and now, as she was being marched through the hall in this way, she saw a virulent strain of gossip germinate before her eyes.

There was a tedious scene at home, and Justine was informed that she would now have a weekly appointment with a psychiatrist.

The psychiatrist was a very expensive private doctor named Dr. Venus. He had a burgundy waiting room decorated by large glossy photographs of Siamese cats. He had beautiful teenaged patients, some of whom had interesting personal habits. He was a large, very happy man with completely flat, almost nonexistent hindquarters, pigeon toes, and curly black hair. Justine thought he was an idiot, but she grew to like him. It was hard not to like someone who desired to talk exclusively about her and who also made her feel superior. She was genuinely touched by his obvious concern for her, his wish that she come into the fold of mental health. He was so pleased when she took an interest and joined in. She even told him the Emotional story, the whole thing, and sat there feeling the same tenderness and vulnerability she had felt for Emotional, feeling his approval, feeling like a little girl as they sat smiling at one another.

This is not to say she wasn't deeply resentful at being forced to see Dr. Venus. She asked her mother: "Why don't you find another mental health center to work at so you won't have to use me?"

The summer was damp and uneasy. Dr. Shade took a month's vacation and slept late every day. Justine's nervous body awoke every morning at six o'clock, regardless of when she went to bed. She would pad through the silent house and make herself a cup of coffee with three spoons of sugar and sit on the back terrace drinking it as she stared at the bright wet grass and the insects walking on the lawn chairs, trying to decide if she were happy or miserable.

. . .

*The following fall*, Watley found a boyfriend. He was new at the school, a handsome, quiet, studious boy who Justine privately considered a little dopey.

At first the boy (his name was Donald) was a lot of fun for Justine. It was a continual source of entertainment planning strategies for Watley to get his attention, ways to let him know she was intelligent as well as beautiful, for example, by carrying around large volumes on Freud. They both knew these schemes were hare-brained and girlish, but that only added to their enjoyment.

Then Watley acquired the boy, and there wasn't much for Justine to do except listen to stories about him or admire Watley in her frilly new dresses as she walked arm in arm with him in the halls. She did admire Watley for pursuing a social anomaly like mild-mannered Donald when she could easily have had a more glamorous consort; it was in its own way as daring as taking up with some menacing greaseball, except Donald was a lot easier to control. His retiring, polite personality, although it contained the requisite intelligence, was like a nice big screen on which Watley could ardently project her needs. He was easy to direct in the big scene in which modestly weeping Watley lost her virginity, a scene which Justine imagined with a mix of interest, envy, and irritation. She felt abandoned by Watley and she began to resent her for it. Her resentment was exacerbated by Watley's behavior when Justine visited her; Watley always wanted them to stand before the mirror with their faces together and then compare them, feature by feature, culminating in an analysis of their respective types, something like, "You're the cute pixie type and I'm the voluptuous beauty type."

She hoped that her envy of Watley didn't play too

great a role in her strange coupling with Rick Houlihan, a senior bordering on greaseballness. It was springtime; he was a big swarthy boy with muscles, cruel lips, and a long gum line. She met him at the cast party for the drama club version of *The Man of La Mancha*, in which he played a rapist muleteer. She was drawn by his large virile oiliness and his condescending manner. A skinny red-headed girl who noticed them talking said, "Stay away from the little girls, Rick." They were sucking face within the hour.

They continued to suck face in the back seat of his friend's car as the friend drove them home, all the while making sex jokes about sophomore girls. Rick joked back as he felt her breasts, and she giggled, feeling like a soft, palpitating baby animal that might be passed back and forth and petted by these noisy humans and then left by the side of the road.

But the way he touched was romantic, his embrace a thrilling combination of condescension, rapacity, and gentleness. She knew he believed her to be too stupid and passive to object to what he was doing, and that, while this made him view her with jovial contempt, it also rather endeared her to him as it meant he could fondle all he wanted and feel superior too, free of the guilt that a more human girl might've engendered. If he'd known Justine's history of basements, rec rooms and johns, it would have been different, but he had no idea.

They dropped her off at her house, and he said, "See ya in school, kid." She immediately called Watley, who was impressed and somewhat chagrined that her little pixie handmaiden had spent time in a back seat with someone so glandular and dashing as the rapist muleteer in *The Man of La Mancha*. All weekend, Justine fantasized him crushing her to his big pink chest while the very air about them exploded in ribbons of delirious color. On the verge of hysteria, she walked around with pimple cream on her face, her muscles furiously coiling and uncoiling under her skin. Monday came; she flew to her beloved.

He passed her in the hall with a smile and hand flap. She was wounded but she ignored that and submerged herself once more in the loud theme song of their great love. She saw him again in the cafeteria, standing in line with a tray. She noticed for the first time the slug-like curve of his fleshy shoulders, the way his bulky legs seemed to have been hastily jammed into his pelvis, but she didn't let these details stand in her way.

She admired his manly reserve in greeting her, the way his eyes slowly dropped to view her hand on his arm and then rose to gaze enigmatically into hers. Chatting happily, she followed him to his table, then out of the lunchroom, into the hall, and to the door of his French class.

They didn't have much to talk about, and the conversation that did occur was strange and arduous. This disturbed Justine, but she found the disturbance easy to ignore. Making out with Rick, his big tongue disporting itself in her head, was a little world which existed beyond the uncomfortable job of conversation and which could be literally touched upon at any moment. Even the distance of reserve and incompatibility had an odd charm; across this distance she could occasionally feel his desultory signals answering her ardent emanation, and the slight tickle of contact was so poignant in contrast with his coldness that it felt to her like a full embrace.

Then there were the hellish fantasies. All day, all night, they battered her until her body was alternately in an agony of sensitivity and completely numb. He lay on top of her in an enormous double bed, cosseted with chiffon and silk, his eyes waxy with desire. Their richly appointed boudoir exploded with flowers; lace curtains flailed the air as the thunderstorm raged outside. Everything in the room became monstrously enlarged and pulsated as the huge event transpired on the bed. He would hurt her but only because he loved her.

However, although her father, who did not like Rick, had intoned that boys that age go out with girls her age to "get one thing only," she felt that she was more interested in that thing than he was. She began to drop hints. "I don't know why people think rape is so bad," she remarked. "I'd like to be raped."

"No you wouldn't," he snapped. "You wouldn't like it at all. You don't know what you're talking about." He shook his head—angrily, it seemed to her. She felt demeaned and hurt. He obviously wasn't attracted to her, she thought.

It was a sticky summer day, just weeks after school ended, that her parents made a social call, and Justine called Rick, invited him to come over, rather bluntly explaining that her parents were gone. There was a moment of silence, and then he said he'd come.

He arrived wearing dark glasses. His whole body had a defensive yet tenacious look, like that of an animal creeping into a bush with a hunk of food in its mouth.

She invited him into the house, but he said no, he wanted to go into the rec room behind the garage. She reached for his hand and, looking the other way, he let her take it, locking a finger around two of hers.

The rec room was a damp space extending off the garage. It was carpeted with unconnected pieces of thin beige nylon and crammed with cheap hideous furniture which had been left by the people who'd lived there before and which was now covered by dust and cobwebs. On the walls were knickknack shelves and a huge plastic salmon. There was a radio the size and shape of a bread box. Rick turned it on and up very loudly, not bothering to adjust the dial, which was caught between two wavering, incoherent stations. They hit the floor almost immediately, he suffocating her with his weight, his shoulder scraping her face. She made what she hoped were attractive moaning noises as he worked her pants down with one hand, swiping at her mouth with his lips. She barely recognized his body. It seemed to be boiling with conflicting impulses contained by ironlike swaths of muscle. A feeling of alarm and disappointment rose in her, and she fiercely jammed it down. He grappled with his pants, raising his pelvis so that his chest mashed hers. A gasp interrupted her careful moans. He reached away from her and turned the radio up even louder, inadvertently adjusting the dial so that a hoe-down cavorted oafishly through the room. She felt him between her legs and in a burst of reflexive panic tried to close them. He pushed them open, gripped her shoulders and, as he had in her fantasy, hurt her, with a great deal of vigor.

"Hurry and put your pants on," he said, easing back from her onto his knees. "You're bleeding." It was true; she sat up stiffly and saw bright red smears on her inner thighs. He was tucking himself away into his pants with a certain tender efficiency, straightening his shirt, standing up. She stayed on the floor and squirmed into her panties with a rocking hip-to-hip movement. She didn't want to extend her curled-up body to get her blue-flowered pants out of their broken twist and put them on but she did. She finally stood. Her underpants were a fetid swamp. There was a rug burn on her lower spine. He stared at her from under his dark glasses. His jaw and lips were stiff and stony as if he were angry about something he couldn't do anything about.

"Okay kid?" he said. His voice sounded like it always did.

She nodded yes.

"Good." He put an arm around her shoulders. This gesture pierced her, and she huddled against him, nuzzling his chest with her nose and thinking at last they could enter their special make-out world. But instead of that remote condescending tenderness she knew and relied on, she felt him squarely there with her, every organ, synapse, and pustule in full operation, the whole hot engine of his body receiving her with utter indifference.

"Come on," he said. "I have to go." He kissed her on the nose and walked out, bearing her with him. When they got outside he let go of her shoulder and walked down the gravel driveway slightly ahead of her, as if he were going to get a beer or something. He turned towards her. "Bye," he said.

She went into the house and into her room. She pulled her pants down and looked at the blood and sperm. Some of it had dried, but the center of her underwear was still slimy and rank. She stared at it a minute and then pulled her pants back on and sat on the bed, feeling the sticky gunk squish against her genitals and thighs. She thought of her little hairs mashed up in it.

The main problem was, she'd told Watley about her planned seduction of Rick. She could lie about what really happened, but at the moment she didn't feel up to it. Instead she listened to album after album of soft music about love that lasted forever as she lay in bed under a blanket, feeling the bleak air-conditioned air all around her.

Eventually she called Watley and told her story, working an element of truth into it so Watley wouldn't be puzzled to hear it was all over between her and Rick. "He probably was afraid of his own feelings, which he projected onto you," said Watley. "He was probably intimidated by your intensity."

Weeks after the event, she told Dr. Venus, not because she needed to tell someone but in response to a series of questions, the first being, "Did you take the miniskirt because you were trying to attract boys?"

The late afternoon light was pouring in like a visitor from space, which after all it was. She absorbed the burgundy atmosphere of plant fronds and crystal paperweights. In the waiting room she had been listening to "Hey Jude" on the intercom, and she felt wrapped in its residue. She looked at the pictures of dreamy long-haired girls on the walls and thought with mild astonishment, "This is what a therapist is for."

So she told him about Rick. He nodded, his heavily lidded eyes widening only in their innermost muscles, which he had not learned to control. "And that has been your only experience?" he asked cordially.

It sounded to her as if she'd disappointed him, that he'd been expecting juicier stuff; what if everybody who came in here had better stories than she? A little cautiously, she talked about her Action adventures, checking his face for reactions all the while, seeing empathy and encouragement in his nods, leg-crossings, and head-tiltings. As she talked she felt as if she were talking about someone else—someone who was complex and interesting, a femme fatale, yet a sad sensitive femme fatale who'd seen and done too much too soon, like one of those teenagers in decadent-society TV specials who drank or something. She recounted everything as matter-of-factly as she could, even the things that had shocked and upset her, like the afternoon with Rose Loris.

Here she noticed a discernible change in Dr. Venus. His whole body seemed to constrict even before Rose had all her clothes off.

"Do you think this is weird?" she asked. She'd noticed an uncharacteristic twitching in his jaw, and it gave her pause.

He shrugged jerkily. "My job isn't to judge," he said.

At the end of the session she felt like a character in a rock song. Even the thing with Rick didn't seem so bad; it seemed very cool to have lost her virginity on the floor of a garage, cooler in its own way than her florid fantasy. Now that was out of the way and she could have one desperate-youth-of-today experience after the next until she met Him, the one who would look past her tough exterior to her tenderness and pain and then—

"Justine, could you tell your mother to come in and speak with me for a few minutes alone? You can just relax and enjoy a magazine. We won't be long."

This was the first time Dr. Venus had made this request, but she didn't think anything of it. She sat in the waiting room listening to the Rolling Stones and thinking about sex for at least ten minutes before the potentially disastrous implications of this unusual move sank in. She remembered the promise Dr. Venus had made early on not to repeat the things she told him to her parents. She was reassured for a moment and then wondered what else he would have to discuss with her mother for ten minutes; she remembered the tic in his jaw. She made eye contact with the young Nehru-collared secretary behind her lavender, triangle-shaped desk. "Sandy," she said as she stood, nonchalantly replacing a magazine. "Could you tell my mother when she comes out that I went to the Burger Boy? I'm really hungry."

Sandy said "Sure," and Justine walked out of the building and down the block until she was out of Sandy's sight. Then Justine, who never ran, not even in gym class, pumped her elbows and shaved knees and flew until sweat ran down her back.

A block and a half later she gave up, suddenly embarrassed, and out of breath. She continued to walk away from Dr. Venus's complex, panting, her heart leaping in her chest, her right foot sliding out of her battered sandal. She was on a sidewalk separated from a four-lane freeway by a thin strip of bright sod, and the rush-hour traffic droned by as she walked against it, its familiar sounds of motion highlighting her aimlessness. She saw the Hudson Mall a few blocks away and walked towards it thinking she'd call Watley.

But Watley wasn't home. She hung up without leaving a message and walked among the counters laden with jewelry and perfume, soothed by the gleam of chromium and the caress of Muzak. She tried to think of what to do. She imagined herself hanging around the mall with her chest out, making eye contact with middle-aged men. Perhaps one would eventually offer to buy her a drink, and they would drive to a motel together. She found a middle-aged man and fixed her gaze on him experimentally. He smiled back uncertainly. Emboldened, she tried another one, a big one with eye-wrinkles and a nose like a snout. His cold eyes zipped up and down the length of her body; his smile was both rapacious and dismissive. She decided she'd go try on some clothes instead.

She returned to the doctor's office imagining the trouble and punishment waiting for her there. Dr. Venus and her mother gravely discussing her incipient emotional illness, the recommendations of intensive therapy, of tranquilizers, maybe of institutionalization! She felt almost tearful as she imagined Dr. Venus advising her mother of her daughter's complex emotional difficulties and needs. How would her mother react? With anger at first, probably a few tears, and then? Justine steeled herself as she walked the last half block feeling frightened, revealed, yet resolute. She opened the door to the office and there sat Dr. Venus and her mother, her thighs tensely crossed, the sharp toe of one fashionable shoe jabbing the air. Dr. Venus rose as she entered, his face consternated, his eyes moving rapidly from Justine to her mother.

"Justine, this is the height of rudeness," said her mother. "Where have you been? I only hope the roast isn't ruined."

Dr. Venus's eyes continued to move to and fro. He lifted his hand in the beginning of a gesture and gave up. "Well then," he said.

In the car they were silent as her mother furiously negotiated the rush-hour traffic, twice hitting the brake so abruptly that she and Justine jerked then stiffly bobbed in their seats. Her mother seemed angry but not necessarily at Justine; she did not seem shocked or worried. Justine waited, her anxious fantasies crowding round, her memory of the middle-aged man with the cold eyes gliding among them. He had been sexy in a way, she thought with a pang of regret.

"What did Dr. Venus want to talk to you about?" she asked.

Her mother tossed a lock of hair from her forehead. "He was just giving me a summary of your progress to date. Most of what he said was encouraging, but your rudeness does not speak well for his treatment."

"He's a shrink, not an animal trainer," muttered Justine.

Her mother gripped the wheel more tightly and didn't answer.

Perhaps Dr. Venus hadn't repeated what she'd told him. Or perhaps he'd repeated it glowingly, seeing in her confession evidence that she was normal after all. Slowly, Justine's images of punishment and drama decomposed, leaving a bewildering cloud of half-formed feelings in their wake. She sat in the uneasy silence of this cloud, relieved but unnerved.

A few days later, her mother told her they were going to end her sessions with Dr. Venus because it seemed she had recovered. Justine felt angry but, as she had always resented and complained of being forced to see Dr. Venus, she didn't feel she could protest being forced not to see him. But after telling Dr. Venus those things about herself, she didn't want to stop seeing him. She didn't see how he could be sitting there knowing all those things about her and not be seeing her. It was like being on the verge of consummating your love and then being snatched from the arms of your loved one and borne out the door. She began to dream about him. Sometimes he would be standing on the periphery of the action, watching her with a mysterious, caring expression. In other dreams he played a more central role, such as the time he stood watching, fatherly and encouraging, while Justine had sex with Rick on his office couch. She had told him her secrets, and he had understood her—or had he? Perhaps he had been the one to end the sessions because he found her stories repugnant. No, she thought. The look on his face had spoken only of understanding and acceptance.

She wasn't trusting enough of his understanding and acceptance to call him and see if it was still there. But it haunted her and she ached to experience it again.

She was at Watley's house, in Watley's bed with Watley, a pale fluffy comforter pulled up to their chests. They ate from a box of chocolates, some of which had ladies' faces imprinted on them, and talked about sex. Watley was saying how unfortunate it was that it couldn't always be like the first time, that possibly it got boring after a while.

"Watley," said Justine, "I didn't like the first time very much."

"But wasn't it very passionate?" asked Watley. "Wasn't it an animal passion kind of experience? I thought it sounded incredible." There was a subtle but firm insistence in her voice; Justine ignored it.

"I made it sound that way," she said, "because I didn't want to tell you the truth."

Watley sat back and looked at her with wide impassive eyes, mouth serenely chewing a chocolate.

"I don't even know if he wanted to do it with me in particular. It was my idea and I think he went along with it because naturally he wanted to have sex with somebody." The truth of this stung her for the first time. "And at the last minute I didn't want to do it but I couldn't get out of it. And it really hurt." This was not like it had been in Dr. Venus's office at all. This hurt too, and to Justine's fright she began to cry. "It wasn't in my bed either," she said in a trembling voice. "It was on the floor of the garage."

"He raped you!" cried Watley.

"No," said Justine, now really crying for the first time in years. "No, that's not what happened."

Like with Rick, it was too late to stop and she told the story in all its terrible physicality. "God," said Watley, "God!" When it was finished Justine did not feel the warmth and mutuality which she had felt with Dr. Venus. She felt uncomfortable and resentful of Watley without knowing why. She snorted prettily, sucked in some tear-related snot, and ate another chocolate.

It was hard for her to call Watley again after that, and an entire week passed without Watley calling her. She finally called Watley, not because she wanted to talk but to be reassured that Watley was still her friend. Watley sounded happy and relieved to hear from her. But when they saw each other, Justine felt discomfort bud between them.

School began. Watley spent most of her time with the enslaved Donald. She and Justine talked on the phone and sat together on the radiator before home room; the discomfort burgeoned. Once Justine saw Watley walking in the hall in friendly conversation with Justine's enemy, Becky Tootle! And when Watley saw that Justine saw them, her face became first guilty, then subtly contemptuous, then friendly. "Hi, Justine!" they cried.

One day Justine was in the bathroom applying Erace to the dark circles under her eyes in the si-lent, bright-eyed company of two mascara-wielding girls. Justine rounded the corner to leave the bath-room, opened the door, and then paused in the short foyer to dig into her purse, letting the door sigh shut without going through it.

"God, can you believe the garage floor?" said one voice.

"And Watley says *she* told *her* that she had to drag him in there, that *he* wasn't even interested," said the other.

"No wonder they made her see a shrink. I don't know how Watley can stand her."

"She can't."

Justine walked out of the bathroom and down a long hall out an exit door into the parking lot. The smell of cars in the sun rose around her. She walked through the parking lot into a stunted huddle of foliage and trees where boys often gathered to smoke. She walked with her arms around her middle feeling loneliness and humiliation coupled with the sensation that she was, at this moment, absolutely herself.

*Her parents got divorced* that winter. They told her of their decision during a long drive that had been taken for that purpose. "Whatever happens," said her father, "whatever unpleasant things we might say to one another during this time, you must know: your mother and I still love each other. And you, Justine. Relationships may not last. But love goes on forever." His voice vibrated in the dry car air. A large muscle in her mother's jaw twitched in smothered anger; her mother's chapped fingers toyed with an errant strand of hair. They silently passed a snowy field in which some beautiful black-and-white cows posed.

Justine waited for the unpleasant things to be said, but they never came. Less and less was said at all as the household felt itself inexorably rearranged by the invisible machinations of papers being processed. The sharp gaze of her father's eyes was focused somewhere far away, and his confident morning cough seemed to apologize for its confidence. Strange bottles of medication with her mother's name on them appeared in the medicine cabinet. Her mother's features seemed to be trying to draw themselves into the center of her face. The voice of the television followed Justine from room to room.

Her relationship with Watley had shriveled to saying "Hi" as they passed one another in the hall. Watley's face would open for a second to allow Justine into her world, her eyes would briefly acknowledge the role Justine had played in it, and then her face would close again. Justine did not make other friends, beyond joking and talking with the skinny raspy-voiced boys who smoked cigarettes behind the parking lot. Her loneliness was painful yet it was strangely satisfying to her; in the same way that she had acutely felt her own presence at the moment of her betrayal by Watley, she now felt herself in her aloneness, and she savored herself bitterly.

When her father moved away to live in a large apartment in Ann Arbor, her loneliness drew her closer to her mother. During the divorce her mother had become swollen, dull-eyed, and unbeautiful. Justine looked at her and thought: this is what it means to be a grown woman. Fleshy, jowly, expensive clothes over big haunches, red veins in the hooded eyes, makeup in the facial creases. Her mother exercised still, and her pelvis and belly were strong and sturdy, full of deep sounds and smells, yet ugly and coarse, helpless and rejected in their ugly strength. Justine looked at her and wanted to be delicate and weak forever, never to have that strong womanly flab packed around her hips and thighs. She never wanted to make the slight grunting noise her mother made when she bent to lift a heavy object, a noise that briskly drew up her ugly pelvic energy and helped her do the things that had to be done. She closed her mouth and held her diaphragm still, shutting the door to her own lower body whenever she heard her mother make this noise for any reason.

Still she liked to sit with her in the evening, doing her homework while her mother read about current affairs in important magazines, so she could discuss events with women at Glade of Dreams. She liked to be in the car with her, both of them in sunglasses, listening to *Adventures in Good Music*. She even liked to shop with her mother sometimes, feeling protective towards this big, chic, but pathetically dreamy woman in the short skirt and knee-high suede boots. Sometimes they would go to Glade of Dreams, and Justine would lie next to her in a lounge chair, aware that they were objects of speculation, the divorcee and her troublesome daughter.

She liked being with her mother better than she liked visiting her father on the weekends. Her father was no longer handsome; his face had been weakened and coarsened by sagging and wrinkles, his body was paunchy and brittle. Their conversations were meticulous affairs about music, books, politics. He didn't ask her about her life, and she didn't desire to talk about it with him. There were occasional discomfiting moments when his sharp brown eyes would swivel into focus and he would seem to be looking right at her, wondering about her, perhaps pitying her. She hated that and tried to distract him immediately. He was easy to distract so they had polite dinners, and then her father kissed her, put his hand on her head and said, "Good night, my beauty!"

Thus she calmly moved from parent to parent to school, counting the months, holding her aloneness around her like a magic cloak.

*When she moved to New York* after graduating from college years later, the cloak was wound about her so completely she no longer knew it was there.

*When I was eighteen,* my father paid for me to go to college in Blythetown, Pennsylvania. His decision to do so evolved over a period of months, during which he would sit at the dining room table with all his bills related to me spread before him, along with my high school report cards. Finally he announced that he would pay my tuition but that I would have to pay my other expenses.

Headley Cramer College was the benign experiment of a wealthy liberal nut who wanted to create an inexpensive two-year school for the working class with all the amenities of a university, including a dormitory, and without the tedious practical bent of the average community college. It enjoyed brief prestige as a uniquely cheap and high-quality institution and it attracted a number of enthusiastic MA's and PhD's with esoteric predispositions, as well as hordes of snobby working-class kids with boxes of art-rock records. Unfortunately Cramer went broke or lost his mind, I don't recall which, and the school deteriorated into a squalid teen slum which occasionally made the papers when there was another stabbing in the special Male Bonding dormitory or something. But that wasn't until much later, and anyway the main virtue of the place from my point of view was that it was a two-hour drive from Painesville.

Immediately after registering, I took a job in a restaurant owned by a stunted creature who sat in the back office with a bottle of whiskey, paralyzed before a color TV for most of the day. I shared a dorm room with a beautiful neurotic who clung to her beauty as if it were a chance piece of debris keeping her afloat on a violent sea. I walked to my classes on cold concrete paths surrounded by yards of snow upon which lay frozen piles of dog shit. There were always other students walking all around me, in groups or alone, a continuous flow of movement in crisscrossing directions. I would close my eyes at night and see a facsimile of this moving grid in the form of endless trails of light ticking on in the dark. I ate alone in a cafeteria filled with lively students who expended more energy in gobbling their ice cream sandwiches than I discharged all day. Their voices echoed in the dormitory halls as I walked back to my room at night to be greeted with a ritual "Hi" by my roommate.

I hadn't thought college would be so like my previous life; there was an awful thematic sameness under the deceptive novelty of the experience. I had so wanted to do well and in a way I did; my passionate papers always came back with A's on them. But something was wrong. Despite my relief at being away from home, I think I missed the dark, rank security of it, the reliability of having it to crouch in, feeling the huge violent energies of my parents encircling me like a fortress of thorns. Walking the concrete paths, I felt the world stretch out before me with sickening boundlessness. The people around me appeared more mechanical and remote every day, even though sometimes I passed by close enough to see their mouths working and their long hair swinging in their faces. I felt myself walking in place through a landscape that pulsed, swelled, and receded like a cell under a microscope.

One day as I walked back to the dorm from history class I began to cry. People focused their eyes on me briefly, then looked away. They probably thought I was crying because I was fat and didn't have a boyfriend. I went into the Student Union bathroom to compose myself, came out, and began to cry again. The next day I made an appointment to see a counselor. I will always remember that kind, watery-eyed woman who sat looking at me with a gentleness and concern that made me cry again. She wanted to know about my family. I told her gingerly, planning to work up to the part about my father and I at night. But the more I minced around it, the more impossible it became to tell her. She sat, furrowing her brows and shaking her head at the scenes I described. I left to go to class and sat looking at the people around me, marveling at my difference from them. I had had sex with my father.

Sometimes I would gloat over this fact in a perverted way, feeling weirdly vindicated and special, enormous and corporeally real in comparison with the hateful skinny boys and girls prissing around me in their fashionable clothes. But most of the time I felt as if my body had been turned inside out, that I was a walking deformity hung with visible blood-purple organs, lungs, heart, bladder, kidneys, spleen, the full ugliness of a human stripped of its skin. I turned the facts over and over in my mind, trying to find some acceptable way to present them to my kindly counselor. But I never did.

It was during the beginning of my increasingly ghastly second year that I rediscovered Anna Granite. One Saturday night when my roommate was out being neurotic, while I sat on my bed with my French homework scattered about, a box of donuts and a bag of potato chips on either side, I heard the sounds of happy people walking past my window. Their warmth and pleasure caught in my protective screen and tore it. I remembered that afternoon, when I'd taken advantage of a quiet moment at work to lounge against the counter with a damp rag in my hand, enjoying the bit of pink and blue sky visible from the front window; during this moment of repose a tall handsome boy walked by and said, "You look like a real winner." His friend said, "Really," and they seated themselves in my section. The words cut me. I wrapped the wound in mental preoccupation, a binding shredded by the voices outside my window. I tried to concentrate on the stiff foreign phrases before me. That only made it worse. I crumpled my papers as I collapsed on the bed, dry sobs scoring my rib cage. I saw my college experience in comic book panels—at my desk in class, walking between buildings, in the dorm—and then I saw the panels come unstuck and spin away from each other, their borders torn, their images blackened and bursting into flames, disappearing into darkness. I ripped the blankets off the bed and sent French book and donuts sprawling (one donut rolling under my roommate's desk, where it waited to start a fight over my loathsome habits) as I thrashed around, snorting and weeping as I tried to think of something that wasn't terrible. I veered forward into the future, imagining myself as a lawyer, a fashion editor, a magazine journalist—all these possibilities seemed like cheap paper cut-outs moving up and down against industrial gray. I clawed backward into the past and found no comfort in anything there unless "comfort" could be had in the excruciating sight of brute, ignorant love, cowed and trapped, exposed by the wildly panning camera of my memory.

I felt locked out of my own fat body, as if I were a disembodied set of impulses and electrical discharges, disconnected rage and fear, something like what real humans feel in abandoned houses and call "ghosts." I remembered my father on top of me, mashing my lungs, making my breath smaller and tighter until it barely existed, opening my body with his fingers, infecting me with his smells, his sounds, grinding his skin on mine until it came off as a powder and filtered into my pores, spewing his deepest poison onto my skin where it was subtly absorbed into my blood and cells and came out in my sweat, my urine and shit, even my voice and words. I felt so saturated by his liquid stench, I didn't even think to wash it off when he left. I let it dry on my stomach or chest or ass, as I lay still with tears in my eyes. I sat in my dorm room and thought of taking a knife and cutting my face. I went into the bathroom and turned on the light and took off my shirt to stare at and hate my body. There were pimples on my chest and I welcomed them, wishing they were boils or scars, anything to more fully degrade this body, loathed even by its own parent. I had the fleeting thought that my roommate could come home at any minute, and I hoped she would so that I could display the truth of how loathsome I was and feel her contempt as well as my own. But she didn't come. I sat on the floor and banged my head on the wall and cried like every homely girl who can't be cute, can't have a "good personality," can't be like the stuck up pretty bitches who throw their beauty away in bored flirtation and don't have to be nice to anybody. Why, why, why can't I be like everybody else?

The sound of my ragged sobs alarmed me, and I realized that my head was getting badly hurt, that I had better stop this now. I had to distract myself. Like someone running to put out a fire, I jumped up and shut the windows, closing out the hurtful sounds of other people. I put on my shirt and paced the room, hugging my poor body as if to apologize for the mean things I'd subjected it to. It was fat and nobody liked it, but it was mine, and suddenly I wanted to defend it and hide it away somewhere safe. I went to my bookshelves, my pulse returning slowly to a normal condition. I remembered how reading *The Bulwark* had made me feel in high school. I picked up *The Gods Disdained* and went to my bed, collecting my potato chips on the way, and sat wound in a blanket with the book.

The first thing I read was how utterly alone Solitaire D'Anconti was in the world and how much pain it had caused her. I could understand that. It described how she'd lived in isolation in the bosom of her family, how she was incomprehensible to her parents and resented by her siblings. I read on. It described her pain as a thing of beauty and grandeur, her isolation as a sign of her innate superiority, and, in fact, caused by her superiority, comparable to mountain peaks and skyscrapers. "Every loneliness is a pinnacle," wrote Anna Granite. I had never thought of it this way before. I read of Solitaire's physical beauty and intellectual brilliance, how she "grimly seized the rapier of hatred thrust upon her by the squalling mob and fought her way out, forcing the hot anger of her pain into the icy steel of her intellect." So, not every social misfit was ugly and/or fat! They didn't all lie on the bathroom floor banging their heads! Some of them ran corporations, which is what Solitaire grew up to do.

The book was about the struggle of a few isolated,

superior people to ward off the attacks of the mean-minded majority as they created all the beautiful important things in the world while having incredible sex with each other. It ended with almost all the inferior majority being blown up in chemical disasters, perishing in airplane wrecks or collapsing buildings, all more or less simultaneously, all as an indirect result of their own inferiority.

My roommate returned that morning to find me pacing our shared unit, playing classical music on the radio, and devouring donuts in a state of exaltation.

The days during which I read *The Gods Disdained* were different from the days before. My life was no longer organized around the meaningless nightmare of dinner in the dorm cafeteria, the walk from class to class, or the classes themselves with their inadequate intellectual content on which I'd vainly tried to ground my flying psyche. Instead, it was the struggles and triumphs of Solitaire, Skip, Bus Taggart, and an array of other characters who now served as the support and metaphor of my existence. Sure, I knew they weren't real people, but they had sprung from the mind of a real person and thus, according to an argument I'd heard in a philosophy class, were possible. These people were possible!

I finished reading at about four in the morning in a state of such poignant excitation that I went out and walked around Blythetown for hours, sweating, smiling, almost in tears, loving even the sight of brutish boys weaving heavily out of late-closing bars and vomiting in the street. The world, previously an incomprehensible prison, was now an orderly place where I could live with dignity. Even what my father had done to me—as a result of his denial of reality—was not too horrible to look at, could be explained and then rejected. I could determine my own world and reject anything that made it an unhappy place.

I skipped school the next day, went to a bookstore and bought everything written by Granite. I stayed home and read for days, oblivious to the histrionic comings and goings of my roommate. When I finished the last of the books, I started over again with *The Gods Disdained*. Between readings I went to classes and walked around the tiny campus, delirious with ideas.

In this state of intellectual euphoria, I found it almost impossible to pay attention to my school work. My new world view, structured through Granite's philosophy, could easily be disarranged by the evil little weavings of the inferior thinkers who dominated my studies, or the noxious barrage of other people's ideas I received when I sat in the cafeteria, or even the complicated probings of my well-meaning counselor. This did not make me think, as it might have, that perhaps my Granite-based structure was unduly frail. I thought the ease with which my new world was imperiled was due to its newness and my own inexperience in fending off challenges to it. I tried to bring it into contact with other people. I introduced Granite into discussions in history and philosophy and was dismissed by my philosophy professor ("I don't deal with the work of dime-store ideologues") and blankly stared at by my history teacher, who'd never heard of her. I was able to talk a little with my roommate, Lisa, as she dragged herself around in the morning in her red kimono and socks, chain-smoking and drinking coffee; she actually seemed grateful when I analyzed her miserable romantic experiences in Granite's terms.

But gradually I had to cut out anything that threatened my new world. First to go was my counselor, with her puzzled assurances that any time I needed her, she was there. Then I stopped answering the letters from my mother, those crookedly scrawled missives whose words careened up and down and across the pages, oblivious to lines. Such urgent, frantic script about such a poor dull life. Finally I stopped opening them. Several weeks of silence brought the lounge phone to life and snotty co-eds into my territory with news that I "gotta call," always from my mother, featuring the occasional tense deranged tenor of my father. It made me almost physically sick to squat on the lounge floor with the phone wedged between shoulder and jaw, corporeally in the sphere of giggling students and canned rock music, and psychically in the realm of my childhood with its listing floors and treacherous light. My mother wanted to know if I was all right. My father wanted to know about my grades. They told me they had new neighbors, and a new paperboy who "missed the goddamn porch every time." I returned to my room in a state of paralysis.

I stopped going to the phone when they called. Soon I stopped going to my classes. It wasn't a decision; I simply couldn't stand going anymore. I couldn't stand not going either. I would pace the dorm room as my aspirations of graduation and success crowded into one corner of my head, yelling and screaming. I thought it was already too late, I was ruining my life, I'd missed too much material. A phantasmagoric comet of historical facts, philosophical yammerings, and French phrases would fly about the room, impossible for me to grab. And then the phantom of my parents' house would appear, trembling and weightless in my skull, and I'd think of the way I'd feel if I went out and walked among the people with their slabs of face and darting eyes. In contrast was the world of Anna Granite, clean and logical, sealed off and growing ever remote, Solitaire, Skip and the others, gazing at me regretfully as they floated farther away. To keep them near, I spent more and more time on my bed, reading Anna Granite while the rest of my life pressed in on me.

Then, within a two-day period, I read two pieces of information. One was that Anna Granite, who never attended college, had left her parents' home in pre-revolutionary Romania, left the country at age four-teen, and never spoke to them again. Two was that Anna Granite was now living in Philadelphia where she was giving a series of lectures at her Definitist In-stitute. It was some time that week, as I lay in bed lis-tening to tinny rock music seeping through the wall from the unit next door, that a path seemed to clear before me, a walkway through the writhing informa-tion I woke up to each morning. If Anna Granite could do it, why not I?

I stopped even thinking about going to classes. I changed from part-time to full-time at the restaurant and feverishly double-shifted. I received a letter from the administration which I threw in the drawer with the unopened letters from my mother.

I threw the letters away when I left for Philadelphia, but not all unread. The last thing I did before fleeing my dorm room (during the dinner hour so my gob-bling fellows wouldn't see me departing with my mea-ger luggage) was to read letter after increasingly frantic letter, the last of which said, "We're worried about you, honey."

The bus trip to Philadelphia was one of the most enjoyable experiences of my life. The vinyl seats, ripped and exploding with dirty foam rubber, the greasy windows, the droopy heads of my companions, the odor of lavatory disinfectant, the merrily sloshing bit of blue at the bottom of the mysterious toilet—the foreignness, the oddity of it thrilled me. I felt I could ride around in the bus forever, going from one dismal, echoing station to the next, eating stale sandwiches and coffee from machines, talking to no one, my identity shrunk to that of fat girl on the bus. Strangely, as I rode through the concrete landscape, dreaming about a life of achievement, beauty, and excellence, I found repose in anonymity and ugliness.

I thought of my parents, fleetingly. I saw my mother standing in the kitchen, her arms limp, her eyes absent. She was exactly the type of person Anna Granite depicted as a vehicle for evil, and she had been. My father's image I had no trouble rejecting. He was a bully, a weak nasty little man who had accomplished nothing. He was a denier of reality who had almost destroyed me. I shut a door on him forever as I rode the Greyhound eating potato chips and Junior Mints.

I ensconced myself in the Euella Parks Young Women's Hotel, a maternal building with round scrolling flourishes on eave and cornice. According to the schedule I'd received via mail from the Definitist Institute, Granite lectured on Wednesday. It was Sunday. I spent the entire first afternoon and evening pacing the room, sorting and resorting my clothes in their rickety new drawers, arranging my few dresses in the closet, studying the traffic on the street below, rehearsing what I would say to Anna Granite when the moment came, and imagining what she would say to me. My heart swelled with anticipation and fear as scene after scene unreeled before me. I'm not sure why fear; possibly because the intimacy and understanding that I fantasized was such that it would rip my skin off. She would look at me and know everything I'd endured. I wouldn't have to hold back; I could tell her about it all, I could allow her to penetrate that part of myself I'd held away from everyone, the tiny but vibrant internal Never-Never Land I'd lived in when there was no other place for me. I imagined how moved she would be by my inner world, how angry she would be at how I'd been betrayed. The mere idea of her powerful emotions were enough to make me weep as I circled the room, running my hands up and down the sides of my body. I imagined myself in a psychic swoon, lush flowers of surrender popping out about my head as I was upheld by the mighty current of Granite's intellectual embrace.

But what if it didn't happen that way? I had never seen this woman; how could I imagine she would care for me in a way that no one else ever had? This question made me feel a loneliness so insupportable that I'd hug my original fantasy until it hurt, then let go into the loneliness again.

At first daylight I rose from my snarled bed clothes (I'd vainly tried to sleep), got dressed and went out. It was a gray dirty morning; squashed milk cartons and eggshells lay in the street. People were walking with their faces against the wind, clothes flapping. I imagined them all in their offices and their apartments, living their fascinating lives (All the little knickknacks! The cartoons taped to refrigerators! The romances, the phone conversations, the families!), occupying their complicated inner worlds as full humans yet appearing in public streets every day to become walking knickknacks in someone else's landscape.

I had spent almost my entire life in rooms, both literally and figuratively, and my awakened sense of private versus public hammered me in the head. I was absorbed by every face that passed me; the jowls, the eye wrinkles, the bumpy noses, the flower-petal quality of young female skin, the parasitic crust of mascara, the leakages of lipstick into tiny mouth lines, the delicate eyebrow hairs, the blue frond of vein at the temple—how could I ever have viewed these organisms as slabs! Even more unlike my campus experience, I didn't feel either isolation or exposure as I walked among the citizens of Philadelphia. I felt as though I occupied a compartment of personal space that they instinctively respected as I respected theirs, out of which I could gaze with total impunity.

I roamed the city in this fashion all day, breakfasting on french toast, riding the bus, sitting in parks, strolling a museum, a department store, a Laundromat. I returned to the hotel with a bag of burgers, fries, and orange drink and slept almost immediately after consuming them. I woke in darkness, shoved out of sleep by a terrifying dream, unable to identify my surroundings or the menacing ear-piercing buzz which was, I finally realized, the big pink hotel sign outside my window. I had dreamed that my mother was under the ground in a container so small she couldn't move. In the slow darkness of my dream landscape, she sent me telepathic messages from her prison. She said, "I'm in hell, Dotty." In the dream this filled me with pain and terror and I tried to find my mother to comfort her. But I could only sense her locked deep underground, away from me forever.

When I recovered enough to turn on the light, I noticed that the Euella Parks Hotel had cockroaches, many of which were forming a living mosaic on my take-out containers. I spent the rest of the night fitfully pacing, thinking obsessively of Anna Granite until the sun came up and I burst out of my cage and went to have french toast for breakfast again.

The next day and night followed the same pattern and the evening of the Definitist meeting found me an exhausted nervous wreck, pacing before the hotel rented by the Definitists, eating from a bag of corn curls to calm my agitation. At eighteen minutes before the hour they began to arrive. I stood holding my balled-up corn-curl bag behind my back, studying them as they walked by, my excitement leveling into delight and solemnity. They were just as I'd imagined: tall, serious young men in suits, sometimes accompanied by a serious young woman. Almost all were handsome, all had a dignified demeanor and good posture. Strangely, I didn't feel embarrassed to be the only fatty in the group, the way I usually did at gatherings of the normally proportioned. Still self-consciousness prevented me from entering the hall until everyone else had and the meeting was about to start.

When I finally did go in, I wasn't disappointed. The Centurion Hotel was of the grand old variety, and the hall in which Anna Granite was speaking was long, thick rugged and crystal chandeliered. There were rows of magnificent chairs placed before a low dais and, on the velvet seat of every chair, a sheaf of vellum note paper and an expensive silver pen that caught and refracted the light of the chandeliers. The solemnity of the note paper, the intellectual heaviness of the pens from which sprang the airy nymph of light— these qualities were such a perfect analogy for the balance of rationality and passion in Granite's work that really, it would've been enough for me to stand there in that room of hushed, attractive people for a few hours and then go back to the hotel and collapse.

But that wasn't all I'd come for, and through a haze of intense emotion I made my way to the nearest chair and seated myself next to a devastatingly handsome man. He glanced cordially in my direction and executed an unnecessary but polite body movement acknowledging my proximity. Then there was a low communal murmur; I looked up and saw that people had appeared on the stage. A tall, broad, handsome man (who I would later know as Beau Bradley) and a graceful woman walked out like an advance guard and

# PART THREE

*It would be an exaggeration* to say that Justine's meeting with Dorothy disturbed the years-old insulation of her cloak of loneliness. But something about the encounter had sent an invisible ray under the cloak, a ray that subtly vibrated against everything it touched before it finally faded days later. During the ten years since Justine had left Deere Park, Michigan, she had had many encounters that were stranger, deeper, or more disturbing than this one, but somehow the interview had the haunting impact of a vaguely remembered dream, the kind one thinks may have been significant because images from it pop up during the day while one's back is turned and then pop back down when one whirls around to confront them.

A week after she interviewed Dorothy, Justine went to Philadelphia for the annual Definitist gathering as Wilson Bean had suggested. She took a train on a gray, damp Saturday morning; it sat in the station for half an hour after she boarded it. She sat with her forehead on the windowpane looking at two fat middle-aged men standing on the platform like two puddings in shirts and baggy pants. They reminded her of Dorothy, and she imagined the teenaged Granite fanatic on a train, going to a meeting such as this for the first time. She smiled with involuntary fondness; it must've been unbearably exciting. One of the men scratched his neck, turned, and walked away from the train. The other stood and looked at it in a heartbroken stupor. Justine thought of Dorothy's father standing like this at a railway station, brooding psychotically over the daughter he had abused and lost. A large boy with a rigid face and distant eyes sat next to her and diverted her attention. The train started to move. She excused her way past the boy's legs and went to the snack bar to buy two chocolate donuts wrapped in cellophane.

When they arrived in Philadelphia, it was raining densely and hard. Justine snapped open her umbrella with irritation; the boy strode into the downpour with stupid determination. Justine walked for blocks, barely able to read street signs, past meaningless houses and nightmare strips of shopping centers, her legs and feet wet and cold, her fellow passenger plodding a few feet in front of her. The hotel finally appeared in its majestic parking lot; she squished in, feeling vile.

The meeting room was large, thinly carpeted and lit with track lighting. People in suits and dresses stood or strolled, holding plastic glasses of mineral water. She was looking for a snack table when she was accosted by a short plump person with bright eyes and tiny hands.

"Justine Shade, I imagine? I expected you to be pretty, but not to this extent."

Justine took his soft claw in a daze; even given the vague familiarity of his accent, he had to remind her that they had spoken on the phone, that he had been the one to give her Wilson Bean's phone number. She was repelled by him, but he was a source of information. Together they wandered through the conference room (which had a table bearing only mineral water, no snacks), Justine trying to form an impression of Anna Granite's followers, as Dr. Bean had suggested. She was struck first by the absence of attractive people and second by the timid, exhausted look that prevailed. They were totally unlike the "cult members" described in the old magazine articles she had read. The men appeared weak but neurotically tenacious, the women limp and dimly pleasant. This was ironic in view of Granite's handsome, arrogant characters, the tall robust males and females who despised weakness, who fornicated with such brutish zeal. She felt curiously fond and protective of the crowd.

"No, I'm not a Definitist in the strict sense," she said to a bespectacled computer expert. "It's just that certain aspects of it interest me."

"What interests you? The emphasis on reason, on cold logic?" He said these words as if they were flags waving in the senseless gray landscape of his life.

"It's more the emphasis on the individual versus the herd," she said. "The concept of the beauty of loneliness."

"Ah," he said.

"Of course, one leads to the other, you know," said Bernard as they strolled away. "To stand apart from the collective is the only choice a rational human can make."

"People stand apart for irrational reasons, too. Sometimes it just happens."

"That's not possible."

Justine said she thought she'd go to have lunch somewhere.

"I shall accompany you," said Bernard.

They went to a Chinese restaurant with broken ocher and black tiles, smeared walls, and crabbed, tiny waitresses. A group of exhausted, sweaty waiters in dingy white kitchen uniforms sprawled around a back table smoking and muttering to each other. They looked at Justine and Bernard with incurious distaste.

They ordered mushroom fried rice with green peas and lurid red spare ribs. They shared from the plates, eating the meat with their fingers. Bernard discussed his endeavors and accomplishments. He was majoring in linguistics at NYU, where he hoped to found a student Definitist group. He was minoring in economics. He was teaching himself Japanese in his spare time. He was studying art history. He was translating *The Hunchback of Notre Dame* into Hebrew. He was putting himself through school by working in computer programming.

"I am taking as my model Jesus Delorean Dilorenzo Michaelangelo in *The Gods Disdained*. Maximum achievement, the highest you are capable of. None of this 'well, maybe I can't.' "

He chewed his rice and peas exuberantly. A kitchen boy tossed a lank strand of hair off his forehead and sneered.

"Although it looks as though I am going to be let go from my job. But, so what?" He shrugged. "Frank Golanka was fired twice in *The Bulwark*, right? For much the same reason. My co-workers do not like me. Very few people like me. Also like Frank Golanka I have no friends."

"Aren't other Definitists your friends?"

"Not really." He looked at her, part of his face bright-eyed and smug, the other part desolate and frozen. "Every now and then a few people come into my life who seem to be friends. But they eventually disappear."

She was touched. The expression on his face suddenly appeared to have been molded by hostile, alien hands, as if he were an unfortunate putty dwarf created to play the patsy in a sadomasochistic cartoon, the jargon he mouthed about the sanctity of the individual part of the mean joke.

"You must be lonely," she said.

Surprise softened his face and made it vulnerable; he wasn't used to hearing concern expressed on his behalf. She wanted to stroke his oily cheek.

"Yes, it is lonely. It is always lonely to stand apart from the crowd. One wishes to meet another with whom one has matching components."

Justine tried to see this as an entertaining experience, but she felt disoriented and sad; she did not even consider the horror with which the Justine of Action, Illinois, would have viewed this situation. Beyond the dirty window pane was gray sky, mist. They and this dingy room, with its sticks of furniture and inhabitants, could be afloat in an envelope of mist, unconnected with anything on earth, as in a serious play about ideas, where tense characters assemble on a bare stage and talk about life or society, with no life or society anywhere in sight. If this were one of those plays, what lines would the kitchen boys have? What would they think of the conflict between the individual and the herd, the choice between rationality and irrationality? She thought of photographs she'd seen of thousands of Chinese in identical gray shirts, thrusting red books into the air. Would their lines give the subject a special Chinese perspective? Or would they remain silent, their presence meant merely to represent society watching as the individuals hashed it out?

"What about yourself?" asked Bernard. "Do you find yourself often alone?"

"Yes."

"I thought so."

"How could you tell?"

"By your arrogance. You are very arrogant. I mean that as a compliment."

Again she thought of Dorothy. She wondered if a large proportion of Definitists were victims of disturbed families.

"What about your family?" she asked. "Do you have a decent relationship with them?"

"Not a very Definitist question. I don't have any relationship with them. They are beaten, weak people. My father was cautious and full of false humility. Of my mother there is even less to say. She peeled potatoes. She wore no makeup. She was religious."

Justine imagined little Bernard in the appalling bosom of his family. The father was a wretch, the mother a shadow. There was a bowl of lumpy potatoes for dinner, shoes left in the middle of the floor, used Kleenex crumpled on the couch, a black-and-white television on the blink. Bernard rarely went outside; he had no friends. Shunned on the school playground, he squatted alone, collecting pebbles and pieces of colored glass. Without naming her, Justine thought of Emotional and felt a pang.

Despite his physical ugliness, surely Bernard wasn't an unpleasant child. There was a gentle, sensitive place in his meaty soul, a place from which he viewed the world as he sat alone on the playground, appreciating its hues of sadness and moments of joy. From this spot he arranged his perception into fantasies of beauty and strength, glory and striving, fantasies he nursed deep within himself. His mother's bleak pain, his father's emptiness, the contempt of his schoolmates, all menaced and tortured his inner self until it developed a callused, horned armor. Through this armor his deformed sensitivity strained to find the thundering abstracts of beauty and heroism that consoled it and discovered Anna Granite.

Justine walked silently beside Bernard on their way to the lecture hall, listening to him discuss the fine points of Definitism. She had rancorous thoughts about the kind of world that could turn a child into a pontificating maniac.

They arrived at the hall late. Dr. Bean was already giving his speech to a crowd of about two hundred people. They sat too far back for Justine to get a good look at him; she could only see a grotesquely tall figure clutching the podium with both hands. He wore glasses and his long hair played with suppressed hysteria about his shoulders. He spoke as though describing something that had been done to him recently at the hands of a mob.

"What we're seeing is a *systematic* attempt to de-rationalize and de-Americanize the educational system of this country. This is something that started in the forties and has gradually wormed its way into respectability. One of the first signs of this change was the mass acceptance of a book by a supposed scientist, Hilma Feeney, who went to live in the primitive island culture of Patagandria, came back, and wrote a book about how wonderful this primitive culture was—implying, quite clearly, that it is better to be a naked, bead-making Patagandrian living in a hut without so much as an outhouse than an American with houses, cars, skyscrapers, shopping centers, and art. That this work was hailed not only by anthropologists but by the public, was one of the first danger signs—recognized as such by Anna Granite herself, who attacked it as the perfidious evil it was when it first appeared. But it didn't stop there."

"I think I'm going to go to the train station," whispered Justine. "I want to get back early." She got up and turned to say good-bye. To her dismay, Bernard stood and said, "I'll accompany you." To her disgust, he put his hand on her shoulder. In this way, they walked out into the rain.

*T he night after I did the interview* with Justine Shade, I transformed it into a wonderful story which I told to proofreaders Debby and Sandra. We discussed Ms. Shade during our break over a metal tray of crumbling company-supplied cookies and Stryofoam cups of coffee.

"Do you really think she's who she says she is?" asked Sandra. "I mean, what kind of reporter would dress like that?"

"And reporters use tape recorders, not note pads," added Debby, picking some chapped extranea from her pink-coated lips. "Did she have any kind of I.D.?"

"No."

"God, Dorothy, I can't believe you let this stranger into your house. Anybody could say they were writing free-lance for the *Vision*."

"But why would anybody want to? She was obviously writing an article for somebody."

"What makes you think that?"

"Because she knew Granite's material so well. She asked a lot of well-thought-out questions."

"That's even scarier if you ask me," said Sandra, jabbing at some tiny cookie crumbs with her moistened fingertip. "She's probably a crackpot gathering information for some sick purpose of her own." She licked her harvesting finger.

"No," I said. "I'm the crackpot. She's the normal person coming to expose me. She tried to make me out as some kind of masochist."

They exchanged glances. "How did she do that?"

"She just said a lot of things implying that Granite's novels are based on masochistic sex, which is totally unfair. Then she tried to appease me by talking about her sex life, about how some guy did stuff to her she couldn't control or something."

The girls gasped in unison and simultaneously picked up cookies which they pried apart, Sandra getting white Oreo goo in the point of a false fingernail. I felt sort of guilty betraying Justine in this way, but I also felt that she deserved it.

"She talked to you about her sex life? And you believe she was a reporter? Dorothy, come on!"

"She even told me about the time she was sexually molested as a child."

"Oh my God, Dorothy. Sicko. Sicko."

"God," said Debby. "What if she wanted to meet you for a personal reason? What if she somehow found out who you are and became obsessed with you? What if she's a lesbian!"

I refrained from suggesting that Debby, who was continually obsessed with virtual strangers, might be projecting. "How could she have found out who I was? I randomly answered an ad on a bulletin board, remember?"

"I don't know, maybe she's a lesbian obsessed by

Anna Granite who fixated on you because you reminded her of somebody."

"Yeah," said Sandra. "You never know with these nut cases. You saw *Fatal Attraction*, right?"

"You really think she might be a lesbian?"

"Could be. Sounds like there was something pretty intense going on there."

I hadn't considered this at all. "She didn't look like a lesbian."

"Well, whether she is or not, if she calls again, I hope you hang up."

"Really," said Debby. She tipped her head back and ferociously expelled her cigarette smoke.

Four A.M. found me in the toilet still wondering about the conversation, undoubtedly the liveliest I'd ever had with my foolish co-workers. Debby's theory that Justine was a dyke seemed ridiculous . . . and yet . . . What did that "Girlworld" on her T-shirt mean? Had it simply been my exhaustion that had given our interview its feverish dimension? I had told reporters about my father before (information which, strangely enough, I found easy to dispense to strangers but never revealed to those I saw everyday), but I had never received such a confidence in return, nor had I ever become so emotional with one of these people before. Justine had said stupid, irritating things, but so had all of them. Was it possible that I had been disturbed because I had been receiving sex signals from Justine? She had referred to her "awful" ex-lover as "he," but perhaps he had been her last heterosexual affair before discovering her true sexuality, which would explain her odd coldness in describing what should have been rapture.

Two proofreaders came in and loudly banged around in the stalls, peeing and yakking about the supervisor's ridiculous infatuation with an eighteen-year-old temp, and what a fool he was making of himself. I sat quietly until they'd finished at the sinks and then emerged to examine myself in the mirror. As usual, my heart sank. I was fat and pasty, with dark bags under my eyes and visible roots. Even if Justine was a lesbian, she couldn't possibly be sending out sex signals to me.

On my way back home to Queens via company car service, I considered my limited experience with lesbians. I'd noticed that things like fat and skin tone didn't seem to matter so much to them as they did to men. There were a handful of lesbians in the Dance of the Spirit and Healing Circle group I went to when I was even more desperate than usual for human contact. They weren't fat or dumpy, but they didn't seem like they'd reject you if you were. I found myself dreamily imagining Justine at a Dance of the Spirit meeting as I lolled groggily in the leathern gloom of the car, my eyes on the aqua-colored bottle of liquid air-sweetener the driver had attached to the center of his dashboard. The convoluted landscape of downtown Manhattan slid by in the emergent light.

Perhaps my attendance at a Dance of the Spirit group would strike some as a contradiction of my belief in Anna Granite, who was an atheist and would probably have scorned auras, healing crystals, and chakra meditation if she'd had the chance to. But one of the central beliefs of Definitism is in the right of the individual to seek out whatever serves and pleases him, as long as others are not trampled upon. Anyway, I enjoyed the meetings, and I thought Justine might too, although I'm not sure why I thought of her when I received my invitation to that month's Dance of the Spirit, two weeks after our interview. But I did think of her, and my memory of her tense body made me feel she might be in need of the kind of gentleness I sought at these fests. Besides, I wanted to know how the article was coming.

I had better luck finding her on the other end of her ringing telephone this time. She sounded disoriented, especially when she realized who it was.

"I haven't even started the article yet," she said. "God knows when I will, there's still so many people to interview."

Her voice was expressionless save that it was sinisterly rimmed with the glowing wattage of raw nerves. It disturbed me; there was something desperate in it. Perhaps she was anxious about the article and my call had precipitated feelings of guilt.

"Oh well, take as much time as you need," I chattered. "These things require a good deal of thought and meticulousness and care. Don't let anyone rush you."

Silence, underscored by the dull electrical pulse of the phone.

"Anyway, that's not the real reason I called. There's an event I wanted to invite you to that I thought might be of interest."

"Yeah?" Her voice swelled with personality.

I described Dance of the Spirit as best I could, emphasizing the healings and niceness. "It's almost all women," I added at the end.

Another silence.

"Hello?" A little irritable, I admit.

"This is a Definitist meeting?" she asked.

"Oh no, no." I gaily laughed. "Not at all. It's something I felt that perhaps, on an intuitive level, you might enjoy."

Another long throb of silence. "Well thanks but I don't think so. To tell you the truth I'm surprised you'd go to something like that. It doesn't sound very Definitist in spirit."

"Well, maybe if you went you'd get a broader picture of Definitism," I snapped. "But maybe you don't want that."

I felt her behind her silence, squirming. "Why don't you give me the address," she compromised. "Maybe I'll drop in if I have the time."

I placed the squares of information at her disposal and got off the phone. Debby and Sandra were right; she was obviously some kind of nut. I was sorry she'd been molested as a child, but ultimately one has to take responsibility for one's self, including one's phone manners.

Dance of the Spirit opened as usual; the Reverend Jane Terwilliger, a tall bright-eyed woman with long, sensitive fingers, stood beaming in the center of her loft before massive vases of roses and lilies, around which were heaped hunks of clear quartz, giant pink and purple crystals. She was further ringed by a half circle of white and blue candles and, beyond that, a circle of primary-colored folding chairs in which members of the group sat, their eyes happily shut, their open hands resting palms-up on their spread knees. Tonal music bloomed in stately bulbs of sound, and the healers moved among the seated celebrants, gesturing earnestly with their hands, pushing auras this way and that.

I have to confess that a large part of my reason for being there was the beauty of the ritual, the solemnity and delicacy of it all. Justine had been right; Anna Granite would not have approved.

The Reverend Jane saw me and floated towards me. "Dorothy, so nice to see you, it's been a while." She rested her long arm across my shoulders, and her body warmth sank into my outer flesh and vanished. I uttered my greeting, and she stepped slightly away from me, her hand still resting on my shoulder. She looked at me, and her expression seemed to spiral inward as her eyes released darts of light that covered my forehead and cheeks with bright barbs.

"There seems to have been a change in you," she said. "Quite recently. Yes." Slowly her eyes eased back into their normal function and she smiled, emitting nothing but kindness and interest. "You're probably not aware of it yet but you will be. A nice opening is taking place." She nodded happily, and I was embarrassed by the little lilypad pulse that answered her from somewhere in my chest, eager for her words and voice simply because they were kind.

I saw Jodie and Marie, a couple that faithfully attended the meetings. I felt for Jodie a strange affinity born of our mutual awkwardness and our politeness in the face of it. We had nothing to say to each other, yet we felt a bond based on the unspoken sense of an elusive similarity between us and the fear that if we actually got to know one another the result would be disappointment. The similarity was not physical; she was a tall, sharp-featured strawberry blonde with an almost expressionless face and stiff Kabuki grace. Her girlfriend Marie, a young, sarcastic, alcoholic Southerner with gorgeous green eyes and bad skin, scared me, but I approached them anyway as they lounged by the snack table.

Marie regarded me resentfully as Jodie and I made our usual pointlessly locked-in eye contact and clumsy small talk. I wanted to talk to them about Justine and the interview but could find no way to do so as they knew almost nothing about me. Instead I made oblique references to a certain "strange person" who had appeared in my life and who was "playing games" with me, a person I could see was trouble, yet felt drawn to. In between sentences I directed hard, confusing thoughts at Jodie, and she seemed to sense the scrambled text beneath my banal phrases, for I could feel a reaction pressing against her austerity like a curious animal. Even Marie seemed sympathetic. "Get rid of her," she said. "Don't cut her any slack."

Reverend Jane clapped her hands and called out, "Okay! Let's begin!"

We sat in our circle of chairs, and Jane began her talk. She'd been thinking about the limitations we place on ourselves. She told of a story she once read in a *National Geographic* which reported that when tigers accustomed to captivity were taken to nature preserves, they refused to leave the perimeters of their cages, even after the cages were removed. My eyes scanned the attentive faces. Who were these people? Mostly attractive, healthy-looking women in their thirties who wore bright-colored clothing. One of them, a Puerto Rican woman with a sternly beautiful face and huge starved eyes, had recently lost her mother to cancer and her brother to AIDS. She sat in her chair as if she were a cactus drinking in the tiny rivulet of nourishment at the center of Jane's voice; it was very little, but she was drawing on it with all her deep plantlike might. I felt for her.

". . . and I just kept seeing that strong beautiful tiger in the midst of that lush greenery, with those wonderful tropical flowers and the fresh air all around him, yet unable to step out and live it. And I said to myself, that's been me. That's been a lot of people I know."

I wondered if it had ever been me. It didn't seem like it. I looked around the circle. People were nodding their heads. Then it was time to link hands, close our eyes, and focus inward, visualizing pure golden light bathing our heart chakras. Usually when we did this I found that while there was nothing much in my heart chakra, my head was a-boil with nasty little memories. The teenagers on the subway who called me "porky," the cab driver who'd called me a cunt, bitchy Ms. Feigenbaum, the lawyer with illegible handwriting, all chattering hatefully to the accompaniment of the Top 40 trash I was subjected to from my work-mate's desk radio. I sighed, linked hands, and encouraged my thoughts to skip with idiotic lightness over my recent plans for joining a gym and losing weight. Salads, I thought. Water. Threads of tonal music penetrated my skull. I must've been tired for I experienced a sudden cerebral dip, the startling change of level one feels when stepping into sleep, not one layer at a time, but down several layers with one elongated step. I yawned. I thought of my mother. This was not unusual; I thought of both my parents on occasion, usually with intense anger. But at this moment I felt acutely my mother as she was in Ohio, still young, still pretty, and in my child's eyes so much more than pretty that "pretty" would demean features that to me were the fine articulation of her deep internal life, which made meaningless the social concept "pretty." I remembered her rubbing my shoulders as I lay in bed ready for sleep, remembered her gentleness, her innocent undefended nature entering my body through her fingers. I remembered my body responding to her. All at once I felt my heart chakra, which was filled, not with light, but with pain.

I must have transmitted this to the women who held my hands, for I felt gentle squeezes on each side. This only made it worse. My mother was swallowed up in black.

"Okay, now we're just going to go around the circle and give everybody the chance to say a few words—maybe to ask for support or to give thanks or whatever you want. If you feel like keeping quiet, just squeeze the hand of the person next to you. Ready?"

I sat shivering and cold as a woman began expressing gratitude for all the wonderful changes in her life during the last year. The image of Justine Shade flitted across my mind, and I wondered why. Was my life so empty? I thought of Anna Granite the first time I had seen her on the dais in Philadelphia.

*I was so overwhelmed* by my emotional response to Granite, that I could only comprehend her speech in fragments. She talked about how tragic it was when the individual was sacrificed for the majority, how the needs of the weak became an excuse for undermining the strong. I wept for the entire time, deep in the turbulent waters of my feelings, terrified by and agog at the fanged and finned beasts that swam by; I heard the speech only when I rose to the surface for air. What I heard corresponded with what I was seeing in my underwater maelstrom. I *had* been stronger than my parents. I had been damn strong to survive a childhood that was completely lacking in emotional or mental sustenance and in fact would've killed most people. And it was my strength that had made my father hate me. It wasn't because I was worthless, not because I was ugly or fat. It was because I *was* worth something and he knew it and he wanted to destroy me for it. I wept with rage, yet with decorum. The handsome man next to me furtively looked, but not with anything but kindness.

When the speech was over, my tears were done. I sat quietly in the back row resting as I watched the audience crowd around Granite to ask her questions and to shake her hand, or merely to look upon her at close range. My emotions gently ebbed as the audience began to filter out of the building, their faces upturned and glowing. I wasn't even surprised when the man who had been sitting next to me appeared in the aisle beside my seat and, putting his hand on my shoulder, said "Goodbye now"—even though no handsome man had ever touched or spoken to me in that way.

I waited until there were only a few people standing around Granite and she was reaching to collect her things as she answered their final questions. Then I rose and approached her. I saw her glance flicker at me and then back to the boy who was telling her of his plans to become an architect. I stood next to him, heavy with determination. I could feel her becoming aware of me, taking me in, trying to interpret the surge of resolve emanating from this silent fat girl. I could see the coarseness of her skin and hair, the deep lines on her forehead, her mouth creases, and the swollen pockets of brown and purple under her eyes. It didn't matter anymore that she was not beautiful. She turned to me. Her aquamarine eyes were shielded, questioning, very tired.

"I ... I ... I ..." To my horror I was unable to speak. She frowned at me, she gestured with impatience. "I just had to tell you ..." My feelings swelled up through my lungs and into my throat. I made a choked noise. My moment had come, I was before my savior, and I was falling away from her as if down a dark pit. Her face seemed to come apart, cracking like that of a witch in a mirror. Alarm bolted from her eyes. My hand thrashed out reflexively, as though to break my fall and then the miraculous thing; she stood and gripped my shoulders with both hands, and I felt her body heat enter my system with the blind muscularity of an eel whipping through deep water.

She said, "I can see you've had a lot of pain in your life."

"Yes I have." People were looking, but I didn't care.

"There were times I didn't know how I would survive. Even recently. I just wanted to die."

Her eyes radiated the gentlest strength I had ever experienced, her tough, hot, callusy hands supported me with the full intensity of her life. "Yes," she said. "I can see that."

"But I did survive, and the reason I survived was you. I had to tell you that. I had to thank you."

She looked at me and, as in my fantasy, she saw me, saw my pain—which no one had ever acknowledged or even allowed me to acknowledge. However, unlike my fantasy, to be seen and acknowledged by her wasn't to be penetrated and ripped apart by an obscene burst of energy. I did not feel her gaze boring through my pores to envelop my swooning spirit; I felt her at the perimeters of myself, attentive, very close, but respectful, waiting for me to reveal myself. So I didn't swoon. I stood and met her gaze and felt my self, habitually held in so deep and tight, come out to meet her with the quavering steps of someone whose feet have been asleep for a long, long time.

"Sit down," she said. "I am very tired, but I feel we must talk."

We sat down to talk as if it were the most natural thing in the world. Everyone else was gone, but I could hear people milling around behind the curtain, occasionally putting their heads out to see what was happening between Anna Granite and the unknown fat girl. She still held my hand.

"Tell me," she said. "Just tell me."

I did. What I had been unable to say to anyone, barely even to myself, came out in normal sentences. I didn't even feel embarrassment, let alone shame. As I talked she sat erect, her whole body in a state of alertness, taking in, I felt, not only my words, but my voice, my eyes, my movements, the invisible mist of my secret bodily qualities, that which makes you sense a person before you've seen them. When I told her that my father had molested me, her eyes became suffused with such an extremity of feeling that they became walls of fierce unfeeling, inanimate as fire or radiation. I told of how I'd read *The Bulwark*, how I'd gone to college hoping to find meaning in my life and had instead been battered by everyone and everything around me, how once again her work had been the only thing for me to hold on to, how I'd come to the decision to leave college, cut myself away from my parents forever, change my name and become a student of Definitism.

When I was finished she stared at me in silence for a long moment, her hand still on mine. She said, "And how will you support yourself?"

"I can type fast," I said. "I'm a good speller. I could be a secretary."

There was another moment in which her eyes absorbed me slowly, and then she said, "Would you like to work for me?"

"Be *your* secretary?"

"Not mine directly. But for my protégé, Beau Bradley. It is part time, I'm afraid, but we are paying almost double the standard hourly wage. And for that we expect double the competence."

She was talking to me as if we were both characters in her novels! I wanted to answer her like one, but I couldn't quite. "Are you sure?" I said. "I'd love to try but I've never been a secretary before and—"

"If it doesn't work out we'll know soon enough. But I think it will. I see incredible strength in you. I also see intelligence, which is proven by the fact that you were drawn to my work. If you could live your life up to this point in the face of such terrible opposition, I think you will do amazing things now that you have removed that opposition. I want you to know that. And I want you to report for work tomorrow."

The last words between us occurred as I was on my way to the door. She said, "Oh, wait, you haven't told me—what is your name? I mean your real name, not the one your parents gave you."

And I said, "Dorothy. Dorothy Never." And she smiled and repeated it.

$And$ *now we're going to open* our eyes," said Reverend Jane.

I opened my eyes to the sight of happy strangers unclasping their hands and looking around. I caught Jodie's curious glance and looked away.

"Why don't we end the service with a little song," continued Jane. "I always enjoy that, don't you?" We reached for our songbooks.

I remembered Anna Granite and me alone in the hotel hall like two lovers clasping hands in a closing restaurant. I remembered leaving her that night and walking through the streets feeling my secret slowly releasing itself from my body. I felt my inner tissue open and lie breathing and restful. I felt yellow flowers blooming on my internal organs.

But now Anna Granite is dead, and sometimes I think my memories of her don't mean as much to me as I'd like to think they do. I remember my sense of release and freedom that night, but only cerebrally. Well, Granite would say that is the most important way, I guess.

We held our songbooks before us and sang: "Happiness runs in a circular motion/Thought is like a little boat upon the sea/Everybody is a part of everything anyway/You can have everything if you let yourself be."

*J*ustine Shade rolled down the cheap black socks of a large male patient. She dotted glue on his thick ankles and applied the clamps.

"Just rest your arms at your sides," she said gently. She moved to glue and clamp his wrists.

What an idiotic thing to spend your days doing, she thought. She looked at the heavy man on the table, exposed in his underwear. He looked calm and potentially very purposeful, despite his passive body. She wondered if he was a Definitist.

"Mr. Johnson, have you ever read *The Gods Disdained* by Anna Granite?"

"No, I haven't. Although I think I've heard of her. Why?"

"I don't know. You remind me a little bit of a character, Skip Jackson. Maybe because your name is Skip, too."

"What's Skip Jackson like?"

"Well, he's an industrialist supercapitalist. He's brilliant and rich. He's one of the only successful supercapitalists left in the world because the liberals and weaklings have pretty much taken over and are trying to destroy the strong, productive people." He looked interested. "Most of the other supercapitalists have hidden out in a capitalist paradise with the head capitalist and are just waiting for the world to collapse without them. Which it does."

"What happens to Skip Jackson?"

"He gets to the paradise with the others and then comes back in the end to take over the world." She worked the knobs of the machine. "Plus there's some romance and some sex."

"That sounds interesting. That sounds like something I might like to read. I haven't read for years now."

"I told Skip Johnson he reminded me of Skip Jackson in *The Gods Disdained*," she said to Glenda that afternoon.

"Ah, what a compliment."

"Now he's probably going to read it and think I have a crush on him."

Glenda laughed throatily. "You know, he really isn't anything like the character. Do you know he is forty-five years old and he lives with his mother?"

"Oh my."

"That's right. His mother is Regina Johnson who comes in about every six months. She is really the mover and shaker of the family. She still manages a floor of Bloomingdale's and she is sixty-seven years old."

"That's wonderful."

Justine filed patients' cards and brooded. According to Definitist thought, for every imperfect entity, be it human or material, there exists a perfect counterpart; a lovely princess for every pimply shop girl. This perfection was not an annulment of the shop girl, but an ideal for her to aspire to, and the clerk who whistled at her in the street could see and love the princess in her, just as she could see the glamorous playboy in him. That is why, said Anna Granite, advertising is deeply moral; its smiling billboards are openings into the perfect beauty that we can all strive for and attain, to one degree or another, depending on our individual components.

Maybe, thought Justine bleakly, there is a perfect Justine Shade somewhere. A tall, full-lipped beauty who wears silk and leather. She lives in a beautiful, austere apartment and condescends to write a half-dozen or so brilliant pieces of journalism a year. They all sound the same, and they are never ambiguous. She has lilac-point Siamese cats and a few strong, handsome, powerful lovers who never stand her up or make her feel awful, instead of a series of eccentrics, instead of a tiny apartment filled with gewgaws and balls of dirt, instead of a job putting clamps on old people and arranging cards in alphabetical order.

This can't go on, she thought. Somehow, I have to get out and Live.

On the other hand, Anna Granite's heroines rarely got out and Lived. They didn't want to either, as it would require that they mix with the herd. They just worked hard at their careers, thought, and were beautiful in grand, square-jawed isolation, at least until the hero appeared who had also, until this point, been sitting alone in his room when he wasn't working hard. Perhaps there was something starkly beautiful about her simple job and her functional apartment, her daily subway ride, her small bags of groceries and neat dinners, her staring vigils over the clanking typewriter. It was possible, except there was nothing stark or beautiful about the gewgaws or the dirtballs. Maybe she would begin sweeping more regularly and throw some things out.

"How is the article coming?" asked Glenda.

"I'm making progress. I'm interviewing people this afternoon, these guys who run a Definitist school."

"That should be interesting," said Glenda, absently examining a postcard from a forgotten patient.

"And I'm trying to arrange an interview with Austin Heller next week."

"Really?" Glenda looked at her with tentative reappraisal. "That would be a feather in your cap, wouldn't it?"

"I don't know. He probably won't understand why anybody would be interested in Anna Granite now. He might not have anything to say."

"But still, just to mention his name in your article."

Justine crouched on the slim ledge of Glenda's validation, her enjoyment of the perch only partially marred by its smallness and flimsiness.

*The offices of Rationalist* Reaffirmation High were located in a small oblong apartment building in Brooklyn. The third floor stairwell had "You Die" written in Spanish on its wall.

Jack Peach, president of Reaffirmation High, was a plump fellow with a proud fleshy chest and a normal smile. He shook her hand and guided her through the functional apartment, which was defined by boxes of files, a desk layered with organized paper, and a glowering answering machine. She sat in a small chair with a vinyl seat and arranged her notebook. "My partner will be joining us in a few minutes," he said. "I hope you don't mind the mess."

She said no and studied the room, its stacks of cardboard files, its blankets rolled on the saggy twin beds, the little bundle of folded socks on the dresser. She imagined two men waking up every morning in this room, walking around in their underwear, drinking coffee, preparing to go and spread Definitism into the world.

"Our office is a little unorthodox," said Jack Peach, seating himself on a folding chair. "Especially for me. Just two years ago, I had an office that was almost as big as this apartment. I had a lovely view of Manhattan and New Jersey."

"What were you doing then?"

"I was a corporate lawyer at Moose Grimm." He grinned proudly. "Quite a change of life-style, wouldn't you say?"

The door opened and a slight man with glasses on the end of his nose entered carrying a box of pizza and a brown grocery bag.

"But it's worth it for the school," said Jack. "The school's the most important thing in my life right now. This is my partner, Dave Fry."

The slender man tugged shyly at the bottom of his suit jacket, nodded, and said, "Hello."

"Would you like some pizza?" asked Jack courteously.

She said no; there was food arranging and jacket removing. Jack gave her a can of diet root beer, and he and Dave sat down to their dinner with an air of gracious ease. Dave picked up his little can of carbonation and fervently began. "I . . ." but Jack cut him off.

"I first conceived of making Definitism the dominant philosophy in our time when I was at Princeton studying economics, and I noticed how two conflicting attitudes towards making money and building commerce were gnawing at the minds of the students. On one hand they were being given the best education that money could buy, the best training to go into business that anyone could have—and on the other, they were being subtly told that what they were doing was somehow base, greedy, even immoral. I saw a dangerous and horribly cruel cultural schizophrenia that needed to be cured with reason. And that's why I started the school."

"Education should make sense," burst out Dave. "It should be about thinking, writing, and speaking within the parameters of logic."

"We had certain problems with the state at first," confided Jack. "We did break a few bureaucratic-type rules. But how could they say 'no' to a high school staffed by teachers who all have such advanced degrees?" He beamed sweetly.

"Can I say something?" asked Dave Fry.

"Sure," said Jack. "I just . . ."

"The bottom line of leftist thought is that individuals cannot know reality or truth, that there is no objective truth. If there is no objective truth, then everything is excused. If we cannot know reality, then to act and build is futile. If an individual is just a collection of neurons and genes, or a receptacle for whatever environmental data that's input, then he isn't responsible for himself. In a world like this, everything's on the same level, whether it's a Bach sonata or a papier mâché pig made by a retarded kid. Everybody's on the same level; you're supposed to care as much or more about thousands of Vietnamese strangers as you would about your own family. In a world like this, what can you value or turn to but the approval and love of other people—*any* other people?"

He emphasized these last three words as though they were steel jaws closing on the horrified face of a victim who has realized too late the trap he's been sitting in. Justine pictured the people on the subway holding shopping bags and reading the *Post.* Jack nodded and beamed.

Justine rode home on the subway in a good mood which was only slightly disturbed by the four ragged, crack-eyed beggars who walked through the cars mutely shaking paper cups of change. Hers was among the arms that furtively thrust coins into the cups while the corresponding eyes scanned cardboard ads for the AIDS Hotline and *Dynamic* Business School, as though it would embarrass the rest of the body to know that the hands had assisted a desperate person, however minimally.

She ate her take-out salad on the floor and was preparing to read an autobiography of one of the sixties' most active rock 'n' roll groupies when she received a phone call from the fat lady interviewee inviting her to what sounded like some sort of group therapy. As in the interview, the woman seemed to get angry at her for no reason; as in the interview, Justine found herself inexplicably intimidated by her. She made a stammering attempt to mollify Dorothy and then got off the phone. Unable to return to the groupie book, she thought of the woman she'd met, the poor bloated creature with her flowered dress and corona of false red, her invented name wafting above her, attached by the thinnest of threads. She tried to imagine this person as a child, to imagine her life. She had a sensation of cold and dark, a dark house, remote, terrifying parents whose faces were somehow blocked from her psychic view, like killers in masks. Dorothy had eaten breakfast with these people, shared the bathroom with them, probably exchanged Christmas presents. It was incredible to Justine.

The hell of it was, the fat woman was obviously very tough in some way. She had that craziness locked into formation, doing drills, getting her up and out and moving through life, with a roof over her head and money in her pocket, instead of roaming the Hades of beggars and bag people, many of whom had had, Justine suspected, normal homes and lives at some point. Where had this strength come from? Surely not her mother; no sane mother could have allowed her husband to sexually assault her child. Perhaps there had been moments of tenderness before puberty, outbursts of love strong enough to support a budding human. Perhaps somewhere deep under the suffocating mud of her parents' psychology there had been hidden pockets of sanity and self-respect that Dorothy had unconsciously sought out with the unerring impulse of a plant root, distant pockets from which she drew enough nurture to survive.

The phone rang and Justine regarded it warily for some rings before she answered. It was her mother.

If her mother's voice had changed during the past twenty years, it wasn't detectable to Justine. It still had that quality of groundless cheer that had inspired, then galled, then depressed Justine as a child. Justine liked and even respected her mother (albeit reflexively), but the sound of her voice always made Justine recoil into some emotionless state in which her own voice became flat as processed air. No matter how she vowed to be kind and warm, no matter how she reminded herself of the profundity of the mother-daughter connection, her mother's habitual greeting—"Hello, hello!"—delivered with that relentless optimism, never failed to transform her into a robot.

"So, dear, tell me what you are doing. I need some excitement in my life. What is a young woman in New York City doing for fun?"

Justine gritted her teeth as she related the only

event that could possibly come under the heading "Fun."

"I'm not going out much now," she finished. "I'm busy working on this piece for *Urban Vision*." Actually, it was fun describing Jack and Dave, and her mother was thrilled to hear of her possible interview with Austin Heller.

Her mother began talking about the wonderful new friend she'd met in her yoga class, the stylish and adventurous Martina, a recently divorced thirty-eight-year-old with whom she was trading books and going to a "really nice little" bar in Deere Parke. It wrung Justine's heart to think of her mother sitting in a pick-up bar with all her makeup on.

"Now we're reading a really *interesting* book about Peggy Guggenheim and her circle. I just love it, but after I put it down, I find myself feeling such envy for all these people and their wonderful lives. Ah, well. Maybe I was just born into the wrong decade."

After she got off the phone, Justine felt the need to go sit in a bar with all her makeup on. She tried to avoid it by grimly walking block after block, handing change to beggars and being called a dyke by a ghostly lurking boy. She was on her way home, having successfully fought the urge to drink, when she was chased into a bar by a man in an Armani suit who wildly waved a broken bottle and yelled "I love you! I love you! I want to eat your shit and drink your piss!"

It was a dark bar with heavy air, tended and frequented mainly by old men whose personalities seemed to have drained from their upper bodies and become lodged in their buttocks and thighs, which, as a result of having to carry that extra weight, needed to rest on as many bar stools as possible. These men turned and faced the bottle-waving screamer and the collective impact of that stultified buttock-impacted energy was enough to make him lower his bottle and slink out the door. Well, thought Justine, that's a relief. Still, you never know; he might wait for me outside. I'd better sit in here for a while. She approached the beautiful oak bar and gazed at herself in the mirror behind it. The heavy, cloudy glass seemed like the deep water she'd sometimes seen herself sinking into in dreams. Alistair, a kindly bartender with a collapsing face, gave her a free scotch to help her get over the coprophiliac assault, and she sat absorbing the hideous modern rock music—"Ohhh! Livin' on a prayer!"—that these old guys apparently had a secret need to bludgeon themselves with.

She'd had two drinks when she noticed that there was a sharp elfin face in the mirror with her. It was such a contrast to the other faces there that she stared at it, uncertain if it were male or female. It smiled at her with an elegant facial twist, and she had the uneasy sensation of someone sliding a finger under one of her tendons and prying it away from her muscle, quite casually speculating on how far it could be pulled before it snapped.

He crossed the room and sat beside her at the bar. "Hi," he said. He expelled smoke from his full lips and sat with his slim, small body inclined towards her as if he'd known her a long time.

Justine felt an odd sensation of excitement, as she gradually eased her tendon back into place, odd because it involved feelings of contempt towards this stuck-up stranger which were somehow playful. She looked into his drunken eyes and found them simultaneously vague and penetrating; she felt that a conversation with him would involve a continual grope for something which would turn out to be, on contact, completely illusory. And there was something else about him, something diffuse and yet heavy and potent infusing his whole presence. He blew a throatful of smoke in her face. "A little young for this crowd, aren't you?" he remarked.

She deftly snatched the cigarette from his lips, dropped it on the floor, and stepped on it. "I only come here when I'm desperate," she answered. "What about you?"

He hadn't quite recovered from having his cigarette snatched so he was slow in answering. "Actually I was going to go to the Hellfire Club down the street, but it turns out tonight is queer night. Want to buy me some more cigarettes?"

"Not if you're going to blow smoke in my face."

"I was just trying to get your attention. Like boys on the playground. When they pull up your skirt and knock you down it means they like you, didn't your mama ever tell you that?"

His voice had the delicacy of a slim snake moving through wet grass. She tried to understand her reaction to him. It was no use; she was dealing with feelings ranging from disinterest and irritation to sickening arousal. He reached out and touched the tip of her nose. "You're really cute," he said. "With those big glasses you look like an autistic kid in a Diane Arbus picture."

"And you're really rude. Why don't you go bother somebody else?"

"I'm not rude, you're just drunk."

She stood up, grabbed for her coat, fumbled, and dropped it. He put his hand on her elbow. "Please don't go. I am rude, but it's only because I'm too drunk to flirt. I've been watching you since you came in. I think you're adorable."

She hesitated, confused. She wondered if he were the person who'd chased her into the bar, if he'd just gone home to change his clothes.

"But if you want to go, I won't stop you. Here, I'll even help you." He picked up her coat and draped it across her shoulders. He got her scarf and was winding it around her neck with a sloppy flourish when she said, "Cut it out. If you want to apologize, buy me a drink instead."

"Great idea! I need one too." He summoned Alistair, who smiled paternally at her as if delighted to be watching an actual pick-up, probably a rare occurrence in this place.

"Jesus Christ," she said. "What a weird day." She remembered her interview with Jack and Dave that afternoon and the phone conversation with what's-her-name and felt like a wild boar crashing through a life of figurines.

"So what happened? You said you only came here when you were desperate. What're you desperate about?"

His voice was soft and gentle in a TV lover-boy style, but his pale eyes glittered with the adrenal malice of a sex criminal who likes to crack jokes while reaming his sobbing victims. She turned away from him. Next to her, one old guy grasped the arm of another and said, "Take care, Jim. Don't let it get you down." The sight of human comfort injured her. The jukebox bawled about sex. She turned again to the smirking vandal at her side. "I'm desperate because I—I'm not actually desperate at all generally, it's just that some mental case was chasing me with a broken bottle so I ducked in here."

"Oh." He seemed disappointed. "You look like you're pretty desperate generally. That's a compliment. I like desperate women."

She tried to read his face, which increasingly struck her as hard and immobile under its thin layer of easy expression. She finally noticed that he was very handsome. "Why do you like desperate women? Because they're easy to push around?"

He smiled. "I like the way you think. What do you do for a living?"

"I'm a part-time secretary and also a writer." She was ashamed of herself for trying to impress this creep, but "writer" had just slipped out.

"Oh yeah? A writer, huh?" He smiled and lifted his drink to his mouth as though to suppress a horse laugh. His slim throat palpitated; she had an urge to touch the exposed vein. He put down his glass, his eyes coolly releasing a jet of sarcasm into her face. "And what do you write about?"

One part of her stepped forward like a first grader in a starched dress with her hands clasped behind her back and, with eager animation, she began to describe the Anna Granite article while another part of her skulked in the background, angrily eyeing the first grader, and yet another part of her tried to puzzle out why she was talking to this prick, let alone exhausting her short supply of charm on him. She was lonely, desperately so; she could feel the loneliness scraping along her insides every time she witnessed the slightest display of human warmth between strangers. But Justine had a hard little spiny pride that stiffly forbade her to talk with people solely out of loneliness, and she wasn't drunk enough to ignore it. What else could it be? She looked again at the boy's face as he listened—actually quite intently, it seemed his snotty composure was somewhat shaken by the Anna Granite article—and tried to feel what it was. Although she didn't remember this, it was as though she and the stranger were doing what she and her mother had done over the phone many times many years ago, as though beneath the nasty and tedious conversation, he was emanating some urgent, insistent signal and was being received by a hitherto slumbering segment of her and answered with a good deal of ferocity. Of course it was sex, but it was something else as well, something that was becoming swollen and unwieldy, like a helium balloon rapidly inflating under her behind. The skulking part of her grimaced to hear her outermost aspect use the word "interesting" again and again with almost the exact degree of irritating elocution her mother habitually used. She struggled to analyze this attraction before she was overwhelmed by it. There was also the contempt; why didn't the contempt kill her interest in him rather than titillating it with a spastic corkscrew jab that first made her shudder, then provoked a sensual, playful hostility that made her want to cuff him like a cat would swat a kitten.

"That sounds cool," he was saying. "I read her stuff when I was in high school. I loved it."

"Yeah?" Her separated selves came banging together in shared curiosity. "Why did you love it?"

"I don't remember." He actually seemed to be trying to talk to her, and this show of respect and humanity after his ugliness made him seem complex. "There was good sex in it, but that wasn't all. I don't know."

The moment of genuine conversation seemed to leave him subdued. He sat facing the bar with his body in a curl, staring at his drink as though he'd just realized he had to be at work tomorrow morning. The jukebox was silent.

"What do you do for a living?" she asked.

"I'm an art director for *Grab* magazine." Without his animating mask of sarcasm, his face was tired and pinched. "It's dumb but I like it. The people are nice."

To her dismay she was afraid he was about to get up

and leave. "My name's Justine," she said with sudden extroversion. "What's yours?"

"Bryan." He turned towards her again, his face regaining its life. "Have you ever been to the Hellfire Club?"

"I don't even know what it is."

"It's an S&M club." He watched her. "You know, master, slave, people being tied up and beaten, women getting fucked by dozens of guys. I'll bet you'd like it."

This was a jarring speech, but instead of pushing her away from him she felt it pull her towards him. A bolt of sensation zipped through her genitals and nailed her to her seat, and she felt much as she had when she was a prepubescent cruising the mall with a pack of boys at her heels; dislocated, aroused, and disturbed to be having such a personal reaction in a public place. Oh Christ, she thought. Not this again. Her heart beat arhythmically against the bones of her rib cage. She looked for Alistair and saw him far, far away, at the other end of the bar, his big once-strong body in an absent-minded slump as he wiped some glasses.

"You *would* like it, wouldn't you? I'd suggest we go except now it's just queers giving each other AIDS."

"I didn't think it was legal anymore, for straights or gays to screw in public."

"Murder isn't legal either, but people do it."

This frightened her. She suddenly remembered where she had heard the name of this club before; it was the last place a beautiful model had been seen before being ritually murdered. "I wouldn't want to go anyway." She frantically tried to make eye contact with Alistair, who smiled and waved.

"Hey, wait a minute, don't be scared. Shit, you're really scared!" He stood and put his hand on her shoulder. She looked at him; his small white face was neither sarcastic nor limp, but taut with an expression she couldn't identify. "Don't be scared, I'm not dangerous, I'm just a nut. Okay, I'm a little bit perverted, I admit it. But I wouldn't really hurt you. I just like to shock people."

"Yeah, you and Richard Speck." She shook off his hand and pulled on her coat, digging in the pockets for dollars that flapped around elusively. Alistair moved towards them, slapping his trusty rag on the bar with a professional flourish.

"I'll get it," he said.

She got her coat and scarf under control while he reflexively navigated the world of commerce and hearty gestures. "Everybody who finds me attractive is a fucking maniac of some kind," she thought. "Every time I meet somebody cute he wants me to pee on him or some goddamn thing." She had the comforting thought that any minute now she would be at home, sobbing on her bed, alone but unmolested. She fought her way through the air, holding back her tears. She had just made her escape out the door when he appeared at her side.

"I hope you were kidding with that Richard Speck crack."

"I just wanna go home."

He grabbed her shoulders with both hands. If his grab had felt like the beginning of an attack she would've run; had it felt like a full attack she would have turned and hit him. But it was just powerful enough to hold her yet tender enough to paralyze her. "Don't run away," he said. "Please don't be afraid of me."

She turned to him and saw his face, drained and exhausted, his eyes wide with alarm. He pulled her to him and she collapsed against his small chest, exhausted. She felt his quick heart leaping urgently. He emanated warmth. His dick hardened against her abdomen. He stroked her hair. She began to cry. "Honey," he said. "Darling."

*My first days of work* for Beau Bradley were so fraught with reverence and vigilance that I existed in a strange state that was both hyperaware and muddled. I arrived that first morning in such a sleepless fever that the physical perfection of tall, smiling Bradley didn't awe or excite me—I, who usually saw beautiful males as species from a hostile planet. He seemed like nothing less than de rigueur for this storybook I'd stepped into. I was trying with all my flabby concentration to absorb the details, to be a good employee. I'm not sure why I wasn't too disoriented to function at all, except that my entire life had been made up of incredible situations in contrast to which this one seemed unusual only in that it was positive. The very bizarre and extreme nature of finding myself employed by my idol the day after meeting her was what made it, in a sense, natural to me. The experience was so charged, so heady that I lived those days in my head, my breath high and quivering on the pinnacle of my deserted body. Anything more mundane would've sunk me back into my chest and pelvis, right onto my legs where I would've felt my old creaking soul slowly doing the hoops and ladders of my life.

But Beau Bradley was anything but mundane. He had black hair, silky, almost feminine white skin, the cleft-chinned square jaw of a movie star, and blue eyes that matched Granite's. Even more unusual, his kindness equaled his beauty. When I entered the office—medium-sized, clean, sparely furnished with modern furniture and stark steel sculpture, located in an oblong building that also housed the Philadelphia Mah-Jongg Society—he smiled at me as if it were utterly natural for me to enter his sphere. His hand enveloped mine with warmth and pressure that was respectful and protective as a father is supposed to be. "Anna has told me so much about you," he said.

I nodded, realizing that he probably knew my secret. I didn't find this probability shaming or even inappropriate. "Then you know I haven't had experience," I said.

"From what I've heard, that doesn't matter. Anna can tell from speaking with someone for five minutes what they're made of, and she says I should jump at the chance to hire you."

The phone rang and Bradley, with an "Excuse me," disappeared into his private office, leaving the door open. I stood in the outer office, in front of what was probably to be my desk, holding my purse against my body, feeling my heart beat against it. I absorbed the cream-colored walls, the skeletal bookcases and their books, the bindings of which seemed to vibrate with color and significance. I stared at a spiney, determined-looking little sculpture of a man hoisting the world on his shoulders and thought, "That's me." I knew it was a silly thought, but I excused it on the grounds that it was emblematic and that it was a pre-figuring of the new direction my life would now take.

Bradley spent about fifteen minutes explaining my duties to me. They seemed, in spite of Granite's description of their arduous nature, to be pretty easy. Answering the phone, typing letters, photocopying, dictation, an occasional run to the post office or deli—all in a quiet office that appeared to receive a phone call every two or three hours. The apparent simplicity bewildered and then panicked me—what if it seemed simple because I was not grasping the entire picture but only seeing the most obvious elements in a complex mosaic! I spent the rest of the morning sweating in my woolly skirt, spot-checking the filing system, cleaning the coffee filter, roaring through a letter, pouncing on the phone whenever I could. Noon arrived and Bradley went out saying, "Take a breather, have some lunch!" I ate my cheese sandwich, potato chips, and candy bar at my desk and allowed myself an hour of feeling superior. If this was hard work then other jobs must be softer than anything I'd ever experienced in my life—and no wonder Granite had such contempt for the common people! I ate my sandwich with one hand and straightened the Rolodex with the other, marveling at my own efficiency.

By the time Bradley had returned from lunch, however, I was again full of self-doubt, which was later exacerbated by a typing mistake which Bradley jovially brought to my attention.

The next two days—half days both—followed the same pattern, except that they were enlivened by the appearance of Definitists from other parts of the country who had long conferences with Bradley. There were three of them, two men—one rotund with a receding hairline, the other weirdly tall, his sensitive brow a-twitch with the weight of heavy glasses—and a big woman with small eyes and a bun of brown hair who breathed in strange broken sighs.

On the fourth day Bradley asked me to join him for lunch. We closed the office and went to a plain, clean luncheonette with speckled table tops. I dimly remember a jukebox playing dramatic love music as we sat across from one another, smiling over our menus. He asked me how I was enjoying the work. I said very much. We ordered our sandwiches. For the first time I felt self-conscious about being fat before him and refrained from ordering the milkshake and double fries I would've liked. We ate without speaking for several moments, but rather than feeling isolated from him, I felt bonded by our mutual silent intensity. Besides, this way I didn't have to worry about saying something stupid.

Mid-sandwich he spoke. "I asked you to lunch for a reason."

I nodded and my heart sank.

"We—Anna and I—need you just now to do more than your usual duties. You've noticed the three people I've been meeting with. They are three of the top Definitist intellectuals in the country, and two of them—Doctor Wilson Bean, the English professor, and Wilma Humple, the banker—will be meeting with Anna and me along with Knight Ludlow, a financier from New York, to do intensive conference work for about two weeks. We would like to have our discussion transcribed, and Anna and I would like you to be the one to do it."

Mentally I reeled while physically I nodded. I put down my sandwich.

"It will be arduous work and will involve long hours—very long hours. Anna can stay up all night discussing ideas; the others will probably sleep in shifts, but you will be expected to stay up as long as there is discussion. Think you can handle it?"

I nodded and said, "Yes." My adrenaline rose, and suddenly, I wanted to order a piece of lemon meringue pie.

"Good." Bradley smiled. "We both know it's a lot to ask of a beginning secretary, but we felt you would welcome the opportunity to learn more about Definitism. It is the chance of a lifetime in that respect."

"I'm ... I'm honored that you asked me," I replied in all sincerity.

"Wonderful." Bradley smiled again. "Let's finish these sandwiches and get back to work." He said it as though we were about to return to the office and do hours of heavy construction.

I bit my sandwich, mentally scorning the lemon pie as a frivolity that would be stripped off the streamlined life of an intellectual.

The conferences began a week or so later. Bradley and I stayed an uncharacteristically full day at the office then ordered sandwiches which we ate with our feet on his desk, then we took a cab to Granite's apartment. I felt extreme anxiety on the way up in the elevator. This was not after all, a fantasy or a TV show, even if it felt like it. I was going to be among the most intelligent people in the world, and I was terrified of disappointing them, even if only in a secretarial capacity.

Out of the elevator we marched, entering the apartment with determined purpose. Granite opened the door, her eyes afire and her forehead locked. Mercifully, we were the first to arrive. Unsmiling, she gestured for us to sit on a stiff square-pillowed gray couch before a small, proud coffee table devoid of anything but a pitcher of water, some glasses, and three ashtrays. I would've sorely loved to see a decorative jar of French creams or even the cheapest peppermints, but I realized that such an item in Granite's home would've disappointed me. Granite left the room briefly, and I noticed that she was again wearing her billowing purple-lined cape. Did she wear it around the apartment when no one else was there? How marvelous! When she returned with a sheaf of papers, she sat in a chair opposite us, gazing slightly over our heads as though she were furious about something. Bradley sat against the back of the couch, very relaxed. I found it odd that on this occasion, the first time I had seen Granite since our original meeting, she hadn't yet spoken to me. But I sat obediently and waited, unable to decide if a slouch or an upright position was most appropriate.

"So, Anna," said Bradley. "What is the topic for tonight?"

"The conflict between the individual and society, focusing on whether or not the will of the individual genius can ever be compatible with that of society."

Having spoken, she sharply adjusted her line of vision to include us and seemed to see me for the first time. Tenderness suffused her eyes as thoroughly as had determination a moment before. "So little one," she said, "how are you?"

Little one! When had I ever been called that? "Very well, ma'am," I answered absurdly.

She smiled at me and then her expression shifted, her eyes again assumed their martial energy, and she began talking to Bradley. I was relieved; her maternal words somehow strained the moment we had had in the hotel.

The others arrived, and the only thing worth noting about their perfunctory arrival, greeting, and seating arrangements was that the wonderful man who had smiled at me at the lecture was among them. Knight Ludlow, financier, nodded at me with incomplete recognition and turned away—then turned back and smiled with full acknowledgment of our last contact.

He turned from me again to talk to Granite, and the room fractured, my ears were filled with the buzz of my own internal circuitry, and I was afraid that the building was going to collapse, catch fire, or be struck with lightning.

Fortunately I went emotionally blank—I say fortunately because the meeting was beginning and my mind is more acute when my feelings are gone.

"Let me introduce to you our new secretary, Dorothy Never." The standing Granite indicated me with a sweep of her arm. "She will be taking notes as the meeting progresses." She then gazed at me, exuding support and confidence. "You understand, Dorothy, I don't want you to take it down word for word; it would be too much. Just the important ideas, yes?" I nodded, heart in throat. I had never taken dictation before.

Granite stood and paced the room as she talked, her cape framing her, a cigarette sprouting from an elegant arm. She spoke at length while the others listened, and I plunged blindly into that state of refined consciousness necessary for taking dictation or any other highly concentrated task. So many words so quickly! All of them seemed to be important! Granite's phrases were so complicated, by the time I had determined that something was important, and went back to retrieve it, I found that other important words had bounded far ahead of me and I was thus in a continual breathless chase. I trembled, my hand sweated and ached, I wanted to cry, I can't do it! I can't! But fast after this feeling came another, a deep dark surge of "Oh yes you can" that seemed to come from my lower body, my stomach, ovaries, and bowels. It was a proud, stubborn, angry feeling that made me picture a harsh thin-lipped mouth setting itself in determination. My will, usually wandering my body in various pieces, suddenly coalesced, and I waded among the words like a Viking in a foreign swamp, sword aloft, striking hither and yon, mercilessly, instinctively, without analyzing whether or not they were important. I felt my pupils dilate. The others began to talk.

"But, theoretically, society is made up of many individuals," said the woman banker. "Theoretically one could pose the problem that it is the violation of many individuals when one imposes his will—"

"Bosh! Illogic!"

"Hitler, Anna, Hitler. Fascism is the antithesis of individuality, yet Hitler was an individual who imposed his will—"

"You have answered the question yourself, Wilma. Hitler was a weak collectivist as is clear from his doctrine of the *Volk*, the blood, the irrational belief in the innate superiority of a nationality. This belief in and of itself is anti-individual."

"It is something you will have to deal with, Anna." Him! His voice! "As well as the misconception that thieves and thugs are truly acting selfishly."

After the first hours had passed, my frayed perception forked into two—one navigating the landscape of words, phrases, and ideas, the other absorbing the sounds, inflections, and tonal habits of the voices. This secondary perception transmuted words and phrases into sounds that took on shapes of gentleness, aggression, hardness, softness, pride, and happiness, shapes that moved through the room, changing and reacting to one another, swelling and shrinking, nosing against the furniture, filling the apartment with their mobile, invisible, contradicting vibrancy, then fading away.

With a half-conscious puzzlement I absorbed these sounds; Wilma Humple and Wilson Bean did not sound like I would've expected, and their voices often seemed to contradict their words.

"We don't have to placate anyone," said Dr. Bean. Yet his voice had the dry raspy sound of defeat and passivity; it moved sluggishly, with a great aggrieved effort.

"Of course," said Wilma Humple, "there is the issue of judgment—the indoctrination of 'judge not lest ye be judged,' the willful paralyzation of the intellect!" She projected the words stridently, but there was an effort in her projection that was like a child yanking its mother's hem and whining, afraid it won't be heard.

Of the three strangers, only Knight's voice was full and buoyant; it reminded me of the easeful support a body of water, miles deep and full of ferocity, can give a human relaxed enough to trust it.

I sat among these diverse energies feeling them clashing against and complementing each other while my mind resolutely held its beam of light on the business at hand. It was beginning to be difficult to go on when Granite called for a break. There was a moment of silence during which Granite lit another cigarette, and then Wilma H. and Wilson B. rose and paced to the windows. Granite asked if anyone was hungry. I was, but when everyone said they weren't, I was too embarrassed to say so. Granite sat near Knight on the couch, and they talked. I was surprised to see a girlish quality come into her face as they spoke; she even slid her feet out of her shoes and flirtily tucked her legs up against her body in my mother's habitual way.

"How're you doing, champ?" Bradley spoke kindly, leaning towards me with an elbow on his knee.

I cringed a little at "champ." "Okay I think."

"Are you able to keep up with the discussion?"

"Pretty much." It amazed me that he was adopting such a comradely attitude and that I took to it so naturally.

"Ah! Dorothy!" Granite got to her feet and into her shoes and joined us on the couch, very close to me. Once again I noticed the dull grainy texture of her skin, the multitude of tiny lines; then I made myself widen my focus to take in the fullness of her face. "You are doing well?" Her eyes were gentle but serious.

"I think so. Would you like to look?"

"Yes, I would." She took my notebook from my hand! I was reminded of the gravity of my position as I watched her eyes rapidly traverse my pages. Her jaw twitched passionately. Bradley and Knight began to chat.

"Pretty good for your first time," said Granite turning to me. "But you are wasting time with asides and extra words. Then you have to waste time crossing out, see?" She pointed to a nasty knot of ink. "Listen as if you were a reporter and wanted to find the main points of this discussion." She emphasized the last six words with a measured up-and-down movement of her hand, fingers bunched together, hooklike. "Also don't worry about the handwriting. I don't need to read it, you are the one who will type it out. Understand?"

"Yes but I . . . I don't know if I'm capable of deciding which are the important points."

"Dorothy!" Her eyes blazed! "That is a weak statement and unworthy of you!" Her severity pinned me through the eyeballs, and we sat staring at each other, she discharging bolt after bolt of sharp indignation. I felt my pores dilate helplessly to receive her until the tissue beneath my facial skin seemed composed of her indignation. Then abruptly she softened. "I know I can trust your judgment. Can you trust mine?"

"Of course!"

"Good." She spoke this word with wonderful finality. "Carry on." These last two words she said with a certain childishness, almost as if she'd heard them recently on TV and had been waiting for a chance to say them, but I didn't mind. The meeting resumed and so did I, my pen flying with renewed vigor. Hours passed. The ashtrays were gradually loaded with pale gray refuse. Wilma's face became soft and ivory with sleepiness, the men took off their jackets and rolled up their sleeves, and still Granite paced and talked. I thought of malteds and potato chips, jelly beans and roast beef sandwiches dripping gravy. I pressed on.

It was one thirty when the meeting ended and I was released into a yellow cab dispatched especially for me. Bradley actually stepped out of his conversation with the still-pacing Granite and offered to go down in the elevator and wait for it with me under the awning of the apartment.

"No, Bradley, it's all right, finish your discussion." Knight was suddenly behind me, manning the buttons of his coat. "I'll take the young lady down, I'm ready to go."

It seemed as though Wilma jerked her head in surprise, but that only added to the pleasure of the whirring fluorescent descent, during which I could not once raise my eyes. I looked at the buttons on my cheap red corduroy jacket and at Knight's shoes, his wonderful sharp-toed gray suede shoes.

He said, "I remember you from the lecture."

I said, "Yes."

"I was very moved by your response."

I gestured with a hand. "I couldn't help it," I murmured at my buttons.

"Yes I know. That's what made it so moving."

I looked up in surprise. The door burst open. We

proceeded through the lobby out into the damp night where the taxi awaited. He opened the door of the car for me, and I got in, looking at him for the first time. According to his face he did this sort of thing all the time. "See you tomorrow, Dorothy."

"Goodnight," I gasped. I was sealed into the cab in a state of shock, staring at the smiling jiggling hula girl on the dashboard and glad to be sitting down. I thought of my former high school companions sitting around their lunch table in their pink and chartreuse skirts, the occasional triangle of pantie, their "Luv" pendants, their stupid dates and proms. Which of them would ever have what I had now?

I rode home obsessively noting the tatty little buildings of Philadelphia, the romance of neon, fluorescence and electricity, even the traffic lights swaying heavily on their wires, the hydrants, the jumbled angles, the splayed newspapers flapping against public benches. I wanted to remember every detail of this night and reconstruct it in miniature, a tiny world into which I could repair at any time.

Beau and I went to the meeting the next night and the next. They followed the same pattern; Granite would prowl the room in her cape, expounding, while the others constructed rhetorical arguments for her to refute or expand upon. I picked out the main points rather timidly the second night and then, emboldened by Granite's approval, more cavalierly the third. Now confortable with what I was doing, I had, to my delight, more time to observe and digest what was going on.

My first observation was the tension between Bradley and Granite. I noticed first that he was the only one of the group from whom she would accept contradiction. Further, when he spoke, her composure fell from her in delicate shudders, leaving her gentle, soft-mouthed, eyes bright and wide. And when she spoke to him, he seemed subtly to expand, to emanate heat, to release some muscles and tense others, as if her voice simultaneously stroked and tickled the length of his body.

Second was that Wilma and Wilson did not radiate any of the energy the others had. Wilson in particular seemed to sit in a patch of personal cold, his thin limbs held stiffly, his comments merely affirmations or repetitions of what Granite had said. To my surprise, Granite didn't seem to mind or even to notice; she treated his contributions as seriously as she did Knight's. Even more puzzling, when Wilma sallied forth, Granite barely acknowledged her or sometimes even scolded her unfairly, it seemed to me. Wilma's pointy brittle face would remain impassive, perhaps tighten a little more, but she never argued.

The philosophy itself was wonderful. Most of it was an elucidation of the points I had already understood from *The Bulwark* and *The Gods Disdained,* but on the third night, a topic was introduced that I hadn't yet encountered: the ultra-real, the apparently patternless structure of the universe that seems random and chaotic (causing some people to despair and turn to religion or nihilistic philosophy) but was in fact a super-rational pattern too intricate to be discerned and comprehended by us right away.

The meetings lasted until one or two o'clock in the morning, and I returned to my bed so stimulated it was hard for me to sleep right away. I was thus sleeping only about four hours a night and skipping my dinner (I considered the sandwich Bradley ordered from work a snack). The happy result was that, for the first time in my life, I was losing weight. The waistbands of my skirts were sliding towards my hips, and my only pair of pants fit loosely. My appearance hadn't noticeably changed, but I nonetheless rejoiced.

On the fifth night, however, my stamina began to give out. One o'clock then two o'clock came and went, and still Granite discussed. At two thirty Wilson Bean went home. At three Bradley retired into Granite's bedroom for a nap. Fifteen minutes later Knight rested in an easy chair to close his eyes. For the next interminable half-hour, it was only Granite, me and the haggard Wilma. The air was heavy with swarming yellow granules, all light was an assault. To my dismay, I saw my dictation stumble, get up, stumble, and proceed along on its knees. Every sentence was a marathon with a lung-bursting explosion at the end. Wilma curled up on the couch and went under. Granite turned to me.

"And how are you feeling, Dorothy?" Her eyes were encircled with bruise-like purple but they retained their intensity. I felt her hot noisy heart pumping in her chest and my own dull organ making its reply. "Are you tired?"

"Yes, Anna, I am." My blood roared in my head; I had involuntarily used her first name.

"Yes, I can see." She leaned forward and turned away, and I thought she was displeased. Then she turned back. "I would like to offer you something to help you stay awake. But only if you want it, you understand?"

"What is it?"

"It" was two small capsules (half midnight blue, half aquamarine) that made me feel as wide awake as I had ever felt in my life. Together Granite and I outlasted everyone, smiling and waving goodbye as one by one, Wilma, Knight, and Bradley expressed their regrets. Indeed, at the very end it was I who fiercely paced the floor taking notes in motion while Granite lay on the couch soliloquizing, cigarette held aloft.

It was seven thirty when she finally gave me my cab fare. "You have pleased me, Dorothy," she said, and I sailed out into the celebratory sun full of get up and go. It was a Saturday, but instead of going home to sleep I went to a large diner with a sparkling, kidney-shaped counter and ordered french toast. I ate slowly as my usually receptive stomach was still taut with excitement. (I didn't make the connection between the pills and appetite loss.)

I looked with great interest at the other people at the diner, thinking about the oddness of fate. Who would think from looking at me as I sat mopping up syrup that I had just, of my own initiative, become part of the greatest intellectual vanguard in the country? I looked at the man just across from me. He was only in his late twenties, I guessed, but grizzled and jowly with tough skin and dully thoughtful eyes. He had a crouched, guarded way of sitting that was wary, weary, and sluggish, yet, because of an alertness in his neck and head, he looked capable of sudden quite vigorous action. I wished I could talk philosophy with him. He looked at me.

"You're a cute little girl," he said.

I stared.

"Do you have a boyfriend?"

"No," I answered. "I don't. I've never had a boyfriend."

"Really?" He picked up a triangle of dark toast and bit off half of it, chewing with loose, loopy movements. "That's a shame. I'd offer to be your boyfriend myself but I'm too old and you're not interested." He looked sadly off into space. "You've got great tits though," he added morosely.

I knew most people would think this was a rude

thing to say, but considering that no one had ever described any portion of my body as "great," it was hard to view it that way, especially given the wistful tone in which it was said. I started to say "Thank you" but then considered how Solitaire D'Anconti would react to such a remark and flushed with embarrassment to think I'd almost been flattered by it. I glowered in the mirror behind the counter, making my features as cold and imperious as possible while surreptitiously checking to see if there was anything there that could reasonably be described as "cute." Drained face, wild burning eyes, pale fat too-wide mouth.

"You don't have to say anything," continued the man, pulling apart his toast with a certain magnanimous air.

I fled to the comparative serenity of the Euella Parks Hotel.

I slept most of the morning and all afternoon but still found myself a little groggy when it was time to return to Granite's apartment at six (she ran the meetings through the weekends). I had barely enough time to heat a can of soup on my hot plate and eat it, along with a few pieces of bread, before rushing out. That night and on many of the nights that followed—whenever the conferences went past one'clock—Granite would secretly share with me one or two of her heavenly midnight and aqua capsules. My dictation became ever more quick and sure, my demeanor so optimistic that at times I feared I was losing my mind. I was sometimes so full of energy when I left Granite's apartment that I walked to my hotel instead of taking the taxi. Knight continued to escort me to the taxi on the nights when we left at the same time and my pill-induced enthusiasm elbowed my shyness to one side. Sometimes when the cab pulled away I would look out the back window and see him turning in the other direction, presumably to walk to his apartment, or perhaps to take a bus. I viewed him romantically, but not with the expectation that anything sexual could happen between us; that didn't occur to me. It was enough for me to be the recipient of his gallant attention, his smiles, his almost tangible warmth and goodwill. Then something happened to awaken another need which, although it initially awoke with only the feeblest twitch, continued to twitch with larger and larger movements until I saw that it was only the smallest foreclaw of a beast that, once fully aroused, would scream unabated day and night—then sleep again forever.

One evening I arrived at Granite's apartment so exhausted that I didn't think I could successfully pick out main points. For the first time I asked her for a pill and she gave it to me. Thus, even though it was only twelve thirty when the meeting broke up, I left with my brain chattering enthusiastically to itself and my body full of energy. When Knight performed his usual courtly gesture, I stopped outside on the pavement and told him I thought I'd walk home.

"By yourself?" he wondered.

"Yeah. Maybe I'll give the cabbie some money so he won't be upset." I did so, shut the door in his muttering face, and returned to my Knight.

"How far away do you live?"

"It takes about half an hour to walk it." We both watched as the cabbie tooled off into the night.

"Do you think it's safe for you to—"

"Mr. Ludlow," I said. "I'm, I, I'm grateful for your concern but I'm really not afraid. I've done it before, even later. I know I must seem very ordinary to you but—"

"No you don't," he murmured.

I hesitated. My stimulated heart ground away, my

stimulated brain spewed words. "Well, I'm not. After what I've experienced, I doubt that anything on the late-night streets of Philadelphia could throw me for a loop." Knight looked at me as if I'd said something curious and very cute. My confidence suddenly felt like a heavy, high structure creaking on a flimsy base. I stared at the sidewalk.

"Well, maybe you'd let me walk you home. I'm feeling pretty stirred up and energetic myself. Besides, I'm a terrible insomniac."

I agreed out of passivity more than anything else; it discomfited me, this familiarity and friendliness. I would have preferred that he remain at a distance, gallant but within prescribed boundaries. I didn't understand why he wanted to step over those boundaries for me. I'd seen movies in which important handsome financiers became smitten by little secretaries—but those little secretaries looked like Judy Garland and Doris Day, not like me. As we walked, however, my feelings began to change. He didn't rush into conversation; he didn't talk at all. He simply walked along, hands behind his back, emitting grace combined with that full and buoyant quality I'd heard in his voice— and now, unlike in the meetings, it was suffused with warmth. I enjoyed his presence in spite of myself. My hopped-up mind spewed words which, since I was too shy to talk, tunneled through my brain and doubled back out until my head was riddled with unspoken words. My thoughts roiled around in such a convoluted way that I wondered how I ever spoke at all. I wished Knight would talk to me.

"Tell me," he said. "How did you come to work for Anna Granite? I know she just met you the night I saw you."

So our conversation began. As soon as they found an opening, the words rolled out in proper form, only more freely than usual. I told him that my life at home had been unbearable, but not why. I expanded more on my life at college, ending with my appearance before Granite.

Then he talked about his life, which included leaving home at the age of sixteen to escape an alcoholic father. This prompted me to ask him questions about his apparently quick rise to success at age thirty-three. I had never had a conversation like this before. Every sentence, from him or me, felt new, wobbly, and vulnerable, waving in the air between us like tiny ant limbs. I felt frightened that I would say something wrong, uncertain as to what was appropriate between relative strangers. I tried to stay with the facts, but even so every new phrase added more footage to a bridge, the length and direction of which I couldn't predict. But despite my anxiety, his voice, as much as the pills, drew me further and further into conversation, unable to resist brushing against this foreign element of gentle strength.

When we reached my hotel, he said good night, smiled, and left. I mounted the stairs to my room, my words and feelings still extended from me like a limb groping the air for something no longer there. I entered my small suite, removed my shoes, dropped my handbag, and walked through the room in the dark to the bathroom (the toilet rather; there was a communal shower in the hall). I turned on the light, stood before the full-length mirror, and, in that narrow space, slowly stripped off my clothes until I was naked except for my socks. I stood for several moments looking, as if I were an adolescent girl just developing breasts. I didn't look to see whether I was attractive or not, I just looked.

Then I turned off the light and got in bed.

The next day, during lunch hour, I used some of

my new financial abundance (Granite's already generous wage was increased with all the overtime) to buy two new skirts, two shirts, and a pair of pants. All were two delightful sizes smaller than my conspicuously loose-fitting older clothes. I also bought a paper, which I immediately folded to highlight the rental ads. I sat at my desk reading coded descriptions of "sunny efficiencies" and "furnished 1 bedrm.," my new clothes bundled in exciting bags under the desk, where I could squeeze them between my knees.

That night the dynamic of the conference was rearranged by Knight's new proximity to me; all night I felt the friendly tug of his warmth, the silent communication of the invisible antennae tickling the air between us. I felt something open in my body, something like a rare flower that absorbs molecules, pheromones, and oxygen, then secretes them in a glittering membrane of vibrancy, fecundity, and power, a membrane that quivered tautly every time Knight's image came into my mind.

The meetings that week didn't run as late as they had previously, and Knight walked me home three times. Each time we sent up new flares which left streams of colored light between us, until there was a cat's cradle of crisscrossing beams that swayed between us.

On the third walk, I asked him, as we stood outside my hotel, why he had said the previous week that I didn't seem ordinary to him.

"Something in your face," he replied. "There's an unusual combination in your expressions. Sometimes you're so blank and remote, you're impossible to read. Other times your eyes are so soft and emotional. But also strong. I think you're very strong."

He stood, serious and tense. I had the almost physical sensation that he was going to stroke my face. My skin drew tight.

"Good night," he said.


*Fourteen years later,* I sat before a legal document, staring into space, stroking my own face with my hand. I had been thinking obsessively of Knight Ludlow for a week, probably because I had seen his picture on a page of the *Times,* which had been pulled apart and spread open on a table in the cafeteria. He was still handsome. He had just been named financial advisor to the mayor of New York City. This information, along with the auxiliary information in the article (which did not mention Anna Granite), put me in a melancholy state, and I wandered the abandoned halls for a good half hour before returning to my station, staring with disbelief at the tiny stuffed animals and smiling pictures on the desks of secretaries. Who among my co-workers would believe me, if I should choose to tell them, that this man had once stood with me late at night, talking to me about the expression in my eyes? I went into a ladies room on the other side of the building where I was unlikely to be interrupted. I stood before a full-length mirror and looked at my huge body, even lifting up my skirt and rolling down my pantyhose to examine the pocked layer of cellulite on my thighs and butt. I looked at it a long time, wondering that this puckered yellow flesh was actually me.

It is probable that the stirred memory of Knight Ludlow played a role in my finally acting on my repeated resolutions to join a gym. I didn't feel as embarrassed as I'd expected, wading in wearing my monstrous cotton sweats. At first I restricted myself to the weight area, the largest place in the gym. The weight area was prowled by huge muscular men in stylish leotards adorned with enormous leather belts at their waists, who looked straight ahead as they walked and showed their teeth as they strained to lift. Our endeavors were performed in decorous silence far from the disco-throbbing aerobics room where squadrons of little creatures leapt and kicked. It was a calming, contemplative experience to be part of the rising and lowering, continually slow-moving machinery, and no one laughed at me struggling with my light weight.

The experience—especially the fascinating dressing room, everyone with their interesting underwear, their unpredictable body combinations, their fussy animal-like grooming rituals—was an active bustling island on the slumbering sea of my daily life, and a reason to wake up. I now looked out my window at the boy exercisers across the street with camaraderie and felt my new-forming muscles.

I had been going for two weeks when I gave in to my curiosity and stood at the aerobics room door watching the classes. They weren't all little creatures. Many were middle-aged and plump, a few were men. There was a certain high-chested majesty in their synchronous movements, their bright outfits were emblematic of sex and fun, the music sang about love and destiny and feverish pleading. The teacher, a beautiful black woman with rosy purple-hued skin, paced among the exercisers crying out, "Up and down, up and down, that's right, that's right, you got it!" her voice like crimson roses burning in the air. I watched voyeuristically, knowing I was peeping at people in the middle of a collective dream. I imagined myself among them, part of the regimental dance, the teacher's rosy heat, the huge mobile hope of happiness and vitality. And as I watched, it suddenly occurred to me I had been merely watching the world all my life. I was angered at the banality of this obser-

vation and walked away from the aerobics room to
push some metal poundage with all my might.


*After Knight described my face* to me, the cataclysm occurred. My sense of a flower living inside me was torn
to pieces and lost forever; I fell in love. The most striking thing about love was its terrible nature. My guts
became black and void with dread while my outermost
flesh came alive with darting insect dots of energy that
boiled under my skin, as if my blood and organs were
trying to get out of my body. My thoughts cracked to
pieces that banged against my skull again and again,
yielding up image after strange, confusing image. I
would see Knight's face smiling at me from that part
of the world where pleasure and companionship were
the norm; then I would feel the darkness of my deep
body go into a slow rolling motion, like the root of a
wave in the pit of the ocean or a silent internal moan;
then I would see my own hand plunging a knife into
my throat. At night I would get under the blankets
and think of him. My insides would soften, my awareness would sink down into my lower body, my pelvis
would open and expand, and then a convulsion would
come from nowhere, and I would emerge from it shivering. I would touch between my legs; my genitals felt
like a foreign object. I would lie this way for hours, unable to move until exhaustion pulled me into a sleep
populated with Anna Granite, Bradley, the Philadelphia bus system, Nona Delgado and my father, always
my father, holding me in an iron grip, his penis, like
rotted meat, pressed against me. I would wake up full
of fear and sit with the lights on while my thoughts
formed and cracked into pieces. And riding a crazy
car around these images and thoughts, screaming and
chattering, or just plain staring, were the people I had

to talk to on the phone at the office, my fellow travelers on the bus, Wilson Bean and Wilma Humple, store clerks, and criminals staring at me from newspaper pages.

I knew this agony had come out of my contact with Knight, yet all I wanted was to be near him. I sat at the meeting absorbing him, pulling his psychic excretions into my body. I told time according to when I might talk to him during a break in the meeting or when he might walk me home.

I don't remember if I longed to hold him in my arms or to feel him inside me. I do know I wanted to be alone in a room with him. It was to this end that I left (not without a pang of sentiment) the Euella Parks Hotel and rented a room. It was a furnished walkup with a private kitchen and bathroom in the hall. The landlady was a rigid white creature wearing a hairnet and a dress covered with nasty flowers; she tried to be pleasant, but she was too unhappy to make it stick. It didn't matter; the place had a certain charm, in spite of a greasy stain on the wall. There was sun, blue wallpaper, flower boxes outside the windows, a quilt on the double bed. In addition to the room, I acquired more new clothes, makeup, and a hair cut.

The night I moved into my new home I didn't get into bed to sleep. I spent the entire night before the mirror trying on clothes and makeup. A young body can withstand a great deal of stress and abuse without showing exhaustion. A few judicious smears of makeup under my eyes erased the circles forming there, pink liquid freshened my cheeks. My weight loss was apparent, and my features had emerged from my face. They fascinated me, although I wasn't yet sure if I liked them or not. My eyes were large without the surrounding fat, my big lips, instead of adding to the previously exaggerated impression of roundness and slackness, added an interesting dimension to the sharpened planes of my chin and cheeks. The shorter hair drew the movement of my face upward and made my skin appear to open out in radiant petals.

Knight came closer; we crossed the catwalks between us and explored our respective inner girdings. He told me about his childhood. I told him everything about mine, except the one thing. We went to the all night diner where the man had told me I had great tits. It was there, over pieces of wonderfully gooey apple pie, that, during our discussion of ultrareality, a phrase leapt from his mouth and shot into the air between us, urgently flashing. It was "my fiancée in New York." This flashing sign effectively obscured the rest of the conversation for several minutes. Knight continued talking, happily manipulating his fork to get maximum corn syrup on it. His words fell one atop the other, forming a senseless pile. I felt myself moving away from him in a square section that became smaller and more distant in evenly spaced pulses, like a photograph inset within a larger photograph. My tiny hands played with sugar packets. Far away, Knight moved his lips in crazy silence. Then I opened my mouth, breathed in and ate the fiancée. Vaguely remembering that Asia Maconda, Katya Leonova, and Solitaire D'Anconti all had more than one lover, I swallowed the fiancée information and held it down. It dissolved in my stomach pretty quickly. I ate my pie and smiled at Knight's ultrareality. We left the diner, and I invited him up to see my new apartment. It was two o'clock Saturday morning. He hesitated only seconds before he said yes.

I don't think I can chronicle the combination of words, silences, and movements that led to him and me on my bed with our arms around each other. Rather awkwardly he stroked my hair, felt up and down my spine, and adjusted himself against me. He said, "This may not be fair to you, Dorothy. I know I should've mentioned Angela before." I shook my head, my eyes half closed. There was more talk but it was immaterial before the feelings emanating from him, the strength and gentleness, warmth and control, the mystery of masculine tenderness that enveloped me like the wings of a swan. We lay on my bed, his body supporting itself above me. The ricocheting chatter in my mind became inaudible, the zipping comets of quasi thought slowed to melting putty. Rivulets of liquid gold, swollen with nodules of heat, spanned my limbs. A glimmering flower of blood and fire bloomed between my legs, its petals spanned my thighs. He kissed me. He put his genitals against me. I contracted; all the light in my body went out. I had a sensation of falling and then a sudden jerking halt, as if I were a mountain climber who had slipped and been caught in my harness, swaying above a chasm. Knight moved his lips over my face, he put a hand on my breast. My brief desire was dead. I shuddered and grabbed his shoulder. He misunderstood and touched between my legs. I thought: If I control my body and follow his movements, everything will be all right, I'll be able to do it. Then he raised himself and looked into my face. "What's wrong?" he asked. "Why are you crying?"

I moved my hand to my face and felt tears. There was an instant of silence, and then I began to cry in earnest. He moved away from me; I had a glimpse of his stricken expression before I rolled on my stomach and curled into a ball. More words: "I'm sorry baby, I don't want to hurt you, forgive me," stuff like that. I gestured irritably. At that moment he seemed almost stupid to me. My heart froze in a desperate palpitation, and I stopped crying.

"It's all right." I sat up. "It doesn't have anything to do with Angela."

He looked surprised. "What is it then?"

I didn't know, but I told him anyway. He sat solemnly nodding while I talked about my devotion to Anna Granite and how I didn't want to be distracted from the important work of her project with an emotional entanglement. I talked about my feelings of friendship for him and how I didn't want to risk ruining them. I told him I'd never had a lover before, which felt true until the image of my father gestured from a corner. I ignored him, continued talking over him, talking about my feelings of respect for Knight's relationship with Angela. Knight continued nodding, every now and then interjecting a declaration or protestation of his own. My father stood mute, listening to me talk. Finally I couldn't talk anymore. Knight talked a little longer while I picked the stuffing from a small hole in the quilt. My body felt wooden. I wished he would go. He stopped talking and sat as though waiting for me to say something. I scanned a list of sentences appropriate for getting him out the door. Then I thought that if he left I would be alone with my father.

"Well," he said standing up. "Guess it's time for me to go."

I cast about for words.

"Dorothy? Are you all right?"

I lunged for a word; it slid away. I began to cry again.

Slowly, I told him. After much more talk, deep under the quilt with our arms around each other, I told him about my father and me. I felt as if there were a hole in my chest and that Knight could look into it as I had once looked into the opened brain of the strange boy sitting in our kitchen. But just as I had felt tenderly protective towards the boy and his poor exposed brain, I felt Knight's tenderness penetrating my wound, curling around my ribs, touching against the vulnerable red sponge of my lungs, mournfully stroking my heart hiding in its dark nest of muscle.

It was six o'clock when we turned off the light and lay down. We lay under the quilt with most of our clothes on. My back was against his front, and he curled his body around me, his strangely small hand holding my elbow. I lay for hours feeling his eyelashes rise and lower against my shoulder, more and more slowly as his breath took him into sleep. My breath slowed and deepened with his, and I lay with my eyes shut watching long loops of gray move around my head. I opened my eyes. Shadows crawled and crept. Knight's penis hardened as he slept, and with a pretty moan, he pressed it against my lower spine before falling back into unconsciousness. I took in the feel of it experimentally. It seemed helplessly outgoing and vulnerable in its blind swollen state, yet fussily and ardently friendly. City sounds and voices came through the window at quickening intervals; the bread truck and its cheerful driver firing jokes into space, the grumbling answer of the restauranteur, the brisk hum of passing cars, the bus doing its noisy duty. Knight's little hand twitched on my arm. All the bones, ligaments, skin, and nerves that felt these things seemed precious to me, and I wanted to stay awake so I could feel them hanging in the hammock of my exhaustion for as long as possible. Knight's dick sat on my spine with all the dumb insistence of life, and I felt accompanied on my vigil.

We spent several nights in this way, until a week after the meetings ended and he had to return to New York. I received one letter from him. The web that connected us, its shimmering gossamer spanning even the state border, finally broke and disintegrated. During the next few years I saw him occasionally at various Definitist gatherings—sometimes with his fiancée, who became his wife. She was a tall, big-thighed thing with thrusting breasts and quick eyes, and she looked at me as if she knew what had gone on. It didn't matter. He would fix his eyes on mine with affectionate pain, he would take my hand, and I would feel as I had when he escorted me down to the waiting cab; distant from him and smaller, but connected by respect and gentleness, even though I had put back all the weight I lost during the fevered meeting period and gained yet more weight.

It is strange that I didn't feel abandoned and betrayed, particularly since, on our last night together, we became lovers. It was unexpected. My body awoke from a shallow sleep suffused with heat, and I pressed myself against him. This time I didn't become frightened, and we continued. His face swam over mine, his breath coiled in my ear. He nestled his body more snugly between my legs. "All right?" he gasped. I arched against him in hopelessly incomplete meeting. My head became a vague blur, my body a thousand cuplike doors opened to receive him. Drool ran in my mouth; I said yes, my voice rising through my body to emerge from my lips a barely audible breath. His fingers gently pulled my stiff nipples, and the outer petals of my vagina crimsoned and curled inward, burned by their own heat. My womb became a supple muscle of fire, expanded and soft, strong as life. I'm going to do it I thought, and in my mind I leapt. Then he penetrated my knot of fiery muscle, and my body went away from me. In my mind were images of my body, arched and abandoned, my neck thrown back, like a surrendering animal, giving to him all the helpless, ferocious, wounded love in my life. Because I wanted so much to give my life to him, even if it were just a moment of it. But my body, still inwardly burning, moved away from me. I could not feel what it experienced and so could not give my experience to him. Hesitant, he pushed farther in, as if he were frightened. My heart hammered in my throat. He pushed deeper. Pleasure rose up through the distance between me and my body and expired. Moaning in sorrow, I held it close as it faded. He kissed my neck; his full, tender, buoyant spirit entered my skin and for an instant I felt my body alive again beneath him.

So it went, the shy beginning and aborted end of pleasure. When it was over I lay confused and relieved in his arms. The next morning he took me in a taxi to a beautiful restaurant with huge feverish bursts of flowers on every table. We ordered champagne with our omelettes. He left the following day.

The next time I saw him, a year and seven months later, I thought with disbelief that this person, so radiant and handsome, had stuck one of his body parts into me, pulled it out, and stuck it in again, over and over. It was wonderful, but I was glad it was never going to happen again. I preferred the elegance of distance, bridged only by an occasional hand touch, which, as the expression of all emotional language, became more eloquent than the confusing overkill of complete body contact.

Last to go were those moments, scattered throughout the years, when I lay alone in bed, motionless except for the hand wandering between my legs, recalling the feel of his eyelashes against my skin, his breath in my ear, his weight, his genitals. Memory playfully tickled my flesh, but the flesh remained indifferent; my mind would wander to something I'd seen on the street that day, radio jingles would fly by, memory would falter and fail.

Sometimes I tried to excite myself by focusing on the love scenes between Granite's characters and then putting Knight and me in their places. But the swollen blossoms of passion described in Granite's novels couldn't accommodate the scratchy old image of Knight's body on mine or the strange attendant mix of cold, heat, terror, love, and need.

Gradually I stopped trying.


*Longingly I stood and watched* the sweating exercisers, slowly rising and lowering, their hands on their hips, their feet flat and thighs spread. Were they people who had had tragic lives, broken love affairs, murdered children, who had, up until quite recently, spent the bulk of their time lying in darkened rooms, just now able to summon the strength to get into their leotards and jump up and down? Some of them looked slightly pathetic in the dressing room, in spite of their rigorous training. There was the thin girl with sharp raw elbows and eyes so one-dimensional in their wounded uncertainty that people probably victimized her reflexively; in the dressing room, she revealed the thick, layered toenails of a dinosaur. Or the gum-chewing young blonde with her bleached hair tortured up on her head and a set of bright rings through her nose, who presented herself, with her ripped flamboyant clothing, as a jangling icon of aggression and mobility, but who sat like a matron, her heavy breasts drooping in her tatty, loose-fitting bra. Or the frail creature with her shoulders hunched as if she was expecting the blows of a whip, burdened with ugly, static, artificial breasts, from which the rest of her body seemed to droop. Did their bodies really register terrible pain, or was I, my own body so muffled in inert fat, simply imagining it? What would it be like to hold one of these complexly injured animals in your arms? Would you feel her slowly come to life as you stroked her bony back, would the innocent ugliness of her toenails scrape you as she murmured in delight, would you see her eyes suddenly expand into beauty as they made room for all the treasures of expression she had held trapped in her frightened heart?

The music asked, "Straight up now tell me do you really wanna love me forever/oh oh oh/Or am I caught in a hit and run?" I kept standing there, inexplicably thinking of Justine Shade and what her problems might be.

*Justine had just awakened* in the hellish but reassuringly familiar suburb of Hangover. Her eyeballs hurt, her vision was static, the mucus in the passages of her head had turned to mud. Insects with many slow-moving legs patrolled her skin. The inside of her mouth and her upper digestive tract felt as if she'd spent the last six hours valiantly vomiting to counter an unsuccessful poisoning attempt. Other than that, she had no idea where she was, and worse, what time it might be. She pictured herself fumbling with the EKG machine, explaining to old Mrs. Hoffenbacher that she was a little hung over; she wondered if the comic element of the situation might mitigate her clumsiness, her possible odor. At the sound of a flushing toilet she lifted her concrete head, squinting into the planes of light and shade that filled the room. A human entered wearing nothing but rumpled socks. He sat on the bed she was prostrate on and said, "I don't know about you, but I have to be at work in forty minutes." Considering the personal nature of the memories that now unfolded in her skull, memories in which this naked person had a lot of prominence, she felt his words were pretty cold. "Don't I even get a kiss?" she rasped.

He pinched his wrinkly face together. "No. But I'll get you coffee if you want. I'm going down to the take-out."

He slowly picked his clothing off the floor and pieced together his own personal puzzle of how to put it on. She fell into a reverie of the recent events between them. She didn't think she'd ever committed such pornographic acts before.

He was moving heavily out the door, a bleary and oppressed look on his face. She sat for a moment, her energies divided between trying to figure out if she were upset or not and attempting to support her monstrous head. A hostile clock said "8:30," and she was struck with fear and shame about failing Glenda and the helpless Mrs. Hoffenbacher.

She was fully dressed by the time he had returned with two cups of hot coffee and a bag of sugars, stirrers, and petroleum milk substitutes. She was waiting for him with uncomfortable questions. He smiled, a bright spark showing deep in the murk of his tired eyes. "Good morning," he said. "It's a nice day out." He sat next to her on the edge of the bed, leaned and kissed her mouth from the side. "I had fun last night," he said. "You did too."

With a conspiratorial air they prepared their coffees, resting the full cups precariously on the rumpled bed while, with mouselike movements, they opened the packets of sugar and petroleum byproducts. Her questions dissolved in the warmth of the moment; she loved the familiarity imparted by having coffee together in the morning. They made small talk and jokes. He hailed a cab for her and kissed her as she got into it. She took it to her apartment, asked the cabby to wait, and remembered, as she ran up the hall stairs to change her clothes, that he couldn't call her, as he'd said he would, because he didn't have her number. She rode to work feeling rejected and exploited.

Glenda was arranging the medical implements on the counter when Justine burst into the fluorescence of the examining room, heroically pulling on her white coat. "Sleep late?" she asked. "It's all right, I have everything under control. But could you make us some coffee?" She looked at her watch. "The doctor is late. Are you feeling well, Justine? Your eyes are very dark."

During the next fifteen minutes of routine, Glenda's presence, the familiar smells and sights, the reassuring sound of *Adventures in Good Music*—still borne along by the same mournful voice Justine had loathed as a teen!—calmed the disturbed pulse of her body and stilled her feelings of abandonment and fear. Well, she thought, he was sort of a weirdo anyway, and, as she remembered their conversation at the bar, an unpleasant one. If she was going to be upset, it should be because she'd gone home with an abusive mental case, not because he wasn't going to call her. She tried to concentrate on how lucky she was not to have to see him again and instead found herself, as she often did, mentally listing all the people she'd screwed since she'd been in Manhattan, and categorizing them in terms of the emotional quality of the experience, good, bad, or neutral. The numbers changed depending on her mood (today, almost everybody had a minus by his name; Eric had three minuses) but even at her most cheerful, there was an abundance of neutrals and bads and, out of twenty-six, only two or three grudging pluses.

No happy person would do this she thought.

Glenda moodily popped her Dexatrim with her coffee and looked at her watch. Two old ladies had come into the waiting area and were sitting with their hands on their purses. One of them, Mrs. Oliphant, walked with a cane. She was fat, and Justine imagined a life made up of the panting, sweating struggle to get from one corner of one city block to the next, your pantyhose gaping between your legs, your ankles leaden in your terrible shoes. For fleeting seconds she saw herself moving around the office like that, only caneless, her bloated legs unable to propel her frantic torso, her elongated noodle arms gesturing impotently. She recalled herself the night before, on her knees with her face pressed into the mattress, Bryan hungrily crouched over her from behind, popping his small penis in and out of her. It was the same numb image of a thousand pornographic pictures, almost consoling in its banality. Show this picture to someone, they know what you mean. His small teeth flashed in his head as he lay on his back and smiled at her. She was telling him a story about an old boyfriend of hers. Ron, a handsome musician with the big-eyed face of a teen fanzine idol, was drinking in a bar in Ypsilanti, Michigan, when he was approached by a middle-aged woman and her visibly anxious sixteen-year-old daughter. After some bewildering small talk the woman asked him to come to their home and deflower her daughter. She explained that the daughter liked him and that she, the mother, thought that he seemed okay too and wanted to supervise the event to be sure it was safe. The daughter was a frail creature wearing unfashionable glasses. Ron, who as Justine explained, was one of the nicest men she had ever been involved with, knew it was sick but he, as he phrased it, "went along with it anyway" because he felt aroused. "That girl didn't know what was happening to her," he said. "She was totally helpless. And I wolfed on her." As she quoted him she pictured him thrusting crazily at the girl on a stiffly made bed in an oblong room with square windows. The mother was waiting outside in the kitchen, sitting with her legs tightly crossed, perhaps drinking a cup of coffee.

"Did he screw the mother too?" asked Bryan interestedly.

"No. I don't think so. He left right afterwards." She imagined Ron fleeing the house as the girl sobbed on her bed, and the mother yelled at her to stop being such a baby. "In a way it was a horrible thing to do," she said. "It was horrible. But I don't blame him. It would be such an extreme, how could you not do it?"

"Yeah."

Miss Stilt, the other old lady in the room, was looking at her quizzically. Justine smiled at her. Miss Stilt was one of her first old ladies. Justine remembered her because of the way she'd stood before the small mirror in the examining room, striking at her mouth with her lipstick as she griped, "I don't know why I bother. I look like hell anyway."

"Honestly, it must be an emergency, I am going to find out," said Glenda, picking up the phone to call the hospital.

Justine thought Dr. Winkgard was probably having an affair, possibly more than one. She thought he loved and respected Glenda but that he believed it was his prerogative to screw other people in much the same way he believed it was his prerogative to keep patients sitting in his waiting room for hours. She remembered her father striding around the house talking about his scrawny broken patients, inert in their beds, totally dependent upon him, this human embodiment of vigor and health, talking as if the world were polarized into those who were weak, ill, and unhappy and those who were not. Justine would imagine him striding among the patients, dispensing wellness and energy; somehow that image became an image of her father roaring through the world in a celebratory rampage of grabbing and eating and expressing himself at the top of his lungs, saying things like, "She's only unhappy because she wants to be."

Dr. Winkgard crashed in through the front door, his eyes radiating fierce outgoing beams, his dark hair ridged against his forehead with the wetness of his morning swim.

Glenda smiled and put down the phone. Justine took Mrs. Oliphant into the examining room and waited outside for her to take off her clothes before she went in to glue and clamp her. She stepped into the bathroom, closed the door, and stood in the hum of the odor-removing fan, looking at herself in the mirror. She scanned her twenty-eight-year-old face for lines and, finding none, concentrated on how huge the pores around her nose had become in the last two years and how ugly it was.

She swam through the day just below the surface of mental alertness, bumping her head on the floating detritus of impressions and thoughts. She woke a little when she went outside to buy the muffins that Glenda and the doctor ate for lunch. Justine bought herself a bag of cookies and walked around the block, eating them out of the bag, absorbing the cacophonous energies of the people around her. A man in rags with one eye gone grabbed at her sleeve as if it were the bow of a lifeboat he was trying to pull himself into. "I'm hungry, mama," he said, "please give me a dime, a nickel, anything, please." She gave him a quarter and the rest of the cookies, and he fell back into the sea.

The most interesting moment of the day came in a

conversation with the generally taciturn Mrs. Thomas. During the cardiogram, Mrs. Thomas said, "Dr. Winkgard is the best doctor I ever had. Because he's not only a good doctor, he's a good man. When I was on the operating table and that other doctor was saying they had to amputate my breast, I could hear Dr. Winkgard fighting for me. He said, 'Don't you take away that lady's breast.' And they didn't. They did have to take a piece out of it"—she indicated the spot with her hand—"but they didn't take the whole thing. And he was right. That was two years ago, and I've been okay since."

Justine wholeheartedly agreed that Dr. Winkgard had done the right thing and left the room with a new respect for her employer. She was bewildered though that while he had been indifferent to Mrs. Rabinowitz who was beaten by her husband, he had respected Mrs. Thomas's body and protected her breast. Well, Ron had made her a birthday cake and stayed up all night massaging her head; he had also assisted a demented woman in the rape of her daughter. And she, Justine, had said she didn't blame him for doing it.

She returned home that evening with a severe headache. Her apartment seemed silent and void. She sat on the foam cushion before her low coffee table and ate a take-out salad from a plastic container. The air between her and the phone was thick and hostile. The bathroom seemed to be at the end of a treacherous tunnel even though it was only a yard or so from where she sat. Her stomach felt too tight even for chewed-up mouthfuls of salad, and she ate uncomfortably, forcing herself because it was good for her. She stared at the clothing she'd thrown on the floor that morning and decided that what had happened the night before hadn't meant anything, that the blade lodged in her chest had always been there, that this incident had just reminded her of it. She adjusted her posture to accommodate the blade and went out for a walk.

The evening was cool and vague. Justine watched everyone who walked past her, and irksome tiny facts about them entered her orbit and clustered about her head. A young couple approached her, the man with his square pink head raised as if he were looking over a horizon, his hands thrust angrily in his pockets, his slightly turned-out feet hitting the ground with dismal solidity, his cheap jacket open to his cheap shirt. The woman on his arm crouched into him slightly, her artificially curled hair bounced around her prematurely lined face, her red mouth said, "Because it's dishonest to me and to everybody and even to yourself." Justine looked headlong into the open maw of their lives; they passed, and the pit closed up again. She looked into the windows of a restaurant and saw in the various wordless postures—a man with his body close in to the table at which he sat, his elbows supporting the intimate lunge of his torso; a woman holding herself in a reserved straight-backed position; a boy displaying himself with an aloof, cross-legged twist to one side as his grinning, socializing head held forth—varying gradations of human relationship that were so strange and unreadable to her, they made her feel like a lost dog. No one accosted or terrorized her.

The next day was a short day at the office; Justine left work at one o'clock. She went to Penn Station and boarded a commuter train to Princeton, New Jersey, to visit Rationalist Reaffirmation High. She had never taken a commuter train to the suburbs before, and the visit seemed like a special outing to her. She brought a bag of cashews, a bag of marzipan, and an apple and was looking forward to eating the treats.

She was startled by the appearance of the train; she

expected anything associated with the suburbs to have a gloss of orderliness, cleanliness, and characterlessness, yet the train was a metaphor for decrepitude. Balled up potato chip bags, bottle caps, crumpled cigarette packages, and cans rolled on the floor or collected in corners under a gray gauze of dust. Foam poked out of the vinyl seat coverings. The cracked and taped-over windows had strange rattling collections of tiny paper wads, food crumbs, and unidentifiable granules in their loose-fitting casements. A businessman seated across from her put his briefcase down, pressed the recline button on his chair, leaned trustingly back, and fell into the lap of the man seated behind him.

Justine was more careful with her recline button, but there was nothing to worry about as it didn't work. How, she wondered, could suburban people tolerate such a level of disrepair? She was disconcerted to find herself thinking that perhaps, since she'd been in New York, the entire country had deteriorated as seriously as Manhattan had, that everywhere people were wading ankle-deep in rolling, rotting trash, that everywhere homeless people pissed in the streets and railed at the well-to-do who slunk shame-faced along the walls. This of course was exactly what Anna Granite had said would happen, due to weak-willed liberals and governmental meddling. For a moment she looked at the possibility of total collapse as if she were a Definitist and found the idea to be somehow dramatically and ethically satisfying.

Then the train entered the fecund green landscape of Princeton, and she was stunned by the order and prosperity, the brightly painted homes, tended gardens, and lush lawns. Flawless sidewalks ran and touched noses, big round mail boxes stood like jolly street corner burghers. Justine had grown up thinking that such neighborhoods were normal places where most people lived, yet this neighborhood seemed foreign and mythic.

Max Nolte, a teacher at Rationalist Reaffirmation High, met her at the platform. He was a tall person with a big bottom and a little head and mild yet intent eyes. His open jean jacket exposed a full chest which, in its fleshy softness, suggested a sensitivity that was almost painfully swollen and tender and yet unrelievedly proud and out-thrusted, like the triumphant guitar chord of the crassest rock song.

He drove with one hand, gesturing with the other as he talked about the school and the English classes which he taught. "You go to most English classes today in the schools—have you? Well you should. Because you'd be shocked at what they teach. Joyce, Kafka— horrible stuff about people's lives being destroyed by a baby crying. Or going to a carnival and getting lost and not being able to find what you wanna buy and getting depressed. Or a guy turning into a cockroach—it's unbelievable. It's all about defeat and helplessness. No wonder the kids hate it."

Justine started to argue for the intrinsic value of beauty in writing, but as he continued, she found herself seduced by his blunt sensibility, so full of feeling yet so dumb, by his cheerful way of going after literature like a dog would a bone, snuffling, turning, chewing, genuinely enjoying it, provided it conformed to his belief. She thought he was a very nice person.

"What I teach is stuff like Ian Fleming, Mickey Spillane, Jack London, Hemingway, Conrad, and, of course, Anna Granite. Literature with clear plots, clear cause-and-effect connections, plenty of action and *heroes*. That's the most important thing. Especially for kids at this age. Heroes who live by clear values."

Justine remembered the man who had picked her

up in the bar, his pale face, the eerie angle of his bones, his glittering eyes, the deliberate way he drew the smoking reed of cigarette to his lips. She remembered herself between his spread legs, sucking his cock, glimpsing his happy rat-toothed smirk with each upward bob of her pumping head. This memory, with its ugly eroticism, was not in the least arousing; however she recognized something compelling in it, a compulsion akin to that of a starving lab animal which will keep pressing the button that once supplied it with food, even though the button now jolts its poor small body with increasing doses of electric shock.

"I have them read Joyce and Kafka and other junk, but I give them a solid Definitist perspective."

"But is a Definitist perspective only looking at whether or not a story concerns happy themes and strong characters?"

"Strong characters, yes. Happy themes, no. Shakespeare is great even though he deals with disaster and betrayal and the worst aspects of human nature because his characters are strong and you can feel something for them when they fall. They at least try for the heroic. When a man tries the heroic and fails, it's a great tragedy. Telling about a man going through a boring day, sitting on a toilet, watching a girl expose herself—what is that?" Max held out his hand and let it drop. "It's nothing. It's antilife."

"But mundane things and even miserable things are a part of life."

"They're not a part of life I aspire to."

The Rationalist classes were held in the rented classrooms of a local community college. The fourteen young Definitists sat on their tailbones, their spines outlined under their shirts. Justine sat in the back of the room, legs crossed and note pad open. Max paced before them, his enthusiasm protruding from him like an invisible spear.

"So what kind of guy is Jake? He's a nice guy, a smart guy. The kind of guy who'd sit for hours in a parlor in Boston and talk about social problems and try to come up with solutions. He's an intellectual, in other words. A liberal in fact. But he's not a phony!" Max's voice went up in register and became both conciliatory and probing, as though he were verbally peeling away the slightly ridiculous outer layer of Jake's character and revealing his deeper, truer nature, while at the same time pleading with the listener to take a peep at this more genuine Jake and not merely laugh at his outer manifestation. "He's really after the truth in life, he wants to experience it instead of just talking about it. That's why he's signed up for this voyage, he doesn't have to go, he's not like the rest of these guys."

Justine looked at the boys and again imagined Bryan, only this time as a young boy, sitting in this classroom listening to Max. What would he be thinking? How would it affect the daydreams he would doubtless be having, sitting on his tailbone in the heavy sun? She remembered Ricky Holland and his gang on a heartless expanse of playground standing in a circle around a trapped fourth-grader who had been forced to lift her skirt. She remembered Emotional and felt a pang of sensitivity and remorse which was so painful it was immediately stamped out by a ferocious burst of internal rock music which, if it had a face, would've been sticking out its tongue.

"So," concluded Max, "that's what you have to do when you read a book. I know it may seem hard at first, but if you practice it, say, when you go to the movies, you'll get the hang of it. Movie after movie, break it down—plot, character, theme, resolution, message. Pretty soon you'll be doing it automatically, and then you'll be able to defend yourself from the crap they'll throw at you in college."

*Justine returned to Manhattan* depressed and nauseous from the treats she had consumed on the train. As soon as she entered her apartment, the phone rang. He said "Hi" as though she was supposed to know who he was, and annoyingly she did.

"How did you know my number?"

"I got it from you last night, don't you remember? Well maybe you were drunk."

*I was at the gym doing lat pull-downs* when I thought of my mother: she and I baking cookies, hula dancing in the living room, making crayon heavens, or together in my bedroom, her tender presence taking me into the night. As I felt these images, weakness spread through my shoulders and the weights became heavier. I thought instead of my mother's voice as I'd heard it from my bedroom in Painesville, telling my father how terrible I had been that day, punctuating and goading his bursts of anger. The strength came back to my arms, and again I pulled down, pushing my breath out between my teeth with a hiss. I remembered her at the dining table, her eyes covered with impenetrable film, her forkful of salad frozen in space. My father told me I was sitting on my fat ass while he worked and slaved with bastards. I pumped at twice my usual rate. A hirsute Hispanic fellow in a leopard-skin leotard glanced, alarmed. "Take it easy," he said. "Don't overwork." I checked my body for stress in mid-pump and felt none; my blood beat like a marching band. My father gesticulated and showed his teeth. My mother's eyes remained unseeing. Then, like the hand of a phantom, a palpable feeling of love and longing extended itself to me. It touched my cheek. Superimposed over my indifferent mother, another mother leaned towards me with tears in her eyes, wanting to protect me, to console me. A chemical release bathed my muscles. I pressed my weight for the last time and let it go. Pain shot up my back and sides. I slumped on the bench, trying to rotate my shoulders.

"Ma'am," said the Hispanic fellow, "I know you're big and strong, but are you trying to kill yourself or what? They ain't gonna pay your hospital bill, you know, remember that paper you signed? Hey, are you okay?"

"Yes," I said, "thank you." He helped me off the machine and advised me to take a steam bath and stretch out. It was only with the faintest twinge of pride that I registered the incredulous remark made by the muscle boy who'd stepped up behind me and seen how much I'd pressed.

I walked into the dressing room, pain and adrenaline vying for bodily dominance. I pulled off my wet clothes with effort, not even trying to hide the grotesque display of cellulite crushed by spandex. The girl next to me was a homely little thing anyway.

I had never used the steam room before, mainly because I had been too embarrassed to sit there unsheathed. Now discomfort overruled embarrassment, and besides I was in no mood to care.

I entered the steam room clutching defiance to my body as well as one of the gym's skimpy regulation towels. I quickly dropped both; there was no one in the room, and even if there had been, I was partially obscured from critical eyes by billows of hot steam. I stood for a moment absorbing the experience and decided it was pleasant. I eased myself onto the wooden bench, leaned back and had the novel sensation that the world was a safe, gentle place.

I had last seen my mother in a coffee shop in Hoboken, New Jersey, where I had lived briefly. Her face had aged shockingly since I'd seen her last; there were dark circles under her eyes. Our conversation had ended with her collapsing onto the table, her head hidden in her folded arms as she wept, the fingers of one hand blindly groping my arm across the table in pitiful supplication. I had sat silent and immobile. She had asked me to come home and see my father who was very ill, and I had refused.

That was not the first contact I'd had with her since I had left home. There had been letters and phone conversations, some of which were with my father. I had seen my mother twice before that last meeting. The first time was in Philadelphia. She had put aside a portion of her weekly allowance over a period of weeks to hire a private detective to find me.

The encounter occurred one afternoon as I returned home from work early, compensating as I sometimes did for a long night of conference transcription. She was sitting on the steps with a newspaper folded on her lap. The crossword puzzle, on which she was writing with a stubby pencil, sat on her knee. When she saw me she stopped, her pencil suspended. If I hadn't been stunned I would've run; I was paralyzed by the certainty that my father was nearby. My mother rose, came forward, and embraced me. "Dotty," she said. "Dotty, darling, thank God you're safe."

It wasn't until we were in my room sitting on my bed that she told me that my father wasn't there, that he didn't even know what she was doing. I was shocked at this information; my mother had never done anything without my father's permission. I listened as she went on, tracing an invisible pattern on my bedspread with her finger. She wanted me to come home, she said. Maybe college had been a bad idea, but I should come home. She knew there had been problems at home. She drew her pattern with meticulous care, examining every aspect of it. But still. Home was the place for a young girl. She looked up, smiled wretchedly, and touched my cheek.

"No," I said. "And you can't make me."

Her expression shrank from me. There was silence, and then she came slowly forward again. She repeated what she had said, adding that they would be willing to "get help" for me. She said my father was "half crazy" with worry. I kept saying no, my conviction that she could not force me growing with each repetition of the word. I was of legal age, and Anna Granite was on my side. If my father wanted so badly to see me, he could have hired a detective; he probably didn't because he was terrified of opening the Pandora's Box of family counseling.

In the end she gave up. She said she wouldn't tell my father where I was on the condition that I write to her regularly and tell her how I was doing. I agreed. We had a short conversation about my job and my life. I told her that I was a secretary for an art dealer and that I had made two new friends—this last out of a desire to reassure her that I was happy, for even then I couldn't be indifferent to the pain I saw her in. She said well, I'm just starving to death and I'd love a grilled cheese sandwich, how about you?

We had a snack at a diner. Our meal was accompanied alternately by bright conversation and my mother's tears. She chewed and wiped at her eyes, then at her mouth, clearing her throat with ladylike sounds.

Once past the initial resentment, I wrote my regular letters with enthusiasm, inventing bright anecdotes I knew would please her. I think I liked writing the letters because they prevented the development of homesickness and remorse, which might have led me to return home. I liked recounting my pretend successes, knowing my real accomplishments were all the greater. I had fantasies of returning home unexpectedly, after a triumph in banking or industry, dispensing munificence and superiority. They would plead with me to stay with them, just for a few days, but I would have to rush off to a conference or something. I imagined my father looking at me with awe, shamed to realize his judgment of me had been so wrong.

The letters from my mother, also full of anecdotes, were small notations of my old life, memories of chili dinners, the evening news, the sound of electric fans and of marching music, the close, dark rooms of the Painesville house, threads worked into the now vaster tapestry of my complex new life—present but safely contained and circumscribed.

This contact alternately fell off or intensified over the years and was, often at Christmas or Thanksgiving, supplemented by phone conversations. During one of those conversations my father came on the line and without warning began talking to me as if he'd seen me the previous week. It was only minutes before the strength of his voice, resonant with the conviction that what he was doing was perfectly normal, drew me into a conversation. I heard my voice change as I talked to him, become small, soft, constricted—the voice of my childhood. His voice was fat with generosity when he said, "Come home for Christmas next year, okay?" and I said okay even though we both knew I wouldn't. I hung up feeling disgust and pain and covetousness—covetousness because part of me held onto the pain like it was a precious pet, the favorite stuffed animal I had clutched as a child.

One day I called when my father was alone. He began talking about the neighbors who hated him and the bastards he worked with, how much he'd like to smash their skulls with hammers. There was marching music in the background. I said nothing.

"And then," he continued, "there's my selfish bitch daughter. Who wasted my money flunking out of college and then deserted us. Who calls us every few months on her royal whim. My daughter—"

"Yes," I said, "your daughter who you raped."

"Raped." My father spoke furiously. "If you think you were raped, you don't know what rape is. I'm the one who's been raped, sister. Raped all my goddamn life by the army, the school system, the bosses, the neighbors—"

I hung up.

For a long time I stopped reading my mother's letters, and I never wrote to her. When I moved I left no forwarding address, and for a time there was no contact at all. Then came the inevitable reconnection, Christmas cards, a birthday present, a shopping trip with my mother, events like a trail of pebbles leading to that final conversation in Hoboken.

I picked at my misshapen bran muffin while she described my father's illness and how her days were spent caring for him. From the moment she told me he was seriously ill and might soon die, I felt my own assumption that I would go home to see him plant itself in my solar plexus. I didn't say anything about it though; I merely listened and asked occasional questions. I could hear in her voice that she shared my assumption that I would come home.

The conversation went on, and I tried to imagine a scene of forgiveness and reconnection. But the stick figures of myself and my father stood mute in the dark rooms of my internal house. I tried to imagine him looking at me with tears in his eyes, speechless with sorrow as he clasped my hand to beg forgiveness. But I could only imagine him with his eyes glassy and glazed, muttering about bastards with his dying breath. "You prick," I said to him. "You ruined me." He didn't hear me.

I looked at my mother. The sentence I had just imagined saying to my father stood between us in full view, but she didn't see it. She began talking about travel arrangements.

"Mother," I said. "I don't want to go."

She didn't look surprised. Her body went into its habitual posture of readiness to receive pain, and then I saw her gather herself to argue with me. She began with the "difficulties" between my father and me. We talked round the fact of what happened; I felt angrier and angrier. I backed away from my feelings, using the conversation to parry and evade them. Unknowing, my mother cornered me, stripping away my defenses as fast as I could secure them. My feelings pressed against my control like the fists and feet of a baby trying to punch free of the womb.

We paused for a moment. There was a light sweat on my forehead. A thin layer of composure constrained my anger. If she had remained silent only a little longer, the layer might have thickened enough to protect us both, but she said, at that fragile moment: "Can't you be big enough to forgive him, Dotty? Can't you stop thinking of your problems just this one time?"

Her face recoiled from my expression, she put her hand to her throat as though in self-protection, and then my words garrotted her. "No, mother," I said, "no

I can't forget about my problems. Because my problems are that my father did everything but fuck me, again and again. You know, incest? You watch television, don't you?"

Her face confirmed my worst fear; she was not surprised by what I'd said, but wounded to the death that I'd said it. Ashy noise rose and died in her throat, and she collapsed on the table like the weak old woman she was.

Some weeks later, she sent me a card announcing the funeral. I disregarded it. Once or twice I worried if I had made the right decision in not going to see him. Then the worry went into oblivion. My mother and I had not communicated since. I did not even know if she was alive.

I left the steam room, my body relaxed and heavy. I didn't bother to clutch my towel over my nakedness; I exposed even my horrible pubic hair. No one gawked. Only another fat lady glanced at me with mild curiosity. A skull with wavy blond hair was tattooed on one of her huge arms. The girl next to me carefully dried her breasts, gently patting the tiny rings that pierced both nipples. No wonder nobody looked at my cellulite, I thought, defiantly assuming poses that I knew would best reveal it. People are used to weirdness, inured to ugliness. It's beauty we stare at, disbelieving and furious.

I lumbered into the street thinking perhaps I should try to find my mother. She was probably still living in Painesville, unless she was one of those old people who moved to Florida. It was also possible she had died and, since I'd changed my name, no one had been able to locate me.

As soon as I entered my apartment I ripped open a

bag of potato chips and a bag of candy, turned on the TV, and sat before it, eating from both bags. The news was on. Two white teenagers who had beaten a black teenager to death with a baseball bat had been fined $100 for misconduct and black people were demanding a retrial. The families and neighbors of the white teenagers were outraged by this, saying that they were being unfairly judged because they were white. A bleached blonde with a huge wad of gum in her mouth spoke to a newsman's microphone. "Cuz I known these guys all my life," she said in defense of the white boys. "They're the nicest, most unprejudice people in the whirl." I hit the remote control button. On the next channel a talk show featured schoolchildren who said they'd been sexually abused by their allegedly Satan-worshipping teacher; they were confronting the accused teacher. The parents of the children stood behind their seated offspring, gripping the backs of their chairs, their faces held in strangely combined expressions of anger, disgust, prurience, and awareness that they were on TV.

"And so Miss Peatrosinski," said the host, stalking the tense young teacher with his mike, "what do you have to say to *that*?"

The teacher blinked rapidly and nervously rubbed the corner of one deeply shadowed eye. She said, "This is nothing but a witch-hunt based on gossip and faulty—"

A child of twelve or so leapt to his feet and shouted, "I wanna say something. How do you think we little kids could make up stuff as dirty as that? How would we know about Satanism and all that other stuff?"

The audience roared in approval, the children

cheered and shook their fists in the air.

I imagined my mother in a room watching television, alone with memories of a rapist husband and a daughter who hated her. I remembered my father as I used to find him sometimes when I returned from school, alone in the darkened house, feeling the hairs in his nose with his thumb, his eyes looking as if he didn't know where he was. His face would come to life as he saw me, a familiar reference point moving through the room. I remembered the way he would lie in the dark in his room before dinner, listening to the soft music emerging through the static on the radio. Sometimes I'd be in the hall and he'd appear, his oiled hair traveling in conflicting directions on his head, his face set like a carving, his eyes totally bewildered. On one such occasion he said to me, "I had a dream. A dream I was back in Michigan at the Bowlarama. Mama and Aunt Cat were alive and happy, and there were flowers everywhere." He put his finger to his nose, turned up a nostril and tenderly stroked the hairs.

My poor father. My poor, poor father. Pity spread through my body, paralyzing me. My father had lived and died in terrible pain. My mother might be lost forever. Anna Granite had not saved me.

The phone rang. I stared in the direction of the ringing. It was my mother. It was one of those instances you read about in *Reader's Digest*; she had been psychically penetrated by the strength of my thoughts and was now trying to reach me. I stood up. Except how would she know my number? I sat down. There were lots of ways! I leapt up and headed for the phone, which immediately stopped ringing. "Shit!" I slammed my fist on the wall and the ringing

*Justine looked* at the Medicaid billing forms before her, fearful that she had filled them out incorrectly but unable to tell how. When she looked at the numbered instructions, boxes to fill in and various codes, she could not see them as specific abstractions with easily understood meanings which began and ended when you put the obvious information in the box. The grid of green ink that made up the form seemed rather the opening of a hellish labyrinth at the end of which sat checks in envelopes made out to Dr. Winkgard. She steeled herself and filled in a code of numbers; immediately the numerals sent out invisible threads attaching them to a machine of paper that ground along on a cloud of thoughts, the now totally abstract thoughts of whoever had come up with this method of defense against a cruel and exorbitant medical system.

Her mind had been moving in this psychotic direction all morning, and it was beginning to alarm her. Even worse, it seemed as though other people could see the distressed twistings and turnings in her head. Patients would approach the desk to request an appointment or to pay their bill; she would look at them and she would suddenly see their facial expressions and body movements as though through the tiny end of a telescope, leading to an infinity of personality, and then beyond personality to a place out of which the personality grew in a thick tough stalk, a place unreadable by even her grossly heightened perceptual mechanism. She would look at the appointment book, and see there a list of names symbolizing people, people who were each as complex as the one standing before her and yet reducible to a list of squiggles in an appointment book anyone could buy in any stationery store. Shaken, she would fill out an appointment card and hand it to the patient and see on her face a vague expression of discomfort and puzzlement, as if she'd registered Justine's weird consternation. When one of them asked her a question and sensed her groping confusedly for an answer, he looked past her to Glenda and said, "Perhaps you could tell me, Mrs. Winkgard?" And Glenda's voice sailed forth, cheerfully acknowledging the chaos that so stupefied Justine, then sweeping it into a corner with the brisk broom of her voice, neatening and simplifying, answering the question.

Probably it was obvious to everyone, on a deep level, that Glenda was a conduit for the forces of order, rationality, and strength, and that she, Justine, was a mere appendage, useful only insofar as she was a conduit for Glenda. Further, it seemed that this had been true all her life and would probably always be true, no matter how many articles she wrote or how old she got. And it was only ten thirty! How was she going to get through the day?

She turned to Glenda, who was sitting beside her

doing some paperwork, her furrowing dewlaps giving her the appearance of a masticating little animal. Surely Glenda would realize that something was wrong with her soon; she thought she'd better comment on her condition so that she wouldn't appear too far gone to have noticed it herself.

"Glenda," she said as casually as possible, "do I seem to be acting weird today?"

"No. Are you feeling well?"

"I don't feel sick. I just feel strange."

Glenda put aside her paper and looked at her alertly. "Strange how?"

"Well . . ." She almost said, "Like I'm going up on LSD" and decided that although it was the most accurate description, it wasn't the wisest and instead said, "I feel like I'm on nitrous oxide, you know, laughing gas? Have you ever had it? It makes your thinking a little distorted. I keep going off on mental tangents, and everything seems to be connected to something huge and complicated."

"Ah," said Glenda, "it sounds like an anxiety attack."

Justine looked at Glenda gratefully. "You don't think I'm crazy?"

'No." Glenda said this as if it were the most obvious answer in the world. "You are perhaps just a little tired and nervous, and I need to take care of you today." She patted Justine's shoulder. "Don't worry."

"Maybe it is just anxiety." Justine cautiously felt around the benign explanation, as if it were a chair that might collapse if she sat in it. "I did have kind of a peculiar date last night."

"Peculiar good or bad?"

"I don't know."

.    .    .

*She had met Bryan* at a Japanese restaurant where they had shared a plate of jewel-like sushi and shiny purple seaweed. She noticed that when he held his tiny cup of sake, he cupped both hands around it for warmth, a gesture she usually saw in women and which she found inexplicably touching. She noticed he didn't eat very much, that he seemed to have little interest in food. His long, black hair fell across his eyes and she wanted to smooth it back. He saw her looking at him and he looked at her, his face infused with a complicated expression of craftiness, interest, and eager excitement. He looked as if he were being drawn into a game that he wasn't sure he wanted to play, and that while this seduced him, it also made him look for a way to give the appearance of full participation while he was in fact scrutinizing her from the sidelines as she charged around after the ball by herself. This expression was frightening but it was also flattering to her because it suggested an extreme and personal reaction.

They didn't refer to their recent heinous intimacy. They talked instead of their childhood experiences, their jobs, her article, and his travels in Southeast Asia. He said he felt greatly attracted to the people who lived in the Patagandrian rain forest.

"They're small and feline and they please me aesthetically," he explained. "There's a sense of delicacy and propriety about everything they do, even the con men. It's partly because their culture is so old, I guess. They have such a strong sense of who they are, individually and in relation to other people. They don't have our kind of demented identity problems."

"Well, if you're talking about a very traditional culture, it's not so hard to find a sense of identity within such parameters," said Justine, happy to disagree so early in the evening. "The more open and diverse a culture is, the less you can rely on the culture to define you, and you have to define yourself. That's harder."

"I don't just mean their culture though. The way they live puts them in direct contact with the most fundamental human needs—food, sleep, shelter. When you talk to those people about supermarkets, they're astonished that anyone would do something like that, going to buy packaged food instead of hunting for it. It's not just a stupid macho thing. They understand the importance of ritual and how it has to be played out in a context of practical need. They don't see how any man with any pride in his masculinity could live such a physically easy life as we do."

"Did you explain to them that men here have ways of shoving their masculinity down the throats of other people?" she asked drily.

His eyes narrowed and his lower lip dropped a centimeter, like the mouth of a cat using his scent organs to test the wind. His face registered that he had taken in the scent and understood it; a smirk flickered in his eyes. "People in this country," he continued, his voice bemused and contemptuous, "have it so easy they don't even know what life is anymore. No one has real problems here, so they have to make them up."

"What do you mean by real problems?"

"Like hunger and—"

"Bryan," she said, "look out the window. There's a guy sleeping on the subway grating. On my way over here I passed two people begging for change. You don't think they have a problem with hunger?"

"Oh, well yeah, but I'm talking about the vast majority of people here."

"Anyway," she said, "there are other problems besides hunger and shelter. Can you really believe that there's no such thing as psychological pain?"

He shrugged. "Well, really, if you want to know the truth, what I like about Southeast Asia is that you can get a gorgeous twelve-year-old to suck your cock for two bucks." His voice was like a tickle on the middle of your back where you can't reach it. "Just kidding," he said.

She decided to change the subject. "So you like Anna Granite's stuff."

"Yeah, I do." He abandoned his orphanlike method of drinking from the sake cup and upended the little bottle, draining it in a gulp. He signaled the waiter for more with a gesture of satirical politeness.

"Why?"

"Mainly because it's a lot of fun. She writes about stuff that's serious and it engages you mentally, but at the same time it's so exaggerated and goofy that you can see the ridiculousness even while being swept up in it. And I especially like the cartoony renditions of the art world, being an artist myself."

"You're an artist?"

"Yeah. I just do that shit at the magazine for money." He grabbed the sake as it floated towards them on a tray, ignoring the sleek waiter's indignant look.

She was relieved to find that his conversation, heard in sobriety, suggested that he had actual thoughts, feelings, and sensitivities, that she might be curious about him. It was also obnoxious, but she was willing to let that pass. She imagined them sitting together in restaurant after restaurant, talking about everything that had ever happened to them, telling each other things they had never told anyone.

"I like you," she said. She was surprised by the sweet tone of her voice.

He smiled, and she saw an expression of tenderness in the center of his eyes. "I like you too." He reached across the table and took her hand. His tender look was subsumed by a strange, forward gloat. "You're like a little girl," he said softly.

"No. I'm really not."

"I think you are. Not a nice little girl though. You're like one of those little monsters who tortures other kids on the playground. I can just see you now making some poor fat kid cry."

She stared at him, shocked, flattered, and slightly frightened. She felt him looking through the layers of her adulthood, peeling away the surface until he found hot little Justine Shade of Action, Illinois, posing on the playground—he was right!—she had never really left. The child Justine pouted flirtatiously as he eyed her.

"Let's get out of here," she said. "Let's go to a bar."

They went to a dark bar with rotting wooden booths and two big pool tables around which men stalked in various attitudes of predatory languor. Cigarettes drooped from their casual lips, their stomachs protruded majestically. Justine watched their deliberate movements and inhaled the reassuring odor of french fries boiling in grease. Bryan was talking about a pathologically violent boy who had lived next door to him when he was ten years old.

"The girls in the neighborhood were terrified of him, and with good reason. I think he might've actually raped a couple of girls. I was with him once when he tricked a girl into climbing down into this hole he'd dug and threatened to bury her unless she stripped and danced naked for us. He even tried to force me to fuck his little sister at knife point."

"Why were you friends with him?"

"I had to be. I lived right next to him, and he would've killed me otherwise. He almost killed me anyway. He beat the shit out of me a couple of times,

and once he pushed me out the third-story window
and I had to go to the hospital—"

"Didn't your parents get upset about this?" Justine
vaguely remembered giggling outside the principal's
office with Debby as they listened to the distraught
Mrs. Wolcott complain about the D girls pulling down
Johnny Wolcott's pants and spanking his butt.

He shrugged. "There wasn't much they could do.
My mother said I'd have to learn to take care of myself. Besides, he was fun sometimes."

"I raped someone once, when I was a kid," said
Justine dreamily.

"Yeah?"

She hesitated; since the vanished Dr. Venus, she
had never told anyone about Rose. She wasn't sure
why she'd started to tell Bryan; she suddenly wanted
to reveal herself to this person who'd recognized the
cruel child of Action, Illinois, and stated that he liked
her. Nonetheless, as she told the story, which was still
painful and sad to her, she disguised the truth of it by
relating it with a smile on her face, as if she wanted
only to excite him.

He received the story with greed in his eyes and his
body in a posture of assessment. "You really were a
mean kid," he finally said.

"It wasn't just meanness," she said, confused. "I
didn't know what I was doing. I don't even know if it
was really sexual." She felt exposed, extended towards
him, and a little sick at having displayed her private
life for a relative stranger's titillation—and yet she felt
titillated herself.

"It sounds like a military maneuver," he said. "You
entered the city, you pillaged, plundered, mauled everything of value, and withdrew."

"Nooo." She ducked her head and giggled. What
he said bore no relation to what she felt, but she was

seduced by the idea of herself prancing through his imagination as a tiny porn queen while the truth of what had happened lay safely hidden in a pocket of misunderstanding. At the same time, she felt a compulsion to make him understand her, and she was disconcerted to realize that the more he refused to do so, the more desperate the compulsion would become. "Really," she said, smiling. "It wasn't like that." And she told the story again.

*Glenda handed her a warm* Styrofoam cup of tea with oil glimmering on its surface. Justine sipped and was comforted as associations with safety and ordinariness were triggered by the sweet taste.

"Glenda," she said, "have you ever had a real anxiety attack?"

Glenda looked at her and nodded; the expression that rose on her face spoke of a deeply disturbing experience, muted with time, and now about to take the tame form of an anecdote. "It happened when I was living in Miami shortly after my divorce from my first husband. I was staying in this sleazy rooming house with cockroaches and I was drinking pretty heavily. One day I made the mistake of calling my ex-husband while I was drinking. He had a woman living with him by then, and I heard one of my daughters call her 'Mama.' It was like a knife in my heart; when I got off the phone I almost lost my mind. I ran to the medicine cabinet and took tranquilizers, and when that didn't help I followed them with sleeping pills. And Justine, when I lay down in my bed I could actually see demons, one black and one red, coming to turn my bed over. It went on for hours, with me fighting to keep them from doing it. And you know, I'm still not convinced that they weren't there."

. . .

"*Have you ever read* Hegel?" asked Bryan.

"I guess. I don't remember." She was feeling drunk; she felt herself slouched on the table in an attitude of belligerent indolence. "Why?"

"I was just thinking of an essay he wrote. I can't remember the name of it. But it has to do with human freedom and its natural limits."

She came out of her slouch to watch as this new vista of his mental processes displayed itself. She felt confused by the ease with which he alternately skimmed and dove into conversation, one moment leading her down into the tunnels and caverns of his psyche to show her the strange stones and stalactites studding the walls and then, without warning, springing up to run away over the barren surface, laughing like a hyena.

"His basic idea is that people crave freedom but that, because of the realities of their lives, they are inherently unfree. And that the only way people can have a sense of freedom is by taking the freedom of others—enslaving others."

"That doesn't sound so original to me," she grumped.

"So that every human interaction, whether on a national or individual level, is a war over who will be enslaved and who will rule."

Justine pictured a bleak landscape occupied by two people, one of whom was groveling in the dirt while the other stood exulting in the vast black emptiness of his freedom. "That sounds hopelessly neurotic to me," she said.

"Well then you must be pretty neurotic to do what you did to that girl in the bathroom. A toothbrush, God." He smiled as he swigged his beer.

"Fuck you," she said, and withdrew haughtily into her booth.

"Don't you think it's true?"

"I told you a personal thing about myself that's actually sort of upsetting to me, and you act like it's some fucking joke."

He inhaled cigarette smoke and aggressively released it towards her. "It's so cute when you have these little moments of self-respect and integrity."

"You're lucky there's a table between us," she said. "If there wasn't, I'd smack your little face."

He smiled like an animal showing its teeth.

Something old stirred in her.

"Have another drink," he said.

*She walked into Dr. Winkgard's office* to put his mail on his desk and heard him haranguing a patient.

"Mr. Nelson, I have told you repeatedly, we have run every possible test, and there is nothing wrong with you. We cannot assume that you are sick because of 'feelings' and the premonitions of your aunt, who is, I'm sure, a wonderful lady."

She lingered in the examining room next to his office to hear the rest of this speech.

"However, one thing is for sure and I'll tell you what it is: If you continue to believe that you are sick, you will become sick. The mind, Mr. Nelson. The mind!"

She had heard this all her life, that if you believe things, they will come true. Bryan had said in a drunken moment the previous night that he could change reality by his perception of it, or something to that effect. Well it didn't work for her; she had believed in things as hard as she could, she had decorated her beliefs with bells, ribbons, and streamers, she had made winged boats for them to go flying out into the world, and although they had looked wonderful sailing into space, they had crashed in a heap.

Dr. Winkgard obviously didn't have this problem. She could hear the rippling muscularity of his belief system flexing through his words, taking up all the space in his office, possibly forcing Mr. Nelson to cower under the desk. This was, she supposed, what was meant by having a strong personality. It galled her to think that Dr. Winkgard had a stronger personality than she. Then she thought of Bryan's nutty Hegelian ideas and was further galled to think that he would see them embodied in the fact that she worked for Dr. Winkgard.

"So," concluded Dr. Winkgard, "stop worrying yourself into illness, Mr. Nelson. Go and be happy and stop thinking about the demons that populate the dreams of your aunt."

More demons, thought Justine as she left the examining room. Demons are the theme this morning. The thought frightened her.

*She was very drunk* by the time they returned to his apartment, and she barely remembered the at first playful exchange of shoves, slaps, and verbal abuse, the escalating bolts of aggression that flew between them.

"I'd like to tie your ankles up by your head, with your legs pushed straight back until I could see up your asshole." His voice jerked as he fucked her. "I'd like to stick a lit candle all the way up your snatch and lick your pussy until it starts to singe."

"An homage to Hegel?" she asked.

She felt the teeth of his ferocity cut open her body, and she felt her poisonous response spill into his mouth like blood. She lifted her pelvis off the bed and fucked him hard enough to rattle his teeth. "Turn me over," she whispered, "and stick your cock up my ass."

"No. I'm going to fuck your pussy until I feel you start to come and then I'm going to cram it up your ass. Then I'll stick it down your throat."

"You stupid prick." But she said it like a caress, slowing her pelvic movement, slowly gripping and releasing his cock with the rhythmic stroke she would use to pet an animal.

"You might hate me but your cunt's begging for it, isn't it?"

She sank beneath the dark current that bore them along, rose and sank again. She saw herself frozen in disbelief at what she was doing and then herself as a child, alone in the apartment after school, running through the rooms, smashing windows and destroying furniture like she had never been able to do, jumping up and down with delight to see big Justine doing the nasty with this dirty boy. The strange thing was that this excitement didn't affect her cunt. She felt it there, but only dimly, as if there was a thin but firm barrier between her genitals and the rest of her body. Stranger still, it didn't matter.

She wrapped her legs around his waist, rolled him onto his back and sat on him. The smell of her cunt floated up to her; she felt like she'd dipped her hand in her own guts. She whispered to him, "I want you to play with my cunt until I'm almost ready to come and then I want you to whip me."

He poked his head up. "You want to be whipped?"

"Yes."

"Then get up. I'll whip you right now."

Fright leapt in her stomach, and she jammed it down. He got a small whip from a drawer across the room. She had never seen a whip before and she was frightened again. Even the rampaging child paused, wondering. Then he grabbed a long candle from its holder and continued towards her.

"No," she said sharply, raising a hand. "No fire."

He stopped. "Okay," he said almost tenderly. "Nothing you don't want." And he turned and hurled the candle against a wall, smashing it.

He pressed her face down on the edge of the bed and bound her hands behind her back. Her knees were bent up to her chest and splayed apart so that her vagina and asshole were pulled open. She thought of her exposed crotch, feeling that these hairy wet holes were her, just as her eyes and nose were her, and yet, seen isolated and up close, they were prehistoric, stupidly impersonal, beastly and irreducible—yet still gentle, merciful and sweet.

She felt him embrace her spread buttocks; he must've been kneeling. She felt him kiss her hips and behind over and over again. "Baby," he murmured. "Baby girl." He dipped his tongue into one hole and then the other. The barrier protecting her genitals fell away; her inner flesh opened to receive pleasure. He slowly fucked her with his tongue, and her mouth released a genuine sigh. Her body opened more deeply until she felt herself split and revealed all the way into the pit of her guts, a place of heat and light that shone with tenderness for the lover who had come at last.

He gently withdrew from her, licked her once more, and backed away. She was aware of him behind her, and although she didn't make this association, she felt as she had when she was alone with her father in his car and he had made her say what Dr. Norris had done; pinned, helpless, exposed. Only now she felt her opened being contacted and stroked instead of coldly regarded. She thought: I love you.

He struck her with the whip. The pain cut her

drunkenness and shocked her so badly she couldn't scream. He struck her again, harder, and she did scream. Her panicked body jerked against its restraints and tried to close in defense; from her depths there burst a terrified creature, all elongated hands and wild distended mouth, its body twisting crazily as it flew into her throat, silently crying, No, no, don't let him hurt me. But it was too late.

*She let her attention wander* to the welts pressed against the vinyl seat of her office chair as she sat, still struggling with Medicaid forms. "I hope you didn't leave permanent marks," she'd said as she lay in his arms.

"Not this time," he assured her. "We'll talk about that later." He turned away from her, his back hard as a door shut in someone's weeping face.

Sleep alternately took her under and released her, tossing her into his room with its staring furniture and scattered bundles of dirty socks, and then drawing her back into her loud and messy dreams.

She blinked and looked up from her Medicaid forms, suddenly recalling: the unhinged Granite enthusiast, Dorothy, had appeared in a dream. Probably, she thought, it was the discussion of Granite's work the night before. A strange dream; they were walking in a garden of blighted flowers and trees that were twisted into aberrant forms, both rotted and beautiful. The gravel path beneath them shimmered with a light that seemed radioactive and frightening to Justine. It shifted as they walked, crawling like the colored sand of a kaleidoscope; Justine was afraid it would open and swallow them. The fat woman seemed to sense her fear and took her hand firmly, giving her to understand that even if the gravel did open under their feet, she would still bear them aloft.

"You shouldn't be involved with this man," said the fat woman. "He is dangerous."

"I know," answered Justine. "But it's something I have to do."

"No it isn't."

They looked at one another, and Justine noticed the clarity and beauty of the other woman's eyes.

"Are you feeling better now?" asked Glenda. "Your face looks very relaxed."

"Yeah, yeah, I am. Can I make a phone call?"

"Of course."

The fat lady's phone rang for a long time with no answer. Justine remembered that she worked on a graveyard shift and wondered if she were still asleep. It was four o'clock already; probably she had dialed the wrong number. She hung up, called again, and was answered immediately.

"Hi, it's Justine Shade. Remember me?"

"Yes."

Dorothy's hollow voice made Justine pause; nothing happened in the pause so she continued.

"Well, I'm close to finishing my article, and I just have a few things I'd like to, er, tie up. I remembered you said you'd be happy to meet again if I needed any more information, and I thought I'd invite you to have coffee." Dorothy was silent. "So we could talk," added Justine.

"Um, yes, that would be—I'd like that."

As she said the last phrase, Justine heard in her voice that familiar disconcerting momentum and was reassured. She hung up strangely gratified, feeling she'd accomplished something useful, related after all to her career.

"Glenda," she said, pushing her chair back. "How about if I go out and get us some cookies?"

tainly novel to be, for just a little while, self-satisfied and obsessed with fashion. Then I would reflect that, fun or not, I couldn't do it because of who I was.

Now though, I had to go into Gran Caffé Degli Artisti, and in I went. Narrowing my focus so that I would respond only to the visual apprehension of one thin blond girl with glasses (I didn't want to stand there gaping at the various types that would doubtless abound), I marched through the place. She wasn't there. I stood a moment, consternated (what if she'd forgotten?) and then sat at one of the cunning little tables across from the door where she'd be sure to see me. I spent some moments arranging myself and then looked up to reconnoiter. I was pleased by the sight of statuettes in niches, candlabras covered with the lavish wax of hundreds of expired candles, and carved, high-backed inquisitor-style chairs. There actually weren't many people of any description there, probably because it was four thirty, an hour when most people are either at work or getting ready to go to work. A table away from me sat a young woman with long dark hair and soft eyebrows. The multitude of finely wrought silver bracelets on her forearm stirred and gleamed as she lifted and set down her cup. She was reading, with great concentration, a book, the title of which I couldn't see. Her blouse was plain and gray, but the jacket thrown over her chair was a beautiful little thing of purple, silver, and mauve, and actually had tiny triangular mirrors woven into it. Was this a signal that she was a fashionable person, or was this jacket a personal emblem, a defiance of the tyranny of fashion, possibly even made by the girl herself? I had no idea.

I looked towards the window. Two plainly dressed women in their thirties talked in low voices, their arms stretched towards each other on the table. Next to them was a table of boys with long hair tied back off their faces, a jumble of cups, dishes, and glasses before them on the table. Their profiles, alternately stiff, gentle or fluid were finely chiseled in the sharp relief of the sunlight, like boys who had just moments before been statues sculpted in honor of youth.

This wasn't what I'd expected, but it was pleasant. I looked at the intriguing glass case of pastries and puddings to my right. I wondered if it would be unseemly to order two. "Hi." Justine's flat chirp announced her presence, and she sat down before me, smiling shyly.

I returned her greeting and immediately felt that she had changed since the last time I'd seen her. I couldn't tell if this change was real or imagined. The waitress, a solemn girl with freckles, brought our menus, and I became too engrossed in mine to examine her further. I would've liked to go and scrutinize the cakes in the glass case and select several by hand, but I was embarrassed to do so. The waitress, however, was wonderfully solicitous in describing the imaginatively named confections on the menu, looking at me as she did so with an expression that suggested not only an intimate understanding and acceptance of my cravings, but also that she was happy to be instrumental in satisfying them. What a wonderful place, I thought, closing the menu. My contentment was interrupted when I glanced up and encountered Justine's face. She too had ordered and closed her menu and, her face turned slightly sideways, was now staring into space, chewing on a piece of lip and covering half her face with her hand. She didn't notice my look for several seconds, and when she finally turned towards me, I identified part of what was different about her. Her air of self-containment, her annoying detachment, and her sharp, out-thrusting concentration, which she had trained on me like a radar gun during our last meeting, was gone. I could still feel her little mind buzzing away, but its rays were diffuse, wandering, seemingly too weak to penetrate anything. In addition, I felt her groping not only towards me, but groping generally and desperately, like a hungry infant futilely trying to work its will by flailing the air with its tiny hands. One obvious difference; she was now using a tape recorder instead of pen and paper.

"So," she said, readying the little machine, "I wanted to talk about a couple of things. Do you remember the last time we met how we got into a sort of argument about how many women perceive Granite's attitude towards sexuality as atavistic and masochistic?"

Her obsession with masochism and perversion was really trying; of course it was her business if she kept it to herself, but for her to invite me out to talk about it was really a bit much, especially since she knew me to be the victim of a sadistic father. She must have noticed my expression because she hastened to make her voice conciliatory.

"You were saying how this isn't what Granite meant at all. Well, during my research and interviews I've noticed—and not just in regard to the erotic aspect of Granite's work—that her followers often seem to derive meaning from her work that would surprise her critics and even Granite herself. It's almost as if her work exists here"—she gestured with her hands as if placing a small package on the table—"and that her followers exist here"—another package—"and that here, between them, is something altogether separate, a mixture of Granite's work and the perception of it. And I was wondering if she was aware of this when you knew her and if so what she thought of it."

Her bland delivery of this brainless assertion made it all the more exasperating. How could someone who had spent the last month studying Granite and her followers not realize that this way of thinking was the very thing she—and we—most despised? But as my anger came forward, ready to smite her, I sensed, in addition to her diffuse desperation, a scary fragility in her, a psychic quivering which vibrated in her smile and even more noticeably in her trembling hand. I had the distinct feeling that I was in the presence of someone about to have a nervous breakdown, and I lost my interest in rebuking her. I didn't lose my interest in defending Granite, but I did so gently.

"Such a concept would never have entered Granite's head. Of course, there were always flakey people around her who misunderstood her work, but if she saw that they were trying their best to grasp it and simply didn't have the mental equipment to do so, she was very kind to them. The others, those who deliberately misinterpreted—"

"That's not what I mean. I mean what happens when people look at a thing and see in it something other than what its creator intended and aren't aware of the difference. That happens all the time, especially to writers. I just think it's particularly interesting in the context of what Granite said about objective truth."

Of course I knew what she meant. But why would she focus on something so trivial when the irrefutable grandness of Granite blazed like the sun, illuminating and upholding the existence of so many people who might have spent their lives metaphorically slumped before their televisions, too despondent to move? (I pushed aside the troublesome thought that Granite herself had espoused contempt for people who fastened their thoughts onto the belief systems of others and would never have done so herself.) It was frustrating to be in the presence of someone so interested in Granite and yet to pass her, ships in the night, but ships that scraped and grated against each other on the way by. I was exasperated to have this strange, nervous, delicate being flitting about me, first jangling the alarm bells of my most personal issues, seeming to offer intimacy and then denying it, stirring up old grief and then skipping off, and now sitting before me like a foreign solar system gone awry, broadcasting signals from her distant station too weak and confusing for me to read and then saying things which could only lead away from serious discussion and which, furthermore, I sensed didn't engage her full attention or express her real concerns.

"Can I ask you something?" I said. "Why are you doing this article anyway?"

*When Justine walked into the café* and saw Dorothy sitting there, she was reminded, with unexpected vividness, of the power of the woman's presence. In the precious café she seemed even more huge than she had in her apartment, even more insistently strange, the emblems of her derangement circling her in an invisible but palpable personal mandala. For a moment she felt embarrassed to be sitting next to a fat lady wearing hideous chartreuse sweat pants, big red hair and the plastic jewelry of a drag queen with an ironic sense of humor. Horrified, she considered the possibility of an acquaintance coming in and seeing her with this person, or even the waitress, who would surely notice how odd they looked together. Then the stubborn kid who had defied society once before spoke up; "I don't care what you douche-bags do. I'm not gonna hate Emotional anymore," and she sat down, smiling.

She immediately noticed a difference in Dorothy and was taken aback by it, although she wasn't sure what the difference was. She surreptitiously glanced across the table as they surveyed their menus; she was touched and amused to see the suppressed excitement in Dorothy's face. Dorothy seemed solid, stronger than she had at that last encounter, during which, as Justine remembered it, the fat woman, for all her weight, had seemed groundless and insubstantial, floating, sometimes flapping as she was buffeted by the abnormal ferocity of her own emotions. She felt the ferocity was still there, but centered this time, shimmering like precious metals in some invisible cache. Her vague fear of the woman appeared behind her like a shadow and tapped her on the shoulder. She ignored it and drew forward, unconsciously intrigued by her strength and where it could be coming from. Perversely, she started with a question she knew would provoke Dorothy. Sure enough, although Dorothy answered the question politely, Justine could feel in her voice and see in her eyes that hornet swarm of anger that had thickened the air during the first interview. But instead of releasing the swarm, Dorothy abruptly asked her that question.

She didn't know what to say, and was glad when their snacks were placed before them and they could become involved in the neutral movements of stirring and arranging. "Just a minute," she said to Dorothy and then saw that it was quite unnecessary; Dorothy was looking with delighted absorption at the huge piece of chocolate cake that had been set before her and was already reaching for her fork. Justine saw her face become immobile and sealed off, as if all reception of signals from outside had become temporarily suspended so that all units could be devoted to the eating of cake. She felt a flash of repulsion at this sight of greed on automatic pilot, and then that was superseded by an odd feeling of tenderness based on her certainty that behind this mask of blind compulsion was a little girl in a state of solemn ecstasy over an extra-special treat—and then she was saddened by the equally strong certainty that food was the only kind of treat this little girl ever got.

"It's good, isn't it?" she said.

"Very good," replied Dorothy. "Really tasty."

They ate in silence for a moment as Justine reflected on something a girlfriend had said once, that men bond when they drink and women bond when they eat dessert together.

"So," she said, "I'm doing the piece because I'm fascinated that people would be so influenced by the work of a fiction writer and would base their lives on the acts of fictional characters. Also I think that in spite of Granite's scorn for collective culture, she in fact embodied—in her work—major contradictions and dilemmas in the way Americans view money and the way individuals interact with groups. And she did so in a very pop culture medium with these archetypal pop characters. That's remarkable to me."

As Justine spoke, Dorothy slowly lowered a fork of cake and fixed her with her large eyes. Justine prepared herself for a burst of indignation and instead felt a chink open in Dorothy's impenetrability; a soft little beam of light came forth.

*She was smarter than I'd thought.* I momentarily lost interest in my cake. Interestingly, once I'd softened in my attitude towards her, due to sympathy for her emotional disturbance, I felt a dispassionate interest in her point of view, which I suddenly saw as an abstract extravaganza of mental reaction, beams of thought darting and ricocheting from one point in Granite's world to the next, growing in heat and light with each connection. "You're right," I said. "It is interesting, and you've hit it on the head when you say she embodied the central moral dilemmas in the country. But why are you paying attention to dumb stuff like people thinking her work meant this or that when the important thing was what it did in fact mean?"

"For two reasons. One is that I think Granite was often attacked unfairly by well-meaning liberals who looked at the work from a shallow perspective—"

Ah ha! She was an ally, a defender after all! An explosion of sweetness went off in my mouth as I chewed, coinciding spectacularly with a burst of mental pleasure.

"—and also because when people adopt a political position or philosophy, they rarely take it into their personality whole hog, whether they think they do or not. It is filtered through a life-long construct of individual perception, emotional needs, and unconscious assumptions about life. That doesn't make the philosophy any less strong or valid. In fact it is a testimony to its vitality and viability that it is capable of subtle transmutation and expansion into various forms without losing its essential characteristics."

This reeked of subjectivism, and I of course saw it as rot. Yet . . . it was interesting rot. I couldn't help but be curious even as I rejected it. "But you are making a mistake," I said. "You are taking sheer confusion for vitality and viability. Yeah, there are plenty of people who misunderstood Granite in many ways but still grasped enough of Definitism for it to be of immeasurable value in their lives. You should focus on the value, not the confusion."

Her back straightened, and I saw her go into that prim boxed-in mode that I remembered. "But I think sheer confusion is vitality and viability. The interplay between the imaginary and the real, the private emotional world and the discourse of ideas ... that stuff. When a person takes Anna Granite's ideas and—well, like you did. When you first read Granite's work, you were living in an unbearable situation in which you were forced to hide everything precious in you because there was no place safe for you."

My stomach shut against the cake, and I put my fork down, pressing my spine against the back of my chair.

"So when you read Granite's work not only did she awaken your sense of beauty and pleasure in life, not only did she illustrate for you a positive use of strength and power, but she provided a springboard for you to create an internal world richer and stronger than the external world which wasn't giving you any support at all. But she was only the departure point."

I stared at her, mortified and speechless. Her impending mental collapse had apparently shattered her judgment, made her reckless, aggressive, oblivious to any concept of the natural boundaries between people, careening into my territory with her wheels spinning. Yet she was right, at least about me. I tried to stir myself into being offended by her reference to Granite as a "departure point," but I was too confused to do so. I felt invaded and imposed upon, skewed, as I had been so long ago by the kind gaze of Nona Delgado in the hallway. This girl was talking to me as I had fantasized Anna Granite would talk to me before I met her, breaking down doors I couldn't bring myself to open and storming in. That wasn't all; when she had talked she was like a tiny magician in a cape and top hat drawing back a velvet curtain and pointing with her wand to the unsuspected tableaux of my life, a place where Anna Granite entered a human woman and was changed into a mythical winged thing

with myriad powers—transformed by me and in fact
part of me. As I say: rot, but seductive, flattering rot.

"Tell me," I said, applying fork to cake once more,
"what do you think of Granite's ultrareality work?"

*Justine had expressed herself* carefully at first and then
more boldly as it gradually dawned on her that as long
as she appealed to Dorothy's taste for drama, maximum impact, and seriousness, she could say almost
anything to her. She wanted to appeal to her intelligence and make her realize that she herself was intelligent too—although she didn't know why she wanted
to do either of these things. She had watched Dorothy's face as she talked and saw a lot of activity transpiring behind its surface, but she couldn't read its
nature. She was a little shamed by the way she was
slanting her words to make it sound as if she took
Granite more seriously than she did; ordinarily she
felt that this was the prerogative of the journalist, but
in this case it seemed unfair. These feelings were further complicated by a skulking wish that she did believe in Definitism in the way Dorothy and Max Nolte
did, and her misleading words were in part a playact-
ing meant to momentarily deceive herself as well as
her subjects.

"The ultrareality theory," began Dorothy, enthusiastically mashing her cake crumbs into the tines of her
fork, "was the most daring and controversial aspect of
Granite's work. It came about in answer to the challenge made to an objective world view by a certain
kind of person. For example, how can you pin reality
down like that, how can you restrict what is real? How
can all the conflict between people be boiled down to
self versus collectivism?"

In between rhetorical questions, she put her fork

into her mouth, suctioned off the compressed cake and began methodically to gather more. With each question, her voice seemed to get louder, as if each phrase carried her closer to the center of her imaginary Definitist world in which she, Dorothy Never, was a participant in a complex drama with global import. Justine glanced nervously at the lone dark-haired girl sitting near them, again embarrassed to be heard and seen having a conversation with this crank in Sears clothing.

"Then there's always the random chaos argument; if logic and reason are the strongest, noblest factors in human life, why is the world such a disaster of chaos and illogic?"

"Well so many people are illogical, for one thing," said Justine helpfully.

"Yes!" Dorothy's eyes bulged with excitement, and Justine was again ashamed of creating this artificial bond of assonance.

Dorothy put down her fork; she had by this time annihilated the cake crumbs. "Now the kinds of objections and points of view that I just listed are—were, I mean—totally alien from Granite's way of thinking. Her thought processes were so clear, so courageous that she simply went straight for the most fundamental elements of human life and psychology and wasn't stopped by the complexity that stymies most of us. Of course there is tremendous complexity in human interaction and many different things going on, some of them apparently contradictory. But they are all—all!—linked to those fundamental life issues and the choice we must make between life and antilife. Every human act, every thought, every feeling has in it a direction one way or the other—weakness, collectivism, mediocrity, death, or strength, beauty, selfishness, life. The connections may not be apparent at first, but they are there. You, for example. Your choice to work as a free-lance writer instead of being on staff—that is a choice that speaks of your strength, your need to be apart from the herd. It is a choice for life." Dorothy took a breath to avoid apoplexy and went on. "Even inanimate objects are statements for or against life. These chairs we're sitting in—which I think are wonderful by the way, as is this whole place; I'm glad you picked it—have certain qualities of refinement, sensibility, *statements* in their contours and curves about the way life should be lived, which connect them to the abstracts of honor and graciousness without which life wouldn't be worthwhile. The desserts we just ate—they embody the qualities of lightness, gentleness, sweetness, and comfort—moral qualities because when you decide whether or not to have these things in your life, you make a moral choice. Moral choice is not ambiguous; it is as concrete as these chairs we sit in. There is no chaos, except that which we create ourselves."

Dorothy's face radiated certainty and pride, as if she were standing on a mountain peak with the sun streaming down on her, as in one of those car commercials that, by some weird twist of sensibility, place a Cadillac on a mountain peak in the Sierras where fawning cameras circle around it as if it had just found a cure for cancer.

Hopeless, thought Justine, as are most attempts to quantify and contain. Still, she had to admit, there was something consoling, seductive even, about this vision of chairs and pieces of cake suspended, along with everything else, in a glistening web of order that connected them to all the morality in the universe. For all Anna Granite's trumpeting about arrogance and elitism and how great it was, her ideas were ingenuously humble and populist. In her vision, there was nothing absurd about a culture that broadcasts images of a car standing triumphant on a mountain peak as if it were a genius who had cured cancer—the car was, after all, connected to the same abstractions of greatness as the scientist and, in a way, represented the scientist! And, after all, you couldn't very well duplicate the scientist and sell him to people, could you?

"I'm glad you brought that up," said Justine, taking the tape out, turning it over and popping it back in, "because you clarified some things for me. But I have to change the subject since I have to go soon."

"By all means," said Dorothy. "I think I'd like to see the menu again."

"I was reading the paper the other day and I came across this guy who's been given a pretty high position in the city financial administration who was quoted as saying Anna Granite was one of his early influences. Did you ever meet Knight Ludlow?"

*When she asked that question,* I had the crazy thought that she knew, that she'd interviewed him and he'd told her, and now she just wanted to watch my face. But then she said, "I've tried to interview him but I can't get through by phone or mail. It's not essential, but since he's so highly placed, it would be good to mention him. So I wondered if you knew anything of interest about him. Off the record, if you like."

Either she had calmed herself, called her blind groping energies to huddle around her and thus presented a more stable appearance, or I had adjusted to her neurotic presence. Because suddenly her white, pretty face moved me almost to tears; the childish sweetness of her demeanor was like silver thread guided by the bright needle of her voice. I wanted to be close with her. I had wanted to be close with her from the moment I met her. "This is off the record," I said, a lump in my throat.

She turned off the tape recorder.

"I had an affair with Knight Ludlow." I had an image of myself sitting there in front of her sobbing but I was dry-eyed. A cup of cocoa loomed in the back of my mind. I signaled the waitress. "It was the only affair I've ever had in my life."

She stared at me, her serene expression scattered by surprise. When her face began to re-form itself, I was surprised that its new expression seemed to be pity.

"I'm not ashamed of it, quite the reverse. It can't be made public because at the time he was engaged to be married, and he did get married shortly afterward. He could be with her still, so I have to maintain discretion."

Justine said she understood.

"It started as an affair of the intellect. He told me about his fiancée before it went beyond that, so I knew what I was doing. Of course, when he told me, I was taken aback and upset. Here I was after all, this naïve little girl from the midwest who knew nothing about affairs, who'd never gone on dates, whose only experience with the opposite sex was . . . you know. But it was the work of Anna Granite that helped me get past all that." I smiled at Justine, giving her a chance to apprehend that she was hearing about a wonderful experience and for her face to change accordingly. It didn't. "For, according to Granite, there is nothing wrong with an affair with a married man, for anyone involved. It would be wrong for the wife to expect the husband to deny himself something that would give him pleasure—it would be very unloving of her. It would also be wrong of me to deny myself the pleasure of an affair with him—wrong also to expect him to leave the wife he loved. I'm not talking about that hippie free-love merde either. I'm talking about passion between responsible adults." The shadows on the wall of the Euella Parks Hotel! The traffic noise outside! Knight happily mopping corn syrup from his plate! The dark-haired girl stared at me as she got up to leave. I stared back, and she dropped her gaze.

"Who came on to whom first?" asked Justine.

"What?"

"Who made the advance? Sexually."

It was uncanny, her intuition for the most irritating question possible. "What difference does that make? We were both passionately attracted to each other, it was obvious. Either one of us could've made the first move."

"Did he know about what had happened to you with your father? Before you had sex I mean."

"Yes and he was wonderful about it. He never made me feel like there was anything sullied or—"

"Big of him."

"—ruined about me. He made me feel protected and loved. He made me feel like a beautiful woman. The way he ended it was so poignant and elegant. He took me to a champagne brunch at the best hotel in town. Can you imagine? This little eighteen-year-old who's never done anything in her life sitting with her lover having champagne for breakfast with a beautiful bouquet of flowers on the table." Again I saw the flowers, saw their bruised petals fallen on the table, soft and full of repose in their delicate death.

"So it didn't hurt you to have this affair with a married man?"

Justine's face had a look of irretrievable sorrow. I resisted its pull. "No, not at all. It was the most wonderful experience of my life."

Suddenly, I was afraid she was going to ask, Well, if

it was so great why didn't you ever do it again? and I found myself without an answer. Instead she said, "I'm always upset by affairs with married men. I'm upset by affairs period."

And her upright posture changed into a soft slump, all the weight of her torso on one slim, exquisitely tapered forearm, the blond hairs of which slowly stood erect. I had an impulse to reach across the table and stroke this down.

"I don't know why that would be," I said inanely. "You're such a pretty woman."

"I don't think I know how to have relationships." She rushed her tone to let me know this was the end of the conversation, pulled the tape recorder into her bag, and looked at me with a hurried sidelong glance, part rueful smile, that was like the light in the crack of a door which is closing shut.

*For weeks this conversation* seeped across the borders of my days. I found myself bursting into extensions of it as I paced my room, preparing for work. "Once you understand the Definitist principles of mutual self-interest, you realize that an affair with a married man is no problem," I argued.

As time went on, my excited soliloquies faded, and I found myself brooding over the fact that it was I, not she, who had asked the question, "Well, if it was so great, why didn't you do it again?" Sometimes I answered, "Because I'm fat," and I saw her face before me, skeptical, as if waiting for me to tell the truth.

I sat in my armchair with bags of potato chips and cookies, flitting from channel to channel with my remote control, pausing long enough to get irritated at the various yakking faces, the muddled blurs of action. I kept coming back to the channel that devoted itself exclusively to videos of bands playing their trashy music amid the debris of images that changed with the rapid fluidity of dreams without the context of a dreamer. I usually passed over this station, but today I found its random faces and movements facilitated my brooding.

The camera was on the chiseled face of a boy whose features were almost distorted with beauty, whose voluptuous lips were an accident of monstrous fecundity in the icy desolation of his cheeks, forehead, and cold empty eyes, who looked as if the hard planes of his face were the direct result of the hard world in his skull.

The camera panned back to show a group of boys much like him, with fetishistic long hair and arrogant childish features. The camera played over their fingers, their lithe arms, the feverish tattoos on their slim biceps (bulging eyes, dripping fangs). The singer's voice plunged into a pit of chemical fire and leapt out screaming. The video told the story of a boy named Ricky who has crossed over into the dreamy world of limitless cruelty with the blithe ease of childhood. He was fighting with his dad in a suburban rec room, the dad a numb fleshy brute whose mind is a blueprint of whatever social rules prevail at the moment. I watched with interest. Dad pushed the kid through a plate glass door. The kid's friend, a pretty, gentle-faced boy, went to help him up and was shoved aside. Both boys walked away from gaping Dad with gestures of contempt. The band threw their hair around, and the singer drew a leash around the throat of his ferocious voice. The next scene was the two boys smashing the meager furnishings of a deserted building, drinking alcohol with head-tipped abandon, and setting the building on fire while the invisible band members screamed and played loud. The boys, silhouetted by flames, leapt into the air to ritually slap their hands together. The band threw their hair again, and I noticed the harshness of their faces was now softened, the singer's especially; his long throat was exposed, his beautiful lips seductively parted. The child vandal pulled up his shirt to reveal a big handgun thrust deep down the front of his pants and then withdrew the gun. He pointed it at his partner, who patted it away with the look of a girl being teased by a boy she likes. The band squirmed against their screeching instruments. The boys pushed and playfully shoved, the gentler one throwing his whiskey bottle into the air for Ricky to shoot. Ricky pointed the gun at him again, and this time the boy opened his jacket to show his chest and dared him to shoot. Ricky shot his pretty friend, and the boy fell in a slow motion slur of open lips and wide disbelieving eyes.

The singer's last screech distended his voice further still. The guitar chords trailed away.

I was remembering the way I had felt with Knight. When he held me in his arms, it felt as though he held my beating inner organs in his hands. This feeling frightened me so much that I could not sustain it while he was inside me. But when sex was over and we lay in each other's arms, the reverberation of it throbbed in my chest like an open wound that only his presence could heal.

I remembered sitting in the hotel restaurant the morning after, the day he left forever, staring at the mass of flowers, all of different demeanor—exploding, rampant, brandishing their bright petals in the air, or frail and delicate, shyly whispering from the vase. There were splotches of light on the vase and on the table. The morning sun was in Knight's face, revealing all his pores and tiny hairs, the slight oiliness of his nose, the rolling motion of his swallowing throat. I had never seen him as quite such a corporeal creature before. He smiled at me and talked about the projects he had waiting for him in New York. I remembered

that in *The Bulwark*, after Frank Golanka takes Asia
Maconda in the art gallery, he walks out sneering and
doesn't think about her, even though it was the best
sex he had ever had, until a few days later when she
crosses his mind during a flight to Los Angeles and
he's amazed to be thinking of her at all. In the book,
this doesn't mean he doesn't love her: they eventually
get married. But Knight was already getting married
to someone else. I looked around the room, taking in
the beauty of the shimmering glass chandeliers, the
velvet curtains, the composed men and women eating
their lunch, trying greedily to feel every iota of the romance and wonderfulness of the experience. I wanted
to fondle and squeeze the experience, to possess it, to
jam it down into every cell in my body, my love affair,
my glamorous love affair, my glass chandeliers and
flowers, stuffed into the locked steel box of memory
where no one could get it. But I couldn't. I had no
context, no reference point, for anything that was happening to me now and could only stare, stunned and
frozen, barely able to feel it at all, almost glad that
Knight was about to go away.

I remembered lying in bed the night after he did
go away. I had lain down looking forward to curling
up in a lone ball, with a sense of goodwill for Knight,
now miles away in the arms of his brilliant and beautiful fiancée. But then I thought of him as he had
been with me the night before, and suddenly it happened all over again, my body swelled open to receive
him, only this time it didn't shut and this time he
wasn't there. I didn't know what to do. My heart continued to thud, saliva collected in my mouth. I lay in
this open position all night, my body receiving only
emptiness and silence.

It did not occur to me to call him or to try to see
him again. I would picture him with his fiancée, who

I imagined as tall, blond, lithe, and thin, and tears of admiration would come to my eyes as I felt the great love between these intellectual titans. I would imagine them in profile, facing the wind together, her blond hair blown back, his eyes coolly lidded, her chin lifted haughtily, his jaw set in determination, and I would think, this is how it should be. And I thought, as I lay in my bed at night, how lucky I was to have been a part of these mighty lives.

When I finally saw them together some time later, I was disappointed to see she was dark haired, with heavy thighs and a fleshy jaw line. It was disorienting to see him after so much time; my dismembered love twitched into life at the sight of him and began to stumble about like Frankenstein's poor monster, who doesn't know why he's alive.

I imagined Knight as he must be today, in his late forties by now, sitting at a desk somewhere, wielding power. I wondered if he ever thought of me. I wondered if he had had other affairs during the last decade. I enjoyed thinking that he had; I liked creating a world of illicit meetings, smoldering glances, feelings too strong to be denied, the powerful businesswomen moaning beneath him, caught in the vise of their doomed love. Gee, I'd been part of it. Except now I wasn't. I had never had illicit meetings, writhed beneath anyone, threatened a marriage. I never even got a chance to writhe beneath Knight; I lay there stiff and terrified. I hadn't been a powerful businesswoman either. How did I fit into this picture? How would he remember me, if he remembered me? What had it been like for Knight Ludlow, superior person, to hold the firm, fat young body of an abused child in his arms, to feel her racked with conflicting impulses, finally coming to a shuddering halt against him, her hot little face in his chest? Had it been pleasant? Had it been a lot of fun?

On the television screen before me a forty-plus woman pranced in garter belt and stockings, displaying the tattoos on her buttocks before an entire battleship crew as she belted out a song.

Why had he done that anyway? Why had he stroked and reassured my frightened body until it felt its need for love and opened up, only to find he had gone? Why did the affair which I had always cherished as the most beautiful thing in my emotional life suddenly seem like a rape?

It was as if I had divided into two people: one hungrily embracing the dangerous world of emotional contact and power play, enjoying the game of move, counter move, the unpredictable changes of feelings, the other a terrified child unable to bear the carnivorous spirit of this world, weeping with fear at the sight of adults savagely copulating on their beds, on desks, in elevators.

I was ashamed of this child and tried to stifle her. She was, after all, the weak, the unable one who must not be allowed to restrain the strong in their thirst for life. Anna Granite was never cruel, never callous, as people believed her to be. She simply loved life, was capable of living it at fifty times the intensity of most people, and could not bear to see the bright beast of desire tripped up in its lunge towards pleasure by some sniveling kid who, if it had its way, would live its life in a closet under a blanket.

But when her affair with Beau Bradley had ended, a kid came roaring out of her closet, kicking, screaming, and throwing things.

"That bastard!" she raged, "that dirty, treacherous little bastard! How dare he! How dare he!"

She had just read the letter in which he informed

her that his love for her, while still strong, had become platonic; he wanted to be friends.

"Tell him to get up here on the double before I drag him up by his ear!"

"Up here" was her hotel suite where I happened to be taking dictation; a group of us were attending a conference in Boston. Bradley was out of his room at the moment and thus couldn't be summoned, and Granite was left alone with me and her fury, stalking the room muttering, actually stumbling once over her cape and flinging an ashtray. I sat silent and still, impressed by the magnificence of her rage and yet puzzled by it. Why, I wondered, was she not happy, in her love for Bradley, to let him decide for his most positive value?

I got my answer when Bradley arrived. As he entered, Granite marched up to him and struck his face so hard he staggered to one side and then to the other as she backhanded him.

"You have betrayed the principle of matching components!" she screamed. "Unless you can give me a rational reason for this treachery, you are my enemy for life—for life!"

Poor Bradley, obviously unprepared for this, fumbled for an intellectual argument to support his decision. Even I could hear the truth in his voice; he simply wasn't attracted to her. So she declared her enmity again, slapped him around some more, and then let him crawl away. I only saw him once more after that, fleeing the Philadelphia office with his box of papers.

Wilson Bean took Bradley's place, and I became his secretary.

After the end of her affair with Bradley, Granite changed. I thought the change was permanent, but it was apparent only for about a month. Her face temporarily lost its hot ferocity, its leonine, regal calm. The circles beneath her eyes became darker, the deep lines running from her nostrils to her chin evinced pain and deprivation, and sometimes her mouth would look like the crabbed, down-pulled mouth of a bitter old woman poking furiously around in a bargain bin for something she doesn't really want anyway.

It wasn't very attractive, but there was something noble and moving about her during this time. I was often with her in the week or so before the advent of Bean, taking dictation from her—notes for the gestating *Gods Disdained*. And it was during this time that I came to feel most close to her, although we talked very little. Her pain was something precious, and I felt I was somehow its caretaker, alone in the rare pain museum, protecting the encased specimens, tiptoeing about with the requisite solemnity, watchful and fussy that everything be just right. I made her coffee, turned down her bed, listened to her dreams.

She felt my protection and vigilance, I'm sure of it. I could see it in her eyes when she looked at me years later, an expression that spoke of her superiority but also of her gratitude for that slim psychic strand between us, along which my protection had once traveled towards her.

On TV more cute boys threw their hair and screamed about love.

*Justine pressed her face* into the floor, rubbing her cheek against the porous smelly wood, trying to scrape through her drunkenness. Darkness moved around her; she could barely feel the welts rising on her back. Her knees hurt, she thought. He beat her as she squirmed on the floor, caught in the steel trap that had closed on her when she was five years old. The upper strata of her thoughts and feelings had ruptured, and the creature long trapped beneath was out and gnawing her with its teeth.

She felt him drop down on his knees to fuck her and she turned away from him, rolling on her back. "I don't want your cock," she said. "I want you to make yourself soft and piss on my cunt."

She lay panting on the floor as he stood at the counter pouring beer down his throat. Silence imploded in her ears. She turned her head to stare at her shoe lying on its side.

·   ·   ·

*That night at dinner* he had told her stories of his travels in Southeast Asia.

He had walked through the Patagandrian rain forest with kind, dark guides who showed him where to find edible plants and roots to drink from, and who told him stories based on their dreams. The paths in the forest were so hard that his shoes were destroyed in a week, they were so rugged that he could not walk on them without falling again and again. If you cut your foot in the forest, he said, you could get an infection and die in days. His guides had feet that were tougher than shoes and they taught him how to walk in the forest, they taught him how to read direction on the bark of trees and the hairs of moss.

He traveled weeks without seeing the sky, when the sun was an article of faith through the emerald roof of the forest. He saw pale-hued flowers that bloomed at night, giant spiders bejewelled with bright hoary pustules, salamanders with tiny palpitant throats, sudden storms of butterflies and plant roots that tore through the earth with erotic violence. He saw a man covered with animal tattoos carrying an old-fashioned washing machine through the jungle on his back. He saw villages where people danced to Prince and Beach Boys tapes, and predicted the future with the entrails of pigs. He hunted boar with parties of men and half-wild dogs. He murdered animals for the pleasure of watching them die. He was mistaken for an evil spirit and almost butchered by a frightened woman with a machete. He talked her out of it, and gave her his Swatch watch, assuring her it would protect her from any cruel spirit.

After two years he returned to Manhattan and was totally disoriented. He felt as if the cab bearing him home from the airport was taking him into hell. It was early December and, trapped in the stultification of the holiday traffic uptown, he viewed legions of shoppers marching the streets at what seemed an insane and martial speed, their expressions of frozen emotion covered with willful oblivion. Mechanical elves and dummy children in the windows of Bloomingdale's beat their cymbals and screamed with joy around the tree. Human beggars extended their hands into the neurotic throng, like thirst-parched men sticking their cupped hands out into the rain which, thoughtless and unfeeling though it is, will provide them with enough drops to survive.

She listened, impressed by his bravery and ingenuity and uneasy with the combination of condescension and fondness with which he described the forest people. She saw him again as she had seen him on their first meeting, a mobile little sphinx with shifting surfaces encouraging her to admire its mystery and then contemptuously shedding that mystery like an old skin, laughing at her as she puzzled over the empty skin. It occurred to her that perhaps he felt so comfortable in Southeast Asia because it wasn't possible to pull this act there; people wouldn't understand it. He was probably forced by language and cultural barriers to interact on a fundamental human level; this being an experience he'd never had before in his life, it was probably a great novelty as well as a great relief.

*He leaned naked against the counter* drinking beer so he'd have some piss when the moment came. His body had a tense, frenetic, rigid quality, it was completely stripped of its animal nature. And out of his face, emerging as if his cells had subtly changed shape, came the stiff visage of something old, mechanical, and unfeeling. She felt that this thing was part of him, and that if it had taken a different turn in its development, it could've been a natural element of his self, but that it had instead gotten stuck in a crawl space somewhere, neglected and denied contact until it had grown into this creature that appeared to come over him like a transfiguration.

"Play with yourself," he said. "Stick your fingers in your cunt."

She did what he said; she was wet, swollen, tender, and numb. She masturbated expertly and felt nothing. She was aware of her humiliation, but it was so far away and had so little to do with her that she couldn't feel that either. Still, she clung to it fiercely, as if it were her only chance to feel.

He pissed on her genitals, occasionally traveling up her body. It felt warm, almost caressing, and for a second she had an unbearable sensation of closeness with him. Then she worried about the mess on the floor, which had smelled bad enough to begin with.

"Tell me you love me," he said.

"I love you."

He pissed in her face.

*After dinner they had gone* to a bar with red vinyl booths and drank martinis as they sat close together, stroking each other's thighs. She had told him about her experience in the garage with Rick Houlihan.

"That sounds a little gruesome," he said.

"Well, yeah." She stared confused at the play of light and shadow on a painfully perfect martini glass. "What do you mean?"

"I mean was it really that bad?"

"Yeah, it was. He was your average jerk I guess." She picked her olive out of her glass and chewed it, savoring its bitterness.

He stared at her until she felt self-conscious as she

hunted for bits of unchewed olive with her tongue. "Most of the men I've ever been with are like that. They're really awful."

His face went into a strange combination; his mouth was as playfully cruel as a child torturing an animal while his eyes were gentle and inviting. "You are so hard and closed," he said. "Don't you know anything about tenderness and caring? Between men and women?"

She stared, incredulous to think that he was on speaking terms with tenderness and caring. "Are you trying to tell me that you do?"

"Yeah, I do." His eyes beckoned her into an Easter egg world where males and females held hands and gazed into each other's eyes while music played in the background. She regarded it suspiciously. "I've had relationships that were close and loving. From what you've told me, you haven't. Why is that?"

His falsely tender eyes mocked her and hurt her; still part of her trembled forward, starving to experience the place of love and closeness he had displayed, even if it was a deliberate illusion created to highlight her privation.

He smiled, and the cruelty of his mouth shadowed his eyes and made their tenderness piercing. "I'm going to teach you about love and closeness," he said.


*They fucked touching as little* as possible; he raised straight up on his arms, she with her legs wide apart and her arms flung open to grip the sheets in an antiembrace. She closed her eyes and turned her head away from him, hurtling alone through her imagination, the furniture of her internal self smashing on impact.

"I'd like to see you on your hands and knees," he

whispered, "surrounded by guys who'd piss on your cunt and jerk off in your face. I'd like to blindfold you in the Hellfire Club and tie you up with your legs spread so anybody could fuck you or beat you."

She imagined the warm piss of strangers between her legs and come running down her face. Split apart and boundary-less, she was sucked into the eye of the storm. She reached between her legs for some tiny memory of pleasure. She floated for a second of peace before she came as if she were being cut to pieces, her cunt and her heart utterly apart.

He continued to flail above her, his eyes closed, oblivious, alone in his private cyclone.

*I don't have a husband anymore* and my kids don't give a damn about me," said the elderly black lady. She regarded Justine with what appeared to be irritation as Justine moved about her, preparing her for an EKG.

"What about friends? Can't they help you out?"

"Yeah, but I'm not the kind of person who likes to always be going to other people with my problems. They've got plenty of their own you know." Mrs. Dubois regarded her censoriously.

The problem under discussion was Mrs. Dubois's partial blindness due to severe cataracts in both eyes. She had begun to find it difficult to shop and to read bills; she had almost fallen down a flight of stairs, a potential disaster for someone her age. She was reluctant, however, to have the cataracts removed; Justice thought it was because she was afraid of having her eyes operated on. "I'm sure your friends wouldn't mind helping you," said Justine, "they'd be pretty mean if they did."

Mrs. Dubois answered her with a look that said, "If you think that's 'mean,' you don't know what mean is, you young fool."

Well, thought Justine, it's not any of my business. Still, she had always liked Mrs. Dubois, a stiff-backed, ill-tempered, good-mannered, ferociously proper little woman who always pulled on her threadbare kid gloves with a wonderful arrogant smartness before she left the office. She hated to think of her alone at home in a small dark apartment, hungry and afraid to go out because she couldn't see. She wondered if her pride prevented her from getting help from her neighbors and children, or if they really were indifferent to her. She applied the clamps to the delicate sepia ankles and thought of herself, alone in her apartment at night, trying to soothe herself to sleep with a fantasy of Bryan holding her in his arms and cupping her head against his chest, which he never did and probably never would do. Her concern for Mrs. Dubois united with her desperation and self-pity and became magnified abnormally. She thought of Mrs. Dubois as a young woman, a romantic and finicky young woman who liked matching jewelry combinations and wanted everything to be just so. She imagined her traveling through the barbed wire and land mines of a racist society which refused to respect or even acknowledge the delicacy of any black woman and insisted on seeing only the coarseness and dullness that it had decreed to be the character of African-Americans, regardless of how it had to distort its vision in the process. Since the neat garden of Angeline Dubois's nature was denied the sun and warmth of acknowledgment, she was forced to turn inward to keep her internal garden alive, to draw nurture from an underground well so deep she couldn't allow her attention to waver from the thread of concentration on which she lowered the bucket, lest the thread break and she be bereft forever. Thus she drew herself in, stiffening the rules, regulations, and visiting hours of the garden, tightening its borders, becoming fanatical over the patterns in which it was allowed to grow until her natural delicacy had assumed the martial uniform of primness, the bitter primness with which she pulled on her battered, once-elegant gloves.

Justine desolately considered the level of insult this woman had had to bear simply in maintaining her true self in a world that denied its existence, and the vicarious pain fell like a piece of granite against her own pain. "Maybe you should get the operation, Mrs. Dubois," she said.

The filmy, half-blinded eyes filled with expressions that rose and were succeeded by different shades of feeling; she saw Justine's kindness which she despised and rejected, she saw also that the kindness was connected to something else, felt curious as to what this other thing might be, then rejected it as well, then felt curious again. Justine could see she felt invaded and oppressed by her concern, and strove to hold it away from her. Then the eyes softened, perhaps because she saw that Justine was essentially harmless and well-meaning, perhaps because she was too old to expend the energy required to reject her; she accepted Justine's kindness and then let it fall away from her with the uselessness of a broken ornament. "Well maybe I will," she said.

Mrs. Dubois *says her children* don't give a damn about her," said Justine to Glenda.

"Ah! That is nonsense. She is probably just depressed."

"How do you know?"

"Because her daughter has come to pick her up here before and she seems to be a fine young person. She wouldn't come pick her up if she didn't care about her."

Justine didn't see that that was necessarily true but she didn't want to argue. Glenda oscillated the radio dial to escape the news for more classical music and was interrupted by a phone call. The dial was caught for a moment on a pop song undercut with the processed mutter of the news broadcast. The song told about love and then the news voice gained ascendancy long enough to mention the latest in a series of incidents in which gangs of young girls surrounded lone women and jabbed them in the butt with needles. So far, the jabbing girls had been black and the jabbed women had been white, and the media was solemnly speculating that the attacks might be racial; one commentator said she thought that perhaps they were making a statement about the spread of AIDS in the black community via hypodermics. The love song swelled forth again, smothering the news with one and only true love. Justine was stung by the sweet, calculated young voice, its high pitch like a tiny knife cutting a valentine heart out of the coarse flesh of love.

Mrs. Dubois emerged from the office, her little hat askew on her head. For the first time Justine saw her composure become undone in embarrassment as she reacted to the sight of Justine's face, which was crying spare, almost dry tears as she filled out Mrs. Dubois's appointment card, talking as if nothing unusual was taking place even as the tears ran over her lips.

*Justine was glad* when they let her leave work early because that way she would have more time to work on her Anna Granite piece. But it had probably made a bad impression to cry at work, even though she had done it discreetly, even though Mrs. Dubois had been nice about it.

She bought a bag of cookies in lieu of dinner and ate them as she sat on the floor with her legs extended before her, thinking about the article. She justified going without dinner by telling herself that preparing and eating it would take away too much of her writing time. The eating of meals had somehow become burdensome to her; she was losing weight and becoming anxious about her health, yet she couldn't make herself eat nutritionally sound food. Well, she'd worry about it later. She wadded up the empty cookie bag and left it on the floor. She put her notebook on her lap, picked up her pen, and began: "The national swing to the right, in progress for the last five years, has developed the skewed, triple exclamation point character of a bad novel."

The phone rang, and she picked it up. "Hi," he said. "Feel like getting your ass whipped?"

"I'm busy," she snapped and hung up.

The phone rang again, four times before she answered it.

"God, what're you so testy about?" he asked. "At least you could say hello."

"It didn't seem necessary."

"You know my nutty sense of humor."

"Okay, hello. I'm working on my article and I can't see you tonight if that's what you were asking about."

"I understand. You're writing really important stuff and you can't be interrupted."

"Fuck off." She hung up again.

The phone rang again. Again she picked it up.

"Is this behavior modification or what?"

"You're acting like an asshole."

"So what else is new? Justine, I don't want to make

you mad. I know you have to do your work. It'll probably be great. I just wanted to see you. I've been thinking about you all day."

"I've been thinking about you too," she lied.

"That's nice."

"I'd love to see you, it's just I can't now. If I get this
done tonight, maybe tomorrow."

They hung up civilly. She continued writing. "This
cultural utopia of greed, expressed in gentrification
and the slashing of social programs, has had its
spokesperson and prophet for the last fifty years, a
novelist whose books are American fantasies that mirror, in all its neurotic excess, the frantic twist to the
right we are now experiencing. Anna Granite, who
coined the term 'the Truth of Selfishness,' has been
advocating the yuppie raison d'être since the early forties; it is only now that her ideas are being lived out,
in mass culture and in government."

The phone rang again.

"How about if I just come over and whip you and
then leave so you can keep working?"

She hung up, cursed, unplugged the phone, and
kept writing.

*J*ustine *had said that* she would call me when the article was going to appear in the *Vision,* and I believed her. I knew that it often took months for magazines to print articles, so I wasn't suspicious or impatient when two months passed without my hearing from her. I kept it in the back of my mind like a present to be opened when the time was right. I imagined reading it and then meeting with Justine to discuss it. I would praise her overall insight and then criticize the finer points of her analysis, instructing her in how she might present her arguments better in the future. I imagined her following my finger with her eyes as it traced the place she had gone slightly awry in her article, I imagined her humbly nodding.

But she didn't call me.

I was leaving work after a grueling twelve-hour shift. It was 10:00 A.M., and I was exhausted. Tiny particles of paranormal light swam before my eyes; the day workers, with their bright, tense faces, their jaunty manic walks, swinging purses and dangling belts were n onslaught. I made my way out of the building, bubles of disorientation popping about my head.

Ordinarily I rode a company car home from work, ut at this hour it was faster to take the subway, so I ent to the nearest noise-boiling pit. The train was deyed, or so I deduced from the mangled voice that oared from the speakers above us. The mob on the latform grew in number, everyone bearing down ard on the track of daily habit, staring into the maw f the impending day, pacing in insect circles, pitchig their thoughts and feelings into the future or the ast, anywhere but the subway.

I spotted a concession stand and thought of little nints and chewy candies. I made my way towards the ooth to participate in the mechanical ballet of giving nd receiving choreographed by the muttering man ehind the counter. As I waited my turn I scanned the nagazines and papers, the horrific headlines and appy faces that help give form to our inchoate and ulnerable mass psyche. I looked rather fondly at the *ision*—yet another headline about the political imort of some rock band—and absently turned the ront page to stare at the table of contents. "Anna Granite," it said, "Yuppie Grandmother—by Justine hade."

The snottiness of it was like a bracing blow to the ace—but I recovered. Probably Justine had nothing o do with the headline, and not everyone used the vord "yuppie" pejoratively. I muffed my part in the newsstand ballet by turning to walk away with the paper without paying, and the newsman screamed at me, cowling at my cheerful attempts at explanation. I aid for it and opened it—there it was again! That classic photograph of Granite's imperial face, so long absent from public pages! My pleasure rose and combined with my exhaustion, and for a moment my brain came undone from its dense gray coils and me[r]rily bobbed in the colorful miasma of irrationality. [I] started to read, and the subway came bawling int[o] view. I folded the paper under my arm and fought sav[-] agely for a seat so I could comfortably read, shame[-] lessly using my size and weight to get my way. Peopl[e] glared, but I didn't care. I was smiling insanely as [I] opened the paper. I was puzzled, even in my magnan[-] imous state, by her first sentence and its metaphor o[f] the bad novel. I was still game though and read on; [I] became even more puzzled. "Yuppies, power break[-] fasts, the leering, double-crossing bed-hoppers of 'D[y-] nasty' and 'Dallas' stalking their victims in glitz[y] gowns, a national obsession with exercise and physica[l] perfection, a riot of matching spider-limbed furniture[,] surreal TV Prayathons . . ." What did this have to d[o] with Anna Granite? She went on in this irrelevant wa[y] until I began to think I was reading the wrong article[.] Then: "It sounds like a bad novel and it is." My dis[-] tended happiness hemorrhaged in inky black spurts a[s] I was lashed in the face with that serpentine phrase "[a] novelist whose books are American fantasies that mir[-] ror, in all its neurotic excess, the frantic twist to th[e] right we are now experiencing."

"That bitch," I said, "that goddamn bitch."

The nyloned thighs to my right shifted away fro[m] me.

I read on, my concentration now razor sharp. Sh[e] went on to describe Granite's influence and its pres[-] ent day manifestations: the taped lectures, the yearl[y] Philadelphian gatherings, the Definitist courses of[-] fered at various small colleges, an expensive three-da[y] workshop held in Honolulu, the Rationalist Reaffirma[-] tion School, and the fact that Knight Ludlow, "highl[y] placed city financial analyst" had been her "persona[l] protégé."

"Her novels," continued Justine "are like phantom comic-book worlds shadowing, in exaggerated Kabuki-like form, the psychological life and anxieties of our society."

"Shit!" I muttered. "A comic book! A comic book!" I turned to the young black woman on my right with some vague idea of showing her I wasn't another subway madwoman. "Have you read this?" I asked.

She glanced at me, more with her face than her eyes, tightly shook her head "no" and returned her attention to her paperback.

"Well if you do, you ought to know it's crap, one hundred percent. I know the writer and I know the person it's about. I was interviewed by this ... writer and it's a vindictive piece of falsification." She ignored me. Well to hell with you, I thought. I looked at the people across from me. They were staring resolutely in every direction but mine. I cracked the paper assertively and continued reading.

Justine went on for several paragraphs in that breezy pop *Vision*-speak, invoking television shows, movies, and media jokes about the inner conflicts of American psychology—the "pop icon" of the lone hero versus the "pathological" desire to be part of the crowd, the assumption that the strong individual is somehow inherently in opposition to society. "This confusion extends most painfully into the conflicting American attitude towards money," pontificated the bitch. "Does an individual with money have a responsibility to society and does the government have a moral right or obligation to oversee this responsibility? This question is overlaid with an almost pornographic fascination with money and people who have it ..."

I had to concede it was interesting; if it hadn't been in the service of trashing Granite, I might've enjoyed it. Why, I thought in anguish, did intelligent people always try to undermine Granite, even now? "Anna Granite's novels not only shadow the back-and-forth, one-or-the-other nature of this struggle, they purport to resolve it." This was followed by an unfair caricature of Granite's theories concluding with "she reduced the complex dilemma of the individual in society down to either/or moralistic terms couched in the dramatic devices and gestural glitz of a soap opera."

"Cunt," I said.

"Excuse me," said a female wearing purple contact lenses. "Would you mind watching your language?"

"Mind your own business," I snarled.

She reared back and clicked her tongue.

"The irony is that, like the wicked liberals in her books, Granite's rational answers are based on illusions. She stood for rationality, yet her novels shamelessly (and what's worse, unknowingly) use emotional manipulation, melodrama, jargon, and sexual fantasy to make her points. While claiming to exalt the individual, she plugged into a mass psyche, using archetypal characters devoid of real individuality, with the same vulgar emotional power as the Wicked Witch. . . . Granite's work is a phenomenon worth looking at as a fun-house mirror for a society that is one part sober puritan and one part capitalist sex fiend. . . . It's an odd thing to watch a culture start to look like the plot of a bad novel."

"Goddamn it!" I yelled.

There was a rustling sound around me as the commuters strained their bodies to put a token of space between themselves and the crazy person. I the crazy person! When obviously demented people got paid to write stuff like this! I felt and stopped the approach of tears. From that point I only scanned the piece for particularly telling and offensive passages, of which there were many.

"She succeeded because she was, however clumsily, onto something much bigger than a first glance at her silly novels would reveal. Her writing was like the broad slashes and gaudy colors of the cheapest comic strip—but it was a comic strip about life and death and everybody knew it."

I inhaled deeply and looked up to be sure I hadn't missed my stop. The doors were rattling open, people were moving in and out, wiping their noses, securing their purses, locking their blank stares into place. I was okay. I looked back down and saw "She was repeatedly molested by her father during what sounds like a horrific childhood, and she says Granite's books were what enabled her to see that life could be other than hideous."

My anger suspended itself as I experienced the strange sensation of seeing my life rendered publicly. It was on one hand a demeaning experience, like seeing myself as a paper cut-out doll, marched by a huge hand through the toy landscape of somebody else's opinions and purposes, unable to register my distaste because my words had been cut into dolly balloons and frozen before my mouth. But it was at the same time aggrandizing. It was only a small part of me, but so enlarged, so magnified, on a national scale, that it was like having a gross image of myself inflated into a giant parade balloon, floating above the crowd, my tubby arms helplessly extended, my face crudely painted in some fiendish expression designed for maximum impact. I watched myself, fascinated, entertained, waving and cheering at the balloon with the rest of the crowd.

I had to admit Justine had quoted me more or less fairly. Of course, my words were taken out of context and distorted as is always the case with such articles, but the quotes were fairly accurate, and I didn't sound

like a fool or a maniac, unlike most of the other peo
ple she'd skewered on paper. She couldn't resist put
ting in snide parentheticals in which she suggested
that my opinions were not well-founded, but there was
still room for the intelligent reader to make a deci
sion. Gingerly I moved from reaction to myself as pub
lic item and into my life again, unscathed, safe, still
me.

Then I read the next paragraph. "Dorothy is a
huge woman, who floats with the slow grace of the al
ways fat in airy, gaudy single-cloth garments of indeter
minate nature. Her face is intelligent, and her
emotional intensity rises from her like a force field. In
conversation, she is incisive, and she displays an acute
sensitivity to nuance and an uncanny ability to read a
situation emotionally by scanning the minutia of ex
pressions and gestures that frame it. When she talks of
the early days of the Definitist meetings, she does so in
symbolic, mythological terms ... when she discusses
the split between Bradley and Granite she is like a
child talking about her parents' divorce a month after
it happened ..."

I looked up and sat still for some moments, my
bulk stewing in isolation from my lone head. I felt
much as I had on first meeting Justine; insulted and
yet seduced. She did not have to refer to me as "al
ways fat," and there was condescension in her descrip
tion. Yet I also felt in her printed words a respect for
me, a desire to understand me, to make her readers
understand me, and I couldn't help being touched by
this. She said I was "intelligent," "authentic," and "in
cisive," yet she compared me to a traumatized child.
Worse, she implied that my fealty for Granite was the
fealty of a traumatized child. I sat still while the possi
bility that she was right hovered about me like the evil
enchanter closing in on Don Quixote.

I noticed that I was three stations past my stop and rose, cursing. My purse fell off my arm and onto the floor, my keys, lipstick, and change poured out of it. All at once I was engulfed by life's physically mechanical nature, all the tiny movements and functions you have to perform correctly just to get through the day, all the accoutrements you must carry which can malfunction at any time. Panicked, I fell on the subway floor, groping for my belongings. Legs shifted about me as the animated forest of humans came to life like enchanted trees; hands shot forth, stealing my change, helpfully extending my keys to me, returning my rolled-away lipstick with an impressive hand-to-hand relay involving several school children and a "Yo! Lady!" I was helped, hindered, patted, pulled up, and nodded at, and then the people turned into trees again, frozen on their straps. I passed through them to exit with the ritual Excuse me's, the doors rattled shut behind me, and I realized I'd left the paper on the train.

My hands made fists, released, and made them again. It was too much, it was unbearable. The darting people about me were like the hurtling debris of an exploded planet, and I could not stand to look at them. I fled the subway and found I was just above East 14th Street, where, I realized I could easily buy another paper.

I made my purchase at a newsstand and was soothed by the ease with which this was accomplished. As my panic receded, I remembered that I was exhausted and decided to sit down in a coffee shop to finish reading the article.

Soon I was seated with the paper open in my trembling hands, a cup of coffee on its way. I read on, my attention caught on the protruding nails of the deliberate meanness that held the piece together. The coffee came and I drank the bitter stuff. The shop had few customers and I was grateful for that. A dowdy woman read a soiled paperback. A teenager stared into space. A handsome boy mutely reached across a linoleum tabletop to touch the hand of his scowling handsome boy companion. The small dark proprietor strolled behind his counter, absently pulling his ear.

If I had been seduced, I had also been abandoned. I thought of Justine sitting in my apartment fixing me with that stare, spindly fingers working her pen. Even then she had known she would write something that attacked everything I had founded my sane life on, even as she allowed our words and feelings to twine and knot, bringing us together again in an effort to disentangle them. She had talked to me, too, exposed herself—and yet not really, because it was ultimately she who walked away and made this house of cards, this article, this canned result of our exchange which had meant so much to me and so little to her. It was she who stepped back, wrote in her notebook, and pronounced me a "child." It was she who, after our intimacy, stroked me with the flattering words "authentic," "incisive," "intelligent," caressing me under the table like a flippant ex-lover, using the remains of her power to invoke the memory of our shared closeness, a memory meant to render me helpless. That was the most painful thing; in this article, in which she used me to further demean the memory of Granite, she also invoked, in an encoded still life, the genuine moments we had experienced. Her sensitivity to me had been real, she had illuminated me gently, with respect, and yet she had done it in a context that made a joke out of everything I believed in, and, indirectly, made a fool of me.

Why did my every close contact become a betrayal?

Why did everyone who touched me desert me? Why was I never able to do anything about it?

The waiter wandered by, leaving a greasy slip of paper on my table, his head turned away from me as if it was a secret note instead of a bill. I stared at the objects before me: cold coffee in a cup of thick white glass, folded napkin, spoon with a liquid coffee shadow on its face. Symbols of order and humility, comfort and banality. These were the things of my life; I had been sitting at these goddamn coffee tables all my life recovering from what other people had done to me.

The anger that had begun on the subway rose like bubbles from a deceptively still pool of chemical waste. That little bitch had to have realized how lonely I was, what an easy target for information and confidence. She knew how much pain I'd experienced in life; I'd told her. But she'd exploited me anyway for whatever piddling advancement this article represented to her. It wasn't the first time; there had been other reporters, other articles as wrong-headed and rude. But I had never had coffee and cakes with any of these reporters, they had never discussed their love lives with me, they had never looked at me with those eyes of hers, those eyes that saw me for who I was, and then betrayed me anyway.

A voice of reason coughed nervously and interjected that perhaps I had misinterpreted the message of her eyes. But I had not! She had silently transmitted promises to me, promises of respect and allegiance and, and ... I felt like there was an animal trapped in my lower body, pacing furiously, wanting to come out and tear the nearest living creature to pieces.

I stood up, wiping my sweating palms on my dress

(a single fucking cloth garment of indeterminate nature) and approached the man behind the counter.

"Excuse me," I sweetly said. "Do you have a current Manhattan phone book I could look at?"

He ran his eyes the length of my body with habitual suspicion and mumbled an affirmative. He found the book in his gleaming cabinets. He handed it to me and leaned on the counter, dreamily gazing out the window. The animal in my abdomen roared and reared as I found the massive "S" listing. I flipped the pages and ran my damp finger down the columns. I was right. There was only one J. Shade. She lived at 33 Charles which, I surmised, was in the Village.

I hurled a wadded dollar at the man behind the counter and I was on the street again, my arm raised stiffly in the cab-flagging salute. This was Monday, the same day of the week Justine had met me at the coffee shop—as she had remarked at the time, her day off.

*Y*ou *cunt," he said.* "You fucking worthless cunt."

She didn't answer him because he had his belt tight around her throat. Her body convulsed and her sight went. He released his grip, and her vision cleared. Her arms and legs were cold; she tried to move her fingers and wasn't sure she succeeded. His face came into focus over hers, wavering out of darkness like a dream. He was saying something, but she couldn't hear, the roaring in her head was too loud. She felt him inside her; her vagina was tight and dry. He tightened the belt again, and again she lost her sight. He released her; first his eyes came out of the darkness, then his face. She tried to tell him to stop, but her voice wasn't working.

He held his hand before her and moved his fingers in a gesture she didn't understand. Then she realized he was snapping his fingers. He grabbed her jaw with a hard pinch, and moved her head back and forth. Her vision started to go blank again and then cleared abruptly.

"Hey," he said. "Hey. Are you okay?"

She put her tongue experimentally out of her mouth and touched her lips. They were so dry they didn't feel like flesh.

"Here," he said. He leaned over her body towards the floor and then rolled back onto the bed clutching a bottle of sloshing liquid. He put it to her lips. Reflexively she tried to take the bottle with her hand and couldn't; she remembered her hands and feet were tied at the corners of her bed. She opened her mouth and the burning vodka made her sputter and cough. He shoved the bottle against her teeth and kept pouring, letting it run down her chin after she had closed her lips.

"Thought you were gone there for a minute," he said. He took the bottle from her, put it to his lips, upended it, and drained it. He emitted a loud "ahhh" noise.

"I wanna get up," she said. "Untie me." She heard the fear in her voice, and it frightened her more.

He leaned back against the wall and looked at her, smiling.

"Goddamn it, Bryan. My stomach hurts and I have to pee."

He extended his hand and began to stroke her cunt. His eyes looked like the eyes of Mrs. Rabinowitz; the iris bristling with dismembered emotion, the whites riddled with yellow veins.

"You look like a lunatic," she said.

He slid away from the wall and put his head between her legs. She retreated further into her body. He followed her. She closed her eyes and imagined leaving her body to float away in empty air, turning somersaults in the contactless ease of space, unseen, untouched, unalive. Instead her body stripped itself for him; her full bladder and all her other organs lay exposed, shivering in assonance with the slow movements of his tongue. She felt she was turning gradually inside out. He could've strangled her. To her horror, the thought excited her.

"I'm your daddy's good buddy," he said, "and your daddy told me I can play with your little pussy any time I want."

"Don't," she said, "please don't."

"Any time I want I can take you out to the park and make you take your little panties off."

"Please, Bryan, don't, don't." Her words were a landslide of pebbles and dirt under someone's foot.

Her buzzer sounded. He turned and looked at the door. "Expecting anybody?" he asked.

She was unable to answer.

He got up and walked unsteadily to the intercom. He looked at her and smiled. "I've always wanted to meet your friends," he said.

*The Village,*" *I said* to the cabdriver.

"Where in the Village?"

His tone opined that I was an incompetent.

"Thirty-three Charles," I shot back.

"Charles and what?"

"I don't know. Isn't the address enough?"

He muttered something, and his little flag went up. For a moment I felt myself engaged with his strange, dissatisfied energies, and then he became merely the back of a head, and I returned to my angry plan.

Of course, she might not be home, but she could be, and even if she was not, I would wait for her. I would come back again and again until I found her. I would ring her doorbell, and if she didn't let me in, I would ring the bell of everyone in the building until someone let me in. At least one thief had gained entry to my building that way.

Once I confronted her, I was less sure of what would happen, except that I would scream at her. I was mad enough to do that, but I so infrequently screamed at anyone that the idea made my heart leap with fear and excitement. I would back her into a corner! If she reached for the phone to call the police, I would knock it from her hand!

I opened the *Vision* again so I could scan the article and encourage my anger. It worked. The second time around, my feelings were not cushioned by shock or the titillation of seeing an interpretation of myself in print, and I felt even more deeply indignant. What kind of person would go around worming her way into people's homes and confidences, filtering their words and images through her distorted cynical vision and then using them as weapons against someone they loved? What kind of person could so twist the truth of Granite's ideas?

"You fucking liar," I said.

The cab driver's eyes flickered in the mirror.

"I don't mean you," I said. "Have you read this week's *Urban Vision*?"

"No, ma'am, I don't read that paper."

His words were polite, but his voice harbored another quality which I could best describe as a readiness to see me as several different kinds of asshole at once. It was different from an assumption in that an assumption is passive; the quality in his voice was watching and waiting. I ignored it and pressed on, secure in the knowledge that I am not an asshole.

"Well good for you," I said. "Because it's a piece of trash. Ordinarily I don't buy it either, but I did this week because there's an article in here about Anna Granite, the most important thinker of our time. Do you know who she is?"

He turned his head to curse at a car which had forced its snout between us and the lane we were rightfully headed for. We jerked to a halt as a dark, leaping boy skipped in front of us and continued nimbly through the traffic, a yelling man in baggy red pants stumbling in pursuit. The driver ferociously manned the wheel; we swerved, and I fell to one side in a rattle of paper. I struggled up and briefly took in the awfulness of the moment, the panting vehicles, their primitive engines covered with a thin veneer of colored metal and cheap style, all tiny compartments for embattled humans on seat-belt leashes, vainly trying to assert their presence with the classical or rap or rock music spilling crazily out their windows to be consumed by the grinding of gears and the clouds of noxious fumes. Construction workers hammered and drilled, bicycle messengers shot into the invisible future of their destination, thousands of faces passed through my line of vision, thousands of expression lines, eye-glints, and hair cuts. An unoccupied strip of street opened before us; the driver gunned his motor, and I was thrown back against the seat.

"Do you know who Anna Granite is?" I persisted.

"No. Maybe I heard of her but I don't really know."

"Well she's a philosopher who stands for everything that makes life possible. She believes in total freedom for the individual as opposed to living for the state. She believes in the primacy of rationality over emotion, although she respects the truth of emotion." I faltered and groped for the words to express succinctly what Granite had been, her hot leonine face in a haze of turquoise light refracting off the crystal chandeliers, the feel of her hand on mine, my life saved, so many lives saved. He was black; I would mention her stand against racism, except I didn't want to patronize.

"She's a Scientologist, right?"

"No, not at all."

"A Moonie?"

"No! She, she was a Definitist, an inventor of a whole movement dedicated to the power and sanctity of the individual—"

"White individuals, I can assume."

"No! Not at all! She was absolutely against the kind of collective tribal mentality from which racism springs!"

He snorted. "So what does *Urban Vision* have to say about it?"

A tornado of explanations, political points of view, sociopolitical lines of thought roared through my head. There was no time to explain it all and anyway, none of it addressed the real issue. "*Urban Vision* ran this article by this bitch who lied to me about everything she believed, who got me to talk to her about the most personal things in my life, and then, then used it in the service of, of evil, of everything that's destroying this society. This person betrayed me, she—"

He sharply swerved and pulled over to the curb. I paused and looked. We were in the Village, but this was not Charles Street.

"Get out of my car," he said.

The chattering voices in my head stopped, confused. "Why? Is something wrong?"

"No, lady, nothing's wrong. I've just been driving around all day listening to the crazy piss-ant problems of white people, and I can't stand it anymore. Get out."

Explanations lunged forward, all talking at once, knocking each other down and climbing over each other. "This is not a crazy piss-ant problem!" To my shame, I heard a whine streaking down the center of my voice. "I'm talking about something that affects both of us, I'm—"

"Whatever it is, I can guarantee it doesn't affect us

in the same way. You owe me three-forty." Smartly, he struck the stop button on his meter.

Shocked, I sat back and reached for my purse. Distress signals flew from my body in bright flares that perished in the dead air between the driver and me. He was a wall, impervious to the stewing explanations, hurt feelings, and angry impulses that hurled themselves at him, tugging at his clothes. I tried to awaken the anger that had so recently reigned in me, but what I felt was the hurt passivity that knew such walls very well. My coins and dollars fell from my fingers and I had to grope for them on the floor of the cab. He muttered contemptuously.

The problem was, when I looked at myself as he probably saw me, I couldn't blame him. A fat white woman with dyed hair who he imagined came from a pampered suburban life and had had everything given to her, but was ranting and screaming anyway. I felt a tingling sensation in the back of my throat, like you get before you vomit. I sat up, the skin on my face hot with sensations. I made myself talk as I thrust the money over the ripped and taped up seat.

"I know what it looks like," I said. "I know what you think. And I don't blame you."

Tears panted in my hoarse voice. His eyes darted in the mirror, eyes of anger, puzzlement, and strangely, an element of fear.

"But if you knew me." I stopped to muffle the tears. "If you knew the truth about me, you would be sorry you are doing this. I'm not your enemy."

His eyes changed, his jaw softened, and in a terrible moment I saw that he was sorry, if not because of my words, then because he was gentleman enough to be distressed by the tears in my voice. It was a terrible moment because neither of us knew what to do about it. He looked away in embarrassment. I dropped the money on the seat and got out of the car.

I stood trembling on the pavement, trying not to cry. I heard his voice behind me. "Charles is just a couple more blocks to your left," he said. I turned in time to see him roll up his window and drive away.

I began walking to my left. The full weight of my exhaustion pressed the backs of my eyeballs. Why had he been so angry? I passed fruit stands, beggars, wastebaskets jammed with trash. The only reason I could think of was the recent acquittal of the white kids who'd beat a black kid to death, an event which had made a lot of people mad. He was right, I thought miserably. If I were he, I'd be in no mood to listen to white people's problems either, however universal they might be. The thought was like a punch in the gut, and I was no longer sure I had the stamina to carry out my mission. My single focus had been cleft in two, and now only half my mind was lunging towards my revenge on Justine, while the other half was riding to Brooklyn with the cab driver to find the white brawlers and beat them senseless or kill them. I sweated in triumph as I imagined the terrified expression on the face of a young thug as I picked him up and pinned him against the wall, fixing him with my righteous stare before I—but although I was big and at that point very strong, it was unlikely I could pick up a strapping eighteen-year-old boy. How would we know where they were anyway? We could find out, but if a white fat lady and a black guy drove into Brooklyn inquiring about these local heroes, we'd probably be set upon by the entire community before we even got out of the car. Besides, the cab driver was long gone.

I couldn't do anything about that atrocity, but, I told myself, I could do something about Justine

Shade; my wavering resolve was strong again as I bore down upon Charles Street.

I was at first glad to discover that 33 Charles was only a few houses down the block, but as I entered the small building, I found myself wishing it had been farther away so that I would have more time to prepare myself for the encounter. I stood before the buzzers wiping my sweating hands on my dress in blank anxiety until I remembered my strategy: first push her buzzer to find out if she was home. Easy enough I thought. I almost cried out in alarm when the device buzzed back. I was not expecting that; surely she wouldn't be stupid enough to admit anyone who buzzed her from the street. To make sure I pressed the button again. Again I was startled by an even more immediate response. I stared at the door. What if she was expecting a friend and thought that I was that friend? That would mean the friend could arrive in the middle of my scene and cause awkwardness. Then I realized that such an occurrence would cause all the more embarrassment for Justine, would mar her social plan. The door buzzed a third time, unprovoked. I shoved it open and began to climb the stairs, my determination advancing and receding. According to the mailbox she was on the fifth floor, and I tried to take advantage of the long walk to rehearse the outraged speech I'd planned. I panted as I climbed, and the panting fed my sense of extremity and imminent crisis. "And then," I whispered between my teeth, "then you have the nerve to patronize a thinker who—"

Like a jack-in-the-box, her door popped open before I'd reached the landing, a pale, mocking face peeked round its corner. Leering, goading, apparently expecting me! I lunged, I gained the apartment, I knocked the face to the floor! "You bitch!" I yelled.

Victorious, I shut the door behind me. Then I

blinked. Embarrassment prickled my face. Before me lay sprawled a naked ratty-looking young man slowly propping himself up on his elbows, a psychotic smile infecting his face. His eyes traveled up and down my body with such aggressive lewdness that I felt like stepping backwards. He spoke to the corner of the room.

"Hey," he asked it, "who's the tub o' lard?"

I followed his gaze, and the air began to ripple like water. Justine Shade lay naked on her bed, her hands and feet tied to its corners, her head raised, her wild mascara-smeared eyes staring at me with utter incomprehension. She dropped her head, muttered incoherently, then raised her head again. "What the fuck are you doing here?" she asked.

"Don't tell me," said the man. "It's one of your diesel dyke girlfriends."

"Eat shit," said Justine.

I saw marks on her thighs and breasts, and dried blood on her lips. My voice came mechanically out of my throat. "I came because of that . . . *thing* you published in *Urban Vision*, that's what I'm doing here." I used the words as if they could insulate me from the scene before me. I realized I should turn and walk out of whatever this was, but I was transfixed by Justine's raised face. Her skin was so red it could have been scalded, her forehead was almost contorted with tension while her lower face was weirdly lax, her eyes were like terrified animals bolting in every direction and finding no release. She looked both inhuman and shockingly human. But when she spoke, her voice and words were clipped, flat, almost rebuking.

"Dorothy," she said, "this is really not the time to discuss it. Why don't you call me later?"

The man rose from the floor into a squatting position. "Why don't you eat her pussy?" he suggested conversationally. "I'll watch."

Justine spoke again, her voice even more absurdly proper. "Actually," she said, "now that you're here, could you untie me? I have to go to the bathroom and this idiot"—she indicated the man with a head gesture—"has gone completely off the deep end."

Her voice held a tea party in the garden while a child was murdered in the house. I could not hear her in her voice or see her in her face and for a moment my contempt for her was almost hatred.

The man stood up. "Are you mad at her?" he said. "Maybe you'd like to whip her." He took a whip from a small table and held it out to me. He was close enough for me to smell the liquor evaporating from his skin, to feel the aggression crackling around him with the electrical force of a bomb. I could feel it pressing around my head and body, wanting to get into me. He stepped closer. I stepped towards the door. "Get away from me," I said. "Just get the hell away from me." My hand was on the doorknob.

"Dorothy," said Justine. "Please."

The brittle control of her voice cracked and I heard her. I looked and saw the strange, serious woman who had come to ask me about Anna Granite. She was desolate and ashamed. My heart opened with a quick, painful movement. I moved swiftly towards her.

The man stepped in front of me and put his hands on me. I pushed him away. He stepped in front of me again. I pushed him. He leaned into my face and started talking to me. His voice coiled round me like a snake. My body stiffened with fear. He put his hands on my breasts and hurt me. And I hit him. His hands flew off my body as he reeled backward, clutching his bleeding mouth; he wavered and fell, banging a skinny hip on a little table. His ferocity fell in pieces around him, and he crouched, looking at me with a slippery grin. He started to say something, but I didn't give him a chance. I kicked him first, squarely in the chin, and then he got up and then I hit him again. It was a terrifying sensation, my fists beating his face, my foot slamming his belly and the knuckles of his hands as he clutched his naked little prick. He hit back, but he was weak and drunk and I could barely feel it. I got his hair in my fist and propelled him to the door, kicking his tailbone to encourage his scuttling cooperation. With my free hand I opened the door, kicked him into the hall, slammed the door, and locked it. My hands were trembling. He had torn my dress and bloodied my lip. My legs were trembling. My whole body was trembling. I felt as if my blood would burst from me. I felt my face with both hands, trying to make myself come back again. I was interrupted by a noise from the bed. I looked up. Justine was wriggling against her bonds. "Hurry! she said. "I'm going to throw up!"

Quickly, I went to her and began to untie her. "Are you all right?" I asked idiotically.

"Just a minute," she gasped.

I freed her and she immediately bounded towards the bathroom, the flesh of her scarred backside jiggling urgently. Outside, the man began to pound on the door with furious vigor.

I sat gingerly on the edge of the grossly rumpled bed and listened to the pounding. The door jumped and shuddered on its hinges, but it held. The man began to yell and curse, displaying a good deal more focus and force than he had a moment ago. I yelled at him to go away. Then I remembered that his clothes were in the room and he couldn't go away. I didn't know what to do. If I opened the door, he could come in full of murderous sobriety and rage; he could attack me and choke me to death. He was, after all, a man and, for all his puny size, possessed of testosterone and the other mysterious chemical and hormonal forces that goad that sex to kill, rape, and commit crimes of horrific sadism; I had simply gotten the drop on him. I felt afraid, more so than when he had been in the room. I thought of calling the police, but it was possible that if they appeared he would charge me with assault—and he had a witness, the unpredictable, perverted Justine Shade who was at the moment emitting unpleasant bodily noises from behind the bathroom door, of no help to me at all.

Then the pounding stopped and I heard another voice, also male, also angry. It said something about "butt-naked" and "jerk-off." Justine's friend seemed to make some kind of response. I leapt off the bed, hastily found the male clothing strewn around the room, and ran to the door. I opened it. His back was to me; he stood, with no shame apparent in his posture, facing a much larger, fully clothed fellow who was half-emerged from the apartment across the hall, an aggravated look on his face. Both men looked at me, the naked one whipping his head around to do so. I threw the clothes. He dove. I slammed the door and locked it. I listened. The shower was running in the bathroom.

"Look," said Justine's neighbor through the door. "I don't give a shit about your problems. I'm trying to sleep. Stop screaming or I'll throw you down the goddamn stairs. Get it?"

Justine's boyfriend seemed to contemplate this silently. I heard the door across the hall close. I heard rustling and floor creaking; probably he was getting dressed. I relaxed slightly.

The bathroom door popped open, and Justine minced out, a towel precariously wrapped about her nakedness. Her short hair was sleekly wet against her head. At first glance she seemed much refreshed. She looked at me, blinking rapidly, rubbed her face, and stood in the middle of the room with her arms around herself, staring at the door.

"Justine," he said from the hallway. "Justine."

His voice surprised me. It was mournful and gentle, full of remorse. It was vulnerable as a child alone in the dark. I looked at Justine. I could see in her face that the voice affected her, but she made no move to open the door.

"Justine," he said. "Honey."

She shook her head and approached the door, her buttocks peeking out of her towel. "Bryan," she answered, "you have to go away."

"Will you call me later?"

"No. Go away."

He made no response, nor did we hear him walk away. Justine listened attentively for a moment, then shrugged. She went to the bed and sat on it, looked at me, and then looked away. "Shit," she muttered. She covered her face with her hands and hunched forward.

I didn't know what to say.

"So," she said into her hands. "I guess you didn't like the article."

"No," I said. "I didn't."

"I'm sorry," she said. "I didn't think you would." She came out of her hunch and faced me. "But I couldn't help it. I had to say my opinion."

"You certainly didn't say your opinion when you were talking to me."

"Well as a reporter I don't have to. And I did say enough that—"

There was a quiet knock at the door.

Her little face coiled furiously, she shot off the bed and attacked the door with vicious, flat-footed kicks. "Dumb fucking scumbag!" she screamed. "Get away!"

She stood combative, panting, I thought rather ridiculous as she faced down the door, clutching her towel. After a few seconds of silence, she daintily adjusted the towel and returned to the bed. She looked at me. "But I don't think I can talk about it now. I'm exhausted. I've been up all night." Somewhat incongruously, she blushed.

"Me too," I said.

In the ensuing silence we heard footsteps retreating down the stairs. "Thank God," said Justine. "I thought he'd never leave." She stood up and walked past me to the kitchenette against the wall. "Would you like some camomile tea?"

I said yes and looked for a place to sit. There were no chairs or couch in the tiny studio, only the bed. I moved to sit on it, and she stopped me. "Wait," she said, "let me change those sheets." She dropped the towel and momentarily revealed her wounded body.

"Why," I said, "why did you let him do that to you?"

She didn't answer me. She took a robe from the closet and put it on. She began to strip the sheets from the bed. I waited, but she just said, "I'm glad you came." Her voice trembled, and she seemed to be trying to hide her face from me. She turned and stuffed the sheets in a laundry bag then drew a folded new sheet from the closet. She cracked it open and let it float over the bed. Then she crawled over the mattress tucking it under, looking like an animal in its burrow. "There," she said. "Have a seat."

We sat against large pillows and drank tea from china cups with flowers on them. We were silent at first, looking at each other, then looking away. I noticed that our hands were still shaking. I said again, "Why did you let him do that to you?"

"I didn't let him do anything," she snapped. She looked at me almost insolently. "I told him what to do." Her jaw twitched violently. "Except towards the end."

"Why?"

She looked away and slightly down and shrugged one small shoulder, the gesture of an adolescent in the principal's office. "I don't know." With tight lips, she sipped her tea. I noted the outline of her naked eyelashes and the fine curve of her cheek. She looked back at me. "Does it disgust you?"

"No. Yes. I don't know. I think so."

"Well, you're probably right. Although it's not as awful as it looks when you just sort of burst in on it like that. I mean *when* you're doing it, it's, you know. Except this got a little . . ." She put her teacup on the table near the bed and lay back against the pillow, curling her legs up and tucking her feet securely under the robe. She didn't finish her sentence.

"You don't disgust me," I said uncertainly. I looked at her cheaply beautiful old vanity with its chipped wood, its carved mirror under a gray veil of dust. On it were musty old perfume bottles with sticky remnants on the bottom, scattered rings and brooches, a piece of ribbon, and different colored candles in holders of all shapes and sizes, all lightly layered with dust. Pasted to the mirror was a black-and-white photograph of a very young child in a bathing suit, posing with a seductiveness that was unsettling in a preschooler. "I always thought you were interesting," I said. "I thought about you a lot."

"Really? What did you think?"

"Just that I would like to talk to you. Of course," I continued, rather bitterly, "that's probably because I don't have any friends. When you came to interview me, it was the longest talk I'd had with anyone for years. So naturally I fixated." I drank my tea.

"I don't have any friends either." She spoke sorrowfully.

"Really?" It was hard for me to believe. I thought all pretty people had friends.

"Well, I know a few people. I go out sometimes. But I don't have real friends."

"Why not?"

"I don't know. It's hard for me to be close to people." She sat up again and allowed her hair to shield her profile.

We sat silently for some time. As my body systems slowly regained their usual stately plod, the adrenaline drained from my flesh, and I imagined going home to sleep.

Then I realized she was crying. Tears dropped from her chin onto her folded hands, and she trembled small and hard. She sat erect and contained, dabbing at her face with the sleeve of her robe and gulping discreetly. I didn't comfort her because her body did not invite it. But I sat with my heart opened to her, feeling her heart mournfully opening to me, sending me the messages that can be received only by another heart, that which the intellect can never apprehend.

Still crying, she said, "I'm sorry about the article. I really am."

"It's all right," I said. "Frankly I haven't had so much excitement in years."

I felt her smile inwardly; her trembling stopped.

"I thought of you too sometimes," she said, tears still in her throat.

"What? What did you think?"

She sniffed and wiped at her nose. "They weren't really thoughts. Just images, feelings. I could tell you were very strong, and I wondered how you got to be that way."

"I already told you how." I spoke rather stiffly.

She smiled. "Anna Granite?"

"Yes. Anna Granite." My irritation with her flickered and died.

"I don't think that's it," she said.

I didn't answer. A cloud swallowed what little sun had come in through her barred window. She settled more deeply into the pillow and stretched her naked legs out from beneath the robe, tautly splaying then relaxing her toes. I felt the last of her tears leave her. She closed her eyes. I sat there watching her hand rise and fall on her stomach, the sound of her breath stroking my face. The hum of her refrigerator crawled up my backbone. I closed my eyes. A cocoon of dreams spun about me.

"Dorothy." Justine's voice woke me. Dimly I regarded her. "I'm going to lie down and try to sleep. I know the bed is small but if you want, you can sleep here."

We lay down side by side, politely observing the conventions of strangers sharing a bed. I could feel her small body bristling with contained fidgets as she lay stiffly on her side, not invading my side of the bed. I too clung rigorously to etiquette, lying with my back to her, curled to take up as little room as possible.

The politeness of course kept us awake; although I had barely been able to keep my eyes open a moment ago, now I found myself trying to soothe my tense body to sleep by parading before it the gray images of ordinariness. Legal documents. Breakfast. Justine scratched herself and sighed. A long moment rolled by. She shifted her legs. I thought: If only I could lie on my back. Exhaustion eased down upon us, dimming mental clarity but not extinguishing it. Asia Maconda's face swam across my mental field.

"I can't sleep," said Justine.

Her voice was so worn that I turned to her with an

impulse to comfort. At the same time she turned towards me. Her thin arms went around my body, her
face pressed against my shoulder. I held her side and
cupped her head, careful not to touch her injured
back. Her body against me was like a phrase of music.
My muscles were calmed, white flowers bloomed on
my heart. Asia Maconda's face still stared at me from
inside my head. I stared back, wondering that this
completely imaginary face had meant so much to me
for so long. I watched it dissolve into pieces as I went
to sleep with my arms around Justine Shade.